The King's Game

Chapter Two Aristocracy

The King's Game
Book One

Richard Light

Copyright © 2025 by Richard Light

All rights reserved.
No part of this book may be reproduced in any form or by any electronic or mechanical means, including information storage and retrieval systems, without written permission from the author, except for the use of brief quotations in a book review.

This is a work of fiction. Unless otherwise indicated, all the names, characters, businesses, places, events and incidents in this book are either the product of the author's imagination or used in a fictitious manner. Any resemblance to actual persons, living or dead, or actual events is purely coincidental.

For more information email: rlight7@icloud.com

ISBN (hardcover): 978-2-6605-0166-0
ISBN (ebook): 978-2-8245-0126-0
ISBN (paperback): 978-2-3759-5964-0

Chapter 1

Now what? What do I do? I can't go back. That's done, and I am done. Right now, I need gas and food. I have a direction and enough cash for a while. At least I have that. South. It's too cold to stay in Colorado right now. I have no idea how the homeless guys make it through the winter, and I don't want to figure it out this week. Hiding out in the mountains is out. I'd get snowed in somewhere then I'd be screwed.

The truck is running. The phone is gone. After the 100th text, it made its way to the ditch. The hell with her. I am done. I am free. What does she want from me, anyway? She has him. She deserves him.

I am out. Out! She would never suspect I would go south. If she had ever listened, she would know but thank God for that. Her head points East or West. New York or Los Angeles. Or San Francisco. Or Portland. I never want to hear about Portland again. I am going south to Texas. I have one friend left who can help me with a job and he's in Texas. There is Paul. He's a friend. But he is back in Boulder, cleaning up the mess he made for me.

I gotta pull over. I am going to fall asleep and kill someone. Maybe myself. Who cares? Dying alone on this road would be OK. I don't want to be some innocent family's fate. God...give me a pull-off. There's one. I'll pull over here and sleep. I need to sleep.

The rising sun beat through his window where his truck had come to a stop the night before. "Where am I?" he muttered to himself. In front of him, a semi rumbled past, shifting through the gears. The landscape to the east opened up as the truck cleared his view. Nothing but prairie. Middle of nowhere prairie. *This is the place I want to be*, he thought, *but eventually, they will find me here. It's too private. With this kind of privacy, I would attract attention. There is no such thing as anonymity in the country. I'd be better off in a suburb. Country neighbors ask too many questions. Maybe they have nothing better to do than try to figure you out. Make sure you fit in. Make sure you become one of them. Eventually, they would find me. Probably faster than I think.* "I gotta piss," he said aloud.

Dave slid out the passenger door to the west where he could relieve himself away from the wandering eyes of passing traffic. There was no passing traffic. He wondered how he could sleep that long without a cop knocking on his window. "They have other things to do," he muttered. Like what? Apparently, these pull-offs don't raise too much suspicion. Nobody cares until they find a reason to and that's usually when they need you to do something for them. "Am I invisible until I am useful?" he asked himself. "Do I treat people like that? Do they exist when I need something from them? Attention? Work? Money? Oh man, I hope not. I am not like that. But here I am, headed to see someone I haven't spoken to in over a year to ask for a job. It was Paul's idea. It's always his idea."

The sun was warm enough the birds had gone off to do what birds do besides chirp happily, or maybe angrily, at the sun from tattered trees by the road. It was desolate and quiet without them. The breeze through the window was light and clean. In the back of his head, his worries were pushing him on. He needed more distance away from Colorado. *Maybe I'll feel better when I am further away*, he thought. He turned the truck engine over and watched the gas gauge rise just over a quarter tank. "Gas. I need gas. What was the last sign I saw? Stratford. I can make it," he encouraged himself.

Dave pushed hard on the accelerator, turning over the rear tires. Dust and rocks shot up behind. A devious, adolescent grin covered his face. There weren't any girls to impress with a truck at his age, certainly not here, wherever the hell here was. "Yee-haw!" he yelled. If he had done that in Boulder County, there might have been trouble. Probably not, but there would have been the anxiety of potential trouble. The social guilt he integrated and was used to. Not on 287 in Oklahoma. It was funny because it felt like getting away with something. *The kids around here probably do that by instinct*, he thought, *lucky bastards*. There it is, Stratford, Texas. When had he passed into Texas? Did it matter? *The difference between Oklahoma and Texas out here is pretty clear*, he thought. That little bit of Oklahoma looked different. *Was there a sign? There had to have been one. Must've slept past it.*

Pulling into the gas station, he reached into the center console and pulled out some twenties. *Thank God for cash. Can't trace cash. The only traceable thing I had was the phone that now lives somewhere along I-70. My license plate and the truck... I gotta do something about those*, he thought.

"Pump 1, can I give you 80 and fill it?" he asked the attendant. The mopey kid set his phone down, nodded and took the cash. Dave pumped 72 dollars of gas, spending the rest on coffee and a burrito. Gas stations in the West can be trusted for burritos. Once you get too far into Nebraska or Kansas the burritos slowly go extinct. The Midwest is useless for them unless you really dig. In that part of the country the burrito is something rare and special; poorly made but special. *How can I be as white as they come*, Dave thought, *and feel more Mexican than all of the Midwest?*

He sipped his coffee continuing south with no idea how many miles he had between the gas station and his thoughts on being Mexican. "Just keep driving and don't do anything out of the ordinary. Don't get pulled over. It's not like there is an APB out for you," he said out loud. But there was no need for a paper trail leading to Somewhere, West Texas. "Is this West Texas or Middle Texas?" he asked himself. "Seems like Middle."

75 mph on a two-lane road. Man, I love Texas, he thought as the miles passed by. *Amarillo is coming up. I can open the package.*

Chapter 2

Amarillo looked brown, cold and generally agitated with itself as it should be in January in the Texas panhandle. South of downtown Dave exited to a Walmart, parking as far away from the door as he could. The truck temperature gauge showed 42. The sky showed dreariness with an occasional hint of hope for the afternoon. He lifted the small package from the passenger seat, studying it in trepidation.

It was pointless to feel worried about the contents. Paul had dropped it off at the house before he left saying, "Don't open it until the day after. It's written on the box, 'After'."

"What the hell could this be?" Dave wondered as he pulled out his favorite elk knife and slit the tape. Inside a pile of packing peanuts was a small, no-frills cell phone with a post-it note that read, "Call me on the alternate number."

Dave dialed Paul's current burner number.

"Hey, where are you?" Paul answered.

"I am in Amarillo, like you said. Have you talked to Duncan? Can he get me a job on a rig or somewhere out in the fields? I can get to Corpus late tonight if I keep at it."

There was a long, pensive pause on Paul's end. "You there?" Dave asked.

"Yeah, sorry, I was thinking about that. You are going to Vero," Paul responded.

"Vero? Where is that, Texas?" Dave asked.

"Vero is in Florida. Vero Beach. Some people call it Zero Beach. It's a seasonal retiree town with a decent sized population of Blue Blood Do-Nothings, Retired Do-Nothings and Do-Nothing Do-Nothings sitting around amusing themselves waiting to die. That's the Zero part of it. They pretty much make three things in that town; cocktails, empty houses, and corpses. Oh, and they make some airplanes but I think those come and go with the economy. They used to grow citrus. You will see the artifacts of that fabled productivity along the railroad tracks. There's also a high-speed rail that blows though town all day long ignoring pretty much everything and everyone blasting a big 'fuck you' with its horn. That town is useless. But the beach is pretty. And it is somewhat quiet. Duncan has a house there again. He is surrounded by some of his best cronies who he never talks to."

"What's the plan then?" Dave asked impatiently.

"Don't worry about the plan. Just go to Vero Beach and call me when you get there. Take 40 east to Memphis then keep working your way east to 95 South. Turn east again when it says Vero Beach. And keep using cash. We'll talk again when you get there."

Dave walked into the Walmart searching for a road atlas. He wandered around the maze of departments until his patience wore out. *I want to get going. A truck stop will have one or a Buc-ee's. Buc-ee's has everything*, he thought. *If Buc-ee's doesn't have a road atlas, I don't need one. Brisket, jerky and an atlas.* He got back in the truck and pounded out more miles eastward. Leaving the West to go to the East felt like failure, like regression. Heading west was like realizing ambition. Even the sun headed west.

The road became one green exit sign after the next as he kept his speed respectfully above the limit. Every car that blazed past received a smile and thumbs up assuming they would draw unwanted attention. Dave had no way to know if a cop had any reason to question him beyond how fast he was going. Paul would know, and he hadn't said anything.

He thought about calling his sister then thought better. The burner phone was for calling burner phones and numbers he had never called before. Besides, Sarah had her own things to worry about. That's probably what Paul had been preoccupied with. Everything should be resolved soon, if it wasn't already. "It's the ex. That's the problem," Dave muttered out loud. "Ex? She's not an ex yet. But she will be." His disappearance would provoke some sort of legal action and Jessica would be free to do what she wanted. What she wanted was undeniable. She could go with her new love and be happy. Dave had no interest in her happiness. His disgust and an absurd fraction of hope for reconciliation was standing in the shadows of his eventual, liberating indifference. She still occupied his head. Indifference was a gift he would have to wait for.

One Minute of Angle down and I could have decapitated that asshole, he thought. It brought a smile to his face. The only reason Stefan Wunderlich was still alive was his marksmanship. Wunderlich blood and brains splattered all over the Wunderlich Campaign Tour Bus would have been a sight; a gruesome, beautiful, vengeful sight. He could still see the image, the crosshairs he had briefly imprinted on Stefan's forehead before readjusting. The first shot had nearly parted that pretentious hair. The next rounds he sent created a circus; everyone running around looking for cover or just running on impulsive fear. He didn't feel proud of the panic he had induced into innocent people. For that and a long list of other sins, he would ask for forgiveness some day in the quiet of the night when he was alone.

Kristian was probably sitting in the County Jail where he should be. *Little bastard started all of this,* Dave thought. Family connections and Wunderlich's local reputation would never have made him a suspect, not in Boulder. The careless investigators had pinned it on Mark easily enough; his brother-in-law was probably about to walk out of jail into Sarah's arms. Dave smiled, thinking about his nieces cuddled up next to Mark on the sofa; his sister relaxed and relieved. It was a nearly perfect operation they had pulled off.

Framing that guilty bastard Kristian had been worth the risk. Dave laughed to himself at the irony of framing a guilty kid. Steve, his accomplice, had to be sitting at his desk at the rifle range pretty proud of himself as the Old Man was screaming at George to call some huge, overpriced Denver law firm. Other than that, Boulder was probably sullen. That town didn't take shootings too well. Regardless of the national gun restrictions, they had had their share of them.

Oklahoma City was up ahead then to Arkansas. He had never been in Arkansas. It was one of those states that people told him was pretty. He would be there in the dark. *Cash is weird at hotels. Do they even take cash?* he wondered. *I'll sleep in the truck somewhere until I wake up.*

For the second time in two days, he awoke in the truck; the windows steamed over from his breath. In reality, he could live in it if he had to. Maybe sub-freezing temperatures might be rough but he had done it while hunting more than once. If it was between putting up a tent or just sleeping in the truck, he had always chosen the truck. A benefit of being only five foot nine. The clock on the burner phone said 4:15. There had to be a truck stop up ahead.

After gassing up and getting some food, he was back on the eastward grind. The coffee was working. He still had no motivation to laze into a state of radio-induced hypnosis. It hadn't occurred to him to turn it on. With so many thoughts in his head, there was no use for more clutter. He drove until the tank warning light came on, stopped for gas and food and repeated towards a place not of his choosing. He had to go somewhere. Paul knew him well enough to know he couldn't live without a purpose. Hopefully, whatever made Paul direct him to Florida would be worth it.

The Florida welcome sign seemed a little over the top, gaudy and extravagantly lit. It was welcoming in the fashion of a gated housing development. Dave had driven straight through the day in a daze and into the night. The Florida sign had stunned the sleepiness out of his eyes, shaking him into coherence. It was dark. The earth and everything around him felt flat. In the shadows, deer grazed along the road next to a sign warning about bears crossing. *How many bears are there? More than deer?* he wondered.

He drove eastward through road-crossing, suicidal bear territory. Arriving outside of Jacksonville, he picked up I-95 south towards Vero Beach. He wasn't going to make it. Thank God for Buc-ee's. He saw the sign of the beaver near Daytona Beach. "That's where I will camp tonight; Buc-ee's parking lot," he decided.

Dave found a spot where he could back the truck in without being harassed by lights all night. Stumbling out of the car, he went in to get something to eat before sleep. This Buc-ee's was geared up for the beach, but the basics were there. The truck was starting to appeal to him as much as a 4-Star hotel, especially when he was tired from staring through the windshield. Jessica would have left him sooner if he had set that low of a standard for her comfort. He had given it everything he had to try to make her happy.

As he lay in the backseat, trying to limit his movements, he felt separated from the world without his phone; separated from the instantaneous and mind-numbing access to information and entertainment. It hadn't hit him until now just how addicted he was to the internet as he lay there, his mind racing. Stupid cat videos would be better than thoughts. His thoughts kept him awake but what difference did it make? He had nothing to do tomorrow other than drive south. Eventually, the fatigue would capture him.

Chapter 3

"What are you reading?"

Dave looked up from his book turning his head deliberately towards the man next to him hoping to express an affected displeasure with the question. The interruption didn't bother him as much as he tried to display. It was expected that at least someone would ask him about a book in a bar. Reading in a bar was peculiar, antisocial. "*The Art of War*," he replied. "Ever read it?"

"Many times," the man said plainly.

Dave got a general feeling of annoyance from this man as if he should test him to confirm they should never be friends. The guy rubbed him the wrong way for some reason. Sometimes he wished that two men could step into a ring and fight it out right away to show who was the more dominant male. Get the social dance over without the bullshit.

"Hey man. My name's Derek," the man said, reaching out to shake Dave's hand. Dave took it and was met with a firm, confident handshake. Was this guy trying to out-man him? He just wanted to read and drink his beer in this nice, overpriced restaurant in the older part of town. No conversation was necessary. Dave knew he was bullshitting himself. He wanted to talk to someone. He had been zombie-like around town for two days sleeping in his truck at the beach. There was nothing yet from Paul. He had tried a few simple text messages using the numeric keypad on the burner, but it was such a pain in the ass he didn't have the patience for it.

"You from here?" Dave asked.

"No, you?" Derek responded.

"I am from Colorado." Dave was warming up to talking. The affected distance he had been trying to put up was becoming weak and beginning to crumble. He really wanted to talk. It was in his nature but it was more in his nature to talk to women. He had very few male friends in the past outside of his brother-in-law and the lawyer who was not taking his calls.

"Shit man. I am from Colorado. Not originally, but mostly. Grew up in the Midwest then moved to Boulder years ago. Spent a bunch of time in Summit County," Derek said, "What're you here for? Vacation?"

"No, I just moved here," Dave repeated.

"Why? I mean, what made you move to this town?" Derek asked as he signaled the bartender for another beer.

"Uh, I have some work opportunities here," Dave replied. He was getting uncomfortable with the questioning, anxious about where it might lead; although he didn't want to get backed into a corner and seem shady. For the last few days, he was coming off as shady by default. It was the first time in his life he felt like he had to look over his shoulder and avoid the police. "What do you do here?" Dave asked, hesitant to draw himself further into the conversation. He felt right on the edge of full commitment to it, as if the conversation would implant itself on him and start controlling him. The whole thing was still very new. He had no idea how uncomfortable hiding could be.

Derek stepped into the question with the least bit of fear, "I came here for my kids. That's the only reason I am here and the only reason to stay. The ex-wife wanted to move out of Colorado to be near family here and I capitulated, but the kids are at an age where they should have me around. Her family is OK. Certainly better than she is. I take that back. Since we divorced, I haven't spoken to her family. So, I'm not sure if they were assholes the whole time and were just faking it. It's a possibility. They were cool for a long time though. As soon as the kids are in college, I am out of here."

"You don't like it?" Dave asked.

"Not one fucking bit," Derek replied just as the now indignant bartender slid him his drink before abruptly turning away. Derek knew she had heard. It seemed amusing to him. "The locals love this useless town," he announced, glancing at the girl. "It is useless. They pump money in from outside sticking it to the snowbird, temporary residents who have nothing left to do in their lives but listen to crappy cover bands, sit on the beach and play shitty rounds of golf. And watch television. Don't forget that. Someone should make a coffin with a television. They all seem like they are waiting to die in front of those, why not take one along?"

Waiting to die, Dave thought. *That phrase must have meaning here.* Paul had used it.

Derek took a sip before relaunching, "It's sad how these useless former wage slaves can't seem to find any real purpose now that they have been emancipated into retirement freedom. There're a few of them who are trying to eke out something, but it's too little too late. What's the difference? They didn't do much back where they were from other than go to work, buy shit and try to entertain themselves through the weekend in order to forget their servitude before the weekly cycle renewed."

Derek looked as if he was ready to pause, but he was warmed up. Bitching about Vero Beach seemed like something he enjoyed. Dave knew little about it. Unfortunately what Paul had described was now partially confirmed in Act One of Derek's diatribe.

"Hmm," Dave managed to get out as he took a sip of his beer.

"Yeah, hmm is right," Derek continued. "If this place actually made anything and had decent factory jobs besides the few airplanes here and there, these old, useless twats would have to start mowing their own lawns and cooking dinner. I should add that if you see a wait at a restaurant you want to get into, don't think for a minute it's because it's good. Most of them act like glorified chain restaurants, all supplied by the same company under non-chain names. They're crap. Even this one." For the good of social harmony, thankfully, the bartender was out of earshot.

"That being said," Derek continued, "if you want to experience all of the basic restaurants around here, just dump yourself on the currently popular dating app and the girls will lead you there. Of the three classifications of dating app whores out there, FB&E, you know the Food, Beverage, and Entertainment class, is the most prevalent around here."

"What are the other 2?" Dave asked.

"That would be Looking For Attention Whores and Only Down to Fuck Whores. I prefer the latter," Derek replied with a self-satisfied grin punching Dave lightly on the shoulder as he said it again. "F, B and E's are the bumper crop here. It used to be citrus in a time when men around here produced something. Anything you see of value was left over from them, the pioneers of this nothingness. Their legacies have been de-treed, paved over and turned into retirement communities. Are you on any dating apps?"

"No, I don't think I am into that. Should I be?" Dave asked.

"If you want to join the legions of feckless chumps looking and hoping for some scraps of female attention, I would say, 'yes'. If you want to keep your balls and your money, just meet women in their natural habitats; coffee shops, the mall, the grocery store, the beach, bars, definitely bars... Correction, not the Mall. You have to see the Mall. It is fucking hilarious; a butt plug store on one end and a huge church on the other as far away from the plugs Evangelical Christians can get and feel safe under a shared roof."

"What about the gym?" Dave asked.

"Fuck the gym. That is basically like being on an app. Use the gym for working out and let the gym chumps live their dreams," Derek replied. "Seriously, the chicks in this town are desperate for any feeble displays of testosterone. Channel your inner James Bond, and they will respond."

"Like be mysterious and like a secret agent? Show you have money?" Dave asked. He was fully embroiled now. There was no slipping out of this conversation. Derek had him. This guy was crass and to the point. There was no way women responded to this kind of talk. It didn't make sense that they would. How could they? This guy made *him* uncomfortable. *Imagine what women must feel*, Dave thought to himself.

Derek continued, "James Bond appears to have money. The appearance of it is just as effective. It's sort of like a guy who has all the stuff to bend her knees, but all that stuff comes with a mountain of debt. And she doesn't want to account for it. She just wants to experience it. You know what

I am talking about." Derek paused to look at Dave to see if he had lit any fires of revelation.

"But I digressed," he continued. "Bond is direct and confident. He can kill any man in the room with his hands and knows it. He is not a big man in stature, but his size is meaningless. James Bond is fit and strong and never seems to work out. He is charismatic and worldly. He is adaptable to any situation. He is in control of his moods and feelings, and he is calculating. He is on a path of justice. All that shit about defending Britain and the Queen is bullshit. James Bond does the right thing regardless of the political benefits. He is stylish because he looks in the mirror and makes himself so. He is self-critical, but he would never denigrate himself out loud to an audience."

Derek took a breather glancing over at the bartender's ass as she bent over to retrieve a beer from the cooler. He gave a brief, calm facial confirmation as to her shape without the eager display of an excitable man. It was as if he was looking at a museum statue, not a living, breathing female. Derek seemed far outside the typical. *Maybe this guy's a little psycho*, Dave thought.

"Anyway, fuck dating apps. However, there is a use for them I have found," Derek continued.

"What's that," Dave asked regretfully.

"Statistical demographics," Derek replied. "You can do demographic studies to see if there is a common type of female who finds you attractive. I happen to attract thin blonds. Mostly chemical blonds and some of the naturals. For some reason the naturals don't seem that thin. Maybe it's the plumping up for winter factor rooted in their heritage? Anyway, the app data is not hard science, but it can be somewhat useful as a starting point. Sends you into situations where your sales pitch might play better. Remember, men sell and women advertise."

"What?" Dave exclaimed.

"Men have to sell themselves. Women just sort of show up like a billboard along the highway. If a decent-looking chick walks in that door and sits down at this bar, she can expect to be engaged by one of these chumps and probably get at least a drink out of it. That chump will start in on his sales pitch, usually leading with his wallet or some other prop like a sports car or god-forbid his job, which he will have to talk about. She starts to formulate a fantastical life of luxury with this chump where he is pussy-whipped beyond belief and she is holding the carrot on the stick just out of his reach. He gets little nibbles once in a while just to keep him around and controlled. Then maybe she gets the burning hots for the pool boy or some jacked dude at the gym. She'd rob a bank for that guy and risk prison while she is robbing time and resources from her chump-assed husband."

"Jesus Christ, man," Dave was in shock, finding the conversation to be getting out of control and too familiar. Derek had him tail spinning into the middle of an ocean full of his past with Jessica. This was not what he wanted to hear, but he instinctually knew that if he stood up and walked out, he would be confirming himself as a chump.

"Sorry man. Did I hit a nerve?" Derek asked.

"Yeah, kinda. My ex, well, not officially an ex yet, was having an affair. That's part of the reason I left Colorado. Just confirmed it recently. I don't want... Uh, I can't really talk about it," Dave stammered.

"That's OK, man," Derek empathized. "My ex had a long affair and I took her ass back. Then, in order to repair her feelings of shame, we opened up a gift shop up in Vail. Gave her something to do while she wallowed in self-pity or maybe in the memory of how exciting it was to sneak around with her chosen, dickhead accomplice. When the inevitable happened and the business failed, I was left with the bills. I was making decent money as a business consultant, so I took on the dual task of cleaning up after her and supporting her. Then we had kids. As soon as my business took a dump for whatever reason I still can't figure out, she ditched with the kids and eventually fled here to be with her top-tier enablers, the parents. Total shit show. Thank God my kids don't know about her past. They'll never hear it from me. Ignorance is bliss and it should stay that way for the good of the innocents."

"Do you think your ex worries about the kids finding out?" Dave asked.

"She is so narcissistic I think she has probably rationalized by now that I was to blame for her affair," Derek responded. "I do hold the nuke in my hand though."

"What's the nuke?" Dave asked.

"I slip the idea to the ex that if the kids were ever to find out. Something like, 'You know. It would really change things with the kids and you if they discovered certain truths about our past together, the extramarital journey you were on, why I am happy being divorced from you and where all the money went.' Let that fester in her little brain and build up the corresponding anxiety. What could she do? Tell them and get in front of the problem? I don't think she is that stupid." Derek paused to consider his last comment.

"No, she's not that stupid," he continued. "It would eat at her, the anxiety, even if she started a full denial campaign. She would be in her 60s, and the thought of her self-glorified reputation with the kids taking a giant shit would be bad for her. It could potentially irreparably alienate her from them."

"Man, that is ugly psychological warfare," Dave exclaimed.

"It is. It's the nuke. A nuke is only useful to blow the shit out of something if you have a lot of nukes and obliterate your opponent before they can obliterate you. Thanks to our glorious, egotistical gringo regime versus Japan, everyone knows what a nuke does. Now, the threat of its use is more powerful, at least psychologically, than its actual, world-ending use. I only have one tactical nuke in my arsenal. I can probably come up with some corresponding smaller nukes to either precede the big one or just blow the shit out of everything. All I would have to do is plant the idea into the ex's head that it's there, and I would be willing to use it given the right circumstances or motivation. All of this being totally and completely up to my discretion. There would be nothing she could do but worry if I would ever do it. The anxious torture of nuclear annihilation."

"Would you?" Dave asked.

"Never," Derek admitted. "I love my kids. It's a truth they don't need to know. But I would let the ex think I would if I had to."

"You are evil," Dave gasped into the top of his beer glass as he subconsciously sipped away what he had just heard. Derek looked over at the bartender's ass again. This time, he smiled a wide, satisfied grin that had nothing to do with its cute little shape.

Chapter 4

"Hello?" Dave whispered into the phone at 4:00 am.

"Dave, it's Paul. I know it's early there but I have this in my head now and had to call."

"Yeah, OK, it's 2:00 am in Colorado; why are you awake?" Dave muttered. He peaked outside the truck into the quiet of the beach parking lot. No cops. He had determined through repetitive observation that shift change was around seven. Frequently there had been a cop car parked and idling between 6:30 and a few minutes before 7:00 when it tore off in a hurry. It was too frequent to not develop a reasonable hypothesis. As long as he stayed hidden in the truck until they left, he felt like he wouldn't draw much attention to himself.

"So, here's the deal. Duncan has this niece he is concerned about. Actually, it's the boyfriend Duncan can't seem to figure out. He wants someone to help him. Anyway, she lives out there near the beach. The parties she goes to, the people she is socializing with or whatever she is doing is unknown to Duncan. He's not very social, and besides, he's Duncan. You know him well enough. I have a guy in California setting up some tracking on her phone. We will text you her GPS coordinates, and you can figure out what she is up to. You can give Duncan a *Dave* opinion on the boyfriend. "

"Why does he care? She's old enough, right?" Dave asked.

"That's a good question," Paul replied. "Duncan has a general and fatherly concern for her well-being. Also, he and I have been brewing up an idea for something else. This is sort of a test run. We don't think this girl is in any danger other than the remote chance of getting knocked up. Drugs and heavy partying aren't really her sort of thing. We know she drinks socially, but how the hell and why are you going to stop that? Like I said, it's the boyfriend who's the question."

"What's your idea?" Dave asked.

"You will know soon enough. What are you doing now? Laying low, I hope," Paul asked.

Dave reflected on his life over the last few weeks. He had been doing almost nothing but working out at a city-owned park and walking on the beach with a few outings to watch bands at a bar. He felt as purposeless as the retirees who surrounded him. He showered at the beach in the dark and shaved in the truck using a dog bowl for a sink. That was his life.

"I haven't really done much of anything. Thought about looking for a job," Dave replied.

"You are not doing that," Paul exclaimed. "There is no way you can. What Social Security number were you planning to use? What the hell is wrong with you? Jobs are not 'laying low'."

"Oh, I didn't think about that," Dave replied. "I obviously can't use mine and have a legit job. That would send an electronic trail right back to Colorado, right?"

"Yes! It will! Instantaneously!" Paul's response sounded

as if he wanted to slap Dave upside the head. He went on to describe the various methods of tracking someone through a Social Security number, then continued on about facial recognition warning Dave to stay out of casinos and government buildings just in case.

"What about dating apps?" Dave asked to provoke Paul.

"NO! Absolutely not! Not even with a fake profile!" Paul screamed. "Stay analog. Meet women at the bar, and don't let them take photos of you and post them. Use cash. If you are getting low, don't worry. Duncan is getting the guest house above his garage ready for you to stay there. He'll explain more when he gets into town next week. Try to keep away from the cops until then. I don't like the idea of you sleeping in your truck. Any cops around at night?"

"A bunch but it's OK. They are doing paperwork or messing with their phones like everyone else. I am pretty sure they only have slightly higher situational awareness than an average person. I see them all the time, head down on the phone. I think the park maintenance guy watches me more."

"Stay away from that guy and old men walking dogs or whatever else they are doing consistently," Paul responded. "They could become a problem. If you catch them looking your way too much, move to a new location. Some of those idiots want nothing more than to be a hero and will make up shit to do it. Beware of them."

"Yeah, I hadn't thought about that," Dave agreed. He had caught the maintenance guy watching him a few times as if he were taking mental notes. Maybe he was just being paranoid. Maybe being paranoid was better than not. It would be smart to stay vigilant and not fall into too much routine. Whatever the accomplishment he was gaining from hiding out, it was psychologically taxing.

"OK, I gotta go to sleep," Paul yawned. "Duncan will call

you next week. Don't be too friendly for now, and try to blend in without being too social."

"I only know one guy. This Derek dude I met at the bar. I think he hates women," Dave replied.

"A true misogynist," Paul said after another yawn. "He sounds like someone I would love to get to know."

The phone connection cut abruptly leaving Dave hanging on Paul's last comment. He knew Paul was joking. Paul could never really hate women enough to be a misogynist or associate with one. Dave wasn't sure how any man could be so damaged and cold as to truly hate women. His thoughts turned again to Jessica, wondering what she was doing. He assumed she was with Stefan. Did she even care that he had disappeared? Why would she? How could she just toss away everything they had for that guy? What was it? Did their marriage mean nothing? Did their past and all the emotional support he had given her have no value? What about the vows? Marriage vows have meaning. Don't they? They did to him. As he sat alone in his truck, he found himself starting to miss her.

Does she even miss me? he thought to himself. She had to be wondering where he was. Wasn't that normal for a person who had lived in the same house for years with another person? Slept in the same bed? How could she be so heartless as to just dump him for Stefan Wunderlich? *We are still married*, he thought to himself. *Doesn't that mean anything?* Maybe she saw him only as a legal problem now. He resigned himself to this last thought. He was just a problem to sort out so she could have what she had already taken for herself. That's all he felt; replaceable and disposable with some additional paperwork. It was absurd to think a woman who doesn't want you would miss you.

The phone vibrated again, "What do you know about the misogynist?"

"Um... I don't know. He's no bullshit. Very opinionated. I think he would nuke all of Florida for fun. That's the general impression I got. Oh, and he is from Boulder. That was a weird coincidence. Why do you ask?"

"Did he give you his contact info?" Paul asked. "What's his name again?"

"He gave me his number. Name's Derek." Dave answered in a half whisper, wary a few cars nearby could hear. That was the direction he perceived his new life to be moving, whispering in his truck like he was on a stakeout.

"OK, Derek the Misogynist. Good," Paul replied.

"Why is that good?" Dave asked.

The line went briefly silent. "Uh, it's good for you to know someone there but don't get too chummy," Paul answered. "I gotta get to sleep. I am starting to hallucinate."

Chapter 5

The passengers in front of him all stood in unison as the plane's wheels came to a stop. Derek stayed put. The awkward hunch under the overhead baggage was pointless. As soon as the line of passengers started moving, he would stand, grab his bag and go. No need to hurry. It was mid-afternoon and he had one place to go. The line began to move.

He cruised through Terminal A, choosing the walk instead of taking the train. It was peaceful without having to look at the herd of anxious people with whom he had just flown. Halfway over the bridge he opened the app plugging in the Hotel Boulderado. His ride was 16 minutes out giving him just enough time for the bathroom. Back in his business days this had been standard procedure for him twice a month. His now-ex-wife hated his traveling. It wasn't that she missed him as much as she wanted him around to help her with the kids. Another of the fatal flaws he had created by having a home office. Real offices were better for marriage for some odd reason.

It had its good qualities. He saw his kids grow up from

babies to tweens before the ex decided to be an ex. What could he do? Unhappiness is grounds for divorce in America, and she was never very happy about anything, no matter how much he tried. Now she seemed happy, especially when he was caught up on the child support payments. If she were truly happy, he didn't care. She had transitioned from someone he loved to someone he paid for services like a private dorm school. The only thing remaining between them was the kids. Eventually they would be adults and on their own. Then he hoped to rebuild real relationships with them without the influence of their mother, who needed to win. Whatever game she was playing to win was open to interpretation.

The car rolled up. He dumped his bag in the backseat and got into the front with the driver. "Boulderado?" the driver asked.

"Yeah, Boulderado," Derek answered plainly. The driver halfheartedly attempted to move him to the back as Derek handed him a twenty and said, "Front." The driver's chitchat Derek tolerated as they flew down E-470 to the west. The foothills grew as they neared. This was the reason for sitting in the front seat. It was important to visually take in as much of the place he loved and had sacrificed. The emotional cost to leave had been expensive to his memories and a potential future.

"David, this is Duncan. How are things?"

"Everything is pretty good," Dave responded. "How are you?"

"Excellent. Do you know where I live? You have the address?" Duncan asked. Dave affirmed he knew the neighborhood well enough to find the house. "Can you come over now? The gate code is 1210."

"I can be there in about five minutes. I am at the beach nearby," Dave replied.

"Great, let yourself in and just park in front of the door near the fountain. The drive loops," Duncan instructed before cutting off the call.

Dave shook the sand off his towel and walked the short distance through a mangrove covered trail to the truck. Duncan's house was an easy walk from where he was, but he would drive. Due to what he imagined was wealthy people purposefully asking the city to block off the street between their houses and the public beach, the drive was longer than the walk. The sun would be setting soon. Leaving his truck in an empty lot, even in this neighborhood, didn't seem like a good idea.

Rolling his tires over Duncan's immaculately designed cobblestone drive seemed invasive. He estimated in his head what it had cost. He and Mark had put in a similar drive at Duncan's ski house in Colorado. He entered the code and watched the gate glide smoothly to the side. *Whoever installed this had to be good*, he thought to himself. He followed the short drive around the circle and stepped out of the truck as Duncan came down the steps.

"David," Duncan smiled, "it's great to see you again. You look great."

"Thanks, it's been a weird couple of weeks. I really..." Dave replied.

Duncan interrupted before he could lament, "I know. It is horrible what happened to Mark. But you and Paul and...?"

"Steve," Dave added.

"Yes, that Steve gentleman from the shooting range. You did something to be proud of." Duncan smiled the way Dave remembered his father had when he and his sister Sarah had done something notable. Emotions were beginning to get to him. He swallowed them deep inside. "Come in, David," Duncan instructed. "Leave your keys in the truck. Ignacio will take care of it."

They walked into the foyer that seemed to soar to an immeasurable height. It was intimidating and inspiring, giving the house an exclamation as you entered then subduing the initial impact with a warm, lived-in feel without pretense. They passed through an arched doorway to a living room that had the feel of a study. It was quiet, the woodwork impeccably constructed.

"Who did the woodwork?" Dave asked.

"I would suspect a local shop," Duncan answered. "I bought this house as-is. The General Contractors here don't seem to have their own fabricating shops like you and Mark did. I could be wrong. But there are a few talented woodworkers around."

They eased into two leather chairs as a pleasant Mexican woman handed both a glass of Scotch before gracefully disappearing. "Cheers," Dave offered with a contended sigh.

"Cheers, David," Duncan replied. "It's good to see you. We have a lot to talk about."

Derek fell back into the bed after a long shower. He had a few hours to kill before his meeting in the Mezzanine Bar. He was starving, hoping the delivery would show up soon with his falafel order. "Back in Boulder," he said to himself. Quirky little Boulder with its outrageously excellent restaurants from the simple mom and pop shops, the family-run taco carts parked strategically throughout the county and the ever-changing high-end dining. For a little city, it had great food. Way better than the standard, overpriced restaurants he had been experiencing in Florida whose purpose seemed concentrated on extracting retirement money from the elderly instead of demonstrating culinary pride. To make great things, profit is an afterthought never the motivator. Boulder seemed to embrace that ideal.

Finally, the knock on the door came, announcing his falafel. The shop had been on the Pearl Street Mall for decades. He had eaten there frequently in his twenties when eating anywhere outside his apartment made him feel less poor. Every bite was a memory, but he didn't dare walk the two blocks to get it himself. He couldn't.

"David," Duncan began, focusing on the main topic of their visit. "You are in a place I can't imagine. You are free and have the opportunity to do something great. I have the means to make it happen." Dave hesitantly opened his mouth to ask Duncan what he meant. "Don't talk," Duncan commanded. "For now, just listen. Some of my friends and I have been kicking around an idea that will take a considerable amount of money and time of which we have. What we need is people like you to implement it. This is not going to be for the average man. From your exploits in Boulder, you have demonstrated you can coldly do what needs to be done."

"I don't know about coldly," Dave interrupted. "I almost let myself and my anger get the better of me."

"Nonetheless, David, you did what was necessary and Mark is free because of it," Duncan continued. Dave sat back a little more comfortably in his chair. It was good to have someone validate what he had done. "For now," Duncan continued, "we have a test project for you. It's not to test *you* as much as it is to gain some insight."

"What's the project," Dave asked impatiently.

Duncan stood up and walked to the window looking out over the courtyard pool. He became pensive and distant in a way he was known to be when something very personal was bothering him. Setting his glass on an end table, he crossed his arms and began to pace in front of Dave recounting a story of his niece and her current boyfriend.

"This young man she has been dating appears to have something going on behind the scenes," he said as he paced. "There is a lot of money and conspicuous consumption that doesn't seem to have an origin from what his business amounts to. We can't put a finger on how much his business is generating in comparison to what he spends. On the surface, he seems to be legitimate."

"What's his business?" Dave asked.

Duncan laughed, "Lawn care."

"What?" Dave sat up. "Like mowing lawns? Gardening?"

"Yes, you know how I have this kind of money. I was very fortunate to be born as I was and given an opportunity to build upon what my father had tortured himself to create," Duncan reminisced. "I struggle to see the margins in this kind of service work compared to this man's lifestyle. It is a little concerning."

"Because of your niece," Dave interrupted.

"Yes, because of her. She and my wife's sister are the family I have left," Duncan continued. "They, and my house staff, are my family. My niece is who I have left from my wife. I know it must place a certain amount of burden on my sister-in-law and niece to be the focus of my wife's memory, but they are very well taken care of. I try to live and let live with them but I have a protective instinct for Kate I cannot ignore. Kate is her name."

"I know what you mean," Dave offered. "Drugs? You think he's dealing drugs?"

"I don't think so," Duncan replied. "It's something else."

"You must be Paul," Derek said as he approached the slender, naturally handsome man.

"I am Paul," the man said as he stood up to shake Derek's hand, offering him a seat facing a quiet jazz trio.

"If you don't mind, I will sit here," Derek requested.

"You like your back to the entrance?" Paul asked with a touch of sarcasm.

"Hardly ever," Derek replied as he opened his photos app. He slid the phone to Paul. "If that woman comes in, let me know."

Paul picked up the phone and smiled, "I know her. I don't know her well, but I know who she is. She works off the mall at a financial firm."

"That's her," Derek replied. "We have a past, and although it was brief, it was..." he paused. "It was excellent, but it was really bad timing. Let's just say, if given better circumstances, I would be here in this bar with her not you. No offense."

"None taken," Paul replied.

"I got the gist of what you and Duncan are up to," Derek said. "I am interested in pursuing this. I have very little to lose, especially as you said there would be an emergency exit plan. Just so you know, I speak fluent Portuguese. I could happily disappear into Brazil at any moment."

"You speak Spanish too, correct?" Paul asked.

"Yes, dormant fluency but very Mexican in slang and dialect," Derek replied. "It has been coming back to me in my current job. I use it a lot, although I don't let on how well I speak it. From what I gathered from our phone conversation, Spanish and Portuguese might be useful. Does Dave speak any languages?"

Paul paused to respond, "To put it in a way, Dave speaks construction Spanish. That being said, he is very smart and can polish up on the language pretty well. He is not at the level you are, but he will be fine. Besides language, what he really needs is some mentoring, especially when it comes to his personal life. It has the potential to conflict with his rational thinking and distract him."

"You want me to be his therapist?" Derek asked begrudgingly.

"No, just lay out the truth to him," Paul continued. "He will be a bit of a problem for a few months while he gets over..." Paul's eyes widened as his gaze raised, sending a surge of anxiety into Derek.

"Is she behind me?" Derek asked. His heart began to race. He desperately wanted to see her. And he feared seeing her. There was no reason to fear her. He feared the possibility of her seeing him and being cold or, worse, neutral. It would be soul-crushing for him. He understood why she had let him go. Their relationship was so brief and so intense, but the potential for them was chemically undeniable. She probably thought it better to just think of him like a vacation fling and move on. He resolved himself to that.

"No, it's Stefan Mother Fucking Wunderlich," Paul whispered.

Derek sighed. The anxiety eased. "Who?" he asked.

"That's the guy whose brain Dave almost splattered all over a bus," Paul laughed. "Now that I think of it, I wish he had. You are about to meet the guy who is fucking Dave's wife. Wait! She is here too. Wonderful."

"You can't just ignore him?" Derek asked.

"Stefan does not get ignored," Paul responded. "He will come up to us. He has to. Image and grand entrances are in his blood. Dave's wife, Jessica, will be pleasant and somewhat in the background. Anyone with that asshole knows their role."

"I want you to follow her, David," Duncan continued. "Find out where they go and who they associate with. Keep a list of people. There are small notebooks in the guest house and a bunch of cash in the safe. If you need more, let me know. The safe code is 2022. By the way, here is your new phone from our technology man in California." Duncan handed Dave a new smartphone. "Use it for whatever you want except for contacting Jessica or anyone associated with your life in Colorado. That's off limits and should go without saying."

"I know," Dave quietly agreed.

"You will get over her, David," Duncan empathized. "You will. It will take time. Give me the old burner with Jessica's number." Dave sighed and handed the phone over. He felt a brief hit of shame throttled by questions.

"How do you know her number is in there?" he asked.

"That's our technical man in California," Duncan replied. "You'll meet him at some point. Our other man you have met, Derek."

"Derek? From the bar? Was he there on purpose?" Dave stared at Duncan.

"He was," Duncan smiled.

"Why didn't Paul say anything?" Dave asked.

Duncan returned to his pacing. "Paul didn't know about him. I sent Derek over to the bar to check on you. To see how you were. See if he could work with you. Right now he is in Boulder so Paul can evaluate him for himself. I have evaluated him in the past. I didn't realize he was in Vero Beach until about a month ago when I ran into him. He did some work for me as a consultant on that ski area I used to own in New Mexico. We hit it off and I wanted to hire him. But he was in a different place in his life and was doing well for himself and his family. For lack of a better phrase, Corporate America dumped him and a lot of good men like him. He was blind to the threat of being outside of the policies, procedures, and social grandstanding corporate types are intent on demonstrating. You have never been there, David. Corporate life is a lot of weak men wielding power they would get their necks cut for in a more primitive civilization. Nonetheless, he was blindsided which led to his divorce and led him here."

"Wow," Dave exhaled, "he seems angry."

"He is not," Duncan replied. "Inside of him is a relatively positive person with a strong sense of justice but also a man who is fallible and knows it. That being said, he has been through a lot of things many men would never get over. His heart and faith are strong and he is not your average man. You will learn a lot from him but some of it might be tough on your preconceptions."

Dave took another sip of his Scotch, sinking further into the armchair. He reflected on yet another twist of his fate this time directed by Duncan instead of Paul. When would he get the chance to lead his own life and plot his own course? *Do men like me ever get that?* he wondered.

"Duncan?" Dave asked. "How did you know I was in the bar?"

"Your phone told us," Duncan replied.

The waitress made it to the table before Stefan, giving Paul and Derek a safe haven for a moment. "Hi Paul," she smiled. "What would you like? Macallan 18, half an ice cube?"

"Yes, Dominique," Paul smiled up at her, turning to Derek.

"The NA IPA in a glass, please." The waitress gave him

an odd look as if he didn't seem the non-alcoholic beer type. Her eyes stayed on him as she turned to fetch their drinks.

"You don't drink alcohol?" Paul asked.

"I do sometimes," Derek replied. "Something about being back here is making me feel sober."

"Why is that? Did you have a problem?"

Derek had been asked the question so many times his answer was becoming canned. He would have found it exhausting, but he understood alcohol was part of the culture. It was natural to think that something dramatic had to have happened to isolate himself from the rest of the party.

"I don't know. There was just a day I decided I didn't like hangovers that much and I like having my head attached when I am interacting with people. It can be an advantage," he explained. "As long as people think you are drinking along with them, they are OK. Thus the glass. Drinking people are suspicious of sober people. They worry you aren't having fun."

"The day you met Dave you were..."

"Drinking a non-alcoholic beer in a glass completely sober," Derek interrupted, "and I had two. I almost never have two. What's the point of it?"

"I think that Dave believes you might have been misogynistic because of the beer," Paul continued.

"Not the beer. And I am not a misogynist. Most definitely not. I like women way too much for that label. Probably too much. Holding them accountable isn't hate."

"Hello Paul, how are you?" Stefan greeted, his eyes shifting from Paul to Derek and back.

"No need to get up," Stefan implored as both Derek and Paul ignored him and rose. Paul reached out his hand to shake Stefan's.

"How are you?" Paul asked. "How have you been since the..."

"The attack?" Stefan interrupted. "I am doing better. I have Jessica to thank for that. She has really been the strength I have needed while I have taken some time to reflect and meditate. Thank God that kid who did it is behind bars. Can you believe it was him?"

Paul shrugged. Derek bit his lower lip, cringing to restrain laughter. Was this guy for real? Dave's wife is fucking this chump? He was a good-looking guy. Certainly, he was well dressed and seemed well-educated and connected, but what kind of idiots back this guy? "Oh right, this is Boulder," he muttered quietly to himself. Stefan turned towards Derek as if he had heard. Had he said it too loudly? He studied Paul's face for evidence, but there was nothing.

"Hello, Stefan Wunderlich," Stefan said proudly, offering his hand. Derek took the hand calmly, feeling like he could crush it if he wanted. The handshake was hurried and anxious in a way that made someone question the resolve and depth of a man.

"I am Derek," was all he offered.

Stefan turned to Paul, looking for support. Paul allowed an uncomfortable pause for the moment to fester. He knew what rattled Stefan. "Stefan," Paul paused again for effect, "you know that everyone knows that you are fucking Jessica, correct? And look, here she is. Great timing." Derek was fighting back tears of laughter as he watched Stefan wither.

Paul stepped around Stefan and greeted Jessica with an uncomfortable, almost lecherous hug. "Jess, it's good to see you. Are you doing OK? Have you heard from Dave?" Paul asked with all the affected concerns he could create. Derek turned and fled to the bathroom.

"Who was that?" Jessica asked, trying to change the subject.

"That's a client," Paul replied. "If I hear anything from Dave, I will call you. We are all praying for him. He was pretty rattled by the footage of you and..." He turned to where Stefan had been, seeing him now across the room, shaking hands and collecting hugs from adoring benefactors. Paul let the stress level build just enough in Jessica to keep her from running when he knew she wanted nothing more. "But anyway, no news is probably good news. Many men do not take that kind of thing very well at all. They do impulsive things. Probably not Dave. Maybe he is in Mexico on the beach figuring stuff out. Who knows, right?"

"Yeah, who knows," Jessica mumbled.

"Everything works out for the best in the long run," Paul continued. "Too bad Stefan ended that campaign. I am sure he needs time to heal." He knew he had lost this audience into a chasm of her anxiety and shame. He felt a bizarre pleasure in causing it. "Again, my prayers are with you and Dave, whatever path you both decide to take. I will support you and cherish the friendship we had. Or, what we have," he corrected.

"Thank you, I should probably go," she replied. "Stefan is not doing well. The whole office is very concerned."

Paul gave his best affected, half-namaste gesture, sitting back down to drink his Scotch and relish in his psychological vengeance.

The western exit of the Eisenhower Tunnel gave way to bluebird skies framing Buffalo Mountain in the distance. It was eight miles down, then up again until they reached Copper Mountain. It was a nice reprieve from the snowy struggle Paul's car had endured climbing up the eastern side of the Continental Divide.

"Man, I miss this," Derek sighed. "I had a condo right there at the base of Buffalo. He pointed towards a rectangular-shaped cut in the trees carved out of the National Forest.

"You'll like my Copper condo. It's right in the Center Village," Paul said. "We got you a flight back out of Gypsum. You'll have one connection."

"Whatever," Derek replied. "When do you think I should quit my job in Vero Beach?"

"Anytime you want," Paul answered as he focused on rounding the curves toward the valley below. His car was a gravity missile straining with every turn. Derek reached over to put the air conditioning on high. "What are you doing? It's winter."

"Helps regulate the speed by putting a little more work on the engine," Derek replied. "It was my Summit County trick. Also, put down the windows and it will increase the drag. You can raise and lower them to change your speed."

Paul lowered the rear windows and adjusted them as Derek had suggested. A huge grin reflected his enjoyment of the trick. "That is brilliant," he smiled.

As they cruised past the first exit and began to climb up a short hill, Derek pulled out his phone quickly typing a text. *Hey dude, I quit. I would give you two weeks, but I don't feel like it. In reality, you should have no problem replacing me. We both know that almost any idiot can do that job. Bye.*

"What was that?" Paul asked.

"I just quit. I am done from that shit hole," Derek replied smugly but relieved.

"You work at a Country Club," Paul exclaimed. "How is that a shit hole?"

"I didn't say it wasn't pretty. It's just full of assholes. Lazy assholes, arrogant assholes, idiot assholes…and general assholes," Derek replied. "The members are pretty nice even though they mostly represent the debt-obsessed aristocracy of professional upper-middle-class America. These are the assholes who have turned us from producers to consumers, and honestly, if I live long enough to see the last one of these cunts die, I will have accomplished enough living. But they are decently nice on the surface. None of them know I used to get them jobs. Most of them were at the corporate management level I recruited, constantly calling me when they got laid off."

"That kind of hate isn't healthy," Paul interjected before Derek could continue his tirade.

Derek knew Paul was right. The shit show his life had become was none of those people's fault. He didn't hate them as much as he hated the fact that they seemed to treat him with some strange combination of pity and leprotic contempt when they engaged him. *Maybe it's in my head,* he thought, *it's probably envy. God, I hope not.*

Paul's condo sat at the top of a five-story building. The view of the ski area was stunning as the mountain's energy faded with the late-day sun. Watching skiers work their way down their last runs was comical and mildly anxiety-producing. Regardless, it was a wonderful place, filling Derek with some of the best memories of raising his girls. He and his ex-wife had spent many happy days on that hill before and after having children. His daughters took their first runs at Copper. The ski area was part of him; he knew nearly every skiable inch of it.

"Here," Paul said, handing him a Scotch.

"Just one," Derek cautioned, "I am not acclimated to 9,600 feet. And I'm really losing my taste for alcohol."

"That's not a bad thing," Paul agreed with what seemed to be a little envy. "Like I said on the way up here, the guy in California has been developing tools to track almost anyone we want. It will be very useful for us."

Chapter 6

"Take a look at this man," Duncan said as they approached a couple walking on the early morning beach. The sun was burning off the haze in preparation for another day. "If I had to guess, he represents the norm. The median that believed it had reached success by discovering the end goal of retirement. Or at least the middle of the curve that convinced himself he had become successful. But look at him. Sloped shoulders bearing the burden of lifelong servitude of some other master never mastering himself, always at the beck and call of his job, his boss's ambition and the expectations of his wife and family. She is now his master."

"Hasn't she always been?" Dave asked.

"She has," Duncan continued. "Her needs have driven him even before they met. He was raised into servitude prioritizing himself to always be the martyr. His education and occupation were chosen in order to obtain her attention. He chose these things to appeal to her before he knew she existed. Before her, he had a few learning experiences with other women. Until he found the *one*. Her. His time was never his. There was always the preoccupation of finding and securing her in order to progress his lineage. She was the vessel by which he could become immortal through his children. It never occurred to him that he could use his time to develop something that lasted longer than a surname. To make something tangible and useful to everyone like art, or music, or invention. He dreamed of these things. Those dreams nagged at him and woke him in the night but he had to maintain the reality that he chose for himself. He avoided striving because of the potential of loss and accepted the common to be safe, and that is what he got."

Dave watched the man pass, his wife blathering on about an event they were to attend later in the day and what he should wear. His shoulders slumped over, matching the weight and shape of his frown. Thousands of concessions in his life added up to his present state like a house built on an eroding bluff overlooking the sea waiting to be claimed by the pounding, unrelenting surf. If his physical state matched the man's inner emotional state, all Dave could absorb from him was depression and the will to free himself. To free himself, to rest and relieve the exhaustion he carried.

"David," Duncan continued, "you have been given a gift. Jessica has freed you. That man was you David. The question is where to go. You probably feel like you are trapped here due to the circumstances you were dealt. In a sense, you are. But what you don't know is that this is meaningful. We are going to do great things. Be patient and you will thrive with us."

"What great things?" Dave asked. "Paul keeps talking like this and you keep alluding to something, but you won't tell me anything."

"All in time, David," Duncan replied. "The reality is I don't know where we are going either. Paul brought up an idea that kindled a fire. There are too many possible directions to begin with impetuous steps. I will know where we are going when destiny presents itself. But right now, my gut is saying to build a foundation. You and Derek are part of that foundation. I want you two to focus on building both your physical and mental strength. Destiny thrives on effort, David. Make developing your inner and outer selves as strong as possible and let fate navigate for you. You will find that faith and fate puts you where you are needed; where you are meant to be. You have to have your eyes open to see it."

Dave felt his heart begin to calm. It had been pumping an anxious tension inside of him since he left Colorado and everything he had known. The nagging anger of Jessica's betrayal still hovered in his head; the anger and guilty self-loathing he had for himself. What could he have done differently? Had he shirked his responsibility somehow and driven her away? Why didn't any of it seem fixable? Even so, how could he fix it from Florida, sequestered from the world? Hiding.

Was this it? Was this the starting line of something new? Could he just erase everything and go forward? The past was a collection of narratives he had always relied on to make sense of the present. It was how he communicated his value to new clients and new acquaintances. It was all gone. It had no meaning; as if it never existed. His past had no value because suddenly no one cared. What would he say if someone asked what he did? Everyone asks, especially women. Would he say I am a retired custom home builder and developer? He couldn't say that. That implied he was really retired with a lot of money or worse, that he had failed, and now he was living on the salvageable pieces of broken past victories. The slumped man they passed was a mirage of his intended future. He was too young to be that man.

"David," Duncan continued, "to be poor and to be wealthy are similar."

"How is that?" Dave asked.

"It comes down to time," Duncan replied. "Time is the only thing of value. How you use it is what matters. The resources a man with means has are of no value if all he does is fill his life with diversions while he slowly fades away. He has nothing but time because he doesn't have to toil for survival. The squandered time and money amongst people with middle incomes and so-called careers is worse than with the poor. After he takes care of his survival, the poor man using his time well is invaluable and worthwhile. His pursuits can create great things as long as he pursues something purposefully with no regard for the outcome. The poor man has to utilize his time efficiently because much of his time is spent surviving. If he is intelligent, he learns from his successes. His demons are the same as the middle; alcohol, games and all diversions. If he is tempted to waste his successes away on hope and immediate comfort or worse on envy, he is doomed. A wealthy man's problem is that he believes his money can buy purpose. You see it at every non-profit gala. Drunks demonstrating virtue, congratulating themselves for making a difference in lives they never experienced nor intend to."

"I have been to too many of those," Dave agreed. "Mark and I had to attend one every year."

"You didn't have to attend," Duncan interrupted. "You attended. Leave it at that. Being there is no sin. It is not much different from paying your taxes so the government can do the helping for you. At least that is how people like to think about it. The difference between a non-profit doing these things and the government is the fact that one of these is asking you to help them and the other is forcing you.

One preys on your emotions and the other coerces you outright.

"The problem with government is that they generally do only a few things particularly well. Taking on too much reveals the errors of their good intentions. A government is average people with average fears, average capabilities and all the normal insecurities who are given far too much power. Power fueled by good intentions or selfish motivations. This is a problem with democratic societies. The voters cannot be informed enough on the real problems and real solutions. When things go wrong, there are many people to blame besides themselves for casting their votes. It is senseless to hold any one person to account, not even a President. The system is too big for one person to hold all of the blame and all of the power, but many average voters have to fixate on one. Government growth run amok is the ultimate hydra. The people believe that they must confront the hydra and cut off its heads. This is a fool's errand. And, fortunately for the government monster, the world is full of fools."

"What do we do?" Dave asked.

"We work around it and find another path," Duncan replied as they stopped in front of the garage. "If you need to go out, use the Jeep and go out the back drive."

"*Miguel,*" Kate texted. "*my uncle is having us over for lunch.*" There was an uncomfortable lag in response, unlike her boyfriend. Kate waited as long as she could stomach. "*Are you there?*"

"*Yeah, what time?*" Miguel replied.

"*Noon.*"

"*Ok, I'll see you there,*" he replied.

"*What are you doing?*"

"*I have some work.*"

"On a Sunday?"

"No different than any other day. I'll be there. Gotta go."

Kate lay back into the bed, relieved and happy. Her uncle would finally be able to sit down with her, and Miguel, and see what she saw. He was driven and handsome. He had built himself up from nothing. Her Uncle Duncan had to respect that. He hadn't always been rich. As the family history was written, her grandfather had cut Duncan off sending him away with nothing. He ventured into the world nearly penniless until a family crisis called him back to Texas and into his eventual wealth. In his poverty, he had been a beach bum living on couches in tiny apartments in California when the beach towns were full of hippies, drunks, and surfers. That's what Duncan was. He painted houses and bartended. He had very little besides his friends and his mind. Now, he had anything he wanted and he didn't seem to care. It was as if he never wanted what he had. Miguel wanted it. He wanted a good life and he was building one.

Uncle Duncan lived in a huge house on the beach with a Mexican family who took care of him. His Texas house was ordinary with another Mexican family attending to it. Same with the house in Colorado. Supposedly, he had a house in Cuernavaca, Mexico too. She had never been there. He didn't talk about it. There was an uncomfortable family joke that he would give all of his fortune to his Mexican caretakers when he died. What did it matter? Miguel was up and coming and becoming more and more hers every day.

Uncle Duncan has to see Miguel's potential, she thought. Potential? He paid cash for a Land Rover, owned a nice, little house near the beach and always had money. He knew how to spend it well. That was beyond potential. That was reality. He expensed almost everything through the company. He implied that he needed virtually everything he bought to reflect his success to new and prospective clients. He laughed about expensing a Rolex and his clothes. Miguel was brilliant, or maybe his accountant was brilliant. It didn't matter. They were in a good place and she was happy.

"Ok, David, make yourself unseen," Duncan ordered. "Kate and Miguel are coming over for lunch around noon. She doesn't know anything about you or Derek."

"What should I do?" Dave asked.

"Get strong," Duncan replied. "You have the gym attached to the guest house. There's an excellent book in there on calisthenic conditioning. I suggest you start reading and following it. I hear it's better than weight training, but if you disagree, there are plenty of weights. Either way, give it a try. You have enough food stocked in your kitchen. If you need anything, call Imelda and she will get it for you. Imelda and Ignacio's numbers are programmed into your phone. Just be unseen."

"Ok," Dave replied.

"One other thing," Duncan continued, "when Miguel arrives, I want you to get a good look at him. There are some binoculars in the desk drawer in your bedroom. Just find a spot where you can see him and he can't see you."

Kate arrived at 11:30 to help Imelda with the preparation. She wanted to make sure Miguel didn't think of her as some spoiled rich girl who didn't know how to do anything. Besides, she liked the Ramirez family. They were authentically sweet to her not just because she was Duncan's niece. Imelda put her to work slicing fruit. Her Uncle was nowhere to be found. *He is probably working or showering*, she thought. She was sure he would make a good impression on Miguel and likewise Miguel on him. Her only hesitation was her Uncle's moodiness and distaste for anything resembling a party. Maybe the description *moody* was more like reserved or pensive but he could make some people uncomfortable. Uncle Duncan never seemed to care. As if it never occurred to him that his personality had an effect on others. The perception he gave people was that he expected them to remain in their own world while he remained in his; to allow those worlds to brush against each other momentarily but never fuse. *What is the phrase? Like ships passing in the night?* she thought. That's what it was. She could not live like that. She had too much to give.

Miguel drove up to the gate. The weight of his watch pulled on his wrist as he reached out the window for the intercom. As he pushed the call button, the gate suddenly lurched, anticipating him. The feeling of being watched haunted as he drove in, his eyes darting around looking for cameras. *The property of a billionaire*, he thought. Every square inch was probably monitored and recorded. He could imagine some fat man in a uniform sitting in a dark room, staring up at hundreds of screens while dropping potato chip crumbs on a control console. What the old man had in wealth, he had in potential and growing power. Fuck this guy. His time and his kind have passed.

Kate stood at the door smiling and anxious. She pecked Miguel on the cheek before leading him in. "What do you think?" she asked, hoping the impression of the house would inspire Miguel.

"Pretty nice," Miguel answered with as little expression as he could affect. It was nice; it was beyond nice. Envy welled up in him. But he was almost there. A few years, and this would be his. He fantasized about buying it when the old man finally went off to Mexico or wherever he would go to die.

"Hello, Miguel," he heard coming from the living room as Duncan entered the foyer. "Come in." Kate's eyes shined seeing her Uncle being pleasant. It was relieving.

"Mr. Westbourne," Miguel said, reaching out his hand.

"You can call me Duncan." The handshake was confident. Duncan had expected that. Miguel was confident. Their brief meetings before had assured him of that. He gestured to a chair while Kate went to the kitchen to retrieve a charcuterie board Imelda had assembled.

"How are things with you, Miguel?" Duncan asked.

"Everything seems to be going well. My business keeps growing," Miguel announced proudly. He suddenly realized he felt a need for validation from the old man. It was disconcerting.

"Amazing," Duncan replied.

"How so?" Miguel challenged. This old man wasn't going to get the best of him.

"I don't mean to be disrespectful," Duncan relented. "I don't understand the business. It seems as though the service industry as a whole is just one cost reduction and labor headache after another. When you get somewhere, there is always someone else outbidding you. Their services can seem barely distinct from yours; labor always the largest, non-depreciable cost."

"That's true," Miguel agreed, "but right now, we are the best and I have control of the costs. I can keep adding as many teams as I need to keep the clients happy and the competition from getting too greedy."

"What keeps your employees from going off on their own?" Duncan asked.

Miguel hesitated. It was a valid question for a valid business. Duncan's money came from oil. He had no control over the market price, only the extraction and storage. The industry was old. Reinventing it came infrequently and maybe not during someone's lifetime. His business was hustle and labor. He had control over both.

"I guess they could. Well, some of them they think they could. It wouldn't be good for them. I literally could crush them if I had to," Miguel replied.

Duncan leaned forward to take a piece of brie from the board, "To crush them how?"

Miguel was prepared for this. He had to be. It was part of the strategy to maintain his grip on the local market. His teams spoke virtually no English, his first line of defense. His second was the commandment that they never speak to clients but refer them to him or his trusted supervisors. His employees knew the consequences of stepping beyond that line. When some uppity client decided to practice Spanish on one of his teams, they were met with well-rehearsed timidity. It would stay that way.

"Crush is probably not the right word," Miguel softened. "I don't see them raising the capital to buy the equipment on $20 per hour."

"You pay them $20 per hour?" Duncan replied. "That seems pretty good."

"It is. They are happy and making a living. It is a decent wage for what is basically a job anyone can do," Miguel continued. "We are proud of that and I got to this point by out-lasting and out-competing the rest. There are a few who give me a challenge once in a while, but it's fine. I have more than enough work."

Duncan agreed, "No one seems to mow their own lawns anymore."

The lunch passed by with common chit-chat about art and social gatherings at the Country Club where Kate had met Miguel in the gym. She could picture the day he walked in stumbling over the threshold as she was exiting. That was the day it began. She moved her workout time back thirty minutes hoping to run into him again. It worked.

You still here? Read the text on Dave's phone.
I am, Dave replied.
Follow Miguel in the Jeep. He is leaving in about 10 minutes. Go out now and park around the corner.

Dave got up from the couch and threw on some clothes. He hurried down the back steps to the garage where Duncan kept his Jeep. A brief anxiety about whether it would start disappeared when the engine turned over. He doubted Duncan had ever driven it. Dave slipped the Jeep into gear and quietly drove out the path to the back service gate; surprised to see it open automatically. He turned right, parking on the side of the street around the corner as instructed. He had barely come to rest when Miguel's Land Rover passed. Jamming the Jeep into gear, he dropped in behind Miguel at what he thought was an unsuspicious distance.

Miguel's use of the turn signal seemed optional and sporadic more than a general practice. He flowed around right turns-on-red with ease and entitlement while Dave tried to keep up.

I think you have a tail, read the text on Miguel's phone.
At the next light, he replied, *take care of it.*
Will do.

Dave was sitting in the right lane two cars back from Miguel when the light turned green. The Land Rover lurched ahead aggressively while the elderly driver in front of Dave slowly turned over the wheels. He was pinned in. Then he heard the whoop of a siren behind him.

"Oh shit," he muttered. He was being pulled over. He felt his pocket for his license. With a prayer, he opened the glove compartment and drew out a small leather bag. Inside was the insurance and registration. His stomach knotted when he realized it was from Montana. Were the plates from Montana? He hadn't looked. He rolled the window down, hoping they were.

"Good afternoon," said the Officer. "You have a brake light out. Could I see your license and registration please?"

"Sure," Dave replied, handing over the documents. The officer strolled slowly back to his patrol car while Dave stared off in the direction Miguel had gone. What kind of luck was he having? He could see the cop fidgeting with his laptop taking what seemed to be more than enough time. The anxiety within him was overwhelming. Was he wanted in Colorado? He was trying to keep it together.

"Here you go," the officer said as he handed back the license and registration. "I'll let you go. Just get that fixed."

"Thanks, I will," Dave sighed.

Chapter 7

"Paul, we have a problem."

"Dominic, you never call me," Paul replied.

"There's a cop in Vero Beach running Dave's license. That is a problem."

"Shit. He got pulled over for a tail light the other day," Paul sighed. "He and Derek checked. The lights are fine."

"Then we have a bigger problem," Dominic replied. "I have a potential solution I have been kicking around, but they should lay low for a bit."

"OK, keep me posted," Paul said as he hung up.

"Dave look, nothing you do is bringing back your wife," Derek said as he leaned on the bar. "Besides, why would you want her back? Done is done. Once they decide to leave, set them free and forget them. They will never respect you if you don't. They can respect you from wherever their choices take them but not anywhere near you. That's a solid rule to live by. If more men did this, and we won't because pussy makes most of us useless and weak, women might behave better but I doubt it. If you took her back, she would tolerate you for a while and you'll feel like you have been vindicated and have won. Forget all of that. It's an odd hypocrisy with women. They can bang the neighborhood and if you forgive them and take them back, they lose respect for *you*."

"You said she looked unhappy," Dave lamented.

"She did and she deserves to be. But that doesn't mean she wants you back. It's certainly no reason to take her back. Screw that chick. This place is full of them. Start thinking of them as a commodity. Go get a new one. Get a whole harem of them. Remember, multiple marriages are illegal in this country not multiple girlfriends," Derek said with a grin.

"Why are you laughing?" Dave asked.

"I am not. I know you are suffering. We've all been there. I left what could have been the best woman I have ever met to move here," Derek said trying to console the man who was becoming his friend. "And her response was to tell me she was trying to replace me. If she is actively trying to replace you, she will eventually land on someone adequate."

They stared at their drinks long enough to ignore a large man in a pressed shirt and tie who slid up to the bar next to them. Derek looked over, making eye contact halfheartedly, opening himself up to conversation.

"Hello, my name's Prescott," the man volunteered.

"Like Arizona?" Derek replied, ready to be entertained. "It's pronounced Pres-kitt."

The man stared at him blankly as if his audience should be more interested to know who he was. Derek could sense the man was already somewhat drunk and ready for verbal combat. He could see the wheels in Prescott's head tightening the skin on his forehead as he searched for a rebuttal.

"I am a very prestigious corporate attorney in this town," Prescott announced.

"Do you work at the airplane factory?" Derek asked in a

voice rhythm he reserved for toddlers. "Are there other corporations around here I don't know about? Are you involved in citrus?"

"There are plenty. I am also a CPA," Prescott went on.

"Wow, a double threat of excitement. Do you do taxes *and* law stuff?" Derek was beginning to like this guy, at least for the entertainment value. He continued to engage Prescott in conversation while Dave slipped away to the restroom.

"There is a lot of money in this town," Prescott spittled as he took a long sip off the top of his overpriced Manhattan.

"There is a lot of spending in this town," Derek rebutted. "I doubt there is a lot of money being earned here. You have seen the local ruins of the last banking fiasco, correct? Or is it normal for pilates studios and home decor boutiques to have drive-through structures?"

Prescott turned towards his drink, muttering. His demeanor had soured, but the ego was regaining traction. Dave returned giving Derek an opportunity to turn away from Prescott. With as much mental telepathy as he thought he could create, Derek gave Dave a do-not-engage warning stare. Dave was content to be uninterested.

Prescott's alcohol-induced irritation found a new victim in the bartender, who was trying her best to avoid him. He waved her over, asking for the tab. With a whip of her hand, she immediately produced it from her apron. Prescott leaned into the bill, writing furiously. He petulantly tossed the pen on the bar, stood up and stomped out.

Derek reached over to read what Prescott had written. *You are a useless bitch. I am not coming here anymore. Tell Andrew I said so.* The tip line said 'ZERO'.

"Fucker actually wrote out 'ZERO'," Derek muttered. "I'll be right back. Pay up and stay here for a minute," Derek said as he slid off his stool. He pushed through a side door in pursuit. "Hey, Pres-kitt. You misspelled 'Fifty' on the tip line," he said mockingly.

"Fuck that bitch and fuck you," Prescott managed to get out as he leaned smugly against his Audi. "What are you going to do about it, fag?"

"Fag? Who still uses that word? What decade is this? How about I kick your fat ass?" Derek replied. With that, Prescott stepped forward, throwing a drunken haymaker swing. As the fist passed Derek's head like a low-orbit satellite, the momentum spun Prescott toward the hood of his car. With a lightning quick motion, Derek pulled one of Prescott's hands behind his back and slammed his face down on the hood with everything he had. Blood spurted immediately, imprinting Prescott's facial features in red against the white of the car; his knees gave out. Derek reached down to pull Prescott's wallet out of his back pocket, relieving it of cash. As he dropped the wallet, scattering its contents onto the ground, he restrained himself from finishing Prescott off with a punt to the head.

"That's one for me, zero for Vero," he laughed as he quickly went to retrieve Dave. Slamming the cash on the bar, he looked up to see tears descending the bartender's face as she read the receipt, "Prescott says sorry. And don't worry about Andrew." He grabbed Dave by the arm tugging him towards the back door opposite a scene gathering around the bleeding and moaning prestigious corporate attorney.

"Get on the plane. You two need to get out of here for a few weeks at the very least," Duncan announced. His irritation with Derek and anxiety over Dave's run-in with the local police was starting to ease, but Paul was right. They needed to get out of Vero Beach for a while. The Gulfstream was ready to be pulled out of the hangar as they stepped on board.

As they taxied, Dave felt unsettled. He had no roots left. Reality was staring at him in the face; his life was shattered. That is how he thought of it. Shattered by a continuous string of circumstances. Shattered by the actions of other people and his willingness to do what he thought was the right thing by them. All it seemed to bring him was punishment and more problems. He looked over at Derek as the plane rotated, searching for reassurance.

"You alright, buddy?" Derek asked. Dave shook his head. "Don't worry. This plane seems safe. We probably won't crash."

"This is starting to get complicated," Paul warned Duncan.

"Are we sure we want to do this?" Duncan asked hesitantly

"It's your call. You and your guys have the money. I just hope I can hold up my end," Paul replied.

"What is your end?" Duncan asked.

"Legal and how to bypass it. Are you getting too old for this? Are you sure you don't want to just fart around playing astronaut with your other billionaire buddies?" Paul replied.

"I am certainly too old for that, and I don't have any billionaire buddies," Duncan laughed. "This idea of yours. What did you call it? Justice in lieu of law? Sounds like vigilantism."

"Something like that," Paul replied. "We got that done here with Mark. As you know, Dave was the trigger man. How is he?"

"He is a mess but he's been a relatively quiet mess," Duncan replied. "That wife of his damaged him; and for some reason, he is acting like he wants her back."

"That's normal man shit. Just get him laid. That fixes

almost everything," Paul replied. "If that doesn't work, we'll keep him occupied doing something useful. Derek will help him. Remind me what he did for a living?"

"He was a Headhunter. He tells people he was a Consultant. That is mostly true," Duncan offered. "He was really good, but his business required guys like me who make decisions, not a bunch of corporate types scared of their HR departments. His business caved in on itself and he wound up here in Vero Beach to be near his kids. What did you two talk about? Anything of substance?"

"I ran a brief description by him outlining the plan," Paul replied. "He seemed interested enough to quit his job. Can he do what we need him to when things get ugly?"

"Given the right circumstances applied to the right villain, he could exact justice on almost anyone," Duncan assured Paul. "Derek would throw himself into the fire for anyone he thought was being oppressed."

"That's what we want," Paul replied. "If my suspicion is correct, this Miguel guy is up to something. To what, is still unknown. Is Kate still dating him?"

"Utterly in love," Duncan sighed.

"She might need therapy after this," Paul warned.

The plane descended towards runway 19 Right. As it taxied to a stop on the ramp, a black car pulled up. The pilot stepped out of the cockpit, giving them the nod that they could deplane and pointing to the car. The trunk popped open; they each dropped in a small bag they had hurriedly packed. Sliding into the opposite sides of the backseat, they were greeted by a thin, curly-haired driver.

"One of you guys needs to be in front," said the man. "I am not a taxi." Derek motioned for Dave.

"Who are you?" Derek asked, "and where are we going?"

"I am Dominic, and we are going to La Jolla," the man replied.

"Wait, where are we?" Dave asked. "This doesn't look like San Diego."

"It's not," Dominic replied. "This is Orange County. We have at least an hour and a half drive."

"Ok," Derek submitted, slipping further down into his seat before nodding off.

Dave tried to engage Dominic in conversation. For whatever reason, Dominic didn't want to talk; he had no idea why. Maybe he *was* just their driver. Whoever he was, he wasn't someone who seemed to enjoy chitchat. Dave relented to stare out the window and think about his life. It nagged at him. He knew he had to find some way to break out of the misery. He needed something or someone to distract him. Maybe Derek was right on the plane. He needed another woman to distract him, fall in love with her, have her dump him and repeat the process until it just hurt less and less. To become immune to rejection or too exhausted to care. *Could I be like that?* he wondered. Derek seemed to be except for the Colorado girl. He said little about her, but the look in his eyes didn't lie.

The sun had set as they pulled into the garage of a small but nicely kept house. Derek stepped out, stretching like he had been on a multi-day bus ride. "Where are we?" he asked.

"This is my place," Dominic answered. "Come on in."

Derek followed on Dominic's heals while Dave lagged behind, taking in the house. It was nice. It was obviously inhabited by a man but thoughtfully decorated. There was no gaming chair or walls of big screen TVs as he expected. He and Mark had built a custom home for a very wealthy kid who had to be prodded by his mother to buy furniture. It was funny and a little sad, but relatable at the time. Jessica had been appalled. Dave was certain she had contacted the young man's mother forcing him into an effort to appear mature and socially adept.

Dominic fell into a chair, motioning for them to do the same. "Ok, guys, you are going to hang out here for a few weeks while your assault," pointing to Derek, "and your tail goes away," pointing at Dave.

"Tail? What tail?" Dave asked.

"The cop that pulled you over. We think he was put on to you by Mr. Aguilar," Dominic replied.

"Aguilar? Is that Miguel? How would he know I was following him?" Dave asked.

"It seems as though the cop was aware of you tailing Miguel and therefore aided and abetted in Miguel's escape from you," Dominic explained. "That's what I could assume from the data. No point worrying about it now. Go get some sleep if you are tired. There are two bedrooms at the end of the hall made up for you and food in the fridge if you're hungry. We'll talk about it tomorrow. I really need to finish up some work and it's late for you east coast guys."

"Good morning," Dominic said cheerfully as Derek walked into the kitchen fresh from a round of pushups and leg lifts. "Coffee?" Dominic gestured to the pour-over pot on the counter.

"Yeah, thanks," Derek replied, taking a sip, "Man, that's good."

"Only way to make it," Dominic said as he looked up from his laptop. "Hey Dave, get some coffee and both you guys go put on the simplest shirt you have and comb your hair." Dave gave him a wondering glance as he turned back towards the bedroom. With both men assembled and the indolence of the morning shaken off, Dominic stood them in front of a green screen to take their photos. They watched as he typed something fiercely then clicked 'send'. "Off to Paul."

"What's that?" Dave asked.

"That is for your new IDs. We are making you guys Brazilian. You speak Portuguese, right Derek?"

"Falo," Derek replied. "Suficiente."

"I don't speak Portuguese," Dave complained.

"It doesn't matter," Dominic reassured him. "If you ever need to, just act dumb."

"Are you calling Brazilians dumb?" Derek exclaimed.

"Definitely not," Dominic replied. "I am saying the best and smartest thing you can do sometimes is act dumb. Stupid is endearing if you do it right. Nonetheless, you guys are going to be unofficial, undocumented Brazilians with documents. You will have your Driver's Licenses, Green Cards and Socials in a day or two."

"Where does Paul get these things?" Dave asked.

Dominic hesitated, thinking whether to tell them but it was something anyone could figure out if they wanted. "He has a guy do it for him; a client he was able to get a reduced sentence for. The guy produces these things with a printer Paul helped him procure. He has a soft spot for Mexicans."

"He has a soft spot for Mexican women," Dave interjected. Dominic laughed. It was true. Paul's legal ethics were exceedingly more flexible when it came to the pursuit of very good-looking Mexican women.

"What happens if we get arrested?" Derek asked.

"Call your Attorney," Dominic replied, "and try to speak as little as possible or speak in Portuguese. What is it, Abogado?

"Advogado," Derek corrected him. "What you said is 'lawyer' in Spanish. I doubt many of the Vero cops speak Portuguese, but there has be at least one."

"You're probably right," Dominic agreed. "I finished up the next line of our defense last night. Let me show you." Dominic spun his laptop around to demonstrate. The screen had a map of Vero Beach with little blue dots moving around, some sitting still.

"What are those?" Dave asked.

"Those are known cops," Dominic replied. "I am still working on data collection, but by the time you guys get back to Florida, this thing should be at least 95% reliable."

Dominic held up his finger to quiet Derek before he could ask the inevitable questions. "Call it AI programming if you want," he said. "I am not sure how intelligent it is. I do this for retail marketing departments. Although, they don't use all the data capability I am using here. They use it to discern the time and frequency a customer goes in and out of their stores, which aisles they tend to go down most, their purchasing tracked through the rewards programs, the payment method they use the most and a bunch of other metrics. It all works using their cell phones either voluntarily through apps and reward programs or through a series of identifiers I made for them. Marketing has become monitoring. And the thing I made creates a habit profile of their customers because people are very habitual. I just tweaked it for cops."

Dominic could see the wheels churning in Dave and Derek's heads. He stood back and let them watch the cop show for a few minutes while refilling their coffees. It was magnificent, simple and effective for someone wanting to avoid law enforcement.

"Look at this one," he said as he zoomed in on a dot sitting still near the highway. It came to life, moving south on I-95 finally coming to a quick stop along the road behind a new dot that lit up. "Someone with a cell phone just got pulled over," he laughed. "The untracked ones only show up when they have been engaged by a cop.

"Ok, before you ask, I'll just tell you. Cops have cell phones. They all have cell phones, and they screw around with them at work like everyone else. They also go to work at police stations, tend to drive furtively and erratically at times, stand around at concerts and do other various human cop stuff. I just take these things they do and create a program that makes an assumption that these cell phones doing this stuff are cops instead of pantyhose shoppers. And voila." Dominic laughed.

"That is brilliant," Derek exclaimed, "and how do you get the cell numbers?"

"I buy the data from the carriers. If that doesn't work, I have my sources who can let me in the backdoor," Dominic explained. "Through the normal channel they won't give me the names of the people, but I have a bot cruising around the internet all the time looking for phone numbers attached to people, and those people are sometimes cops who get into news articles and receive awards and other crap they have to post on the internet. Honestly, most of these guys seem to post themselves because they think they look good in uniform. I pull their names off social media and make a list. Then, I associate that list with the phone number. If they responded to a scene and it gets on the internet through the news or whatever, the programming goes back in time, looks at the photos, identifies the cop and saves his photo. They also own houses and drive their cop cars home. That makes it really easy, thanks to county property records. And this is the guy who was tailing you, Dave..." Dominic pulled a photo out of a manila folder, slamming it triumphantly down in front of Dave, "Vero Beach's finest Officer Marco Sandoval."

"That's him," Dave confirmed.

They passed the next few days in La Jolla at the beach, running and working out. For Dave, it was good to feel free from the confines of Duncan's estate. Dominic left them to themselves, only warning them to mind their manners and not get arrested. On a beautiful Southern California afternoon they strode into the house refreshed from a run to find an opened FedEx envelope on the table. Sitting on the envelope were Green Cards for João and Benison Abreu.

"What is this?" Dave asked. "Is that me? How do I pronounce this?"

"Jo ah ooh," Derek explained, trying not to laugh as Dave slaughtered the Portuguese name for John. "Try it more nasally."

"This would be better in Spanish," Dave lamented.

"It would be more common," Derek corrected. "Besides, maybe you can land yourself a Brazilian girlfriend who will teach you the important things you will never learn from a gringa."

"What do I need to learn?" Dave contested.

"More than you can imagine, buddy," Derek laughed. "You have an idea about women I wish I still had and I wish were true. Maybe you can find that in Brazil, but I doubt it. At their core, they're also women. Just Brazilian. But in comparison to us, they are unique."

"I have no idea what you are talking about," Dave replied with a smile. He was beginning to see Derek differently. He wasn't a misogynist. He was something else. What it was wasn't clear.

Chapter 8

Chez Laurent was about as good as it got for fine dining in Vero Beach. It was set apart from the nauseating, extensive collection of restaurants and bars, all vying to be unique while achieving paradoxical similarity. The majority had lines of snowbirds processed quickly through the hostess station to a table before their hips gave out. Speed-to-seat was more important than culinary standards. With low standard demands, there wasn't enough sophisticated pretense to justify the development of better restaurants. Chez Laurent was the risen cream while the rest of the town did its best to make banality excessively expensive, equating price with an illusion of quality. It was another facet of the Zero of Vero everyone seemed to tolerate.

Miguel refused to meet Kate at a restaurant bar and wait to be seated. It had become a ritual for her friends to join her as she waited for him to leave work. Barely warmed up in conversation, Miguel arrived unusually early. He was socially pleasant and handsome, keeping Kate on guard against other women. Her friends were, after all, women and known to have snatched away boyfriends in the past. She was not allowing it this time, for this man. At twenty-seven, she was old enough to know what she wanted. Following her instincts, she stood up to hug him and take a firm grip on his hand.

"Hello," Miguel smiled. "Have you been nice to Kate?"

"Hi," they replied almost in unison. Kate's friend Courtney gave a synopsis of their conversation up until his arrival while Miguel eye's searched for the Maître d'. Catching his glance, he signaled to be seated and rescued from further societal pleasantries. They were quickly led away from the women still trying to talk to Kate as she lagged behind.

Miguel was unusually quiet as they sat listening to the rehearsed specials. As the waiter took a breath, Miguel put up his hand to end the monologue. "A bottle of the Tuscan Merlot," he ordered. He looked back at his menu, assuming Kate's approval.

"Excellent choice, sir," the waiter replied as he backed away a step, his head slightly tipped downward in submission, before turning on his heals to leave.

"Are you OK, baby?" Kate asked.

"We lost one of our guys today," he explained.

"Lost?" Kate asked. Miguel gave her the grim look of bad news. "Do you want to go?" Kate asked. "We can have something at my place," her face showing concern. She bit her lower lip slightly as if to pause before asking what had happened.

Miguel leaned forward to tell her, looking around for potential ears. "He just didn't show up. We thought he may have been illegal and picked up by Immigration. Then about three hours ago, we heard that he had been found along a road pretty beat up. He died from his injuries at the E.R. before he could tell anyone what happened."

"Who would do that?" she exclaimed, quickly calming herself as she became aware of the other people around them.

"There are plenty of people who would," Miguel explained. "The cartel, maybe."

"What cartel? Here?" Kate seemed incredulous that the cartel, or any cartel, could exist in Vero Beach. "I mean, I heard that the airport used to have some drugs flown in but everyone says that was taken care of a long time ago."

"For the most part, it was, but traffickers don't give up on markets entirely," Miguel replied. Kate gave him a confused look. "For the most part," he repeated. "There was a crackdown on the airport about the same time the Navy and Coast Guard were putting pressure on Columbian cocaine being smuggled in through The Keys. That's what helped the Mexican cartels become more powerful. Why bother with a bunch of islands and airports when you have almost 2,000 miles of border to smuggle across? Florida has many places to boat or fly in drugs, but it only has one way to go from there. North. Trafficking is logistics. The only reason it became an import area long ago was because it was easy. Both the DEA and the smugglers got smarter but the smugglers have businesses and the Feds have jobs and retirement plans. Who do you think really got smarter?"

He sat back to let her ponder as the waiter arrived to pour their wine. Miguel gestured to be left alone for a few more minutes while they read the menu.

"You think he was dealing drugs while he worked for you?" Kate asked.

"Possibly," Miguel replied, "you never know what these guys are into. His paperwork was all checked out. Had a Green Card." *That should keep her occupied for a while*, he thought, *Give her something to think about.* She would forget soon enough. Kate was a spoiled, rich girl whose preoccupations were dedicated to appearances and comfort. He was doing his best to continue spoiling her, but he needed her out of his business. She had been a little too interested the last few weeks. So was her Uncle. The old man was probably just interested in the business because he thought he knew how to run everything. Old businessmen were like that, always looking for an ear to reminisce and a past to feel validated.

"Wow, wait," Kate asked between sips, leaning forward to be discreet, making it obvious they were talking about something private. "You think the cartel is still here?" she asked in almost a whisper.

"Maybe," Miguel replied. "Like I said, they don't like to give up markets."

"But the cocaine people were Colombians, right?" she asked, "Aren't the new cartel people Mexican?"

"I guess, but I think cocaine comes from Columbia or maybe Peru," Miguel replied innocently. "It probably stops off in Mexico to be smuggled in from there. It's not just cocaine they are trafficking." He knew very well who the cartel were and how narcotics entered the United States. Giving Kate the example of cocaine was easier for her to relate to. Although she stayed away from drugs, many of her acquaintances proudly bent the knee to the powder. Miguel signaled to drop the conversation as the waiter returned. They placed their order before Kate stood up to go to the restroom. As she rounded the corner out of sight, he slid the phone on to the table to text, *Dead. Confirm?*

Dead, came the reply.

Did he talk?

Nothing we know of. Was tailed by the usual.

Someone in his family needs to pay his debt. Get someone new, and don't fuck this up again. Find out how he got to the hospital. That was a huge fuck up.

We are on it Jefe. Sorry.

He slid his phone back into his pocket, expecting Kate to return. Sipping his wine, he reminded himself to relax and act like the name he used for his clients, 'Typicals'. The typical gringos. The typical upper-middle-class idiots who worked themselves silly to leverage a lifestyle they used for the show. *What the fuck do these idiots do that they can't mow their own lawns?* he wondered. Whatever it was, he didn't care. Running a gardening business with trafficked workers was profitable. He was out of the day-to-day drug business, taking only his cut for higher-level management the others were incapable of. For now, the DEA seemed occupied with other things leaving the legacy drug business alone. ICE was malleable when he needed them. The local cops were occupied trying to make headlines busting small-time dealers or their attention was purchased. It seemed like half of them were on his personal security force. It wasn't half, but there were enough. And Kate, he liked her. She was hot enough but what did that matter? She was replaceable. The more she believed they were monogamous, the better things would be for him. It was good PR to date a billionaire's niece and could have future benefits. It leaned towards credibility.

"Dude, it's five. Let's go down to that bar on the corner and talk up some women," Derek suggested. "It'll be good practice for you. You can be Dave."

"I'm Jo ah ooh," Dave replied as he distinctly pronounced the three syllables of his Brazilian name in a broken, staccato enunciation.

"You are not João. Not yet but there's potential," Derek laughed. "Let's go."

They walked the few blocks to a trendy local hangout behind a couple of young professional men in suits. *Lawyers,*

Dave thought. The place was about half full, but from the antsy demeanor of the hostess, it seemed like it would fill up soon. Derek led the way to the corner of the bar motioning for Dave to occupy the seat facing the length of it.

"You don't want to face the crowd? Don't you feel paranoid when your back is to everything?" Dave asked. He was more than willing to give up his view of the bar and face the racks of spirits.

"There's a mirror," Derek replied, pointing to the field of view reflecting in it. "I can see enough. Besides, chicks who go to the bar together seem to like those small, protective high tables where they make you swim up like it's an island and you just crashed your plane off shore. You crawl up the beach to be met by a tribe of cannibals, not a lust pack looking for your seed and someone to exalt."

Dave paused, letting the island description fade. "You don't care? Why are we here?" he asked. "I thought we were going to 'talk up some women' like you said." Dave had the feeling that Derek's strategy was to get out of Dominic's house for a while, baiting him with potential diversions.

"You meet women when they want to meet you, Dave," Derek explained. "I am not opposed to walking up to a woman cold but, in my opinion, you are better off knowing their attraction signals than trying to force something out of thin air. It's more natural, less awkward and she thinks it's her idea."

"I thought approaching women was a thing. Like some sort of rehearsed art form," Dave said.

"It is but they let you know," Derek replied to a confused Dave. "Women will always give you a sign they find you safe at the minimum and attractive enough to sleep with at best. They will do this immediately. If they don't, you are more than likely invisible to them. Move along. Anything you do to change that means you are chasing and chasing is a waste of your time. But there is also the strategy of being around. Like in small social circles where you can exhibit competence. That takes consistent mental fortitude or, in most cases, nothing else to do. Most of time, the best thing to do is to do your thing and let them show up."

"I sort of chased my wife," Dave recalled.

Derek looked at Dave in a way a father looks at his kid who knows he said or did something wrong. Sternly but patiently waiting for the kid to come around. As Dave's eyes widened in response to the realization flowing through him, Derek could feel a new surge of potential. Dave wasn't lost to a stubborn, defensive ego like a lot of the men he knew. He was smart, but there were still petrified layers of conditioning and willful ignorance to chisel through.

A pretty blond slid up to the bar next to Dave. He turned towards her briefly enough for her to say, "Hi." Dave responded, turning away from Derek to face her. They spoke while the bartender poured her wine. Once she had it in hand, she patted Dave on the shoulder and returned to her friends at the small, high table they inhabited.

"Huh," Dave said with a smile. She seemed nice.

"Yeah," Derek agreed without a hint of emotion.

"You don't think she was nice?" Dave contested.

"She was pleasant. Most people are relatively pleasant especially when your personal space is overlapping. It's how society works to keep us from kicking each other's asses all the time. Right now, you are conflating *pleasantly social* to her being *into you*. Maybe possibly, if you had another chance to talk to her, blah, blah, blah," Derek replied.

"No, I'm not," Dave denied.

"You were. It's OK. She is one of millions of women," Derek eased his response.

"I could go talk to her," Dave defended.

"You already signaled your interested when you turned towards her. You think you could walk up to her and her friends based on that conversation with nothing more?" Derek asked.

"Yes!" Dave exclaimed.

"Fuck me, I have to see this. Go!" Derek challenged giving Dave a little shove.

"Fine, I am going," Dave stood up, determined and confident, he started to walk toward the woman who adjusted her body language as he approached. He continued to walk past her straight to the restroom. When he returned, Derek was quietly laughing to himself.

"Thank God you have some sense to pull up when you are about to crash and burn. Good job fighting your ego with your feet," Derek laughed. "She's not into you. At least not right now."

"That's obvious," Dave relented. "I just kept going like you said, fighting my ego with my feet. Nothing. Not into me at all. She didn't even look up as I passed. Is this what single life is going to be like?"

"Yup, and it gets weirder. There's shit you can't even imagine at your age. What are you? About forty?" Derek asked.

"Thirty-eight," Dave replied.

"That's a good age to be. To be careful," Derek warned. "You pretty much have a dating pool between twenty and sixty, and in that pool, the women are nothing alike and everything alike. Because they are all chicks."

"They are not all the same," Dave contested.

"They are not individually the same, but they all have chick instincts. It's their motivations that will vary," Derek replied. "They are the female animal to our male animal.

Remember watching animal shows when you were a kid? Did the female animals act like the males? Did the male animals desperately chase around the females? They did when the alpha male wasn't around. When he was present they either challenged him for his status or they calmly stepped away and submitted. The females were waiting around to see who won. We do something like that and you can see it when it's happening. Once you see it, it can't be unseen."

"What are you talking about?" Dave lamented.

"Mating, Dave. Mating rituals. We have them just like other species but in our own way. Instead of asses getting all puffed up and red when they're ready, our females are more subtle in their mating signals. But they signal, sometimes loudly, and you signal your value to her through your words, your actions, and how she receives it in the *feelings* part of her brain." Derek took a sip of his non-alcoholic beer, opening up space for Dave to respond.

"You think I could get her number?" Dave asked.

"Who? The blond?" Derek laughed. "Not today. I would let that one go. You're too fixated. Not on her specifically but you are fixated on the win. You're doubling down on getting somewhere just to get somewhere. Like a guy looking to score points."

"Points for what?" Dave asked.

"You know, points. Attraction points. Men do this all the time. It's like they calculate a potential lay price and work towards gaining enough lay points to get the lay. Dinner: 50 points. Flowers: 20 points. Texting her nice things: 5 points each. Texting her too much: negative points. When you first meet her and she gives you attention, you immediately assume she is into you, explain your fucking job with esoteric flamboyance and subtly, or not subtly, explain to her that this job will guarantee her survival and the survival of your future children: 85 points.

"You keep earning points until she meets your preconceived lay-award level. Call it 100 points for this part of the story. If you go whizzing past 100 points, you start to realize that it might not happen and you might be getting played. You are in purgatory between your waning patience and her manipulation. You might start bugging her to allow you to cash in your points which gets you more negative points. At 150 points, you might turn into a creepy stalker because you are so fixated on the lay point price being 100. Why won't she relent? Then she says some shit like, 'let's be friends' after you have invested time and resources into getting with her. You are back to zero points, where you will stay forever. You still think you have the accumulated points, but she has reduced you to the equivalence of being one of her girlfriends and no longer a romantic possibility." Derek paused.

"Oh, and women seem to have their own point system which is where the friend-zone is. The idiot living there is unknowingly trying to reach her infinite point threshold. The other idiots are working towards a level of points fluctuating with her moods. If one of these fools gets to the right number, where he has waited and performed long enough, he wins the prize. That's what the girls call 'making him wait'. It's like training your ass off for a race then coming in second and that satisfies you. It becomes your prize and you happily quit. It's a stupid way to live, Dave. Let that fester around in your head for a while."

"Do you think men and women can be friends?" Dave asked.

"They can," Derek replied. "It helps if she is hideous, entertaining in some way and you have no physical attraction to her. Or maybe you have so many options that having female friends is a condition of your social circumstances. What I am talking about is reverting to friendship when you are into her just to keep her in your life. You know, staying friends at her request while you think she is a potential romantic possibility and you just have to ride it out. That's sad and desperate. It broadcasts your lack of options. You just gave her permission to cry to you about her future, shitty boyfriends while you sit there listening, thinking you are the magic remedy for her bad decisions." Derek stared impatiently at Dave. "Let's get the fuck out of here."

As they left, a pretty woman seated with Dave's blond made eye contact and smiled at Derek. Waiting at the door, Dave watched Derek talk to her briefly. Within a minute, he handed her his phone. She keyed in something and handed it back. With that Derek smiled, gave her a fist bump and walked straight out the door past Dave.

"What was that?" Dave asked.

"She gave me her number," Derek grinned, holding up his phone.

"What? How?" Dave pled.

"She gave the signal. I responded," Derek replied.

"Straight to 80 points," Dave sighed.

"I don't need points, Dave." Derek laughed.

Chapter 9

"I got them to the plane about an hour ago."

"Thank you, Dominic," Duncan replied. "Were you able to extract what you needed from Kate's phone?"

"I got the whole thing, texts, contacts, emails, everything."

"We won't need much, right?" Duncan asked.

"I glanced through it and ran some software I developed to find keywords and phrases. I also added all of her saved cell numbers to the monitor program. Not much came up except for one curious item," he hesitated, hoping to avoid delving into Kate's personal life.

"Just spit it out. What curious item?" Duncan implored.

"It seems like one of her friends spends a lot of time with Miguel," Dominic revealed.

"Which one?" asked Duncan.

"Her name is Courtney."

"Ok, we will keep that to ourselves. Maybe I'll have Dave and Derek check up on her after they get back from Colorado," Duncan replied.

The Gulfstream turned for its final approach into Rocky Mountain Metro. Derek stretched out. His thoughts were tracing the few months of change in his life; how his path had veered towards a completely different direction than his expectations haphazardly tried to force. His shit show parade of a life, consisting of one bad circumstance after another, seemed to be coming to a close. Nothing he tried put him anywhere near the past when he had everything a normal, working father and husband wanted. It was one dilemma after another, leaving him feeling hopelessly replaceable. Even his relationships with new women he liked had suffered. It didn't matter how much he liked a woman or how much fun they had together. Once she realized she was with a man who seemed to have bad luck, she opted out like it was contagious and permanent.

But things were turning around, it was incredible that he could do a little work for a nice older man ten years previous, not speak for years, then wind up in a clandestine organization formed with no defined purpose other than following around a boyfriend. And getting paid for it. Although he had yet to get paid. *Are all people with money this petty about controlling their families?* he wondered. *Is that what this is with the niece?*

Not only was he technically unemployed, but he had received word that his driver's license was about to be suspended because some busybody county government employee could not read and interpret his court-ordered garnishment. *Monica Del Valle, total idiot*, he thought. Another bullshit thing he had to deal with. The garnishment was a moot point. He quit the job that was supposed to pay it. *What can I do to pay the child support and look legit?* he thought as the plane came to a stop near a hangar. It was a pressing topic to bring up with Duncan. Although he hated the insidious way his ex-wife alienated him from his daughters, she needed the money. It was his duty to pay her, regardless of the little time he got with the girls. Paul came into view through the window, waving from inside the hangar. He would know what to do.

"Dave," Paul smiled, holding his arms wide to hug his friend. "Welcome back. Did you miss it?"

"Have I ever," Dave sighed. "It's good to see you and breath this air."

"Come on, you two, let's get up to the ranch," Paul said as he led them to the car. He studied Derek a moment before opening the car door.

They began the 30-mile drive with Dave recapping his impressions of Florida and California. Derek interrupted every so often to recall his memories from the back seat. It was impossible to hear his voice and think he wasn't conflicted. As they passed through Boulder, Derek looked more melancholy with every stoplight.

"What's the problem?" Paul asked.

"Duncan was able to get my mail and forward it to California. This woman in Child Services is getting my Colorado license suspended. It's the only tangible thing I have left from here. And now I sort of have a job, whatever this thing is, but no cash flow to pay the support," Derek lamented. "Do we have a solution for that? I appreciate this opportunity, but I need to have some income."

Paul stared out the window in thought for a moment. "Duncan has been covering all of your day-to-day living expenses, but I understand the problem. You need to appear more legit. I'll set up a shell company. You guys will be house painters. You'll never have to paint. You'll just collect the normal amount a painting company should every week.

I'll have my assistant make up invoices, billings, etc, and buy paint and supplies so it looks real. We'll get an account with a local paint store and stick the paint in a storage facility then sell it later, if ever. We can probably run this temporarily until we get through this boyfriend problem with Kate. Then we'll reassess and I will come up with something else."

"How do you think up this stuff so fast?" Dave asked.

"Experience and defending the right kind of clients, Dave," Paul replied with the best evil grin he could derive. "Is this county woman Monica Del Valle?"

"That's her. Know her?" Derek asked.

"Oh yeah, she has been a pain in the ass for a few of my clients," Paul replied. "I am getting a little irritated and have a plan to mess with her. I wonder how many ex-husbands her letters have been the final blow."

"Final blow?" Dave asked.

"Receiving her letter and ending yourself before you realize it was nothing you couldn't handle in a better frame of mind," Paul replied grimly. "Regardless of the fact that she is part of the wider problem, I would guess her incompetence has been complicit in at least a few suicides. I'll deal with her in the way I know best. Impersonally and justly."

"Impersonally?' Dave asked.

"Impersonally because when someone does their job as a drone of a system and brandishes that system's power it does not exclude nor insulate their soul from morality, ethics and justice," Paul replied. "You are human not a job."

They drove the final few miles to Lefthand Canyon. Dave and Derek were tranquilized by the scenery. Florida had nothing in comparison. Everything was nearly at eye level, giving it a two-dimensional feel. At best, Florida was a painting. Colorado was sculpture. They turned off the road at an automated gate driving up a steep mountain road through an open field then into the aromatic stands of ponderosa pines. Dave knew the property well, better than Paul.

"Dave," Paul interjected into the quiet, "I added some new things recently. There're more shipping containers and they are habitable."

"Really? Like tiny houses?" Dave asked.

"Yes, and off-grid completely. The only thing I need anyone up here for is putting propane into the big tank. The one that has survived all of the fires. And someone to clean out the septic tank."

"You got a permit from the county for a septic tank?" Dave asked.

"There was the old one my father had. We just revamped it. County doesn't know it's there and I am keeping it that way," Paul replied. "You and Mark left me with enough subcontractor contacts to get anything I need done without permits. Cash and quiet are King and Realm, Dave."

Dave winced at the thought of bypassing the county. He and his brother-in-law Mark had always done construction through the proper permitting, but they built for other people. Paul built for Paul.

The SUV came to rest on a small, flat area peculiar to the surrounding hillside, cut into the slope before the current generation of trees. In front of them, four dark green shipping containers appeared as though they were being used for nothing more than storage. Dave stepped out of the car, taking in the cool, pine-scented air. He was back.

"Uncle Dave!" he heard behind him. He turned, dropping to his knees to hug his two nieces who dove into his outstretched arms. The tears welled up after months of being away from his family with nothing to hold but memories. Behind the girls, his sister and Mark appeared.

"Why are you crying?" Becca, the youngest, asked as he stood up to embrace his sister. Mark stood back while Sarah looked her bother up and down like his mother had. Dave took Mark's arm, pulling him towards him into a brotherly hug.

"I can't believe what you guys did for me," Mark sighed. "You put yourselves into so much risk."

"You're out of jail. You are free. I didn't care about the risk," Dave replied.

"But it up-ended your life," Mark protested.

"My life was up-ended anyway once I knew what…" Dave paused before saying Jessica's name in front of the kids. He didn't know what they knew or had been told about their aunt. "It's OK. It's done," he finished abruptly.

"Come on," Sarah said, taking his hand to lead him to the shipping container. Paul opened the steel doors to reveal a glass slider leading to a small kitchen. As Dave stepped inside, the aroma of Sarah's cooking welcomed him. He was overwhelmed with the emotions he had suppressed, buried in a place he had tried to forget. The tears he shed were a long time coming. They were necessary.

The kids ran around through the trees as the sun was giving up its last rays to the east. Mark and Derek watched while Paul uncorked wine and poured Scotch. He was pleased with himself and the task he had designed for Dave. The time had finally come to celebrate the success of their plan to free Mark. Duncan's new involvement brought possibilities for greater things. Now when he concocted a plan, the resources he had at his disposal overwhelmed his imagination. He only had to sell it to the money and it would happen.

"I don't know, Courtney," Miguel protested as he slid out of bed. "I don't know when or if I can just dump Kate."

"But why not?" she whined. "She is going to find out."

"She had better not. I told you. At this point, I have no reason to get rid of her. You knew the deal when we got together. It's open on my end and on your end. Kate doesn't like that kind of thing and I want to keep her around. I have my reasons. Don't do something stupid and tell her about us or you will lose. I will replace both of you. Then what are you going to do?"

Courtney slammed her head back into the pillow, staring at the ceiling. She knew the deal. She hated the deal, but she knew it. When she needed money or someone, Miguel was there. The sex just happened one day. That was the rationalization. It just kept happening.

Miguel threw on his clothes, stopping to kiss her quickly before turning to leave. She listened for the door to close, the sound of the deadbolt punctuating the end of another few hours spent with Miguel.

"I have some things to show you," Mark said as the kids helped Sarah clean up. "Come on. You too, Derek." They walked down the hill about fifty yards to another three shipping containers pushed together. Mark opened the door. The light revealed a well-equipped machine shop.

"Those are yours from your garage," Dave exclaimed.

"Yeah, Paul moved them up here while I was still in jail. Made it look like Sarah was giving up and selling off my stuff. He started on the day you left," Mark replied as he spun the dial on a safe in the corner. Mark leaned into the safe, pulling out two pistols resembling Glock 19s. Opening the chambers on both, he handed them to Derek and Dave.

"Wow," Dave exclaimed, "you did it. You made aluminum Glocks." Derek quietly studied the gun in his hand, his thumb releasing the slide with a pronounced slap as the spring slammed it forward. "You still had the parts?" Dave asked.

"I had them. Paul had some and we made the rest," Mark replied proudly. "Something new, that little button right there on the cover plate, full auto."

"Shit, you guys are relentless in your disregard for the law," Derek laughed. "Who does this? Especially now with the Firearm Storage Law."

"I would guess a lot of people," Mark replied. "When they did the initial search and seizure, we had a fair amount of firearms stashed in my house in a safe under the lawn." He went on to explain the hidden space he had built and how it was accessed. Paul had assured him that Derek was one of them and could be counted on. "The guns are all here now except for one of these I made for myself. With this shop, I can make more. I can 3D print polymer versions too. I just like the feel of aluminum."

"How did you make this receiver?" Derek asked.

"I made foam blanks then cast them up here with scrap aluminum I had around. Then I finished them up with the mill," Mark replied holding his hand out to take the gun from Derek. "There are suppressors I made for them too, plus a bunch of ammo. Getting the ammo is the problem, that's where Paul is most helpful. Somehow he can get brass, powder, primers and bullets. I don't want to know where or how he does it. Some of the stuff I made is subsonic. They are pretty quiet coming out the bad end but you need to be close."

"I like to call it the 'see you in fucking hell' end," Derek smiled.

"Hopefully, you won't need them," Mark said.

"What do you mean?" Dave asked.

"These are yours. Paul thought you might need them so I

made one for you and Derek. That's all I want to know," Mark repeated. "I tested them both. Obviously, they aren't official Glocks, but they are Glocks. You don't need to test them. I have never had to test-fire a Glock in my life. They just work right out of the box. These are no different even though they are technically a patent infringement. Pull the trigger if you have to. They work."

Dave slept through the night better than he had in months. The effects of the elevation and Scotch could not defeat the ease he felt being around his family. Cold, dry mountain air seeped in through a crack in the window connecting him to the wild beauty outside unlike Florida air conditioning trying in vain to replicate it.

The morning sun put the birds into a frenzy. Wild turkeys roosting up the hill from the container house cursed the rays that warmed their wings. Dave slipped outside to relieve himself the way men enjoy most as a light breeze flowed down along the surface of the slope, moving east to greet the sun. About two hundred yards down the hill, a small herd of elk grazed between the trees. He felt content. One more day lazing around with Paul on the hillside was not enough, but there were things to do.

"What is going on with Miguel?" Duncan asked.

"He has been spending some time out at a farm west of town," Dominic replied. "Looks like from the map it used to be a citrus farm. It has five long buildings, and you can sort of see where the trees were planted. Oddly, there seems to be a lot of cell phones on the property; two or three per building. The satellite views are a little older, but they show some gardening trucks and a bunch of vans."

"That is probably his father's old place. He mentioned something about it," Duncan responded. "A small grapefruit farm. You said the phones are signaling from the buildings?"

"They are," Dominic expanded the map view where he had the cell phone locations pinned. "Looks like they are in the buildings then leave around 5:00 and head for the island and some of the larger developments. What time is it there? About 8:00?"

"It is," Duncan confirmed. "That must be where he keeps his trucks and congregates his employees for the day."

"The historical records show the cells leaving early during the weekdays but I only have data that goes back about a month. I'll set the program to track that area throughout the next few days to see if that looks like a pattern," Dominic suggested. "It's curious that all of his employees don't seem to have phones and the images don't show the employees' cars lined up. Maybe it was taken on a weekend; I don't have a date stamp. There have to be more people getting into the trucks, right? The trucks and the vans have one phone each, sometimes two. Maybe just for supervisors?"

"That is curious," Duncan replied. "The guys will be back here later tomorrow. Why don't you start strategizing where they might be able to sneak in there to have a look around? Can you detect cameras? Also, fences would be good to know about or dogs. Any dogs in the satellite photos?"

"None that I have seen," Dominic replied. Dominic sensed that Duncan was getting anxious to get some real information on Miguel. *Who cares*, he thought. The old man was overpaying him. Whatever the client wants. If he can provide it, he will. If not, he will figure out how.

A day well spent, Dave thought as he dropped into a recliner. Derek seemed restless after their hike. He was fine during Dave's tour of former hunting spots both on Paul's property and the government land surrounding it, but now there was something going on with him.

"OK, thanks," Dave heard Derek say from the other room. *He must be talking to Paul on the burner*, he thought to himself.

"Hey," Derek said as he came out of the bedroom, "I am going into town. You OK here alone for a while?"

"Which town, Boulder?" Dave asked.

"Yeah, I should be back before it's too late. Don't worry about me if I am not. Paul knows where I am going," Derek replied.

Dave shrugged off the impulse to ask what the secret was as Derek took the truck keys from the counter, stepping out without a word. There was something important going on. He slipped back into his book, content to be alone for a while.

Derek started the truck, pausing a moment as he convinced himself to shift it into Drive. "Just go," he said to himself. The butterflies in his stomach were desperately attempting to get him to turn around as he entered Boulder. Nearing downtown, he forced himself into a myopic get-it-done mode. He would do it. It had to be done. And right now, he had the opportunity. There was no failure in the outcome. It would be resolved, either way, today.

He parked near the Pearl Street Mall and walked onto the bricks for the first time in over a year. The cold shadow cast by the Continental Divide bit into him as he squinted against the last rays of sun. Office buildings began to empty their manicured and well-dressed occupants, seeking relief from a long day of work. Derek leaned against a slab of rock pretending to be a statue and waited. *This is destiny or idiocy*, he thought.

After what felt like an hour, the sun had given up and left

him in the cold. This was unfinished business. It would have less meaning without suffering. It felt good to have his stomach knotted up; his nerves stretched tight like a bowstring. He assumed most people were smart enough to avoid these feelings in whatever way they could. Anxiety wasn't something he had the luxury to feel in the last year as he survived day-to-day on faith when he had run out of ideas. Every advantage and opportunity that popped up was the tiniest of miracles meant to see him through another day. There had been so many. He found it impossible to deny that something was keeping him alive for a purpose. If that something was God, he was ready for whatever came next. The anticipation he felt at this moment somehow lacked fear. The resolution he hoped for would free him either way.

The door of the building opened as three men in suits stepped out. The last one spinning to catch the door as it began to swing shut. She stopped, framed in the opening, as her surprised eyes met his. The man's grip on the door held as the moment became timeless. Derek stepped forward, taking the door in his hand and her in the other. He said nothing as he pulled her to him. He could feel her breathing heavily as he held her. She held on to him.

Chapter 10

"I don't want this to happen again, Miguel."

"Sergio, it will happen again. I can't control these people all day," Miguel replied.

Sergio sat back in his chair, sizing up Miguel. Was this kid still worth it? So far he was and he wasn't a kid anymore. Sergio had to remind himself of that. Miguel was making money and paying his share like he always had. "Your job is to control them all day, every day. Make sure you are getting in front of the problems," he lectured. "We know your operation is getting bigger. You have this town mostly maxed out."

"I have 80% of the gardeners, nearly 100% of outsourced hotel housekeeping, enough private housekeeping, the roofers, a lot of the construction labor. More than I want of that shit, I don't want to deal with much more construction and roofing. They get hurt too often. I can expand the other services into new markets. I have to. I just need you to keep feeding me labor. This service work is a lot better than that other bullshit. I don't want any more of that shit." Sergio responded to Miguel's recount with a sinister sneer, ready to remind the kid who he was.

"I know," Miguel recovered, "I know what you are going to say. It's still good business, but this service work doesn't kill stupid white kids and make headlines. And you have to admit, it's profitable. The protection money I pay covers the dealers we have left. The protection network I pay for is still picking up the drops and they do the necessary enforcement. Eventually, my gardening foremen can pick up all of the drops and bring them back to the farm. Then I can get the cops out of the money part."

Sergio leaned in to take a drink of his beer. "I hear you saying 'I' a lot. You remember that we made you. You work for us. Without us…"

"I know," Miguel apologized, "I know you got me started."

"We made you," Sergio corrected. "You are not the college kid mowing lawns anymore and pushing shit in school. If we have to, we will make you go back to dealing. You know how this works."

Miguel felt his chest tighten at the thought of going back to moving drugs. It was so basic. He was past that line of work and doing better things. His business was growing. He found it comical that his empire was built on moving people now instead of drugs. It wasn't much different. Drugs had supply problems and no feet. Supply problems from manufacturing, supply problems on the streets and supply problems for the people to move them. Why waste time on that? An illusion of the American Dream, government corruption and poverty supplied him labor. There would never be a shortage of that. He just had to move them, put them to work and keep them under control. The one advantage drugs did have, they were simple things. They had no opinions, no motivations, no aspirations and didn't fight back. Keeping his people from fighting back was working for the most part. You only had to know how to finesse them. It did not sit well, in what was left of his soul, that fear was the primary instrument of finesse.

"We're not going to have anymore problems like that," Miguel assured Sergio. "When does his replacement arrive?"

"A couple of days. We got him across the border once, but ICE nabbed his group. Fortunately he told them he was from Mexico, like we told him to, so all he had to do was walk back across. At least this one listens. If he said Honduras, he would be sitting in Guantanamo or some other bullshit cage waiting to be processed by your fucking legal system." Sergio stood up and dropped a twenty on the table. "I have to get going. When he gets to the farm, have your men get him situated. There's a group of women coming along with him. I have told you this before, but I will say it again, keep the women and the men separated. We don't need pregnant housekeepers and we certainly don't need them anchoring some baby here. That's one legal loop hole I wish they'd get rid of. I don't have to tell you what could happen to one of your women if she gets pregnant."

Miguel cringed at the thought of what he would have to do. She would be lucky to get away with an abortion. It was cold, but the security of the business came first. Replacing her took less time and money than waiting for her to give birth and get back to work. What would they do with the kid? The best case scenario would be a Fire Station drop-off and run but that involved cameras. Getting rid of her altogether would be more practical. It was a painful, learned experience that once one of them produced a headache, the trust was gone. They were, like their work, commoditized. Plow-horses at best. Easy jobs require easy, low-skilled labor. The strenuous work they performed hurt only until they rested or were aged-out. Their heads were never going to think themselves into something better. And he kept them too busy for aspirations. Gringos loved to lionize the strong immigrants who did the tough jobs. They weren't tough. They were beneath a threshold of humiliation most Americans would sink. What you can't put machines to, you put hands; the cheapest, poorest, neediest, least educated hands you can get.

With Sergio back in Mexico, he could breathe a little easier. Having him around created tension not only for him but for everyone on the farm. The way he looked at them, especially the way he looked at the women, was inexpressible. It was a feeling the word 'repulsive' didn't describe well enough. If he had become cold to his laborers, Sergio was arctic.

"Ok, I will be back when I need to be," Sergio warned. "Don't make me need to be."

Miguel sat a moment longer to finish his drink. He thought about making the rounds. It would be good to see the teams working and his phone was full of Kate. She texted too much, but ignoring her was easy. *Probably too easy*, he thought to himself. He motioned for the waiter as he dropped some more cash on the table. "Can you have the valet get my car?" he asked. Another couple of sips and the car would arrive.

"Dave," Derek said with a pause, foreshadowing a strong statement. "Hit the guy like you are trying to punch his nose out the back of his head with the heal of your hand. This isn't a fucking karate class." Derek stepped up to the dummy to demonstrate. The force he generated into the dummy's head was enough to make the weighted base nearly topple over. "And don't be afraid to use an open-handed slap on his ear. If you land the punch with your fist, you run the risk of injuring your hand. The face and head are full of hard bones." Derek took Dave's hand putting pressure on the ring and pinky finger knuckles. "If you use your fist on something like the solar plexus, make sure to keep these knuckles out of it. Punch through the guy, focusing the strike with the knuckles that are in line with your forearm."

Dave stepped up to the dummy again, planting his feet as Derek had taught him. A firm connection with the ground put power into the punch. He looked into the dummy's eyes, envisioning Stefan Wunderlich. With a coordinated hip rotation, he slammed into the bottom of where the sternum would be sending the dummy into the wall behind. It was satisfying to stand over the dummy laying face down on the floor.

"That's it," Derek complimented. "Now, we aren't talking about a bar fight here. When he's hurt but can get back up, stomp his fucking head into the ground. Bury your heal into his chest. Kick him in the ribs. This is battle, not drunk-sport."

"Are you teaching me to fight or kill people?" Dave asked.

Derek's response was a look he reserved for questions undeserving of answers. "Let me tell you something," he sighed. "There have been times in my younger life when I have had to fight. Now that I am older, I understand what my Shaolin instructor was saying when he told me, 'If someone wants to strike you, consider it deadly. Respond in kind. Finish it.' Then he would say, 'Firm your resolve. Focus your intent'."

"What does that mean?" Dave asked.

"It means firm your resolve and focus your fucking intent, Dave," Derek replied plainly. "What is your intent?"

"I don't know," Dave replied. He was growing tired of the intensity. Something seemed to be bothering Derek, and it was being taken out on him.

"Let me make this easy on you," Derek continued. "Your

intent is to survive. Fuck the guy who has other ideas about your survival. Fuck that guy straight to hell. If he wants to hit you, assume he wants to eliminate you. If it is you or him, it's gonna be him. Put that in your head right now."

"I don't think I can kill someone. I had the chance once. You know that. I couldn't do it," Dave replied.

"Some peacockish dipshit fucking your wife is not justification for killing. Sorry to bring that up, but you have to be clear on what is, and is not, a reasonable response to unreasonable people," Derek said. "If someone throws a punch at you, consider it a threat to your life. Kung Fu is not a sport. It is a martial art. 'Martial' is synonymous with 'war'. In almost every aspect of daily life you will never need to use your training. People are generally docile, but they can become savage once in a while. If you want to test this shit, go to a small-town bar and hit on some of the local sluts. One of the hillbilly retards will come out of the woods to defend her honor or her perceived chastity or some other drunken hillbilly bullshit. Fortunately, most of these idiots can't punch. They send these round-the-world flailing swings at your head that almost give you time to laugh. You just deflect and control the incoming fist, then give the guy a heel of the hand to his nose. Then get the fuck out of there. Those idiots multiply when they smell blood."

"Do I want to know how many times you have experienced this?" Dave asked.

"More than enough to make this a generalization," Derek answered. "We are done for now. Let's go do the push-up walk on the beach and get some fresh air. Duncan wants us around for dinner tonight."

Miguel pulled his Range Rover to the side of a heavily treed street a few hundred feet from one of his crew trucks.

The neighborhood was nice. It took almost a million to buy the poor house on the block, plus ample available credit to put the right cars in the drive. These were the bulk of his direct clients. The rest were HOAs. The HOAs were easier. Their expectations were based on committee. Between what he charged them to cover expenses and keep his crews alive, they were a consistent money stream. It was eye-rolling when they threatened to move to another company because, more than likely, he owned it.

When the HOAs wanted bids, he sent three different representatives out to propose them. Behind each LLC was him and his army of workers. Different changeable, magnetic signs on different trucks, same employees. The gringo wives watching out the windows couldn't tell the difference from one of his crews to the next. If he kept rotating the workers, they spent less time becoming friendly. When they got too familiar, it was time to move them out and move new labor in. He had learned this from the sex traffickers in the strip joints. Keep the workers moving around, keep them isolated and keep them in line. If they established roots, they grew in place and became a problem. Fortunately, if they were caught, ICE was more inclined to deport them than to waste resources investigating them. That was an advantage he had over the imbeciles selling sex to the pathetic assholes who got their rocks off on young girls or boys. Those guys made headlines and promotions for cops. There was nothing sexy or socially rewarding about investigating trafficked gardeners and housekeepers.

There was no end to how useless humans could be when they had all their basic needs met. These clients weren't too much better. In their desperate attempt to seem rich, they held jobs to pay for services the idle wealthy would never think to do. Even worse, they didn't make their kids do them. There wasn't a kid in the area who knew how to push a lawnmower. And there weren't many parents who wished their precious little shits learned. God forbid if their children were seen mowing their lawns by the neighbors. That would be a serious reputation blunder; the neighbors wondering what might be wrong. Did something happen? Are they poor and common now?

He provided the First World's social problems with Third World solutions; low priced, menial labor. Just how low the price was, these idiots had no idea, and it would stay that way. Who cared if the Suburban Aristocracy funded his empire? They didn't know what was going on and they wouldn't want to believe it if you explained it to them. Denial was as powerful a sedative as the meds they all took for the anxious inner turmoil of buying their free time and appearances with debt.

He certainly wasn't Robin Hood protecting the poor, but maybe if he thought about it in the right way he was similar. Maybe not. Governments were the real Robin Hoods. At least, that is how they branded themselves. Take from the rich and support the poor. It appeared virtuous and democratic. It was all a scam. He did what governments really did; take from the middle, skim off his cut and exploit the poor like any other economic system. It all made the clueless gringos feel superior, giving themselves a dose of pride in what they had accomplished in their mediocre lives. They thought they were too important for most of their household menial tasks, too educated. "Total denial," he muttered to himself, "just completely clueless and arrogant".

The recruiting pitch was easy. We will get you to America so you can have the opportunity to become something more. What they didn't know was they would be living a Third World life in the First World. They would be servicing a system but never fully partake in it. Keeping them in debt bondage was critical. It was the leverage the cartel had over them and their families. It didn't matter if the leverage existed. It only had to exist in the minds of the trafficked. If you don't pay your debt, grandma gets a bullet in her head. *That is a strong motivator*, Miguel thought. His conscience rebelled quietly against his ambition. It ate at him.

His father came to the United States on a temporary visa to pick fruit. That was the story he had been told. What was the point of coming here to pick fruit? The real strategy was to work for a while on a farm, slip away from the temporary visa status and take a step into a better life. The boundless opportunity of the America everyone seemed to envy enticed him to do whatever it took to get here. *It was a lie*, Miguel thought to himself. It was the same lie that drinking a particular beer made you attractive to blonds with big tits. The lie of attaining great things by conforming and adapting to a system. The lie that told people to take guarantees in life and expect to win something big beyond the risk they put in. It was penny slot, half-assed gambling.

No matter what, the lie brought him labor. Kidnapping people outright to mow lawns didn't work. People knew when they were being kidnapped and resisted. They became resentful, full of fight and hard to manage. That shit was reserved for hapless kids peddled as sex toys. The cartel used American opportunity to entice people in a bait and switch. It found them when they were the most vulnerable and gave them an out. It was his part to get as much as possible out of them. He wasn't the one closing the borders and limiting work visas. Did the fucking gringos understand that their gluttonous lives depended on cheap labor whether it was manufacturing their Asian-made things or through the Spanish speakers reroofing, cleaning their hotel rooms, cleaning their homes, mowing their lawns, washing their cars, building their houses?

Some, if not most, of that labor was done with outright modern-day slaves. To eliminate it was to eliminate the lifestyles of almost every American. The entire system would collapse the day they lifted the blindfold, saw the light and were stupid enough to repent. They would never repent. They never had. They only changed the appearance of slavery. *These fucking people*, Miguel thought, *they are all complicit and fully invested*. The irony of it all was the clients were all just debt slaves themselves with slightly better mobility. There was a class hierarchy in everything, even slavery. He would continue to take from the middle, use the poor, and become one of the rich, free from bondage.

Then there was Kate. She was another gate between himself and another life. By the time her uncle was dead and buried, he would have enough to be enough for her. She already saw him as enough. That was evident. In truth, she had no idea. He was more than she knew, and he was less. There could never be full disclosure or any form of confession. Never a pillow conversation to placate his soul. He would simply transition from his world into hers when the time presented itself and leave this life behind. If he were to continue his lineage, it wouldn't be with a woman like Courtney. It would be with Kate. She would set the standard for his future generations, forever leaving behind the bullshit he inherited from his father. The heritage best left where it was placed, rotting in a drunk's grave.

"Oh, hi Jefe, I am glad you are here."

"Nacho, what's going on?" Miguel asked as he walked into the old house at the farm. He gave his Office Manager the concerned look he had come to rely on.

"We dealt with that bitch and the others," Nacho replied as he looked up over his computer monitor. "They should be halfway to Nashville by now. Jose will take care of them when they arrive or find a way to get rid of them. He knows what to do."

Miguel nodded, his brows furrowed at the thought of getting rid of them. *Hopefully*, he thought, *that means return to Guatemala*. "We have enough new work there now to keep them busy," Miguel added. "How are things going?"

"We could use some more private customers paying in cash," Nacho replied. "HOA income is good. No problems with the equipment. I think we should take some of the trucks off and buy some new ones. It will be good for depreciation."

"You know what you are doing," Miguel replied. "As long I look small, we are OK. You know that."

"No problem, boss. We know how to do that."

Chapter 11

"I would like to see you married before I am gone," Duncan blurted out as he poured himself some Ginger Ale. The bottle he set on the counter was snatched up and tossed in the recycling bin before he could turn back towards his niece. "I can do that Imelda," he said.

"I know, Señor," Imelda responded, "but I have to do something."

"You do more than you need to. All of you do," Duncan smiled. "When would you like to go to Taxco? I can have the plane ready whenever you want."

"My cousin's wedding is in a few months. We will go then. Are you going to have Alfonzo and Alejandra here from Colorado when we are gone?" Imelda asked.

"I don't know. I think I can manage for a few weeks by myself," Duncan replied.

Kate sat quietly watching the interaction between Duncan and his Housekeeper, content with the distraction away from the topic of marriage. The interaction was in deep contrast between what she saw in her mother who remained distant and authoritative over their cleaning lady. *Maybe the differ-*

ence is living in the same house, she thought. It was excessive to hire someone to come clean. Her mother didn't work. She didn't have to. What was the point of having someone clean for you when your daily duties included ordering grocery delivery and making the rounds at the Country Club? They were very different, her Aunt and her mother. If it were not for Duncan, they would have very little. When her father died, he left some money but nothing like the trust Duncan had set up for them. Even before Aunt Catherine died, Duncan had taken over the patriarchal void left by her father. He didn't have to take care of them. Her mother wasn't related to him through anything but marriage, but he assumed the role.

Kate watched Imelda move through the kitchen finishing up her morning tasks. Once Imelda left, she would respond to Duncan's marriage statement. Maybe he would just let it go. Miguel didn't seem to be in a hurry to ask, and she was in no hurry herself. He was everything she wanted. He was like Duncan. He built himself from almost nothing, but in contrast, he had started with much less. Miguel's father had nothing and died of liver failure when Miguel was only 11. He never talked about him. He never disparaged his father to her, but even a hint of the topic imbued tension and avoidance.

"Thank you, Imelda," Duncan said as she exited to an apartment behind a secretive door built into the cabinetry. He turned back to Kate laying his hand over hers looking into her eyes with all of the concern of a father. "You know that wherever your path takes you, I will be present when you need me," he said.

"I know," Kate replied quietly. She knew her Uncle would do anything for her. She felt as though she was more connected to him than anyone else. She was the one he was most open with. He always had concern for her future, worried about her choices. They were made not only for her but for his legacy. She would inherit generational wealth to be managed and distributed to her children and grandchildren. The underlying reality of that kind of wealth was incomprehensible even to her. It was easy to say it was just money, but there were unborn children to consider.

"Kate, look at me," Duncan requested. "You are a very intelligent, grounded woman. I have to remind myself of this every day because you are always the little girl to me. You will always be that sweet, little girl with the big smile and joyful spirit. Keep that in you for the rest of your life and share it with your children." She stayed silent, knowing he would continue. She loved it when he gave his philosophical life lectures. It was something he needed to do; to hear himself validating his thoughts and feelings out loud to someone who would listen. "Life is a path you take that was given to you by whatever created us. There is one good path. Your free will can and will divert you from it, but your free will will also redirect you back on if you let it. Your direction in life is always calling you back even when you go astray. Sometimes, it has to scream at you. Sometimes, it whispers."

"I am not quite getting what you are saying," Kate stated. "Are you saying that we are on the good path or not?"

Duncan paused. He was trying to express something he deeply felt but had not yet conceptualized fully into the right words. Kate watched him. She knew from experience to give him room to speak without filling the void. He had taught her since she was a child that silence in a conversation was not an invitation to step in. It was more likely an invitation to practice patience.

"I sometimes find it difficult to express what I am thinking," Duncan continued. "What I am trying to say is that I believe God gives us a path for our souls to follow. God, being all-knowing, gracious, and merciful, also gives us free will or at least the illusion of it. The path God creates for us is a perfectly straight line for our souls to return. Our free will," he paused searching for more poignant words but in failing continued, "sort of makes us follow that path in the general direction, veering on and off of it. We are not perfected enough to follow a direct line. I think what I am saying is that a perfect being would travel through time along a perfect line. But perfection is reserved for God, alone."

"What about people who do not believe in God?" Kate challenged. "What path are they on?"

"Whether you believe in God or not is a moot point," Duncan continued. "Assume God is the creator of all that is seen and unseen. Your belief or disbelief in God makes no difference. There are the humanists who believe God is a function of our imaginations. Does God exist because God exists, or does God exist because we think and hope he does and therefore we created the illusion of him?"

Before she could say it, Duncan knowingly interrupted, "I say 'he' only as a simplified reference. God could not take such a simplistic human form of one gender or another. It is ridiculous to believe he would. Even neutralizing the pronoun to 'it' demonstrates our human imperfections in perceiving God. Maybe 'The Creator' is a better name for God. Or maybe referring to God as we look for and apply the powers we attribute to him, such as the Healer. The Redeemer. The Merciful. The Most Just. Or as the Muslims refer to him as Allah, The God or The One. Singular. There are so many ways to express how a Creator of all that we experience, even with our limited consciousness, could be described. It is common to believe we are all gods in some way. It is ridiculous to compare ourselves to something that has no known beginning, creates everything seen and unseen, and has no apparent end. That is how I think of God and cannot fathom an existence where my ego compels me to believe that I am in any way comparable. I have been a fortunate servant but a servant nonetheless. Many times not a very good one. Hopefully God will allow me to live out the rest of my life serving his creation so I may die in peace one day."

Kate's will to attend to the conversation lost its strength with his last comment. She knew she would have to divert her Uncle back to the ground he stood on. "What do you think of Miguel? she asked.

Duncan hesitated as he usually did before replying. It was his way of maintaining order in conversations that weren't under his direction. It was a skill he had learned from his father that had been practiced to near perfection in business. "I think Miguel is very intelligent and seems nice enough; how do you feel about him?" he asked. Another of Duncan's communication tactics was the ability to take a question and revert it back to the questioner. Duncan observed early on that most people asked questions not to seek answers or truth but to open a channel for their opinions. Perhaps they craved to be heard by anyone who would listen. Regardless, listening to people helped them feel validated, relevant and happy.

"He is very sweet to me," Kate replied. "I feel like he respects me, for me. I like that."

Duncan's phone rang as Kate was about to continue pitching Miguel's attributes. "I am sorry; let me take this. Can you wait for me out by the pool? I want to hear more about him," he asked. Kate smiled, leaving him to take the call.

"Dominic, is something wrong?" he asked.

"Something interesting in the data," Dominic replied. "I have a program running looking for anomalies, I won't go into detail, but it found one."

"Tell me," Duncan ordered.

"Ok, there was a cluster of phones around a road about 20 miles west of where you are. Farmland area. It's not too far from the Miguel's farm where we think his crews gather every day. The road is next to a canal. This is historical data. I have exact dates and times, but again, I will keep it short like you prefer."

"What's the anomaly?" Duncan asked.

"One of the phones stayed in place for a few days next to the canal until it appeared to have gone dead. All the other phones that we have tagged as being Miguel's employees went back to the farm. That was weird in itself. What were they doing out there? Normally, I would just think that it was dropped on the ground and lost. But who does that, especially in a random, nowhere location like that? People are too obsessed with their phones to just drop them and leave. They panic and go search for them. I know I do."

"Ok, I agree. What else?" Duncan asked impatiently.

"The phone came back on yesterday at the County Sheriff's department. It stayed on there for about an hour, then traveled back to unite with one of Miguel's employees along the road heading towards the farm. So, therefore, I assume a Sheriff's Deputy delivered it to someone. Excuse me, I know one did because it was traveling alongside a phone belonging to a Deputy in the same car. It was then passed to one of Miguel's employees then it traveled back to the farm."

Duncan went uncomfortably quiet as he tried to think through the scenario. "I don't get it," he stated. "That is a strange occurrence. Maybe someone found it and turned it into the police."

"Maybe," Dominic replied, "but then an Officer tracks down someone from Miguel's business and hand-delivers it at a random spot along the road to Miguel's farm? That would imply a high level of knowledge of the general public around there and a higher level of service."

"OK, I see the problem you are having with this," Duncan responded. "Suggestions?"

"I have been thinking about this for a while," Dominic replied. "We assume that the farm is where the gardening crews congregate. The phones we have tagged as Miguel's employees tend to start moving at the same time but in different trucks. Some go to private homes, and some go to the HOAs. You only see one or maybe two phones at each job site. Would he be sending only one or two people to each location?" Dominic paused to allow Duncan the choice of whether to answer what was obviously a rhetorical question. "There has to be more. And everyone has a phone. There should be more phones because there should be more people working."

"Doesn't seem realistic to me," Duncan replied. "It seems too amateur for what I know about him. He is young, smart and presents himself well. I wouldn't be running a landscaping business like that. My own garden here is a full-time job. My neighbors are similar. If you recall me saying, I met him when he pitched his business to me. He didn't describe it being one man doing the work but as a full team. This person wasn't of concern to me until he showed back up with my niece," Duncan whispered.

"I know. There is something off about this. I have heard you say that enough times to believe you," Dominic interjected. "Can I suggest something?"

"Go ahead," Duncan replied.

"Let's do what you were thinking a while back and have the guys go out to the farm and take a look around as soon as possible." Duncan considered the idea, visualizing an operation in his head. Dominic broke the silence. "What do you think?" he asked enthusiastically.

"I think that is a good idea. Sorry, I was just running it through, considering potential details," Duncan apologized. "I will talk to them and get them prepared."

"How are they?" Dominic asked. "Is Dave coming out of his funk?"

"He seems to be," Duncan replied. "Derek has taken him under his wing, keeping him busy working out and learning some martial arts. I don't think he has the strength left at the end of the day to do much more than close his eyes."

"That's good," Dominic replied. "I got the feeling Dave needed more exercise."

"I don't know if he told you, but he was quite an endurance athlete in the past. Never professional but certainly capable. Also, one of the best hunters I know. He and his brother-in-law can melt into the woods like they were raised there. And shoot. Paul says he could have been a sniper. He can be exceptionally calm, robotic."

"That could be useful," Dominic said. "I will keep you informed if anything else pops up. So far, I am pretty happy with the algorithm's functionality. But I won't bore you with that."

"Thank you," Duncan replied. "The tech world is confusing enough to me without you trying to explain it." Duncan ended the call refilling his glass before joining Kate by the pool.

Chapter 12

"OK, gentlemen. There is something I need done," Duncan began. He paced the floor in front of Dave and Derek like a tenured professor intent to inspire a half-interested sophomore class. They had just come in from a beach run to find Duncan in the apartment quietly mumbling to himself. Derek watched intently, thinking he had seen this activity before, but he couldn't remember where. *This is about money*, he thought. Dave politely watched, his eyes following Duncan's momentum.

"I need you two to go out to a piece of property Miguel owns and snoop around," Duncan continued. "And I want it done very quietly. You can't be seen. If Kate were to think I was spying on him, it would create havoc."

"I know you have your reservations about Miguel, but what's up?" Derek asked.

"Dominic has collected some information that seems peculiar," Duncan replied. His lecture shifted from business to the tone of a spy movie senior leader briefing agents. It put Derek on the edge of hysterics only controlling himself through an inner dialogue, *focus, focus*. He was living on a billionaire's property, doing nothing but working out. His bills were paid by a fake painting company set up by a lawyer in Colorado who seemed to be trying to get disbarred. Life was good. It was strange, and it was good. He could hear the ghost of his ex-wife's voice cringing in anxiety, but she was paid. The child support was up-to-date and his kids seemed to still like him. She was silent. Paul had taken care of the obnoxious Child Services busybody in Colorado, leaving him to life as it was now. Whatever his life was supposed to be in this comfortable limbo. Babysitting Dave? Distracting Dave from driving to Colorado to win back his wife? That was an easy billable thousand dollars per week.

"What do you want us to do?" Dave asked eagerly.

"I spoke to Paul at length. He gave me the details on the Colorado operation you pulled off, David," Duncan continued. "I was impressed with how you performed."

Derek stared at Duncan. He thought, *this guy is turning into a character. Is he always like this? He must be completely stressed.*

"I have collected the necessary equipment from a list provided by Paul. We have reviewed the aerials and determined how to gain access to the property." Duncan held up some printed photos.

"Can I see that?" Derek asked. Duncan handed him the photos, continuing to pace quietly while Dave leaned over to get a look. "What's this 'X'?"

"That is where we believe you can wait and take notes," Duncan replied.

"That looks like a fair distance. Are we taking photos?" Derek asked.

"No photos," Duncan replied emphatically, "only observation and notes. We don't want any discoverable evidence in case you are compromised. Mental notes will be sufficient. There are two of you to compare what you see. I have taken the liberty to buy some ghillie suits for you as well as well as some good boots. I have also procured an exceptional spotting scope. You will be going in the late afternoon, just before Miguel's crews end their day and before sunset. According to Dominic, they are exceptionally consistent." Duncan handed Derek and Dave copies of a list of the items they would need. Dave scanned his quickly, setting it down on the coffee table while Derek ruminated.

"Is there something missing?" Duncan asked.

"Yes, bugs," Derek declared. "This godforsaken shithole of a swamp has bugs. Not so much out here on the beach, you know the lipstick portion of this pig, but that far inland? There's going to be bugs biting the hell out of us."

Duncan paused to consider a solution. "We will get some DEET, will that suffice?"

"For mosquitos. I am not sure about those little No-See-Um twats. If the day is cool and there is some wind, we might be OK, but you got us down in bug town," Derek replied. While Duncan considered the bug problem, Derek looked up Special Forces insect protection on his phone. "DEET, permethrin, and picaridin," he read off.

"It will be done, thank you Derek. I don't want anything obstructing your ability to focus," Duncan sighed. How could something as simple as watching his niece's boyfriend become complicated by such easily overlooked things? The logistics Paul had gone through seemed fraught with potential problems. Thank God for Dominic. His data capabilities were world-class. His ability to obtain real-time access to the major cell carriers was still a mystery. It had cost more money than time. *Dominic must have some compatriots inside the companies*, Duncan thought.

"You two continue doing what you have been doing, and be ready. We will wait for favorable weather like you said Derek, cooler temperatures, and hopefully some wind. That, with the repellent, should be adequate to allow you to remain in the field for a few hours. Now I have to go. Kate is coming over for dinner. You two continue to stay out of sight. Only the staff and I know you are here. Keep it that way." With that, Duncan left.

Derek looked at Dave, "Is he losing it?"

"I don't know. I haven't seen him like this. He was your client you should know," Dave replied.

"Didn't you and your brother-in-law build him a house?" Derek asked. "How was he then?"

"Honestly, he was hardly ever around. He was dating some woman at the time who seemed more interested in the project than he was," Dave replied. "It was a six thousand square foot doodad to him. I have known him a long time but not like I am beginning to know him now."

"Only six thousand," Derek mocked.

"You should have seen some of the ten and twelve thousand square foot monstrosities. I remember Duncan saying he didn't want it to be ostentatious and," he paused to reflect, "cumbersome. A lot of those clients liked buying or building something to add to their collections. Duncan wasn't like that. It had to be livable but it also had to fit in to the neighborhood. He had more money than the neighborhood and one of the smaller homes."

"My dealings with him were strictly attached to his work. Nothing in his personal life," Derek recalled.

"He was different. Duncan never worried about spending money; he worried about trust. If you broke that, he broke you," Dave warned. "I saw it happen to the contractor we replaced. Utterly destroyed the guy and honestly, he deserved it. Our business was full of people who needed to find a new occupation. Money draws in the greedy idiots; building codes exist because of them. I think there might be dead people somewhere behind all the codes."

"Well, buddy… Whatever this is, we both have a new occupation," Derek added. "It could be entertaining."

A few days passed with nothing. The sense of urgency, compared to Duncan's briefing day, eased. The temperature remained well into the eighties, even on the beach. Inland, it was oppressive. They would wait for the day to come while continuing their training, uncertain if they would ever need it.

As they walked quietly back to the house, cooling down from a run, the tide was on its way out. Derek was following the tiny footprints of a child in the sand as the waves worked to erase them. They reminded him of his daughters when their little feet printed up the beaches on family vacations. The joy they had at the ocean running full speed ahead of him and his wife. The girls were the only remaining threadbare bond between them. Soon, they would be in college and his ex-wife would go into the graveyard of his memory where she would rest in a state of near-perfect indifference. The same woman he swore an oath to in front of both families. *That was a very real oath for me*, he thought to himself.

Unfortunately the oath his ex made was non-binding and eventually an inconvenience. *Humans are too full of options and too aware of their mortality to make binding personal oaths to each other*, he thought. The best someone can do is find love when it presents itself and ride it as long as it lasts. Real love, whatever that is.

The closest he had to *real* love was in Colorado. He had let her go before, and he would again if he had to. He loved her enough to free her no matter the self-sacrifice. For now, he remained in Florida to be near his children who he would finally get to see again the coming week. It had been too long. As for Colorado, the distance would become an excuse to end their relationship unless he could find a way to be there. The reality was that eventually she would meet his replacement if he failed to be there distracting her. The opportunistic nature of women can destroy the delusional ideal of a man's concept of love. If he allows himself to step into her line of thinking, she is easier to forgive. But who is he to have the right of forgiveness over nature? It is harsh, but truth.

Dave had stopped to look out over the horizon. He had seen the little feet in the sand. Jessica had been reluctant to discuss having children, always pushing it off into the future. Her resistance multiplied after she took the job at Stefan's firm. She was relatively young. It made sense to wait a while. What was thirty-two today, anyway? Near-death a few thousand years ago? It was nothing now. He would probably never have children. He felt deceived into thinking that marriage put a priority on creating a family. It meant that to Mark and his sister. Unfortunately, his life hadn't aligned like theirs.

He was 38, estranged from his wife and hiding out in Florida under the suggestion of a potentially insane and scheming attorney. He thought he had been sent to Florida to be part of something bigger than spying on the boyfriend of a billionaire's niece. What these people did to maintain their money seemed completely ridiculous. Was this little operation just a way for Duncan to verify if Miguel was an inheritance risk? What are the rules for choosing a mate for the ultra-rich? The primary rule had to be, *don't lose the precious money*. Kate was certainly attractive from the pictures he had seen and the few glances of her out the window. She could get almost anyone she wanted. The question was whether she could she get who Duncan wanted and still be happy with her choice. It was a complicated life plan to have to think about who you should marry to protect a family fortune.

"Gynoid fat," Derek said in a hushed voice discernible enough for Dave to hear over the breaking waves.

"What?" Dave asked.

"That special squish that gives women that thing we like," Derek explained. "The woman we just passed was well-proportioned with it."

"You mean boobs?" Dave replied.

"Yes and the other parts we find appealing," Derek continued. "What drew you to your ex-wife?"

"Not an ex," Dave protested knowing the end of the marriage was an eventual formality. His denial was becoming rehearsed. Although, his banal protest lacked the heartfelt defensiveness he displayed only a month before. It was over. It had occurred to him two days prior that he had lost track of when he had put much thought into Jessica or of any regard for her wellbeing. It felt like she existed less to him now than she had the day before he met her. He labored with a mental image of her trying to convince himself she had really happened. It was getting easier. She had happened. But now he couldn't find even a trace of hate for her. His loathing was for himself; for wasted time. He could only conjure a speck of hate for Stefan. It was a feeling of justified vengeance more than hate. A lesson another man should be taught when he steps over a firm boundary; a lesson he should remember well.

"True. Not an ex officially," Derek agreed, "but I haven't heard you say anything about her in a while."

"I was drawn to her smile, the way she moved," Dave replied, focusing on the original question. "She had a way about her that was hard to describe. She really seemed to love me for a long time. I don't know if any of that was real. That's the part where my brain just stops."

"Like your inner voice goes catatonic?" Derek asked. Dave nodded halfheartedly "What do you think happened? What made her attach herself to that douchebag Stefan? And I apologize if I am digging at any scabs you still have," Derek stated as empathetically as he could.

"No, dude, I think I am good," Dave relented. "It is getting easier but I don't see myself being interested in any women for a long time. Jessica seemed exactly like the kind of woman I should be with. If I was so wrong about her,…" Dave appeared strained by an absurd, self-afflicted torment meant to awaken him and punish him for something he thought he had caused. "After a while, it got weird like I was losing who I was to fit into a mold she came up with for me," he sighed.

"Did you find that you were conceding parts of yourself to keep her happy?" Derek asked.

"I felt like it was my job to make her happy," Dave replied regretfully.

"I have been there," Derek consoled. "It's an impossible task. Ironically she asks for the concessions to make her feel safe and secure then WHAM, you are not the man she married. See ya later or worse; she sticks around and turns into a roommate. Either way, a chick always has options, even one who loses her looks. There will always be some dude willing to pay for date night and give her that exciting, new-guy attention. And if you don't mind me saying, your ex-wife is not ugly."

"No, she is not," Dave agreed. "She won't have any issues with or without Stefan."

"That depends on what she wants and what a man can provide at the time," Derek replied. "As far as Stefan goes, I think you may have wounded him for life with your little stunt. The Stefan I saw in Boulder was not cocky like you described. Healed scars are sexy to women, but lingering, festering wounds are not. That dude is scared shitless, totally wounded."

"Good," Dave smiled. Vengeance felt good.

Derek's phone buzzed. *Come back to the house, we are going.*

"Ok, Paul, thank you," Duncan said as Dave and Derek entered. Duncan was seated on the sofa looking like an amalgam of triumphant and anxiety. "Just send the amount and get the deal done; $40 million or so is fine. You can mail me the deed or hang on to it until I see you next."

Dave and Derek fell into chairs, waiting for another of Duncan's pre-mission lectures. After a few moments of watching him listen to Paul, their impatience was building. Finally, Duncan ended the call, took a deep, self-soothing breath and gave them his attention. "Gentlemen, we are going today. Go get ready, we will be out there by the farm around five. I will be driving." He stood up to leave them to their preparations.

"Duncan," Derek interrupted, "can I ask? $40 million?"

"I bought an island near Eleuthera," Duncan replied without a hint of excitement.

"Where?" Dave asked.

"It's way out on the eastern side of the Bahamas. Basically, the border of the Atlantic and Caribbean," Derek explained. "Fantastic place."

"You have been there?" Duncan asked.

"I have. Many years ago, when I worked for a resort company," Derek replied. "It's not Nassau. It's like the backwoods of the Bahamas. Like I said, wonderful place."

"Well, maybe we will go out there together," Duncan suggested. "Now, let's focus on today. We leave in two hours."

The time dragged on as they waited to leave. The first half-hour after Duncan left flew by as they gathered their gear. It was a hurry up and wait game they had not expected or wanted to play. Dave paced until Derek forcefully told him to sit down. Tossing Dave the TV remote, he reclined as far back as he trusted his chair. He was asleep within 10 minutes leaving Dave to anxiously flip channels.

Landing on a news channel, he stared blankly at the screen as a panel of anchors explained to him what was going on. It was then he realized that he hadn't watched or followed the news in weeks. If this was news, it seemed to be on repeat. Finally, there came the knock on the door they had been waiting for.

"OK," Duncan began as they crossed the bridge to the mainland, "we will get out there in about twenty minutes, thirty depending on traffic. I will drop you off at the insertion point. From there, you step off the road and put on the ghillies. Make sure your phones are muted. I will drive around until you signal me. Dominic will watch what is going on as best as he can and feed me information as needed. I will relay any pertinent information to you. You focus on watching what is going on with the scope."

"Why aren't we taking photos?" Dave asked.

"As I said before, they aren't necessary and I don't want any physical evidence," Duncan replied. "Both of you take turns looking through the scope and take mental notes. I trust you to recreate an assessment of what you see. We will debrief later tonight."

They drove through town out past the highway into an area that had yet to be suburbanized. A few more miles to the west, Duncan turned south down a sand road. Slight openings in the mess of foliage along the road flickered the scene of an open field where citrus trees had grown decades before. Few stubborn trees remained.

"This is it," Duncan said as he pushed hard on the brake pedal, "GO!"

Dave jumped out the passenger side of the Jeep with Derek just behind toting the bag of ghillie suits, two rucksacks and spotting scope. They slipped into the bush, immediately ambushed by waiting insects.

"Fuck this shit," Derek muttered. He reached into his rucksack for the repellents, handing some to Dave as he slathered on enough to repulse the most anemic mosquito. The combination of ghillies and repellent seemed to be working as they eased through the brush along the edge of a forgotten field. Their line of sight proved to be better than they expected. A convenient game trail led them closer and closer to the farm buildings. Settling down behind a stand of tropical brush neither of them could identify, they waited in the quiet shadows.

"Can you imagine hunting here?" Dave whispered.

"What would you do?" Derek replied, "Just sit, right?"

"I guess so. Walking around would be a waste of time. Just learn their patterns, let them come to you and take the shot," Dave contrasted his memory of Colorado hunts and what lay before him. An open field that must have creatures in it all night. The game trail indicated deer or maybe wild pigs. He hadn't considered deer would live around there. *Why not?* he thought. *They live everywhere.*

"Wake me up when something happens," Derek said quietly as he leaned back against a tree. "Ah fuck!" he exclaimed as he shot upright. Dave instinctively grabbed at him to keep him down. "Red ants. We gotta move."

They quickly gathered their bag and scope, moving back down the game trail away from the farm but still within a line of sight. Derek surveyed their new location carefully before settling down again to wait. Within a few moments, a female figure moved through the farm lot. Dave followed her with the scope as she entered the door of a long outbuilding.

"That sort of looks like barracks," Dave mentioned.

"I think they used to have migrants out here," Derek replied, "to pick fruit."

"Look, some trucks are coming," Dave whispered.

They watched as multiple crew trucks entered the farm gate, backing into neat rows. The passengers climbed out, stretching off a long day before making uninspired steps toward the buildings. Most of the workers wore a lycra balaclava concealing their faces.

"I do not understand the special gardening forces thing these guys are into," Derek snickered. "Isn't it hot enough in this fucking swamp? Fuck the balaclava. The guys I worked with at the golf course said it was for the sun."

"I don't get it either," Dave replied. "It's weird."

"Duncan!" Dominic exclaimed. "You have a cop on you."

"I do? There's a truck behind me about a quarter mile. Doesn't look like a cop," he replied.

"That is a cop," Dominic repeated. "I have that phone verified. Take a left and head east."

Duncan turned his Jeep onto another white sandy road, spinning the tires as he shifted into third gear. The truck followed, speeding to close the gap. "What do I do?" he pled with a hint of desperation that felt foreign to him. The countryside he was in, the circumstance, the anxiety was something he hadn't had to feel since he was young. Its memory lost to the repetitive luxury of a privileged life no matter how hard he had worked to achieve it.

"Stay calm," Dominic reassured, "just drive. I have something I can do." The truck came to a halt in the middle of the road, fading into the dust of Duncan's tires. "Ok, turn right at the next road."

Duncan followed Dominic's instructions. As he made the turn, he saw the truck speed by towards the east. He slowed the Jeep to a stop, his hand clutched to his pounding heart. Another sensation from younger days. "What did you do?" he asked.

"I sent the guy a text from one of the Florida numbers I have. I can't believe that worked," Dominic laughed. "He is on his way to the hospital to be with his grandmother. She'll be dead in about 30 minutes. So he thinks. That is going to be one pissed-off cop when he runs into the ER. Poor granny."

"How do you know he has a grandmother?" Duncan asked.

Dominic laughed, "His name is Scott. He is one of the cops I was able to gather a lot of information on. Your digital footprint can be very detailed."

"Hmm," Duncan replied, "what should I do now?"

"Stay where you are for a while. I will let you know if I have any other known cops or anyone else heading your way."

Three white vans pulled into the farm along with two gardening trucks. The female occupants filed out of the vans walking in groups of two and three to a barracks building opposite that of the men. Where the men's postures expressed that of a beaten team, the women were lively, almost hopeful. As they approached the door a stern woman met them, defeating their brief, joyful camaraderie. Each lowered her gaze as she filed past the woman.

"They don't seem to like that one," Dave muttered his report from the eyepiece of the spotting scope.

"I can see her bitchy posture just fine without the scope," Derek agreed. A few more work trucks and vans arrived, releasing their human cargo to repeat the scene.

"That's a lot of people in those barracks if that's what they are," Derek observed as he took over the scope.

Dave laid back to rest. It felt good to shift his posture and stretch out his legs. He held up his hand between the sun and the horizon to get a feel for the remaining sunlight. "45 minutes," he stated.

"What?" Derek asked.

"There's about 45 minutes left before the sun is gone behind the trees," Dave replied, "a little less actually."

"How do you know?"

"Each finger is about 15 minutes. We have about three between the tops of the trees and the sun. It's a hunting trick. You never learned that?" Dave asked.

"Nope," Derek replied from behind the scope. "Good trick. I will remember that. Huh…"

"What?" Dave asked. "You see something?"

"There is a guy in the back of one of the work trucks. In the cargo space. He just poked his head up from under all the shit piled in there," Derek reported.

"Under the palm frond mess?" Dave asked.

"Yeah. He's looking around like he is up to something," Derek replied. "Ok, he's climbing out."

"I can see him now," Dave said.

"He is sort of creeping around like he doesn't want to be seen," Derek reported.

They watched the man make slow progress around the line of trucks. From their vantage point, he was alone in the farm yard. His motion said otherwise. As the man snuck back behind the last truck, he began to pick up his pace. He made a few hurried looks behind before committing to an all-out run in Dave and Derek's direction.

"What the fuck?" Derek exclaimed. "He is heading right for us, and he looks scared as shit."

"Sit tight," Dave cautioned. "There's no way he can see us."

"I agree," Derek replied. "Fuck me, he looks scared. Oh shit, I see why."

As Derek spit out the last sentence, a man on the flat roof of the farmhouse came into view leveling a rifle at the runner. The end of the barrel was fat with a suppressor. The shot was nearly inaudible to Derek and Dave at their distance; but as the bullet skipped off the ground near the man's feet, it carried enough speed to remain supersonic splitting the air with a crack as it pealed off leaves from above.

"Jesus Fucking Christ!" Derek yelled. "Get behind something!" They both dove for the trunks of two large Live Oaks as the bullets increased in frequency. Dave peaked out from behind his tree to watch the man running a haphazard zigzag pattern in a desperate attempt to dodge bullets now coming from three rifles. His only saving grace being a combination of distance and frantic weaving.

"Call Duncan! Get him back here!" Dave yelled.

Derek fell back from the spectacle, burrowing in tight against his tree as he fumbled with the phone. He managed to text, *get us out now,* as the bullets stripped away more leaves;

the rounds cracking loudly as they pierced the foliage around them.

"He is still coming. What do we do? They're all running this way," Dave screamed.

"Duncan is coming; he says he is fucking 10 minutes out," Derek yelled. "Sit tight!" They could hear the men yelling now, taking brief pauses to fire as they attempted to close in on the runner. For a moment, the yelling and firing seemed to take on its own slow pattern of time as Dave and Derek waited for the man to reach them.

"Duncan is going to have to hold off. By the time he gets here, he will roll right into this," Dave warned.

"I am on it," Derek said, feverishly texting.

The man came crashing into the brush amongst a hailstorm of bullets. Instinctively, Derek stuck his foot out, tripping the man up. With a furtive dive, he piled on the man before he could rise, placing his hand over his mouth. "No te muevas," he whispered. "Calla-te, tambien." The man struggled a moment before relinquishing his instincts to flee for an impulse to freeze. "Shhhh," Derek reassured him. The man lay face down, Derek draped over him, the ghillie concealing them both. Derek could feel the man's heart beating against his rib cage in sync with his own. He had no idea what had become of Dave. Had he run?

For what seemed an eternity, they waited. "No te muevas, todo va estar bien," he continued until a crescendo of footsteps came to a stop a few yards away. The man tensed as if he were willing to give flight again forcing Derek to slide his arm around his neck demonstrating the seriousness of the situation. The man's trembling shook the ground under Derek's arm.

Voices uttering desperate plans with little direction could be heard over a breeze batting at the underbrush. Steps were drawing closer. The scraping of flora against pant legs announced the uneasy declaration of their approach. For Derek and the man, the sound meant capture. One of them was the prey; the other an unexpected discovery.

"Duncan," Dominic yelled into the phone. "That cop is on the way back and he is driving like he has a siren on."

"I am almost there," Duncan replied. His nerves were fully engaged. His hands shook on the wheel as he rounded the final turn to the pick-up point. A half mile down and he would have the guys back in, then a stop at the Country Club on the way back to celebrate. He hadn't been there in years. It would be worth sitting down for a drink among the do-nothing wealth he abhorred to debrief at his favorite corner table. He rolled up to the location and waited. Where were they? They should be less than a hundred yards off the road.

He saw someone coming through the brush, relieving his tension. Three men stepped out rifles ready. It was a brazen and peculiar display in the post gun law era. Duncan froze as one of the men stepped up to the window the other two blocking an escape. "What are you doing here, old man?" he sputtered in a heavy Mexican accent.

"I just stopped for a moment to get my bearings. I see you are hunting?" he asked.

"The fuck you care?" the man replied. His hostility for Duncan seemed deep and historic.

"No worries," Duncan complied. "Do you know how to get to the highway?"

"Yes…" came the reply. "I do…" The pause was unnerving, foreshadowing bad intentions. The other two men watched, smirking at the interchange.

"Did you see someone running down the road?" the man asked.

"I did not," Duncan replied.

"You sure about that? You are not here to pick someone up and bullshitting me right now?" the man growled.

"I am quite sure," Duncan replied. Duncan's phone rang. It was Dominic. He had ignored the flurry of text tones while being questioned, letting them go unread.

"Someone is calling you," the man said as he waved for his cohort to close in on Duncan's Jeep.

POP!, POP!, POP!

Duncan's heart jumped as he clutched at his chest, convinced he had been shot. A barrage of reports came from an unseen gun. Next to the road, what appeared to be a standing bush held a pistol hot from firing. Three Mexicans dropped to the ground. The man threatening Duncan had gone first, his chin glancing off the window frame as his knees buckled. The other two lay squirming in the road, not yet dead. Dave ran around to the front passenger side as Derek shoved the runner in the backseat of the Jeep.

"Get the fuck out of here, Duncan!" Derek yelled.

Duncan slammed the Jeep into gear, billowing dust behind as he bounced the wheels over the legs of a corpse. The phone rang again.

"Duncan!" everyone could hear through the speaker. "That cop is almost there. I see you're moving finally. Turn right, now!" Duncan spun the wheel onto an eastbound road. The Jeep's tires bit into the sand as they slid through the turn, catching before they were nearly sent into the ditch. He shifted quickly into third, then fourth. "Ok," Dominic calmed, "you should be OK. Just stay on that road into town and calm your driving. Good job, Duncan. I am three time zones away about to piss my pants. I'm out. I will call you tomorrow."

Dave pealed the ghillie off his head and turned to face the startled runner. "Hola," he managed to spit out.

Derek was still fully engulfed in his ghillie, laughing hysterically. "Jesus Christ, Duncan! What the hell did you get us into? And congratulations, Dave. You are homicidal."

Dave slid down in the seat as reality took over the moment. He had more than likely killed one or all three of those men. He didn't have the stomach for it. Again, circumstance had put him behind the gun. This time, he wasn't able to walk away without blood.

Chapter 13

"What the fuck, Scott? Where were you?" Miguel yelled as he stepped carefully over a blackening slick of drying blood, irate. He had lost two supervisors; another was drugged into a coma in his infirmary. The patrolman he relied on had not been making his rounds.

"I am sorry," the cop apologized meekly. "I got a text that my grandmother was dying at the hospital. It turned out to be a hoax."

"A hoax?" Miguel glared into Scott's eyes. "A fucking hoax. How does someone know you have a grandmother and have your number? And how do they know to text you when they are fucking around out here by my farm shooting my men? Does that make sense to you?" Miguel kicked at the dirt, his mind trying to work out what had happened while Scott subconsciously mimicked, kicking sand over the blood. "Stop!" Miguel yelled. "There is no use trying to cover it. Go get a fucking shovel and put it into the ditch."

"You know," Scott said sheepishly, "maybe the text didn't have anything to do with this."

"Stop being an idiot. I pay you to fucking think once in a while," Miguel hissed. "Shut the fuck up and go get a fucking shovel. I am not going to tell you again."

Miguel stared down the road to the north. Some of the vehicle's tracks were still visible, taunting him in the headlights of his Range Rover. How did they know where Scott was, a tracker stuck to the car? How would they know who Scott was to track him in the first place? FBI? ICE? Whoever it was, he needed to be cautious. If he had to get some workers deported as a last resort, he would. Maybe buy another farm. Multiple locations to house his crews could work. The best thing to do right now was to shift some, if not all of them out of state to one of the other regions and replace them. Something was off about this crew; they had been a series of headaches.

That fucking Brazilian, they knew he would be trouble. Mexicans, Hondurans and Guatemalans were easier to manage. There were ways to keep them in line. Fuck the Venezuelans, Colombians, and anyone else south of Panama. Purge them and get a new crew from another region until this was sorted out but the grass still grows. He had to think intelligently, with a strategy. "I don't want to see Sergio again," he lectured himself. "I can't deal with him right now. I have to keep this problem quiet and not overreact."

"You OK, Dave? It's been almost a week," Derek asked as they walked the beach at sunrise on a Sunday. The tide was out; a light breeze blew in from offshore.

"I am coming to terms with it," Dave quietly replied.

"This is what I am going to tell you then I won't mention it again," Derek said. "Think about those three idiots. They were going to do to Duncan whatever they wanted. This large Foliage Sasquatch starts shooting at them with a pistol that no private citizen in this country can legally own or carry anymore outside of a registered gun range. They had numbers but the fight was weighted to your side. You had the element of surprise and you were justified. That is all you need to come to terms with. Those assholes were trying to kill Gilberto and nearly did. You did the right thing. You eliminated three scumbag losers. This country and the country they came from are better off without them."

"I wasn't even thinking," Dave replied.

"I can imagine," Derek continued. "You reacted. You protected your tribe and sent those fuckers straight to hell where they belong. I am proud to be part of the tribe with you."

"Thanks, dude, but I am not feeling too proud of myself right now," Dave muttered. The last few nights he had awoken soaking wet from dreams felt but thankfully unremembered. Somewhere deep in him, they wreaked havoc on a conscience lacking a capacity for killing. He had never been in the military. Soldiers had to be immune to what he felt, right? Did popular culture try to make us believe they were so we hope they could robotically kill on our behalf? To kill without the anguish of a spoiled sense of morality? He was not proud of himself.

"It will go away," Derek consoled. "To deny your emotions right now is not human. You will let this go eventually. New events will take their place. Just give it time and don't be too hard on yourself. If it is any consolation, I would have popped those fuckers too."

Duncan sat back in his chair, sipping coffee while Kate busied herself making eggs. There was something wrong with her Uncle. He was deeply thoughtful. She had seen him like this before when he had to make difficult decisions at the company. She knew to leave him alone. Eventually, he would act on his thoughts.

"Here, Uncle," she said quietly, handing him a plate, "I have to be going. Mom wants to go to church today and I said I would go with her."

"Have you seen Miguel lately?" Duncan asked.

"Why do you ask?"

"No reason," Duncan lied.

"He has been busy," Kate replied. "He has some staffing problems to work out. That's what he said." She paused to examine her Uncle's reaction. He usually took the conversation bait when something business-related came up. He remained uncharacteristically quiet giving Kate a rush of anxiety. "Do you like him?"

"What?" Duncan replied hurriedly.

"I asked if you like Miguel."

"I like him just fine," Duncan lied again. "We should get together with him again. Maybe I can help him with his business."

"Yeah," Kate mocked, "you can help him with a gardening business. Your advice might be a little overkill. Don't you think?"

Duncan shrugged, "You know. People are the business in all businesses. Oil doesn't extract itself. I know it's not the same but every business runs well or poorly because of the mix of different people you have and can keep. The worst kind of business runs OK with OK people. If they are motivated and bought into the mission, they will do what it takes to keep things moving from the lowest level employee to the highest. But you have to be ethical and act within a framework of social, legal and spiritual justice because otherwise the best people will discover you, discover themselves then they will abandon and avoid you. And you will suffer the people who are still with you and you will deserve it."

Kate paused, considering the last comment. It felt baiting. "You eliminated half of your staff once with new equipment," she redirected. "They weren't the *best people*?"

"I eliminated dangerous and outdated jobs. I kept most of those affected or gave them the option to retire. And that was a long time ago," Duncan defended.

"I know. You told me," Kate replied. "I gotta go. Can we talk about this later?"

"Get going then. Thank you for breakfast," Duncan managed to smile, "and tell your mom I said, hello."

He finished the eggs as he walked around the kitchen island, sliding the plate and coffee cup into the dishwasher. The house was quiet, only the sound of his mother's clock ticking out the seconds. His footsteps on the hardwood floor happily diverted him from the monotony of the clock as he stepped out to visit the three men hiding in the guest house.

"Mister Duncan," Gilberto smiled as he looked up from the laptop. "Rosy, mira. Eu vou trabalhar por ele na ilha. Também vocês vão comigo." Gilberto spun the laptop around to show his wife the man who had changed their lives. She waved at him happily. "OK, Eu vou. Falamos mais tarde quando os filhos estão em casa. Beijos, amor." He closed the laptop to properly greet Duncan, who motioned for him to remain seated.

"What'd he say?" Dave asked Derek.

Derek leaned over to whisper, "He told her he is going to work for Duncan on the island and she and the kids can come too."

"Is she amenable to leaving Brazil?" Duncan asked.

"She is. She will go where I go," Gilberto replied. "Thank

you. I can't believe how this has happened. I couldn't speak to her for many months. I think she thought I was dead."

"So, as you said," Duncan began, "you were trying to enter the US through a smuggler. A coyote, right?" Gilberto affirmed with a nod. "Then he abandoned you and the rest of your group somewhere near the border. Then another coyote took you across."

"Yes, we entered the United States somewhere in the west of Texas, maybe in New Mexico. I don't know. I was listening to the Mexicans talk and I didn't understand them well," Gilberto explained.

"Tell me again what happened after," Duncan asked.

"They told us that we get jobs and we go to Florida or maybe Tennessee or some other place. They say they will give us documents. They explain to me that they have to hold my passport to show to officials. I never see it again. When I ask, they tell me it was in a safe with the others. I asked the others. None of them had one. It seemed strange. I got into a van with many other people and arrived here in Florida."

"And they told you that you had a debt to pay off for the coyote, transport and documents?" Duncan asked.

"Yes, so I have it still. The Mexicans and others were very scared of their debt. They worry a lot. I didn't understand how they can pay it since they make us pay to live at that farm and give us no money," Gilberto continued. "They tell us they are saving for us for when we go back. After the debt is paid. I didn't have money to send to Rosy or anyway to communicate with her so I make the decision to run."

"Do you think Rosy may be in danger?" Duncan asked.

"I don't know. I heard them complaining about me in Spanish. I was beginning to understand them better, but I didn't let them know it. The Mexicans and especially the Hondurans were always worried for their families. They say things about the debts and the gangs threatening. We don't have that in Brazil. We have our own gangs."

"Gentlemen," Duncan announced, "we have a problem we must address. What do we do about this?"

"Can we go to the Feds?" Dave asked.

"We can," Duncan replied. "Then we might have to explain the three dead men. We would have to explain a lot of things to a justice system that wants to discover and prosecute on their own. Then, we enter into the world of politics and federal law. We already assume there are a significant number of police officers on Miguel's payroll here. Who else? We don't know. The Mayor? City Counsel? County officials? Feds? There are three police officers who are confirmed to be close to Miguel. Dominic is tracking them and says to assume that every cop around here is on the take. And every politician. It is better to assume and avoid them than look for a reason to trust any of them."

"So what are you thinking?" Derek asked.

"What I am thinking is something beyond the scope of this issue but related," Duncan replied. "I have the means and know a few others in a similar financial position who will contribute. Paul and I have toyed with this idea for a while in the abstract. Now, it seems as though it is calling us. We will begin creating a private organization to serve justice and protect the vulnerable and oppressed. It is going to take some time to accomplish. I don't believe we will have any trouble recruiting talent to help us. The French Foreign Legion is potentially a good example, although we will not be bound to a national government. We are bound to justice. Instruments of it and in fear of God's judgment alone."

"So, what you are saying is you are going to start a mercenary special forces group whose purpose is punish those who deserve it?" Dave said. "How will we determine who deserves it?"

"That is a difficult moral question. We don't know yet," Duncan replied.

"I know," Derek spoke up. Duncan looked up at him, wondering whether Derek would say something ridiculous. "The leader must have a basis in justice from an ethical, moral and spiritual position. Drawing on the basic tenants of the major religions and the ideal that not one soul is more valuable to our Creator than another. Someone or a group of people who can identify the oppressed and punish the oppressors. Make an example of them. Someone who wants nothing more than to remain in the good favor of God who is the ultimate authority. This person, or group, will do what they believe is the will of God in the service of God and bear the wrath of God if they stray onto the path of their own temporal desires. Like you said, 'in fear of God's judgment alone'." The group stared up at Derek absorbing what he said.

"Do you believe these people exist?" Duncan asked.

"Probably not," Derek conceded, "but that would be ideal. Obviously, we need to be able to influence and recruit like-minded people. And to build a tribe of justice-seeking mercenaries. Like you said about the French, I think if we start looking at mercenary organizations that already exist or have existed, it could be a good place to start. The one thing they all have is resources. The begging question becomes whether the ones providing the monetary resources also provide the direction. Potentially, you could wind up with an organization of thugs paid to defend and coerce for the resource provider's whims and greed. Like a bad atheistic, plutocratic government who deals in social or legal justice that serves its own purposes. This is a very idealistic vision you have Duncan. I have to say, I dig it."

"Well," Duncan replied, "we are a long way from realizing this. Now, we have an immediate problem to deal with. We are sitting in the middle of a trafficking organization. One that nearly every one of my neighbors supports. Everyone who likes clean hotel rooms around here. The roofs and most of the construction. I am sick inside knowing that it's so close. Much of the privilege here is built on and supported by nothing more than coercion and modern slavery. These people are sold the idea of the opportunity to have jobs and make American dollars to support their families. I cannot blame them for that. But what some of them are getting is no better than what they would have if they had stayed where they were. You can thank Miguel for that and all the other Miguels out there." Duncan looked over at Gilberto who nodded in agreement.

"Politicians close the borders to appease voters, which increases trafficking to provide these same people to mow lawns and do jobs that the voters won't do themselves," Dave spoke up. "So what does that mean? Is everyone who lives in suburban America somehow benefiting from trafficking?"

"Yes," Derek stated plainly. "Not just suburban America. All of us, in some way, materially benefit from this. It even comes down to everyone who buys food from the grocery store."

"I think I am going to puke," Dave lamented.

"That is the problem with real truth," Derek said. "Once you see it, without your self-interest filters, you can't unsee it and it makes you sick. It should make you sick. If not, how human are you? And what do we do about this little fucker Miguel?"

"That is complicated," Duncan replied. "I am not sure yet."

"It might be time to get Paul involved," Dave suggested.
"He will be here soon," Duncan revealed.

Chapter 14

"Grab the bag with the fins and shit," Derek said to Dave as the Jeep came to a stop within the ruins of a Bahamian resort razed by a particularly angry hurricane. Dave jumped out while Derek stared through the windshield. Closing his eyes, it came back to him. He was young and full of ambition, but for a time, he let serendipity take him. This place had been built to make people happy one week at a time. The guests always said they envied him. They ironically coveted his relative poverty, living on a beach at a place he couldn't have afforded to visit. Then, one day, it was over. What he thought was the real world calling him home was only an echo of repetitive generational wisdom with no capacity for adventure. He was different, at least for a while, giving his family much consternation. Submitting himself back to the real world for them eased the imaginary worries they created for his wellbeing. With him back in the US finishing college, they could rest. They had pulled him back in for a while.

For Derek, this island resort was the first truly remote and exotic location in a pattern of them to come. He had learned to snorkel here. What was there to learn? Face down, breathe through tube and kick the fins. After a year and scores of coral formations, learning to snorkel turned into pushing himself a little further under. He had increased his ability to hold his breath another second, then another. In what was left of the pool in front of him, he had become inspired by a French Free Diver demonstrating physical and mental control beyond human. He learned to relax, to flow with the currents, to glide along with Eagle Rays as long as he could. In those moments, he was free and indifferent to the kind of normal he was supposed to be.

"What happened here?" Dave asked.

"Hurricane decimated it," Derek replied. The scene in front of him was enough to elaborate on what he felt.

"You were here?" Dave asked.

"I was. A long time ago, when I was in my early twenties," he replied letting his eyes wander through the wreckage. The images of buildings regrew from what was left of their foundations. He motioned for Dave to follow. "Come on. This was a pretty great place, but there is something that a hurricane couldn't destroy." He led Dave up a series of cracked, eroding stairs to the top of a small dune overlooking the Atlantic.

"Wow, look at that," Dave exclaimed. In front of him a pink sand beach arched a small bay full of coral heads nearly to the shoreline. He stood in awe of the beauty. Its isolation was akin to places he had hunted with his father years before the gun control law when all someone needed was a way to become purposefully lost. In Colorado, it was easy. You needed a four wheel drive and the intention to use it. Here they were about a mile off the main road that ran the length of the island; lost on a conveniently forgotten beach left for them to rediscover.

"Yeah, like I said on the way here, this beach is indescribable," Derek commented happily. The best thing about it was sharing it. *Thank God it hasn't been exploited*, he thought. There was enough of that. Other Caribbean islands from his past were so developed he had no desire to return. This one was special. Fortunately, the threat of another total destruction kept banks and developers away. Looking with open eyes free from unrestrained greed, there was good in everything even hurricanes. "Come on Dave, we'll snorkel around that closest head. There are a lot of barracudas here and sometimes sharks. They shouldn't bother us, but it's a good idea to look behind you once in a while. One of the guests had a hammerhead following him around. The dude nearly shit himself when he finally saw it. He said the shark looked pretty surprised too. They left on good terms."

They spent an easy hour floating around the coral close to the beach, accompanied by schools of Sargent Majors. The sun was past noon when Derek left the water to sit on the sand. Dave stayed facedown with a Parrot Fish he had befriended. As much as Derek felt the joy of sharing this beach, Colorado kept prodding. This beach had been the leap he made away from every comfort he knew and thought important. He had never thought he would see it again.

It was the way he thought of her. She would eventually find his replacement deep in the distractions of life. Someone better and more available was going about the day, unaware of how beautiful she was. It was a matter of time. Whoever he was, he would be someone better. Derek had never experienced losing a woman to a lesser man. It didn't happened. It wasn't in a woman's nature to downgrade. It made no difference if the better man was putting up a good show; in her eyes and in her feelings, he was better. That was all that mattered. Whatever made her happy at the moment would legitimize her decision. What could he do? The answer was simple and painful. Accept defeat, mourn through the steps, and move on. *If you love someone, set them free,* went the cliché. In their last encounter, he had left the door wide open for her to stay in or step out. He had things to do and Florida to endure until the kids were in college. Maybe it would be different in a different reality. Right now, his time belonged to his girls, then to Duncan. She had to wait and get him in electronic doses through texts and calls. Maybe that would be enough for a while.

Uncle Duncan, I put the Jeep back in the garage. Sorry, my car battery was dead. I had to go to an appointment, Kate texted. *Love You!*

Duncan read the text. The image of the Jeep splattered with blood weeks before plagued him. The guys had washed it thoroughly, proudly showing him the results. The stain was physically gone. His phone buzzed another text. *What could it be now?* he thought as he picked up the phone. *Call me.*

"Dominic, what is it?" Duncan asked.

"A cop tailed Kate. Same one who stopped Dave," Dominic reported. "I was out for a while and came back to an alarm from the program. Maybe it's nothing. For whatever reason, he tailed her right to your property. He came all the way from the other side of town to follow her. Seems weird."

Duncan set the phone down, clasping his hands on his face, "No, no, no," he lamented.

"DUNCAN!" Dominic yelled into the phone.

He picked the phone up momentarily catatonic and immune to Dominic's yelling. "I am here," he murmured finally.

"Is there a problem?" Dominic questioned. "Maybe

Miguel was just having this idiot check up on her. You know, like a jealous or protective boyfriend."

"Unfortunately no, Dominic," Duncan's tone was measured as he sheepishly hoped he was dreaming. "She was driving the Jeep."

"Oh," Dominic replied distantly, "hold on a minute." Duncan heard a rapid firing of keystrokes as he remembered Kate's text, punctuating the lapse in time with an uncomfortable silence. It felt comforting to share his anxiety with someone else. Perhaps this would provide solutions his emotions were unable to discover.

"Ok, this is what we know so far," Dominic stated. "On the topic of cops, a cop followed you and then he went to the hospital. He has to know that was bullshit because his grandmother is not dead, nor was she ever there. That doesn't place you or the Jeep back at the killing site. There could be suspicion, but who would think that a septuagenarian would knock off three scumbags. We know the cop knows about the shooting. He was with Miguel on the road, but that is not the cop who followed Kate. That was Scott, not Marco. Marco is the Kate-following cop and Dave-stopping cop." Dominic paused to see if Duncan had anything to add. The old man was silent.

"If I may continue?" Dominic asked into a quiet phone. "The Mexicans are, we assume, buried with their phones somewhere on the farm. There were only two phones on the three. We know that. There are way too many details to put together to link you. I just ran through the data. It's pretty obvious they picked up the Jeep on their license plate reader system, which means they were specifically looking for it. A curiosity about Dave maybe? After she passed one of their cameras, Marco the Kate-following cop, like I said, came from the other side of town to follow her. After pulling Dave over, all he would know is that Dave's Montana tagged Jeep was driven by Kate to your house making it your Montana tagged Jeep or a Jeep that is at your house for whatever reason. But Scott, the grandma-having cop, would not have been close enough to see your plates. And seriously, have you seen how many fucking plates that ridiculous State of Florida offers? Even if he, Scott, caught a glimpse of the color from a distance he couldn't determine Montana from whatever stupid, fucking Florida fish, manatee, bird, bear, turtle, deer, swamp critter or other random benefit plate it might have been."

Dominic continued, "There is a ton of plausible deniability in case of any links they would find to you and the dead Mexicans and Dave. You're old. You were lost. The Jeep is not linked to the shooting. Yeah, it was followed by Cop Scott. Maybe it was followed, maybe not. Maybe the tire tracks you put over one of the dead guys looked like they were from a Jeep. Again, potentially deniable. And who cares? It's not like this shooting was reported by dead Mexicans or Miguel. And the local cops, the ones who might not be corrupt, don't seem to have anything to investigate. These Mexicans just ceased to exist; poof, off the planet, if anyone actually cared about their existence anyway. Whether or not they had friends or families outside of there, we don't know. Let's assume they did. They would be the ones looking to find them and probably only Miguel knows where they are."

"He does," Duncan replied. "And he knows now that the Jeep is on my property. The same Jeep that was tailing him with Dave driving. When the truck was following me out by the farm, it was quite far behind. Like you said, probably too far to see much of the license plate. The question that can only be answered by Miguel, is what will he do now? At this point, even if he does nothing, he is doing something. If I were him, I would take no obvious action but I would open my eyes and available resources to start considering contingencies. And try to figure out who Dave is, where Dave is and what he has to do with my Jeep. And potentially what he has to do with Kate."

"Jefe, he's awake," the medic reported.

"Ok, I am coming over," Miguel replied. He stepped away from the meeting with his crew leaders into the dull air of the yard. The smell of antiseptic seeped through the door of the makeshift clinic hitting him full in the face as he opened it. "How is he?"

"He can talk. He is waiting for you," the medic replied.

Miguel walked into the patient room. They were almost completely autonomous from the world around them with the addition of emergency care. Delivering this case to the hospital would have been reckless self-immolation.

"Who did this?" Miguel asked.

"I don't know," the man replied hoarsely. Miguel handed the man a glass of water.

"What were you doing on the road? Are you guys stupid? You were standing in the road with rifles. Then two of you were dead out there, and you should have been dead too. What were you thinking?" Miguel screamed as he yanked away the glass. The man recoiled into his pillow, expecting a beating.

"There was a man in a Jeep," the man remembered.

Miguel hesitated, thinking. Opening a photo on his phone, he shoved it towards the man's face. "Was it this Jeep?"

"Yes, that is it," the man replied, hopefully believing his identification would spare him from another tirade. "It had those plates. Not Florida."

"Who was driving it?" Miguel asked. "A thirty-eight year old fucking gringo?"

"I was in the back. You know, behind it like that photo. Enrique was talking to the driver. Some old man. I couldn't see but he sounded like he was nervous," the man replied.

"Some old man? Who shot you?"

"I didn't see him. I didn't see any other person, just felt the bullet hit me. It wasn't the old man. I know that."

Miguel's phone rang. "Marco," he answered, "Paco is awake out of the coma. I am talking to him now. He didn't see the guy but he said it was an old man not that fucking Dave guy. Same Jeep that was tailing me. They stopped him on the road."

"That was Duncan Westbourne," Marco replied.

"What? How do you know?" Miguel asked.

"I just tailed that Jeep with the Montana plates back to his house. Kate was driving it."

Miguel's face twitched as the news boiled within him. Marco knew not to say anything while Miguel seethed. He waited.

"Thank you," Miguel answered, "we will talk about this later." He hung up and turned back to Paco.

"You know the man?" Paco asked.

"I do," Miguel replied confidently. His demeanor softened, turning to comfort. His wounded crew leader's eyes alit with ambition.

"That's good. I can help you find him when I get better," Paco offered trying to sit up. "We'll take care of that fucking gringo."

Miguel pushed him gently back down onto the bed. "It will be awhile. Don't get up."

"You know I want to help, Jefe. I have to. There's a lot to do," Paco lamented. His desperation was so poorly veiled it made him pitiful. Miguel loathed a plea for pity more than anything.

"Don't worry," Miguel consoled him again. "You have been very helpful."

Miguel gave Paco a reassuring pat on the shoulder as he turned away to leave.

"If you see he is taking a long time to recover, give him the injection. The longer he sits in here, the worse it will be for us," Miguel said to the medic as he left.

Derek pulled into a parking lot across the water from Duncan's new island. The illusion of how close it seemed would be evident once they were on the water.

"Duncan really likes Jeeps," Dave commented as they boarded the boat. "Forty million for a compound on your own island and you get a Jeep."

"He does seem to like them," Derek agreed. "I was surprised he could drive like he did."

The Boston Wailer engine started up. Derek slammed the boat into gear, planing out in a headlong assault at a choppy sea. Dave gripped a handle happily watching the island grow in front of them. As they cruised into the tiny harbor, Derek pulled back on the throttle easing into the boat lift. Dave jumped onto the dock to spin the lift wheel as Derek stepped off, confidently satisfied with his seamanship.

"Gilberto should have dinner ready by now," Dave said as they climbed into a golf cart. "I am actually looking forward to getting back to Florida. Hope he doesn't go completely insane on this island before Rosy and the kids get here."

Chapter 15

"This is a beautiful place," Paul said as he leaned over the railing of Duncan's deck to get a better look at a woman walking along the beach. She was alone, swaying her arms happily to music, oblivious to the eyes taking her in.

Duncan sat up in his chair to pour a little more Scotch. He was sullen, unable to enjoy his drink but optimistic of its effects. That night still haunted him. The sudden surprise of pain on the man's face who wanted to cause him harm was etched into his mind. Duncan's shock was the last thing the man saw as his head crashed against the window, his knees buckling in slow motion underneath. Had they widowed someone and left children without a father? Nothing was in the news. Every day he awoke expecting a headline or maybe a knock. Missing men, bodies found on farm outside of town, nothing appeared. Those men had once been children. They were carried and nurtured by mothers who praised their accomplishments as they grew from boys into men. Were mothers waiting for calls? It was too much for Duncan. They had to have rules. This could not happen again.

"I want a code of conduct," Duncan blurted out, "rules of engagement."

Paul turned to face him, waiting for a follow-up. His friend was in a state of emotional anguish. That was obvious. He was a man who had built a fortune with no direct heirs. The estate plans Paul had made for Duncan over the years and remade then remade again were a testament to his shifting moods. The anxious pain in Duncan reminded Paul of this. His niece gets everything; she gets nothing then she gets part of everything with contingencies. In the latest version, Kate would have enough to provide for generations. Duncan had assured Paul the last iteration of his will would stand. Or until Kate had become a potential problem again. She was a sweet, kind young woman. Her childish whims had evaporated. If the estate were left only to her, there would be no questions.

How could I break the news to Kate that her boyfriend is a modern slave master? Duncan thought to himself. When was talking to someone about the person they love anything but an avoidance exercise in temporary, affected positivity? It was probably best to trust in an inevitable breakup; then the truth could be revealed. Hiding opinions was good for social order. *It's OK Kate, I never liked Miguel anyway, and besides, we didn't tell you he was a human trafficker who we have tied to a known Mexican cartel boss. We knew this for a while. And we assume he has killed some people. We never liked him that much. You can do better.* The script ran through his head.

"What kind of code?" Paul asked.

"I don't want any killing," Duncan sulked.

"Duncan, I have never seen you like this. You are one of the most stoic, rational men I know. And I am going to lecture a bit," Paul replied. "The opportunity for the virtue you want is, for a lack of a better phrase, dead and buried. Thanks to Dave who, I have to remind you, saved your ass."

"We don't know that," Duncan protested. "Those men may have just been being harsh with me before telling me to leave."

"There were three Mexican men, who had been trying to kill a Brazilian, brandishing illegal, suppressed rifles. They confronted you on a desolate road, and you think they would tell you to just move along? Nothing to see here, gringo." Paul mocked. "Do I have to remind you of federal law? No guns outside of the certified locations. Ninety-five percent of that means gun ranges, not dirt farm roads in the middle of mosquito-infested buttfuck Florida. Before that law was passed, just having a suppressor without the tax stamp was a felony. You were having a chat with three felons. Fuck them straight to hell where they belong. No shooting. Sorry what did you say?"

"No killing," Duncan replied.

"I wish it were that simple, Duncan," Paul consoled his friend. "Justice doesn't always come from the apprehension of a perpetrator and lengthy court fiasco. Sometimes, it is rather abrupt and bypasses the assumed monopoly of justice."

"It was rather abrupt, as you said," Duncan replied. "I am talking about the future. I don't want to be involved in killing."

"Then this idea of yours should just end. Get it together, Duncan. Human nature is ugly and sometimes some of us are tasked with making it prettier. You will be involved when it happens because leadership takes the blame for everything. Real leadership does, anyway. The people you want to help are oppressed by people who don't have the capacity for reason. They're idiots. They have no use for discourse. They understand power," Paul lectured. "If you were the President of the country, you would be involved in legalized killing; regardless of whether it was justified.

"Do you think some fucking idiot politician and his bureaucrats are better equipped to decide who deserves to die than you? 'So fight you against the friends of Satan'…Isn't that what the Quran you love to read, says? Doesn't it reference that you have not killed them but Allah has allowed them to be killed by your actions or something like that?"

The idealistic organization Duncan had envisioned was unraveling as the reality of death became evident. He wasn't ready to front an organization that may sacrifice some of its members consciences. Could he send someone like Dave or Derek into a life or death situation? Ask them to kill? Was he capable of being the responsible, assumed leader who could do that?

If he led an autocratic organization, he would be placing himself as the sole authority of justice and ethics only answering to God or maybe some sort of rebellion. Who died and who lived? What would they do with captured enemies? Was the government so inept that he couldn't just hand this problem off to them? He knew they were completely capable of taking on the problem. But how could they tip them off, who would they contact? Was this important enough? The same government that used to use legal and biblical justification for the rights of slave owners? The government that repeatedly favored the lives of some people over others based on religious or political opinions? The government that favored land and expansion because imaginary boundaries are more important than lives and historical traditions? The government that uses terrain as a deterrent for migrants then ignores the bodies the harsh conditions create? Other perspectives of the truth were an inconvenience for those who wished to maintain a status quo of relative comfort.

Dominic had already confirmed that nearly everyone in the county and city governments, as well as the Federal, County, and City Prosecutors, were employing Miguel's crews directly or indirectly through their HOAs. They were all complicit in human trafficking. The embarrassment would be unfathomable. In Duncan's youth, he had dreams of becoming a journalist, breaking open cases of corruption, embarrassing officials and trying to force change by provoking the public with truths they willfully resisted. His experience running an oil company told him that politicians in the US and abroad were scared to death for the health of their reputations and easily bought. As nauseating as it was to interact with them, it was better to have them on your side than to hold their noses to the shit they created. He quietly believed the word 'politician' equaled 'scum' regardless of their good intentions. His conscience had had enough of doing what he thought best through political mechanisms.

"Look, Duncan, you can take this event or trauma or whatever you want to call it and look for some level of comfort to hide in, or you can get pissed off and go to war," Paul continued. "Seeking comfort is for the weak. You know that. Comfort is a warm bed that breeds regret. Comfort is the pacifier for those who sit around and wait to die. Without some discomfort prodding you, you are jellyfish enslaved to the currents," Paul paused as he stared down at Duncan, waiting for a rebuttal. "Do you want me to keep making up fucking motivational quotes for you?" he threatened.

Duncan smiled finally, "No, thank you, but no. That's enough. You are right. Let's proceed with the planning. I don't have the time left to procrastinate and avoid what I have to do."

"Excellent," Paul replied. "I think the first thing we need

to do is get the guys some passports from somewhere else. Where are yours currently?"

"Paraguay, Dominica, here, Malta and Turkey," Duncan answered. "Malta might be the most useful one I have. It basically says I have a ton of money and am a citizen of the European Union but it comes with agreements with our government. Vanuatu doesn't have an extradition treaty with the US. Let's see about that or almost anywhere in the Middle East. Their distaste for America could be beneficial. Maybe the BRICS if possible."

"Babe," Miguel said, "it would be good for him. He is hiding in that huge house. I know he plays golf once in a while. Just propose it to him. It's a charity tournament at the club. We need a fourth."

"Ok," Kate relented, "I'll ask."

"Good, tell me what he says," Miguel replied before hanging up. "Ok, Scott, that should work. We'll get the old man on the team and warm up to him. See if he squirms at all around us. Sergio is coming in for it."

Scott nodded, stood up and walked to the window to look out at the housekeeping staff coming back from work. *There are a few I would bang*, he thought. "Why aren't we doing the escort thing?"

"We talked about that. Let the Russians have it and let the Chinese massagers jerk off the rest of the fucking losers. We do service labor and construction, period. And we aren't going back to dealing. I am done with that," Miguel replied. "If the gringos want to feel rich while they work jobs, let them. We will do all the shit they won't. We will do the shit their soft little useless kids whine about. They can live in debt, playing rich while we take their cash. The common serfs are building an empire right underneath them. Eventually when I marry Kate, I might pass this on to you. If you're lucky and Sergio approves…" He paused, looking up for Scott's reaction. "By the way, I didn't tell him about your fuck up, so when you do it again, it will be fresh. He'll be disappointed instead of pissed off. It's usually the same result with him."

The cop relished the idea of running the little empire, but Sergio scared the hell out of him. The cartel was far away but was known to close the distance in an instant when problems arose and the flow of money slowed. *Does Miguel tell this Sergio guy anything?* he wondered. Miguel was probably screwing with his head about passing on the business. His promises were always big.

"Yes Uncle. It is a charity event," Kate begged. "You need to get out of that house and do something social for once."

"I'll think about it," Duncan answered before hanging up.

"What was that about?" Paul asked.

"Apparently, Miguel wants me to play golf with him at a country club tournament," Duncan replied suspiciously.

"Wow, country club tournament. That sounds awful," Paul replied snidely.

"These things are a joke," Duncan continued. "It is basically just a bunch of assholes looking for an excuse to demonstrate some virtue they think they have. Tournaments, Balls, Benefits and Galas. All the same. What do you think it means? I mean, why me?"

Paul thought a moment before answering, "It's hard to tell. Is he cozying up to you to gain the approval of his relationship with Kate? Do you think he really likes you? Is he checking out where he stands with you after this Jeep thing? Who knows? The guy just lost three of his employees and he seems to be taking it in stride. No big deal. Mourning time is over. That's powerful stoicism or maybe a lack of compassion or a psychosis."

"If they had families…," Duncan replied.

"Everyone has some semblance of a family, Duncan," Paul half-heartedly scolded. "Regardless, you should go. There will be security. You aren't the only ridiculously wealthy guy around here. Although, besides the house, you hide it pretty well. A lot better than the conspicuous consumers with their far-too-young-to-be-anything-but-whores girlfriends. That is comical. What do they call that? Sugarbaby arrangements? It's just hilarious when you see it out in the open. Whatever, it's not my money. I like my whores to demonstrate a little more enthusiastic dedication, a little less transaction."

"Ok, Paul, back to business. I appreciate you being here," Duncan interrupted. "What do you suggest?"

"This is what I would do. Go play golf and let these idiots do the talking. You should be good at that. Unless you are leading, you are an exceptional listener. Ask 'who', 'what', and 'how' questions. I would ignore 'why' questions. They can be an endless pile of desperate validation. One 'why' stacking on the next before the honest 'I don't know' answer finally appears. Just go with the flow and play golf. If they have an agenda, let them run with it. Don't feed into it. You can always use elicitation too. You know how to do that."

"Good advice. Thank you, my friend," Duncan replied.

The morning of the tournament was quiet. A nice breeze blew in off the ocean cooling the house as Duncan slipped into the Maybach next to Ignacio.

"Do you want me to wait for you Mister Duncan or come back?" Ignacio asked.

"You can come back to the house. This tournament should take a few hours. I'll text you when I am about done," Duncan replied. Ignacio nodded easing the car into reverse.

"We never go in this car. Usually just the Jeep," Ignacio commented.

"The Jeep is going to stay in the garage for a while. Maybe we'll ship it out to Eleuthera to be with the other one. In fact, that is a good idea. Can you ask Paul to arrange that? We'll get something new to drive here. Maybe one of those Broncos. Paul can set it up. Ask him to register this one in Florida."

"Yes, sir," Ignacio replied.

The golf course was 15 minutes from the house along the main road. The Maybach had never been up to speed. It was a pity such a beautiful car couldn't stretch her wings once in a while. It was nothing to worry too much about. None of the sports cars in the area ever went much above 60 unless they made the trip out to the interstate. Like retired race horses, they loped around looking nice from one stoplight to the next while the potential of their drivetrains sat around gaining weight.

Ignacio turned into a gated housing development surrounding the course; the guard stepped up to the car, ready to flex his authority. "Mister Westbourne is playing in the tournament," Ignacio announced. The guard looked in the back window, seeing no one. "He is here," Ignacio gestured to the front passenger seat. The guard, looking incredulous as he could, peered in at Duncan.

"Mr. Westbourne?" he asked.

"Yes," Duncan replied frankly.

"We haven't seen you here in a very long time, Sir. Enjoy the tournament," the guard said.

"Thank you," Duncan replied with a smile.

Ignacio drove up to the Bag Drop and popped the trunk. Before Duncan could step out, his golf bag was whisked away somewhere into the line of carts. He kindly patted Ignacio on the shoulder. "I will text you," he said.

"Mr. Westbourne," the Golf Pro beamed. "So nice to see you."

"Thank you, Gerry; it is nice to be back here for the day. You look good. I don't think I have seen you in about two years," Duncan replied, "How long has it been?"

"I believe six," the Pro said.

"It has been that long?" Duncan questioned.

"Hello, Mr. Westbourne!" Miguel called from the practice green. He pushed the ball he was intending to putt away with his foot as he approached with two other men. "Mr. Westbourne, this is Sergio, a long-time family friend and Scott, who helps me from time to time with the business." Duncan smiled, cordially grasping their handshakes.

"It is a pleasure to meet you gentlemen and an honor to spend some time on the course with you," Duncan said.

Miguel was demonstrably upbeat, happy with his triumph. He had landed one of the least-seen billionaires in the area on his team and now he was in the middle of it all soaking in the atmosphere of their friendship. Someday, maybe they would be like family. Hopefully, the day would produce something further when it came to Duncan's influence on Kate. Moreover, why was Duncan out by his farm? There was no chance of cornering the old man into a confession. Duncan was there, his now-deceased supervisor had all but confirmed it. Who else could it have been?

Miguel suggested Duncan and Sergio ride together as they began the drive out to the Fifth Tee for a shotgun start. "You never saw him in the Jeep?" Miguel asked quietly.

"No," Scott replied, "I saw a Jeep ahead of me before

going to the hospital. I couldn't see the plates. Paco didn't see him either, right?"

"No, but it was him. Marco tailed that Jeep to his house when Kate was driving it. How many Jeeps are in Vero with Montana plates? That Jeep is at his house. That same Jeep was following me when Marco pulled over that Dave guy. Whoever the fuck that is. It doesn't matter that Paco didn't see his face or remember the plate number. It was Duncan," Miguel seethed. "He is up to something."

"What's going on, Dominic?" Derek asked.

"He is with Miguel but he is riding in a different cart. The cop from the shooting night is with Miguel. The one with the grandma. Not the one who tailed Kate in the Jeep."

"What?" Dave exclaimed. "Kate got tailed in the Jeep? Duncan didn't tell us that. He just said not to use it."

"I didn't think that was a secret," Dominic replied. "Why would it be? Anyway, Kate took the Jeep to go somewhere and the cop tailed her back to the house. Happened a few days ago. Same cop who pulled you over, Dave."

What Duncan was keeping to himself was beginning to bother them. They were discovering there was a secretive side to him, then he would drop information bombs normal people would stew over and share for reassurance. Duncan would just do something and then tell them about it. Forty million for an island and a house in the Bahamas. One day, he just blurted it out and then sent Gilberto to live there. It felt like their job was to hide in the guest house, workout and wait for the next flurry of his whims. The continuous anxiety of not being in control of his life ate silently at Dave. Derek seemed to take it all in stride.

"So the cop is there, who else?" Derek asked.

"A cartel guy we traced a while back," Dominic shared nonchalantly.

"What? There's a cartel guy with them?" Dave yelled at the screen. "Dominic, what the hell?"

"We know Miguel is associated with a Mexican cartel guy named Sergio," Dominic answered.

"You knew this before you sent us out to spy on Miguel?" Dave asked.

"Yes and no," Dominic answered. "It took a while to confirm who the guy was."

Dave stomped away from the video call. Dominic could hear a door slam. Derek stepped into camera position. "He's a little on and off about that day," Derek explained. Dominic said nothing, returning to his monitoring. "What are they doing?" Derek asked.

"Nothing new right now. Just driving around the golf course," Dominic reported. "Paul should get to them soon."

"Ok, wait. There's another thing you didn't tell us," Derek said. "What is Paul doing there?"

"He's taking pictures," Dominic replied.

"It always interests me how people get their start," Sergio said as they sat in the cart waiting for the group ahead to move forward on the course. Duncan showed no reaction. It had been an obvious attempt at getting him to speak. After an uncomfortable silence, Sergio continued. "How was it when you started your business?"

"I inherited my business from my father," Duncan replied. He hoped his abrupt response would drop the conversation so they could continue making golf-related chitchat.

"I inherited mine too," Sergio blurted. "Logistics. We were in logistics."

"You are not doing that anymore?" Duncan asked. He figuratively pinched himself for taking the bait.

"I passed that on to my nephew when I retired," Sergio answered. "I am happy he has it now. He can worry about it. My biggest problem was my competitors trying to steal my employees. You have that problem?"

"No, but I have had competitors lament that I stole their best people," Duncan replied. "You can't steal people. You steal things."

"Hmm," Sergio replied.

"Gentlemen, how about a picture for the newsletter," Paul asked as he raised the camera.

"No, thank you," Sergio responded.

"Come on Sergio, smile for the nice guy. It will be a miracle if they use our picture," Duncan said. Sergio reluctantly gave in.

"Thank you, gentlemen. Say, aren't you Mr. Westbourne?" Paul asked. Duncan nodded. "And you, sir?"

"This is Sergio," Duncan paused, looking at Sergio, waiting for him to fill in the blanks.

"Villanueva," Sergio stated impatiently.

"Mr. Villanueva," Paul asked, "are you a member here?" Duncan looked over at Sergio hoping to influence an answer.

"I am a guest," Sergio replied trying to remain as casual as possible. "I live in Mexico most of the time."

"Well, welcome to Vero Beach. Enjoy your visit," Paul said cheerfully as he stepped over to take pictures of Miguel and Scott.

Chapter 16

Derek watched through the guest house window for Duncan and Paul trying to decide what to do. He and Dave had had enough. No man feels fulfilled in a role of servitude and restricted movement just because he is being paid. The people who ask for this always follow with an appeal for the virtue of patience. They felt no purpose without knowing the direction they were expected to take, living in the wake of Duncan's whims. Three men were dead. Although they rescued Gilberto, corpses are credited with victim status. Governments prefer to bury men behind bars, not in holes. Prisons are the red herrings of repentance concealed behind piles of money. The Maybach pulled in.

Derek stepped away from the window to conceal the anxiety he was stirring up before an inevitable confrontation. As footsteps ascended the stairs, he took one last look at Dave before positioning himself. Paul stepped through the door first into an energy that put him on alert.

"What are you guys doing?" Paul asked.

Derek held up his hand to Dave asking without a word to

talk first. "We are wondering what is going on," Derek replied.

Paul's sense for verbal sparring was readied. He relished the chance to take on an emotional opponent. He waited in silence hoping to provoke Derek into eruption. As Dave timidly began to fill in the uncomfortable silence, Derek again raised his hand silencing him. He stared at Duncan and Paul. It was Duncan who broke first.

"What are you wondering?" Duncan asked.

"You just played golf with a Mexican cartel guy," Derek responded. Dave sat up straighter taking on a physical posture in solidarity with Derek.

"Ah," Duncan replied, "Dominic told you who that Sergio fellow is. Yes, he is from a Mexican cartel. As to your question, we don't know what we are doing."

"I have a suggestion," Derek said. "Why don't you start talking to us about your plans a little more. We talked about this when Gilberto was here, but then everything went quiet. We know you are bankrolling this Duncan, but what this is we have no clue and we are getting impatient."

"Fair enough," Duncan replied as Paul handed him a glass of Scotch. "What do you suggest?"

"I think for starters, we need to discuss the end game here. What are we trying to accomplish? Are we trying to liberate these trafficked people from Miguel and his organization? What do we do with them, assuming we did that? What would happen to them?" Derek asked.

Paul stood up to answer offering Duncan relief from the initial confrontation. "That's it really. We don't know. We don't know whether we should get involved or not. Let's assume we tip off the Feds and they raid the farm. The history of traffickers getting any real punishment is almost nonexistent. The people held in what we believe to be debt bondage would, more than likely, never testify out of fear. They would most likely be deported, turn around, come back and be victimized again. Miguel could just disappear along with his organization. Maybe he would pop up somewhere else. The business is highly profitable. I doubt they would just let it go. I have to assume they have more cities than Vero. They could have multiple states. We don't know."

Derek stewed over Paul's answer. Finally, Dave stood, "We don't have a strategy, so we don't know what our tactics should be."

"Exactly," Duncan spoke up.

"We honestly don't know what to do," Paul reiterated.

"Monitor their moves and react," Derek said.

"That is about all we can do for now," Paul replied.

"What's more, Paul and I have been discussing the foundation of the organization I hinted at a few weeks ago," Duncan said. "The foundation in terms of conduct."

"What conduct?" Derek asked.

"Whether or not we take lives and create mayhem for these people," Duncan replied bluntly. "How do we do that, and who makes the call?"

Dave raised his hand to speak. As the eyes in the room fell on him, he said, "Have a panel. A death panel. A leadership group that looks at the evidence and determines whether or not we use lethal force and on whom. Like a tribal counsel."

"That is an excellent idea," Paul agreed, "Duncan?"

"Yes, I am in agreement," Duncan replied.

"We all agree on that," Derek interjected, "but what about the victims of these assholes? What do we do with them?"

"Money solves a lot of problems, Derek," Duncan replied. "I think we need to see about helping these people on a case by case basis. Talk to them about what they need in their lives and determine how we can help."

"Duncan," Derek responded, "I hope you understand that we can't really grasp how much you can do with a checkbook, nor will we ever know how much influence your wealth has."

"I understand," Duncan replied.

Miguel paced the room while Sergio blew smoke at the ceiling. "What do we do about the old man? He is snooping around in my business," Miguel asked.

"Find a way to get rid of him," Sergio replied.

"What about Kate?"

Sergio silhouetted himself against the window facing the barracks. The workers were quiet on a Sunday; too hot for them to walk the yard. The soccer game had been voted down. They stayed in watching television. Some huddled around tables watching the farm's masters of dominos, hoping to find some new trick to the game.

"Kate," Sergio muttered, "who cares about Kate?"

"I want to keep her around," Miguel replied as nonchalantly as he could. Sergio would never be amenable to his marriage plans. She was the pull he needed from outside the organization, the minute hope buried inside that resisted giving everything up to them.

"En serio," Sergio replied, "you don't need a girlfriend as much as you need to be focusing on your fuck-ups. Buy some pussy. It's cheaper and less hassle to rent it. Get one that's consistent and it's like having the best part of a wife."

The conversation was taking a turn in favor of Miguel feeling like the scapegoat. His responsibility had limited authority. Did Sergio forget that his workers were people?

Each of them presented a problem. Maybe that was it. Sergio transported them. He didn't have to manage them.

"You should stay around here for a while and help me," Miguel proposed. The backhanded challenge pushed the limits of Sergio's temper providing a boost against Miguel's assumed inferiority.

"You know what you are doing," Sergio replied. He knew what he was. There was no interest in the finality of what his cargo did. He was a mover, a transporter. It was completed when they arrived in decent health, ready to work. A man whose ambition out-ran himself reached his level of incompetence too quickly. "Find one of your cop friends to take him out. You're paying them. Make them do something for once."

"An assassination? That's too blunt," Miguel replied, rejecting the idea.

"So, what do you do?" Sergio prodded. "Come up with something and surprise me."

Miguel thought through potential scenarios. There were many ways to die, but the story leading to death had to be believable and ordinary. Too much plot would ruin a simple accident. "I got it!" Miguel interjected. "He will fall. He will drink too much and fall. The fucker is old. It happens all the time, especially in this adult diaper town. He will crack his fucking skull in half."

"How will you do that?" Sergio challenged.

"Scott will do it. He will sneak in on a Saturday night. Kate told me Duncan likes to sit around drinking Scotch on Saturdays and read. He doesn't drink that much, but we'll pour some more down his throat before pitching him off the balcony. His fucking head will pop."

"Can you sneak in there?" Sergio asked.

"Easy," Miguel smiled. "Kate has a path she showed me that bypasses the cameras. She used it when she lived there to sneak out to the beach. 16 year-old girls are fucking clever when they want to party."

"OK," Sergio said as he stood up, "Get it done."

Oh Scott, I'm dying. I think I have terminal chlamydia from all those senior dance parties. Have you ever heard of twerking?

Fuck you! Scott replied.

"God damned it!" He screamed as he threw his phone against the wall. His neighbor pounded in retaliation, followed by a muffled "Shut the fuck up!" Scott seethed. The messages came at random intervals throughout the day and into the night. They seemed to be especially prevalent while he was in his patrol car, responding to a call, always when he was well over the speed limit. It was as if the person on the other end had a sense of the worst times to fuck with him. He would be sitting at the bar talking to a girl and he would get a text *I think I have a kidney stone. Or maybe it's a urinary tract infection. Anyway, I can't pee, and I hurt. Save me Scott. Please. Love, Grandma.* Who was it? Some asshole kid he had arrested? One of those fucking computer dorks jerking off in his mom's basement? He had already changed his number once. That held off the asshole for about 12 hours, then *Scott! Scott! How can I die if you didn't know about it? Don't change your number without telling granny. Now be good and come over here. I have fallen. I need you to fetch my undies.* So far, nothing worked not even blocking. *The asshole must have one hundred numbers*, he thought.

His phone vibrated an incoming call. *This better not be him again*, he seethed.

"Miguel," he answered, "I am glad it's you."

Miguel paused to wonder what Scott meant by that. He needed him engaged and undistracted. "I need you to do something for me." Miguel outlined the plan. "That is it. You will do this. It'll gain points with Sergio. This is your chance for redemption."

Dominic sat back to review his Fuck-With-Scott program. It had been operating flawlessly. It understood the opportune times to send random messages from scores of phone numbers. It was, by far, the most obnoxious programming he had ever developed. As the numbers got blocked, the program waited and then sent another message. His new voicemail feature was excellent and ready to go live. Various generated granny voices leaving messages at odd hours on random days. It was beautiful. It was what Artificial Intelligence was meant for, the complete mental and emotional destruction of an asshole. No sane person had the patience and fortitude to mess with someone's brain like this. But the computer didn't care. It didn't even have to be told it should care or that it might be doing something illegal. It did what it was told to do regardless of ethics, morality, or conscience. Dominic felt like an evil genius as his imagination envisioned Scott the Cop completely losing it.

It seemed like you should be heard or seen walking on the beach at night. The waves crashing against the shore distract the sounds while the plainness of the sand and backdrop absorb your image. Couples sat cuddled against each other as Scott walked behind them yards away that could have been miles. The glow of the house ahead tensed and readied him. He was hyper-aware of every sound he made while affecting a casual gate towards the slit in the mangroves that would guide him onto the property.

An alarm went off on Dominic's phone as he leaned in on his date; her eyelids heavy, her mouth expectant. His instinct to ignore it and continue his move brought his lips just to hers for an instant. "Hold that," he told her as he tamed the hand sliding up her blouse. His phone was going wild with alarm. "Jesus Christ!" he exclaimed as he ran out to the street to call Duncan. "Come on Duncan, answer," he repeated hopefully as he paced the sidewalk. Couples passed him, giving him a wide berth to avoid flailing arms. Wishing the call to connect wasn't enough, he dialed Derek.

"What's up?" Derek answered.

"Scott is on the property," Dominic yelled into the phone.

"Where?" Derek asked in a panic.

"Northeast side, towards the beach. He is at the house now. Go get Duncan!"

Derek tore down the steps of the guest house with Dave in tow. The front door was locked. He shook the handle, kicking at the door in desperation. Duncan was awakened. The beating on the door went quiet. He wondered for a moment if it was something he had dreamt as he pulled himself upright in his chair. *I haven't drank that much*, he thought. He steadied himself, feeling the Scotch play tricks on his balance. *Maybe I have*.

Scott was through the window Miguel described making his way to the stairs. The noise of the pounding door urged him forward. Halfway up he saw Duncan walk out of the study. The stunned old man turned to run, finding nowhere to go as Scott caught him. As Duncan tried to put a door between them, Scott's foot caught it. A shove sent both the door and Duncan back and out of options. They faced off.

Derek ran to the side door by the kitchen while Dave ran in the opposite direction, looking for another way in. It was locked. His foot came up for a solid kick, splitting the frame, crashing the backside of the door against the counter. All the noise was enough to awaken Ignacio who stumbled out bleary-eyed in front of Derek only to be pushed aside. As Derek crested the top of the stairs, he heard the thumping of fists against a withering opponent. He burst into the door to find Scott dragging a badly beaten Duncan to the balcony overlooking the pool. Duncan's collapsed body proved too heavy to push over without significant effort. As Scott bent down to hoist a leg, a foot connected with his head. He looked up, startled to see the bottom of a shoe impact his face. Instinctively, he reached for his gun only to have his head stomped again. The impacts came furiously as he slipped into unconsciousness. Derek slumped to the ground next to Duncan, feeling for a pulse as Dave entered with Ignacio.

"Get an ambulance!" Derek yelled.

Ignacio dialed 911, looking to Dave for the story to tell. Dave waved him off, whispering, "Just send someone; tell them he fell, head injury."

Derek picked up Duncan, carrying him down the stairs. "Ignacio, he fell. That's all. Don't speak too much English. You heard him fall," Derek instructed. "Come on Dave."

They ascended the stairs to find Scott's limp body oozing blood onto the marble. Dave ran to get as many towels as he could find as the ambulance sirens grew louder. "Open the gate!" Derek yelled down to Ignacio. "Dave, close this door and lock it!"

They slumped back against the railing, hearts pounding as they listened to the paramedics ask Ignacio what happened. The cops would come at any moment.

"Dave, climb down and close the kitchen door as quietly as you can," Derek whispered.

Dave slipped over the railing, dropping into the shrubs lining the pool. He crept under the windows out of sight on his way to the kicked-in door. The pieces of the door frame littered the floor in jagged, jigsaw order. As he pushed the splinters into place, the lockset looked as if it would hold as another set of flashing lights came in through the gate. There was a siege in the middle of the house. His only escape was to the guest house to wait and pray.

In the study Derek remained frozen, listening to questions from inquisitive police. A small whimper to his right put his hair on end as Scott began to stir. Scott's eyes opened to see the hand that would end him clench his throat and spin him around. He writhed as Derek put a chokehold on him, sending him back into the dark.

"We had to do something with the guy," Dave said into the phone as they drove back to the house.

"I guess what you did will work," Paul replied. "I just got back to Boulder. How's Duncan?"

"We don't know," Dave replied. "We haven't been able to go to the hospital."

"Right, I will call Kate," Paul said as he hung up.

"Marco, I want that fucking house watched!" Miguel yelled. "Put our guys on the accounts we have around it and keep watch. Find out where Scott is. I am going to kill that fucking idiot!"

Miguel threw his phone down. How could Scott fuck this up? He wasn't answering his phone. Nothing. The old man was beaten to a pulp, lying in the hospital comatose. The stairs? He fell down the stairs? Bullshit. None of his informants had seen the Jeep. A Bronco came and went from the house now with Florida tags tracing back to another LLC. It was always the gardener or his wife driving. What the fuck happened in there?

Chapter 17

"Coming here to work like this," Miguel said to himself as he watched one of his crews mowing, "You leave with no skills, and you come here. What do you expect? The worst are the construction. Fucking total shit. Who cares? The greedy fucking gringos want huge houses built fast. Fuck 'em. They get what they want. Cheaply built, overpriced shit built with material no Mexican would think to use in Mexico."

He seethed at the failure of the previous night, still wondering where Scott was. Maybe he was hiding. He had better hide. Fucking idiot. *If he weren't such an arrogant gringo, he would only be working for me*, he thought, *instead of wearing a badge. Fuck him, I hope he's dead*. He lowered his windows to let in some air and watched. *If I didn't control them, they would overrun this town with secondhand push mowers. Whatever, it keeps them in line and keeps the work to a standard. How would they even communicate? They're all fucking illegal and uneducated. What are they going to do, go door to door with a translator app until ICE finds them? They fucking need me and I don't think they know it. Pendejos.*

A patrol car turned down the street towards him. As the car neared, he lowered his window, his eyes remained fixed on the crew.

"Everything looks OK with the other crews, jefe," the cop said as their open windows united.

"You checked them all, Marco?"

"No problem, they let me through all the gates. They have to…," Marco replied.

Miguel continued to stare straight ahead. His demeanor deflected any positivity Marco could project. He was a seemingly calm, visible expression of rage. "Any news?"

"Of Scott?" Marco asked.

Miguel continued to focus his burning gaze forward, ignoring the question. Inside, he wanted to strangle Marco for asking such a stupid thing, of course of Scott. They were all idiots and they were all too easy to buy. It made him sick, but it was a necessary expense to have them on his side. It made a lot of money for him and for them. Not the kind of money Duncan had but enough to keep the cartel happy and keep them mostly in Mexico far away.

Marco's insides twisted with anxiety in the face of Miguel's cold hatred. The boss would find a way to kill him too if things kept getting fucked up. Miguel would never use his own hands, but he would be dead nonetheless. Or worse, on the run constantly looking over his shoulder for the inevitable. That would be worse. His throat was drying up. Finally, he was able to respond, "Nothing about Scott, boss."

"I want that motherfucker found," Miguel hissed.

"His truck was still…"

"I know where his fucking truck was," Miguel interrupted. "What the fuck do you idiots do around here besides drive around? You don't even pull over the old white drunks. You're all fucking useless."

Marco slunk in his seat enough to make the grip of his gun cut into his side. He knew enough to shut up and let Miguel get through his hateful mood. It was rarely expressed, but when he had seen it, it was intense.

He is going to be OK, but still pretty bad, Kate's text said, adding insult.

"You want to get the fuck away from me right now, Marco." Miguel seethed.

Marco put the patrol car into gear inching down the street at the low speed he used on the island for watching rich people's daughters. The parade pace he was accustomed to was solemn today. The bikinis would have to wait. Thankfully, Miguel's Land Rover shrunk in his rearview mirror along with his tension.

"Oh, Uncle Duncan, what happened? You poor thing," Kate lamented as Duncan slipped back into unconsciousness. She held his cold, weak hand in hers. Her tears had finally run dry. Now, she waited for him to open his eyes, stand up and command the room like he did. The doctor said it would be a while before he was lucid. The sedation gave the impression of imminent death. In his semiconscious state he had asked for Dave. She didn't know *Dave*. Did he know someone by that name? It was so common. What could someone named Dave do? There had to be hundreds within 20 miles of Vero Beach. He was dreaming, hallucinating, she consoled herself.

That's great! Miguel replied to her text. *Can he talk?*

He is pretty out of it. Only said Dave. Hallucinating?

Miguel relaxed slightly for the first time since that night. *Dave. Motherfucking Dave*, he thought. Thank God he wasn't saying Scott. Duncan had only met Scott once. Would he remember him?

OK, mi amor, I will come join you, he texted back.

I will see you in the lobby. They won't let anyone up here unless they are approved by his lawyer Paul, she replied.

Miguel felt the anger welling up in him again. He took a deep breath before responding. *Would a pause in replying be construed as anger?* he asked himself. Without emojis a text was just words, right? All perceived emotion was deniable.

Ok, I'll see you tonight then, he replied. *I love you.* The heart response came a few moments later. Slower than he expected.

"Guys, let me explain this," Paul said as he stood in the window watching the fountain below. "Duncan is, or was, trying to get his head around what to do if this thing blows up."

"Blows up?" Dave asked.

"Get's bigger," Paul corrected himself. "He is not the only one who is interested in this idea. If it takes off there will be more funding than you two can imagine. He has silent partners. These are men like him who want to do something big with their money. Something good and worthwhile. These are not the billionaires farting around with the Moon or Mars or rising sea levels. Between you and me, I am rooting for melting ice caps. I would like to see a lot of this useless swamp we are in right now reclaimed by the Atlantic. But to be serious, what I am saying is that they want to take politics out of justice and do what is right for the majority of the people. That being said, there is some hesitance. They can't come to terms with who determines what is right. They are stuck in a state of ego check."

"Wow," Derek said, "I had no idea billionaires could check their egos. What's in it for them?"

"The ones I know are good and relatively humble guys," Paul replied. "Do you think something different of Duncan?"

"Not at all," Derek stated. "I have always seen him as fair and on a straight path. Never felt ego from him as a client or a friend. He just wanted shit done well and honestly."

"It seems like," Dave spoke up, "it might be putting them outside of the law; creating legal problems."

"Exactly," Paul replied, "That is the primary problem. Governments own justice."

"They own law," Derek disagreed.

"For all intents and purposes they tend to want to conflate those two things," Paul replied. "Our government's track record on justice is a giant pile of steaming shit if you ask around the world. This brings us to the current problem. We have a small war going on here with a small arm of a cartel. What do we do about that?"

Derek stood up and poured himself some coffee, waving the cup as he spoke, "If we are talking eye for an eye justice, I would guess we may be about even. I am not sure what Miguel thinks."

"He's probably not going to meet up with us for a conference to talk about it," Dave inserted.

"I don't think he knows you two exist," Paul stated. "I believe you can get some more information. Put on some basic clothes and go use the Brazilian credentials I gave you. Try to talk to some of their men in the field. There will be just enough understanding and language barrier between Portuguese and Spanish to enhance the facade. Derek, you do the talking. Dave just play shy and dumb. See if you can get jobs."

"It's clear," Dominic said, "You can head that way. The cop is headed back to the station."

"Thanks," Derek replied, "we're ready." He motioned for Dave to follow. They had rehearsed their Brazilian personas ad nauseam. "I talk," Derek reminded Dave. The crew was laying in the shade during a break as they approached. Derek eyed the meekest one he could identify, walking straight up. The man looked at him with concern.

"O senhor, desculpe. Eu não falo…no hablo? Espanhol." He pointed to himself, "Português. Você fala?"

The Mexican man seemed to understand him by the nature of the similarities between the languages, but not fully. His initial apprehension eased.

"Nos estamos buscando trabalho," Derek stated, pointing to a mute Dave who smiled, affirming with an eager shake of his head.

"Trabajo," the man replied. "You speak English? Work?"

"Eu não entendo inglês," Derek lamented. "Você pode me entender?"

The Mexican man hesitated a moment, "Si, te entiendo poco. I understand."

"You espeaky engleesh. I no espeaky engleesh," Derek replied suppressing the internal laughter desperately trying to make him break character.

"Tu no hablas inglés," the man replied.

Very slowly Derek enunciated, "Você," pointing to the man. "Tu?, estão contractando pessoas para trabalho?"

The man understood well enough to give Derek a so-so response that he wasn't sure if they were hiring or not. A white pickup eased up behind the three of them.

"Señor Poncho, elles quieren trabajo. Son brasileños." the man spoke into the open truck window.

"No mas, pinche brasileños. ¡No!" The man said as he slid out of the truck. "¡Trabajo!" he commanded as the crew snapped to attention. "You two, Brazilians?" he asked.

"Sim," Derek replied. "Nós queremos trabalho."

"You won't get it here," the crew leader stated with a heavy Mexican accent. "Go away. No more Brazilians. No más fucking brasileños."

Derek affected what he internalized as a confused and dejected look on his face. He stood his ground, waiting to see what the man would do. Against his nature, he tried to appear meek while Dave slunk back a few steps.

"Onde…donde? Nós buscamos trabalho?"

"¡Vete a la chingada!" the leader yelled. "Fuck off!"

Derek gave the man a stare. His eyes pierced like an ice pick thrust into the man's forehead, about to twist and scramble his brains. Dave reached out, grabbing Derek's arm to pull him away. Derek leaned into the man, finally relenting to Dave's pull. Around the corner, out of sight of the crew, Derek relaxed. It had been all an act. His phone buzzed.

Cop coming, the text read.

"What's that?" Dave asked.

"A cop is coming. Just walk and he'll pass us," Derek reassured him.

The cop rolled up behind them, chirping his siren. They stopped and turned to respond.

"You two, stay right there," the cop commanded as he stepped out of his car. "What are you doing here? Do you have a reason to be in this neighborhood?"

Derek looked at Dave inquisitively.

"You understand?" the cop asked.

"Brasil, Português." Derek said, pointing to himself and Dave.

"Papers," the cop requests.

"Papers?" Dave asked Derek.

"Carteira de identidade," Derek said to Dave, pulling out his Green Card. Dave dug around in his pockets, pulling out his along with his driver's license. The cop studied the documents as Derek and Dave nervously waited.

"I don't want to see you around here unless you are with a crew," the cop commanded bluntly.

Dave and Derek looked at each other. Playing stupid was quickly becoming second nature. "OK?" Derek replied, "Tchau?"

"Ciao," the cop mocked, pointing to the west, indicating where they should go.

Dave and Derek walked towards one of the bus stops as the cop inched along, confirming they were leaving. They sat down on the grass to await the bus. Satisfied, the cop sped away climbing the bridge to the mainland.

"Vamos. Let's go, João" Derek said, pointing towards home.

Dave gave Paul the recap as Derek cooked dinner. It had been a fruitless effort. Dave lamented the waste of time while Paul attempted to extrapolate useful information from the recount. Paul paced, thinking of the next move, sipping at his drink. Their goal was still unclear. Without Duncan, there was no strategy. They were at an impasse.

"We need to identify where Miguel is in this organization," Dave spoke up. "Who does he report to? This Sergio guy? Or is Sergio just a messenger for another?"

"I am going to see what Dominic can do to figure this out," Paul replied.

Chapter 18

"When the conversation stopped, I knew she had finally replaced me," Derek sighed, giving the sand a half-hearted kick, remembering, not knowing what it was that prodded him into talking about the first attempt at his relationship with the Colorado woman.

"How often were you talking to her?" Dave asked.

"Every day, and then there was a week she just dropped off the planet," Derek replied. "It was uncharacteristic of her. I made up as many excuses as I could, but ultimately I knew."

"You knew she had moved on," Dave finished the sentence.

"Yeah, moved on somehow," Derek sighed. "It sucked. I heard the words but when I remembered to look past them at the actions, it was apparent. But I was relying stupidly on the words and giving the benefit of the doubt. Then finally, I got the text. Some BS about wanting to be friends and how she couldn't do anything romantic anymore. She obviously found someone else. Do you know any women who don't line up their next one before dumping the current guy?"

"That sucks," Dave sighed.

"She probably, at least, had an idea of someone else who she wanted," Derek continued. "The fact of it is, she can probably get whoever she wants. Men are easy to get. And we are easy to dispose of."

"What did you tell her? Did you call her bullshit?" Dave asked. "Didn't you want to at least be friends?"

"What was the point? Didn't we have this conversation before? Men who convert that easily to being friends are men without options, or they are planning a sneak attack." Dave looked at him, wondering. "A sneak attack is when the guy friend waits for her to have a weak moment then he attacks her with a profession of love. He has been faking being her friend the whole time. It's a weak move. In all seriousness there are just too many women out there to bother with one who doesn't want you. If she were repulsive, she would have a better chance to become friends with me."

Dave laughed. As the waves chanted their mantra, calming him, he reflected on his own experience. Jessica was long gone. Paul had told him about the missing person report in the Boulder newspapers. She was preparing to divorce him and he could do nothing. He wasn't even around to fight her for half the stuff. What was half the stuff, anyway? She had done most, if not all, of the choosing and buying. He couldn't visualize what half of it was. It was really her stuff. It was easier to agree with whatever she wanted to decorate. It was her stuff, her house. Now, he remained in limbo above a billionaire's garage waiting to see where he fit into a secretive, grand plan. That's all he had.

"In my rational brain and at my age, I know that it is probably not worth the effort to have relationships with women, not even with her. All relationships have tragic endings, especially the ones that survive til death. It's an irony of Shakespearean comedies; eventually, if played out, they will end in tragedy. Shakespeare was smart enough to end writing his comedies before the inevitable outcome so his audiences could walk out happy," Derek paused, his mind searching. "For whatever reason, I still get involved with women like I am trying to break some new ground. I only have myself to blame when they don't work out."

"Was it the distance? That hasn't changed," Dave asked innocently.

"Yeah, that was one of the reasons," Derek replied quietly. "I often wonder if a man can go off to war and expect a woman to wait, especially now. How fast could she be set up on a dating app while he is dodging bullets? Pretty cynical, right?"

Dave laughed uncomfortably, "It is cynical."

Derek continued, "They have so many options to get attention from men. I remember when I worked for the resort. We had a joke that the girls were all there to hook up with us and their boyfriends should be at home tossing their shit in the street. Fuckers probably drove them to the airport. I can tell you that if my girlfriend wanted to go on a beach vacation with her friends where I worked, she would come home to changed locks. I know all too well how that goes down. Poor bastards think they are being supportive when she wants some space and a vacation at the beach. Women don't want space. They want freedom from you while they come to terms with their current feelings. Space is just how they make it seem less destructive. Makes them feel better.

"They are definitely slaves to their emotions. And I am cynical enough to say that 'I love you' really means 'I feel like I love you right now while you are entertaining me or providing for me or until I find a way to manage the social implications of abandoning you'. They have a way of squandering a good thing for new attention when attention is what they build their self-worth on."

Dave spoke up, "I think I am beginning to believe that attention is such a cheap commodity for women. They don't realize what goes into creating it. We bust our asses to provide it." Dave paused to see if Derek would react to his newly expressed opinion. "We could go out to one of the bars around here, right? Maybe chat up some women to get your mind off of it?"

"Man, I don't know. We have killed three people and I beat the shit out of that idiot lawyer. I feel a little conspicuous just walking along the beach. It seems like it's the only place with no cops in this shithole town," Derek replied gruffly. "My kids are here, there's that. It's the only reason I am not in Colorado right now getting dumped by her in person."

"You think she would still dump you?" Dave asked.

"I don't know," Derek replied. "Maybe. If I am disposable to her here, aren't I disposable there? I might be being cautiously paranoid."

"Long distance doesn't work," Dave added.

"Not for long," Derek agreed. "I'm not around to fend off the willing attention givers. And there are thousands of them. This time around with her, I am expecting an unpreventable reality. Unless something changes, she will disappear again." He paused, his eyes searched the horizon. "Women will never know what it is like to not get free attention. Even the hideous ones. In hindsight, I probably projected a lot of virtues onto her that I wish she had. She's human and I like the human she is. She had her reasons. I am kind of happy in a way that she didn't tell me what they were but I would assume it was another guy. I guess I am at peace with that, for now. We'll see what happens. The reunion sparked something. But I am suspiciously cautious."

"You have everything you need," Duncan said. "You have too much."

"What do you mean, too much?" Kate asked.

"You will never know hunger, Kate," Duncan sighed. "You will never know how to rely on a man who provides for you."

"That's good, right?"

Duncan pushed the button, raising his bed to get a better look at Kate's face. As the bed rose, he withheld his response. "Can you hand me that water?" he asked. Kate passed him the container, watching him sip, hoping the topic would shift. "Of course, it is good, but with all good, there is bad. With all bad, there are good lessons. I fear that you will be like your mother." Kate stiffened. Before she could rebut and defend, Duncan continued, "A life of luxury chasing nothing but stimulation to distract you from reality. Fretting about luxury problems most people in the world can't imagine."

"You know I am not like that," Kate muttered indignantly.

"People only know who they are when they have nothing. When the comfortable world you live in is gone, you are forced to build something or perish. That is not the experience most women have. The world is kind to them or tries to be, especially the world you live in," Duncan replied.

"Uncle Duncan," Kate said firmly, "I don't like this. I don't like this from you."

"What would you do if I had to take away your inheritance?" Duncan asked. "To allocate all of it to a bigger cause?"

"Why would you?" Kate contested. "You wouldn't do that."

"Hypothetically, what would you do?" Duncan asked.

"I don't know. I guess I would get a job. I went to college, remember?" Kate replied. She was suppressing a deep, internal tension, waiting for whatever this joke was to end.

"Eventually, you would get married, Kate," Duncan said. "That would be the solution. It was the solution for women for tens of thousands of years. To bind themselves to a man for provisioning and protection; to lean on him as he fulfilled his promised duty to you and the children. Now you have jobs. You all have entered the world of men, of careers. The place where men went to gain the provisioning for you. The archaic patriarchy, as you call it, has become women's surrogate husband. It leaves no time for a woman's true role in a family while she chases a career and money. I blame the suburban nuclear family. It isolated women away from their extended tribe."

"You think I should be a housewife?" Kate spat.

"I think you would be a wonderful wife and a wonderful mother," Duncan replied. "The value of that has been vilified for many women. It's sad."

"This is ridiculous," Kate protested as she went to the window to cast out the rage she was feeling. *He must be going through some sort of life crisis*, she thought. *He can be such a control freak.* Would he really write her out of the will? What had she done?

"Darling, I am being hypothetical," Duncan conceded. "I didn't mean to upset you."

"Well, you did. I don't like this," Kate sulked.

The graceful young woman he knew was slouching like a spoiled child. It was a horrible thing to hold someone else's future life in your hands. Kate's luxurious lifestyle could be erased with the stroke of a pen. In truth, he didn't have the heart to torture her this way. He felt dizzy putting her into a thought experiment she had no business enduring. Kate would never know real hunger nor would her children. Their privileged lives would be filled with whatever whim they chose and enough cushion under them that failure, or the fear of it, could never survive long enough to learn from it. Listening to the trust-funded gentry talk about appreciating the little things in life nauseated him. He had had enough of being around them. Their petty problems were like spitting on the graves of regular people's unrealized dreams. Time in solitude without distraction is needed to create. Everyone needs more of it and only a few could find or afford it.

A deep sadness fell over him as he lay in his bed thinking. Conquest made men. If she had boys, the possibility of them conquering anything substantial was nearly impossible. They would never know what he knew deep in his soul. They would never know hunger. *Is it really necessary*, he wondered to himself, *to know hunger?* Millions of Americans knew nothing of it. Not hunger nor conquest, just mundane, cautious baby steps from the cradle to the grave doing what they should in a country that assumed the rest of the world were underlings. Americans lived average lives wracked with fear imprisoning them inside the walls they built for themselves. He had had enough of it. There had to be somewhere else.

"Besides," Kate spoke up, breaking the uncomfortable silence, "Miguel will probably ask me to marry him. He is a lot like you. That's why I love him." She stepped away from the window; her mood improved with the announcement. Putting her comforting hand on his arm she smiled the way she always had when she was sweet to him. Duncan stared at the hundreds of puncture holes in the ceiling tiles, looking for patterns to distract him from the topic of Miguel. In their seeming randomness, the tiles were all the same.

Kate felt the awkward distance in Duncan's silence. *He likes Miguel*, she thought. *He should like him.* Miguel built his business from nothing. He was the son of a hardworking immigrant family. His father was a mess but he hadn't been the only one guiding Miguel's early life. There were virtues in him Duncan was known to praise. Perseverance and grit. Myopic focus on a goal. Miguel had that. His business was small, but he was determined and it would grow. He saved his money and bought a decent house on the island. It wasn't a mansion, but it was respectable for a young man on the rise.

"He's just like you in many ways," she repeated.

"I suppose he is," Duncan replied quietly. The state of remaining neutral required as much acting as he could affect. He leaned on his condition for sympathy hoping to escape the topic. "I am getting really tired, dear. The medication is getting to me." Crushing his niece was not something he could do from a hospital bed. It would have to wait. Thankfully, there was a knock on the door. As it opened hesitantly, Paul stepped in.

"Is he awake?" he asked.

"He is, but he is getting tired," Kate replied.

"I am OK for a while," Duncan mumbled. "Kate dear, can you come again tomorrow?"

"Of course, I can bring you the donuts you like," she replied kissing him gently on the cheek below his bandages before stepping out.

"How are you, my friend?" Paul asked.

"I am OK. A little drugged up," Duncan replied. His demeanor improved without the need to act out a part. "Everyone keeps saying 'stairs'. We know that's not true. I have just been quietly listening to them make up a scenario of how I ended up here. I don't remember a lot. Just a face…"

Paul looked around the room for anything resembling a recording device before sitting down next to Duncan. He leaned close to speak loud enough for Duncan to hear him.

"Derek took care of that cop," he replied.

"The one from the farm? The grandma cop?" Duncan laughed quietly, raising his hand to cover his mouth. It was absurd to laugh about such a thing. "He was the one at the tournament. I remember now."

"That one," Paul replied. "He is gone and the town is looking for him. The news is running around interviewing people who knew him. There is no trace. I would guess they have his phone records already."

"Are his texts in there? Voicemails?" Duncan asked.

"They were," Paul smiled. "We have a Dominic, remember? He left enough to give them something but nothing to implicate or trace back to Miguel."

"Why not? "Duncan asked.

"This town is corrupt to the core," Paul answered. "An investigation would go nowhere. If the feds were to get involved, we could lose our momentum. We will keep this little story for us. Like you said to me the other day, we will own the justice. Fuck the bureaucrats and politicians. Let them have their laws. If they want to use their legal system, they have to catch people."

"I believe that more now than ever," Duncan replied. "I am beginning to understand and respect vengeance. I have a new appreciation for it. I have been taking soft vengeance in the business world for years. This will be real and permanent. There can be no truce with these kinds of evil. When we identify it, we will crush it." He looked out the window towards the west as the sun was setting. Paul remained respectfully quiet. "I intend to stay alive long enough to see this through. When I am satisfied the organization is in good hands, I will step away. Hopefully, for good."

"What does that mean?" Paul asked.

"It means I have asked God to allow me to do what is

right before I am taken from this Earth. If He wills it..." Duncan replied. "However, for now, I want to tread lightly and be sympathetic to what Kate is about to go through."

"Understood," Paul replied.

There could be no good in telling her outright that her boyfriend was a minor cartel member enslaving people for his own profit. As far as Paul was able to piece together, there was enough deniability built into Miguel's operation to give him an opportunity for escape.

"How did that cop get in?" Duncan asked.

"He found a path through the mangroves that the cameras overlooked," Paul responded. "We traced his footsteps backward from the window he accessed. Why that was unlocked, we don't know."

Duncan sank into his bed. "I know the window and the path," Duncan sighed. "Kate used it as an escape route when she was a teen thinking I didn't know. I thought nothing of it. She probably told Miguel about it."

"Why would she bring up something like that?" Paul asked.

"She could have been recalling her teen years innocently adding to a conversation," Duncan replied. "Whatever you tell a monster like that goes in a file to be exploited later. Innocence never assumes evil is sitting across from it absorbing ammunition. Either way, there is no need to speculate. It is done, and we will take the appropriate precautions."

Chapter 19

The paranoia is stupid, he thought to himself. *I am just a random guy standing in line at the Post Office. Who is going to recognize me? The cop that pulled me over months ago? I am anonymous. Worse, invisible. I could stand here all day. People would come in, do what they needed and walk out past me.* He thought about the implications of loitering. Not doing anything in the same place for too long would make him visible. That sort of inactivity offended people; made them create laws. Regardless, the Post Office lobby was about to open and he was just a guy in the back of the line waiting, not loitering. *Why am I obsessed with this thought of loitering?* he asked himself. He looked at the rows and columns of Post Office boxes where people staked their claims on the island. It was disheartening to think he had no claim anywhere. Even a tree dislodged and toppled over still had some of its roots in the ground half grasping the earth, the others reaching up towards heaven. *Here I am, standing in line, thinking up tree metaphors to explain my life.*

"Are they closed?" a feminine voice behind him asked.

"They open in a few minutes," Dave replied, barely turning to look at the girl. She had to be a girl. Her voice sounded innocent, but something implied experience.

"There're a lot of people in this line," she said.

"Yeah, with email, I sort of thought paper was going away. Like the trees were winning," Dave responded over his shoulder.

He heard her laugh. A tentative silence fell between them offering an easy opening to talk to her. A chance every guy gets once in a while. A chance that can have lasting consequences if he doesn't get in his own way. The moment was his to take and perform or let it sink into regret as he kicked himself later for fear of engaging. *What's the difference?* He thought. His inner dialogue was desperately coaxing him into action, taunting him for not turning towards her obvious interest. The more he procrastinated the more excuses he created. *She is probably just friendly*, he demurred defeatedly. *She is like this with everyone. Some people are.*

"You don't have a return address," she mentioned.

"Oh, right, I'll do that inside. Thanks," he lied. He looked down at the postcard for his nieces. There was no return address.

"The trees are winning," she echoed whimsically. "That's funny."

Dave laughed a little, proud of the little quip, thinking he should store it in a file for later. Like memorized lines, it had already lost the power of spontaneity. As much as he tried to resist, her energy was commanding him, against his better judgment, to face her. His affected, nonchalant attitude was making him feel standoffish and rude. Her voice was too sweet for that; it pulled at him, tormenting his cowardice. Finally he half-turned towards her, his eyes seeking hers.

She seemed so close to him. Brown and happy eyes full

of life. It was true. He looked straight into her soul; eyes were the window. He had no cognizance of how long their eyes fused, eternal.

"Hi," she said, offering her hand to the space between them, "I'm Kate."

Dave winced. The spell snapped as he reached for her hand, desperately running an escape plan in his head. "I'm Dave," he answered, his subconscious prodding his feet into action. The distance between them grew by inches.

"Are you from Vero?" she asked.

"No, Colorado. I'm visiting for a while," he replied, now fully aware of his entrapment. His internal panic was buried well beneath the play-acting of simple social interchange. The door to the counter area finally unlocked. It was as if the entire line breathed a sigh of relief in sympathy for him. He quietly rejoiced at the good fortune. He had been gifted an out by the Post Office or God or the Post Office through the will of God. This thought raced through his head as he turned away towards a stamp. *All I need is a stamp*, he thought, as he plotted escape from a woman who had no idea of the power she held over him. For the first time in months, he had become recognizable. What should make him feel accepted was pure dread.

Dave did everything he could to ignore her until another man engaged her attention with a premeditated compliment. He felt a tinge of jealousy before it washed away with tactical opportunism. She was distracted. There was nothing. She was just a nice young woman. She is probably like that with everyone. Sweet and wonderful and beautiful. He paid for his stamp giving her a quick smile as his feet dragged him out.

"Bye, Dave," she said smiling.

He halfheartedly waved goodbye, stepping through the door into the sun.

"You know, Duncan. I can empathize with the people Miguel uses. Before you came to me to meet up with Dave, I felt like this country had used me up and spit me out. I imagine they felt like that before coming here. Probably most of their lives. They wanted opportunity and someone sold it to them. So they went for it. Now they're fucked and enslaved in a country far from theirs performing bullshit work for elitist assholes who will deny, to their death, how elitist they really are."

Duncan walked around the kitchen island, setting a coffee mug in front of Derek as he took a seat next to him. His battered face was stitching itself back together well enough. The tingle of an occasional nerve was all that was left of the pain. "I know what it is like to be hungry for more," he replied to Derek. "I can't say that I have felt what it was like to worry about eating for a very long time."

"I can," Derek stated. "There were times I had no money and no food. I would go for days on water hoping to sell off some shit I had collected when life was good. You remember. My business was great. Until it wasn't."

"You are very good at what you do. There's no doubt," Duncan agreed.

"Being good and being valuable to a fickle, disloyal Corporate America are different things. They didn't give a shit if I was good. The clients had no budget they could spend for me. It had been expropriated by other departments claiming they had a better way. My clients happily retired leaving a bureaucratized shit show that was already out of their control. I don't blame them a bit. It's not like they had any idea how fragile I had allowed myself to become. I was becoming bitter when I ended it. My last hold-out was telling me he could engage me on a project if he got permission. I don't think he liked my response," Derek lamented.

"What was that?" Duncan asked.

"I told him he was the definition of a corporate slave," Derek replied. "He had all the responsibility to get the work done and none of the authority of how to do it. He was in a constant state of asking for permission from other departments who took away his authority so they could seem more valuable. And they were mostly pure overhead. It offended him and the self-perception he had of himself as a leader. I really didn't give a shit anymore."

"That is a common problem," Duncan said. "One that allows my company to walk all over most of my competitors. Not the huge ones. They are in a different game. One we will eventually have to deal with. Nonetheless, while my peers have meetings and in-fighting for attention, we have action and results. We eliminate people who think the company exists for them and their careerism. Our company exists solely for our customers. I control enough of it to avoid this idea of existing for the so-called owners who think they have enough shares to speak assertively for them."

"I know. It was a great pleasure to work with you. I really appreciate what you did for me then and now," Derek smiled placing his hand on Duncan's shoulder. "You have always been a friend and mentor to me. And I can't thank you enough for this opportunity."

"I am a sucker for love," Duncan replied.

"When Alyssa texted me, I knew I had to go. I can't describe this thing I have with her. Chemistry? That's probably the best single word to describe it. Life keeps throwing us back together and now we have a chance to see what can happen."

"I had that or thought I did long ago, the chemistry,"

Duncan reminisced. His expression distanced. Derek sipped his coffee, knowing Duncan was in a faraway place for the moment. What kind of man or friend would he be to intrude into the silence with his own words and thoughts while his friend's thoughts carried him back to a love long ago? The quiet would resolve itself when it was ready. Duncan stood, leaning straight-armed against the counter, as he journeyed back into the present.

"You will go. Paul can use the help," Duncan said. "When you come back here every few weeks or so, you and the kids will have the beach apartment in town to pass the time. Nobody ever uses it. I like this idea, it's good for everyone. Bring Alyssa. I would love to meet her."

"I will. It might take a little convincing. I haven't been a very good representative of Vero Beach. Funny how opportunity and money changes the way you look at a place. It puts a silver lining on about everything," Derek smiled.

"It insulates you from reality," Duncan interjected. "It can expand the world and draw you out of it at the same moment." The mood of the room changed. Derek imagined the wheels churning in Duncan's head. Miguel had gone quiet. His entourage of paid-for cops were sticking close to him constantly patrolling the roads out by the farm. The crews were working. Nothing had changed for them.

"I will let Dave know tonight," Derek spoke up. "He's going to be left alone here to deal with immediate issues. I doubt he will be too happy about it, but as you said, I will be on call to come back whenever you need me."

"Yes," Duncan answered pensively, "go let Alyssa know it's official." Duncan patted Derek on the back as he stepped out the kitchen door towards the guest house. The sun was warm, the breeze off the ocean calming. Derek felt excitement welling up in his chest as he called.

"Hi," Alyssa answered in her sweet voice. "Good morning."

"Still in bed?" Derek asked. "Are you going to work?"

"Of course, but not until later. I was having a dream you were cuddled up behind me, your breath on the back of my neck," she answered.

"We haven't had enough of that," Derek replied gently.

"I know," Alyssa whispered. Derek could hear her stretch and readjust in the bed. The thought of kissing her and pulling her close to him after a long restful sleep… His head was swimming in anticipated scenes of a life with her. All the expressions of love he had stored up for the right one were ready to give to her. She was the one. When he had met her, he was convinced there was no 'one' woman for him; there was only an endless parade of counterfeits he force-fit into the role. With her, it was easy. Their separation brought them closer as she tried to replace him and he tried to distract himself. They never really spoke of it in detail. He didn't care to know. Whatever the forces were that brought them back together, they were stronger than those trying to pull them apart. Finally, they would have their chance.

"Baby," Derek spoke gently, "I know we have had some tough times, mostly because of the distance between us. It's the only thing we have ever fought about." He paused before letting out what he had to tell her, "I am moving back."

The phone line was quiet. Derek waited. He could hear her sit up in bed. "What? What do you mean? Here?" she asked.

"Yes, there," Derek replied. "I worked it out with Duncan. I can float back and forth between Colorado and Florida for this work and Paul needs some help. You remember Paul."

"Oh my God," Alyssa gasped.

"Are you OK with that?" Derek asked with the same anxious anticipation a man gets when he proposes.

"Are you kidding? Of course, I am. I love you, I love you," she replied excitedly. "When? When are you coming?"

"I'll be there in a few weeks," Derek answered.

"Where are you going to live? Wait, what am I saying? With me. You are living here with me," Alyssa exclaimed.

"No, it's still going to be an adventure, but I am living up at Paul's ranch at least for a while," Derek cautioned. "I think that would be better."

"It's OK. We'll work it out," she replied. "I am too excited to think right now. And I have to go to work."

"Go, we'll talk later," Derek replied. "I love you." He imagined her bouncing out of bed. Dancing around the room hurrying to get out the door. It was finally going to be a reality. The distance would never be the excuse. The only gift he had not been able to give was hers now, the feeling of his presence.

Dave worked his way along the beach ten pushups at a time, thinking about his mistake. His cell phone sat on the nightstand back at the guest house. He had no access to Dominic and no warnings. The only electronic signaling device he carried was the tag on his set of guesthouse keys. No way for Dominic to warn him, 'KATE IS NEAR, 'RUN!' Did it matter? She knew nothing of him. She didn't know that he and Derek had saved her Uncle twice in the last few months from a monster Duncan hesitated to drag her away from. Dave couldn't put together what the problem was with telling her. Was Duncan going to let it go all the way to a proposal? A marriage? At some point, he had to give in and do the difficult thing. Dave felt for her and what she would go through. That beautiful, sweet young woman is going to be crushed. What if Miguel found a better way to eliminate Duncan? Who would step in and tell her?

He pushed hard against the sand, forcing his intent out to the horizon to maintain his planked form. Had he done ten? It felt like it. He did three more. He stood to walk another hundred or so yards until the next set. Duncan's house was in the distance 50 or 60 more pushups away. *My focus is off*, he thought.

She was sweet. If he hadn't known who she was, he would have been much more gregarious. He knew that look. The eyes searching each other. The tension. The feeling of something new in another's hopeful expression. *I am ridiculous*, he thought as he pushed against the sand. *She's just nice. She is like that with everyone. She has a boyfriend.* He knew he was lying to himself. There was something. Given the right order of things, maybe there would be. But the order of things was not for him; not now. He had no business thinking about her. The pushups were automatic. The house was near. He ended his last set trying to remember how many he had done.

"Hey, you're back. You left your phone on your nightstand. It's losing its shit," Derek announced as Dave stepped through the door. Dave expected criticism for leaving it behind. Derek offered none.

"No worries," Dave lied.

"Bullshit, Dave. What was that about?" Derek asked. "Dominic, or Dominic's AI, whoever it is, doesn't lose its shit unless there is something important. Did you do the scan before you came on to the property?"

"I did," Dave lied again. He had forgotten. There were only elderly couples walking the beach. He was probably safe.

"Who was near you?" Derek asked.

Dave sighed, not wanting to come clean. "Kate," he finally confessed.

"Did she see you? I mean, did she see you enter the property?" Derek asked impatiently.

"No, I saw her at the Post Office. I really didn't know who she was at first. She was in line behind me. Didn't recognize her. I mean, I have only seen her from a distance and in photos," Dave replied. "Then she started talking to me." He saw the alarm on Derek's face forcing him to react. "She has no idea who I am. I was just some guy at the Post Office."

Derek studied Dave's face, knowing there was more. Quiet, scolding eyes were enough to punish him for now. He had more to think about. "I am going to Colorado," he blurted out.

"How long?" Dave asked.

"Mostly permanent," Derek responded.

"What does that mean? Mostly permanent. Are you leaving?" Dave grilled, visibly irritated by the news. "What the hell, dude?"

"It's OK," Derek replied calmly. "I will be back but my main operating location will be with Paul. I will be back a lot for my girls. Also, if anything starts getting weird around here and you guys need the support."

"So far, it has been weird all of the time," Dave countered. He was not reassured. Until now, it had not occurred to him how much he relied on Derek for friendship and camaraderie. Forced together into friendship by circumstance, they had become like brothers and now they would be separated, by what he could only assume had to be a woman.

Derek let the tension hang. He couldn't get himself to interject the real reason. There was a code amongst brothers, no woman shall come between. None shall split the group, especially during a battle or hunt. It was their unspoken code of honor always broken with good intentions and the feigned support of the squad. A man who abandoned his brothers-in-arms for the arms of a woman was never to be fully trusted again but they wouldn't tell him that. He would enter a state of suspicion. Anything they told him, probably had an extra set of ears. For the man who willfully took another's woman, he was to be beaten and cast out. There was no nuance to that. That was the code.

"You're going back for her," Dave blurted out into the silence. "We were just talking about how you would probably break up. It would be over."

Derek said nothing. He felt the parchment of The Code going up in flames as he sheepishly avoided Dave's stare. "Yes," he answered finally, "we were."

Dave walked to the window, glaring down at the circular drive below. His eyes followed the path around and around as if the motion would soothe him into something to say. His head searched for a stabbing insult he knew would come too late and out of context. Derek, of all the stoic, independent men he had known, had succumbed. He tried to feel betrayed. It was all an act. Everything was an act. There were no hard truths. He turned to Derek, expecting to see less of a man. It was still there; confidence, masculinity, strength. Dave had to surrender his resentment. His friend was doing the right thing. At that moment, he felt ashamed of his thoughts. He felt selfish, needy and at a loss for people and friends in his life.

Dave turned towards Derek. "One of my friends asked me on the way to my wedding, 'Dude, do you have any dreams? I said yeah, of course. Don't you? He said he did until he got married then his dreams became her dreams and his became stupid and unsupportive of their future together'. I don't know why I am remembering that right now." The jab hurt his own soul as he flailed to thrust it into his friend's side. His emotions were taking over his reactions. It might have been envy.

"The dreams you are talking about are a waste of energy. They're only useful to temporarily medicate idle minds. I would take a bullet for her the same as I would for my principles and my brothers," Derek stated, glaring up at Dave. He didn't need to say more than that.

Dave sighed and fell deep into a chair. His fingers beat the devils tattoo on the armrest, still searching for some righteous outrage. "I would do the same," he relented. "I would do the same thing. You're not abandoning me. Who am I to think that? I abandoned everyone in Colorado. Who am I to judge?"

"Dave," Derek leaned forward, "you did not abandon anyone. It's not in your nature. You are at an impasse in life. A circumstantial impasse. Don't start thinking that we can predict or control the future. And for that matter, we can't allow the past to shackle us in fear hiding under a rock from shit that no longer exists. It's not living."

"I feel like that's what I am doing," Dave grieved. "Hiding."

"And I feel like a puppet," Derek interjected. "Circumstances have been pulling me this way and that for a couple of years since everything went to shit. I am done giving up my life in service and martyrdom for nothing other than feeding money to other people. There are better ways to demonstrate to my kids that I love them than just being a plow horse harvesting money for my ex."

Dave looked up at Derek, surprised to hear him say that about the kids he loved enough to forfeit his own happiness.

It seemed inconsistent. Was what he said one day, to be contradicted the next? "What do you mean?" he asked.

"I mean, I love my kids but how can they respect me for sacrificing myself when they don't need the sacrifice?" Derek replied. "It's teaching them that men are disposable. There's been enough of that bullshit lesson. Yeah, I need time with them. That is certain. Sitting around here waiting for little scraps of time isn't noble and good. It's pathetic. Who can respect that? A father and brothers are the only men most women have in their lives who will tell them the truth. They need me around. But, what is done is done to the family. It is torn apart. They are living that unfortunate legacy of family life in a country that values the feeling of happiness over duty."

"It's bullshit and damaging, but we had our own versions of bullshit growing up. My parents stayed together until death, but their marriage died years before. This shows my kids that life is in the present because all life is lived in the present. When I see them next, it will be in the present. Fuck the future, and fuck the past. They are both meaningless wastes of thought. Alyssa is my present. Everyday I wake up, and she is there, it confirms that we have one more day together. What better way to start the morning? My kids are always and forever will be my present.

"Right now, Alyssa and I have the opportunity to take what we have together and be together. Now. Who knows? It could explode into a giant pile of bullshit over toothpaste or some ridiculous chimera we project blame on. It would be an insult to the gift of meeting each other not to explore it together."

"I get it," Dave acquiesced. He stood up and stretched out the exercise haunting his shoulders and chest. "I am going to take a shower. Maybe a nap."

"Do that then later we'll go down to that weird café bar for a drink," Derek suggested.

They walked down the beach towards the tourist shops along the concreted sand of low ride, reminiscing about Colorado. Dave halfheartedly buried his envy for Derek's good fortune. He wanted to go back too, for good. Maybe when things calmed it could happen. For now, he was stuck. They stepped out of the darkening shadows of condominiums cast across the beach into a procession of tourists looking for food and evening entertainment. The eccentric little bar they targeted was packed with a mix of sunburns and lifelong tans. Choosing a table away from the bar, they watched. Derek's phone exploded.

What are you two doing?
You are at a bar?
This is uncommon.
Kate and Miguel just arrived outside.

Derek showed the text stream to Dave. They, along with known threats, were under constant surveillance. "We'll finish this and leave," Derek said calmly. "It doesn't really matter, anyway. We are just two dudes in a bar. Keep your back to Kate."

Kate walked in ahead of Miguel who stopped to talk to a man near the door. She was quickly pulled into a group where two other women looked to outnumber and resist hovering, inebriated men. Dave turned away to conceal himself as Derek calmly observed the chatter, taking in Miguel's mannerisms. He was confident or he had the kind of arrogance trying to disguise itself as confidence. Derek consciously moved his observations around the room, not landing on anyone too long. His eyes followed a cute waitress as she passed.

"Hi," a female voice said as she tapped Dave on the shoulder. "Remember me?"

Dave knew the voice. Quickly gaining his composure, he turned to her. For the second time in the day their eyes met. "Kate, right?"

"You remembered," Kate smiled. Dave quickly introduced Derek explaining the circumstance of how they met. Derek took over the lead as Miguel stepped up behind Kate his arm snaking its way around her waist. "This is my boyfriend, Miguel."

Derek stood to shake his hand while Dave took the hint to do the same.

"So, how do you know them?" Miguel asked Kate.

"I was talking to Dave today at the Post Office," she explained. Miguel took over the conversation, unleashing his well-rehearsed social and gregarious personality. Kate faded back an awkward step, her glances innocently bouncing off Dave subconsciously seeking his approval. Miguel continued to command the center of attention by sheer will. Their submission to him was presumed. Derek had seen this thousands of times. To a trained eye, Miguel was superficial, potentially covertly narcissistic. Twenty years of working with corporate executives taught Derek to identify these types quickly enough to ignore second-guessing himself.

It had been his role to resist their charms while keeping them wiggling on his hook. In the game of perceived social hierarchy, Derek was a master, an undercover agent. The details of Miguel's expressions, his tactics to grab on to attention, the grandiosity and body language were being filed away for evaluation of what his intuition already knew.

The best way to be gaslighted and taken in by someone was to gaslight yourself through the benefit of the doubt. A social order in our civilized world arises through subtle power struggles where might is wielded by physically weak people in control of paychecks and their willingness to take them away. Not enough corporate types knew what it was like to have their noses broken. It was unfortunate. The meting out of justifiable, real pain would fix a lot of social problems and restore order.

Miguel, satisfied with his dominance over the conversation, excused himself taking Kate by the hand back to the bar to be near familiar faces away from Dave and Derek. Miguel continued to glance towards them, his fingers furiously pounding a text message into his phone.

"Let's get out of here," Dave whispered. Derek nodded, dropping a fifty on the table for the waitress they slipped out a side exit unnoticed. The air outside was cool and welcoming in contrast to the breath-filled smog of the bar. As they walked the beach back towards the house, Derek texted Dominic his impression of Miguel.

Chapter 20

Courtney leaned in to make her question clear and discrete. The coffee shop was half-full of people staring into screens. "Is there something going on between you and Miguel?"

"What do you mean?" Kate replied.

"It seems like you two aren't the same lately," Courtney answered. She was stirring something up, fully conscious of the motivations commanding her to pry. Injecting a little doubt was known to have positive effects.

Kate hesitated to answer. It was working. She felt the excitement she craved and the consistency she needed, although he had been acting differently in the last few weeks. Something was troubling him. He was more quick to be jealous and protective. She felt it in the bar when she was talking to the two guys in the corner. That Dave guy from the Post Office and whatever his friend's name was. She had felt something from Miguel that seemed like possession when he stepped up behind her. She had never felt that before. It was as if Miguel feared those two for some reason. Maybe he was jealous of their attention towards her. If that was the problem, she liked it.

"I think everything is OK," Kate replied.

"I don't know," Courtney tilted her head affecting concern. Looking directly into Kate's eyes, she said, "If he were my boyfriend, I would think something was going on. I am just saying this because you are my friend."

"I know," Kate smiled reaching across the table to take hold of Courtney's hand. "You are sweet and care about me." Courtney smiled as contentedly as she could. She hadn't seen or heard from Miguel in days. He barely acknowledged her at the bar. He walked in, glanced at her then went straight to where Kate was talking to those guys. It wasn't normal for Kate to talk to tourists. They were probably the kind who are in Vero for a few days, looking to get laid, then bailing out of town. Nobody seemed to understand that the town wasn't like that. It was mostly conservative and reserved; the heavy humidity of conservative Christian shame hovered over it. As much as the town yearned to have a party vibe, the aging snowbirds didn't have the energy and the locals were mostly raising kids. These two demographics dominated the population, keeping the town horrifically mundane and predictable. Miami was the place to live. Vero Beach was a nice place to end life slowly and quietly. Courtney wished she could leave. Her relationship with Miguel was her relationship with the town; not on her terms.

Derek felt the caress of Alyssa's breath gently massaging his chest. The sunrise was impatient with him as he nestled his face towards a hint of perfume on her neck. He could sense the deep contentment she felt in his presence. It was hers to cue him. Love or coffee. It didn't matter. To make love to her again this morning or make coffee, he was there with her. She wiggled slightly to bury herself deeper into the soft feathers as Derek gently kissed her on the neck and slid out of bed.

He pulled on his pants then heaved a thick sweater over his head. That would be enough to get him to the store and back. The town usuals were walking their dogs as he ducked branches on the tree-lined path. The birds roosting above readied for the day with chatter of self-encouragement. The familiar faces hadn't changed since he was a family man living two blocks opposite the market from Alyssa's condo willfully unaware of her. Life had dragged him to Florida to do the right thing. Now, he was experiencing the curse of Chief Niwot. That's what they called it. The curse that says you can never leave. It hangs on to you or pulls you back. He was thankful for it.

Since his divorce, circumstances had pulled him back into the town twice. It was a curse that was impossible to regret. Chief Niwot had warned of the alluring beauty of the Boulder Valley and how it would tempt anyone who saw it to stay, filling the land with settlers until the land had been overrun; it's beauty trampled under hooves and wagon wheels. It had happened but as much as people had tried to exploit it fully, something compelled them to protect its open land. Voters were consistently against the interests of infuriated residential developers. Boulder County was unique. It had conviction. With all of its wealth, it tried its hardest to hate profit and especially profiteers.

Derek paid for the two breakfast burritos and quietly walked back to the condo. The Colorado air was pure and crisp, unlike the stagnant, pungent smell of rotting mangrove swamp he had learned to tolerate. Alyssa was awake, standing in the kitchen, as he slipped in the door as quietly as he had left. She wrapped her arms around him. Holding her against him, running his hand gently on her back, she relied on him to stand. There was nothing to disrupt or distract them from each other. All time was theirs. Like the beauty of the valley Chief Niwot had contemplated, their chemistry compelled them to be there with each other. It was an undeniable blessing to protect.

"When is Derek getting here?" Dominic yelled over the knee mill chopping through an aluminum block.

"He'll be here in a while. Said something about mid-morning," Paul replied stepping away from Mark's side. He gestured for Dominic to follow him outside.

They sat down in camp chairs next to the shop facing east as the sun's rays forced their way through a notch in the foothills. The resident wild turkeys were shaking themselves awake up the hill behind them, disgruntled by the intrusion of surviving another day. Paul tapped Dominic on the shoulder, pointing down the hill towards an opening where a bull elk stepped into full view. The elk calmly resumed grazing, uninterested in being watched. Out of respect, they remained quiet. Their dialogue was not urgent enough to disturb a morning meal. The crackle of truck tires over gravel alerted them to Derek's arrival as the bull elk stepped out of view.

"Good morning," Paul greeted.

"Good morning," Derek replied. "Hey Dominic, I didn't know you were here."

"I am," Dominic said standing up to greet Derek with a friendly handshake while Paul positioned another chair.

"What's going on in there?" Derek asked gesturing towards the noise.

"That's Mark working on something for us. He should be done in a few minutes," Paul replied.

They sat chatting about Derek's homecoming; how he and

Alyssa were getting along while the mill churned out its last few cuts. The three of them watched the door of the shop, anticipating Mark. A blast of compressed air broke the silence while simultaneously turning on the compressor in a shed down the hill. Finally, the door opened. Mark stepped out handing the part to Dominic.

"Perfect," Dominic smiled. "And you'll inset the plate here?" he asked.

"Yeah, this will keep the weight down and still force the blast in this direction," Mark explained.

"The blast? What is that?" Derek asked.

"Sort of a flying claymore," Dominic grinned. "It will be after we attach it to a drone."

"Who is on the other end of this?" Derek asked.

Paul stood up offering his chair to Mark. "Whoever we think needs it," he replied. "What was the range you predicted?" he asked Dominic.

"Depends on the drone, but at least five miles with some added hover time," Dominic replied confidently. "The drone uses GPS to travel autonomously then once it's there, we can take over or just give it instructions to detonate based on certain criteria and visual recognition. The more criteria, the more detailed the onboard programming will have to be, but Duncan doesn't seem to care. He is obsessed with accuracy."

"Duncan does not want any collateral damage," Paul interjected. "The target is the target. Any fuck up, and we are at risk of Duncan or his partners pulling the plug on the whole thing."

"So we are finally getting to the point where this thing is real," Derek stated.

"Duncan feels obligated to do something. He is looking at this as a calling for the last period of his life. The last time we spoke, he was adamant about taking action. He said that he has the means; therefore, he has the obligation. He has no interest in involving the authorities who he believes will only, as he put it, 'usurp the responsibility for political grandstanding and get nothing substantial done'." Paul looked around at the faces, contemplating what they had heard. There was rebellion in their eyes. These men were well-chosen. Each had a strong sense of justice and a healthy, general distrust in politics.

"Let the politicians placate the common rabble with laws, as Duncan told us," Paul continued. "We will work the ethics and justice side of things. Apart from that, he had me form a non-profit to aid the innocents who will be affected by our actions. Instead of a general welfare organization, we will be able to focus on their short and long-term needs. Even if they wish to return to their countries of origin."

"Like what?" Derek asked.

"Like building and operating schools and health centers. We will aid in economic opportunities they can exploit for themselves; things they can do with their families and friends instead of risking everything to become slaves here. The first people we will try to help are the ones living on Miguel's farm. If we simply eliminate the force that keeps them there and the government steps in, they will be locked up and eventually sent back with nothing. Their debts will survive and they will be compelled to return.

"These people were sold a lie to enslave them. We have to break that lie and those in control. We will break the organization with pinpoint accuracy and induce fear into the oppressors. These cartel idiots won't know who is after them. We assume and hope they will think it's a clandestine government entity. Let them chase around scumbag politicians as much as they want, paying them off and putting them in political pressure. We'll remain small, operating with precision. There will be no rest for these assholes. The minute they feel comfortable, we will strike again and again. This little, shithead Miguel is itching to become our test subject."

Derek laughed. His life had turned into something like a teenage daydream. Out of nowhere came the reality of justice being served by people on a righteous path. The romantic ideals he used to dream about were real enough now to believe they could have been true all along.

The social pressure of placating yourself with comfort while you hoped to ease into a comfortable grave didn't exist in the adolescent mind. It was unique to those who learned to disbelieve their own daydreams. Seeking and wishing for comfort in conformity. It's the average man's curse to seek pleasure and happiness. To avoid the suffering and experience that creates contentment.

Suffering was an unavoidable circumstance presenting itself when it wished. The only thing anyone could do was learn to think of it as a lesson. It was the unfortunate reality of life. When suffering slept, life was a blessing. Those who sided with injustice and exploited innocents deserved to be punished and made to suffer by the hands of the righteous. There was little hope they would learn anything.

Dominic stood up, holding the claymore casing for everyone to see. The bloodshed this innocent piece of aluminum would be capable of was unapparent in its present form. "In here, there will be a C-4 charge, buck shot embedded in epoxy, and a 3-volt detonator. The cover is a thin sheet of steel. In order to get as much force forward the drone will detonate as it approaches the target at max speed. You know, an attempt at equal and opposite forces. A feeble attempt.

"But it will be effective enough just hovering in place. In order to get as much out of it, I have designed the program to rush the target and drop it right before detonation. That should allow the drone to escape the blast, maybe. The drones have a camera that feeds back to the operator as well as feeds into the software to verify targets. There's an automatic abort function if there are unrecognized individuals within the blast range such as children or wives. We don't care if we make them cry for their lost assholes. We just don't want to kill them. We don't have any guilt by association in our code of ethics, assuming they are innocent."

"Where do we get the C-4?" Derek asked.

"Duncan owns an oil company," Paul replied. "We could just make it if we had to. It doesn't take any extravagant chemistry. The average terrorists seem to have that capability."

Derek held his hand up. The men all looked at him, waiting for his comment. "We are terrorists," Derek announced coldly.

"For the most part, I would agree," Paul replied. "In the mind of a terrorist, he is a freedom fighter. Those who he believes oppress him call him a terrorist and easily control that narrative. The sloppiness of his operation makes him a terrorist when he harms innocents. I don't believe anyone can justify harming innocents just because of their national identity. We are all subjugated to some extent to the whims of our governments, to their idea of justice. Let's face it, governments are horrible at defining justice. It usually has some self-serving bullshit propaganda attached to it and more than likely money for a few. Governments are good at making laws, turning common brains into mush and holding on to power. Real justice is too simple, too straightforward for them. It can be found in the Ten Commandments and theories of Natural Law. Unfortunately, many laws tend to create favoritism and privilege better than they protect the majority of us.

"I am not talking about simple, preventative laws like speed limits. We can all agree that suppressing human stupidity, arrogance and greed for the greater good is reasonable. But a lot of laws protect a few people at the expense of others. Politicians rely on law and hope for a public that has little understanding of them. Behind every law, there is an opportunity for exploitation. Even speed limits created radar detectors. The personal firearms ownership law created revenue for shooting clubs and eliminated the freedom to hunt with your friends and family. It created the paid guide system that sent the expense of hunting into the stratosphere of elitism. Mark and Dave know that very well. These are just a few examples. You cannot unsee with open eyes.

"The immigration laws created more and more exploitation of those seeking better lives here," Paul continued. "It helped give rise to the trafficking of people as a profitable enterprise for gangs and cartels. Why move drugs when you can move people who can carry drugs for you? A drug is moved at the expense of transport, sold and then replenished to be sold again due to demand. Now the carrier is also the product. In our country, we demand the luxury of cheap roofs, construction, gardening, plucking chickens and labor we don't want to do. That is a drug in and of itself.

"While the idiots grandstand about illegals taking those jobs, they do nothing to step in to perform them. So, the result is a political bandaid called a closed border then sections and sections of wall for opportunistic contractors to erect. Trafficking people across a closed border is profitable. Trafficked people are treated with less care than trafficked drugs. They have a debt and a high cost of transport assured by threats and extortion. If you want to get a debt paid, hold a debtor's family members hostage with a gun pointed at their heads. That's pretty motivating for the debtor. What they don't tell these people is that their debts will probably never be paid. If they are caught here illegally, people like Miguel will let the system take them, deport them and then replace them."

"Technically, they would still have the debt," Dominic inserted. He was incensed by Paul's diatribe. Something struck a nerve in him the rest of the men had never seen. "They are still on the hook. So they have to come back, incurring more debt so they can be exploited over and over. It is like the system is in league with the Miguel's of the world. It makes you wonder how many politicians on our side and the other side of the borders are getting something from this. I have no problem detonating this over their useless, fucking heads!"

The men all stared agape at Dominic's uncharacteristic outburst. The mild computer guy was expressing himself like a fanatical assassin ready to lay waste to his enemy. In his shaking hand, he held the claymore casing aloft, prophesying the hell it would unleash. Throwing the casing onto his chair, he stomped off into the woods to be alone. The men looked at each other, knowing to let him go.

Paul steadied himself before continuing, "We are in uncharted waters here. We could be labeled a terror organization. That is why extreme secrecy is a must. Duncan and I discussed bringing on a few retired Special Forces, but honestly, we can't trust them. Their oath to the country makes them a potential liability. If we bring on anyone, we have to go with our gut and vet them out for a long time. That being said, it is probably a matter of time before we are discovered by either the FBI, NSA or CIA. We will deal with that when it happens. It's something to think about. In the meantime, you all will be getting as many passports as possible. There are a number of countries that will issue them for a price. In the next few weeks, the nonprofit I mentioned will be operational. We will run it like any other. It will seem like do-gooders with money congratulating themselves. We will have events and silent auctions and all the bullshit that makes people congregate to applaud their own benevolence. This is the only seemingly legit thing we will do. I will head that as CEO."

Derek drove east out of the canyon. The road wound its way through the green fields of early June past horses and grazing cattle. As the road jogged to the south, he looked out at the snowy peaks of the Continental Divide in contrast with the early summer of the plains. He felt at ease that he could tell Alyssa what he was up to. She was a comrade. He had never felt so content.

Chapter 21

"Alyssa asked me, 'what grounds you?'" Derek said, continuing a conversation Duncan had started earlier on the topic of women asking about things inhabiting their thoughts. Were these tests or did women really want to know what a man thought?

"What do you mean?" Duncan asked.

Derek hesitated to continue as he sat down in the beach chair next to Duncan. His daughters were splashing around in the tiny harbor with relentless joy. "Grounded. What keeps you calm and peaceful? You know, contented," he replied. "I had to think about it. I was looking for something external like the kids or my family or friends. It comes down to me. I ground me. Maybe it's the stoic nature I am always trying to cultivate. Or practicing being non-reactive to life's constant bullshit. But I think it has a lot to do with being able to pick my battles. If you have to fight everything, you are most likely fighting your own demons not for your cause. You are constantly reacting."

"What's your cause, then?" Duncan interrupted.

"My cause is the constant pursuit of truth. Whatever that

may be," Derek answered. "And when I see an innocent person being treated poorly, I feel compelled to step in. This was a problem when I first met Alyssa. There were a few times I didn't. I didn't choose the battle that was affecting her. The battles she expected me to take on. Shame on me. I didn't recognize how she felt about some things that happened. At the time, we barely knew each other. It's not a good excuse, but I think I need to be with someone for a while to understand what affects them and where I can assert myself. There were a few instances where I was unaffected by a situation and she was hurt. It affected her deeply enough for her to hold on where I would just let it go. You know, bounce off."

Derek's gaze wandered over his children, then out towards the horizon. The memory of the pain he had caused Alyssa when they were new to each other came to him. How they had come together, he could not comprehend. They were friends. That was the foundation of their relationship. They enjoyed talking to each other as much as they enjoyed being wrapped around each other in bed, searching for another way to find pleasure for the other. Their relationship was like a child they had created. Each nourished it with the best they had in themselves while trying to protect it as best they could from the darkness of their own unresolved issues.

"What do you mean by 'you barely knew each other'?" Duncan asked.

"It was like any other new relationship, but we were separated almost immediately," Derek replied. "I moved to Florida to be near the kids. The circumstances of Alyssa and I being able to experience each other for only a moment were unexplainable. Everything seemed to align at the last minute. It was like God throwing a curveball. 'Here you go Derek.

Here is the woman you have waited fifty years to meet. You get her for a night.'"

"Was that a one-night stand that turned into a relationship?" Duncan asked.

"It sort of was," Derek let out a sigh at the irony of his life. "Who knows when you are going to get with a woman and then develop feelings for her when a relationship is completely impractical? It was torture. She was hurt. I was awestruck. She doesn't know how much confusion I went through. How much second-guessing went into my decisions. When it came down to it, I did what my duty to my children called for. I thought they needed me so I left her in Colorado hoping to build something long distance."

"Romantic relationships die with distance. Real friendships don't. There's something better about friendships. They endure. As far as your girls are concerned, I think they do need you around," Duncan counseled. "Look at them. They seem very happy."

"Yeah," Derek replied, "they are. They have always been content around me even when I was still married. If my wife was away, the girls were calm at home. I think it sort of irked my ex that they didn't go running to the door when she came home. They are at ease around me. But now they are older. Their friends and activities take up most of their time and I only get to see them in doses. Thanks to you and Paul, I get them more than before. God knows how isolated I was from them when I was struggling to feed myself. I would bank enough gasoline to get to a soccer game and eat the cheapest food I could get, if I ate at all, just to be there. I felt pathetic; like a complete failure for a long time."

"You should have called me," Duncan said.

"You know, a lot of people say that and I don't doubt the sincerity, but nobody really wants to deal with a broken man and I was broken," Derek replied. "Broken men are tossed aside like lepers."

"What kept you going?" Duncan asked.

"Faith. Hope, I guess that things would work out," Derek reflected. "You have to pick yourself up. Nobody does it for you especially as a man. We're disposable. Look at these people trying to emigrate to the US. Is that their last hopeful effort before the world shits them out? They don't seem to arrive starving. So what is it? There has to be something else. Something more than material opportunity. At least, I hope so."

"I have been considering that for a long time," Duncan replied. "Ignacio and Imelda came to the US through me. They worked for me at the Cuernavaca house. They seemed happy there, but I needed someone in Vero Beach. So I proposed a deal with them and they accepted. We have spoken about immigration at length. Ignacio is rather cynical about it. He thinks the lure and perception of relative luxury that Americans display is stronger than the reality. Then there's the currency exchange. This makes sense to me. If you can earn US dollars and send them back, you will be ahead. At least until the US dollar falls against your currency. Gilberto can attest to this. The dollar converts well into the Brazilian Real. It is an extreme advantage for him to earn US currency. Things are expensive in Brazil though. The import taxes are very high. But their government has a lot of social services to pay for. The money has to come from somewhere. This is something Paul and I have been putting a lot of thought into. Anyway, enough about that. How are things now with Alyssa?"

"Great," Derek answered. "If we had met ten years ago, she would have hated me. There's still some of that guy in me though, as much as I try to erase him. What it came down to with the initial problem is that she didn't feel safe. She felt all of the excitement of a new relationship, but after a while women need more than that. We didn't have enough day-to-day life experience together for me to show I could protect her. And the few instances where I failed to choose the battle stuck with her. The only reason she seems to have stayed connected is the fact that we seem to have something really rare together that can't be denied. When you let go and tolerate the few negatives, it is really beautiful what we have. It is easy. The more we spend time together the safer she seems to feel. That little scar we have from the beginning of the relationship helps me. It makes me reflect on the bullshit I carry and have carried throughout my life. It, so far, keeps me from taking her or our relationship for granted. Just that little bit of fear of losing her is enough."

"Fear as a blessing," Duncan said.

"Yeah, fear as a blessing," Derek repeated.

"How is living up on Paul's property?" Duncan asked.

"It is peaceful. I spend a lot of nights down in town with Alyssa, but the mountains are there waiting for me. It's hard to take them for granted," Derek said. "I like my solitude but Dave's brother-in-law, Mark, and I have spent a lot of time together. Mark is an excellent guy. He went through a lot of the same shit I did with his business, then the bullshit that happened to him."

"Dave saved him from that," Duncan replied. "Paul was the mastermind."

"I know," Derek answered. "For a lawyer, Paul seems to come up with some far-out and spectacularly manipulative plans when we need him to."

"Best lawyer I have ever had," Duncan stated. "I have no love for lawyers. They mostly seem like lazy, low hanging fruit pickers. If it doesn't seem winnable in a legal sense, they are useless. Unless they think you'll pay them a ton of money then anything is possible. With Paul, he determines how justice can be served regardless of whether or not it's legal. Legal, he says, is for politics. Justice is natural and objective."

"He was good with the law when he negotiated my new parenting agreement with the ex," Derek smiled. "That is really all I needed. Someone to talk to her lawyer and more income to pay for it. I have you to thank for that."

"You earn it," Duncan replied. "Both you and Dave have earned it many times over."

Dominic and Dave settled into a brisk pace through the brush. The GPS waypoint was only a mile or so away from where Ignacio dropped them off. The late afternoon sun was oppressive; their water supply felt like it forced their steps deeper into the desert sand with every step.

"Once we get there, we can fly them out to us and set them up," Dominic said in a hushed voice.

Dave acknowledged with a nod Dominic couldn't see under the camouflage. The terrain was rough; the brush caught them from every angle.

"Stop for a minute," Dave commanded. He pulled the hood off and began to strip out of his suit.

"What are you doing?" Dominic asked, surprised at Dave's cavalier attitude.

"Take off your ghillie. We can put them back on as we get closer. Sometimes these things are stupid. Besides we can use the terrain for cover. We'll go faster. There's no one around here, and I am getting sick of snagging on all of this shit."

Dominic complied, begrudgingly stripping off his ghillie suit. He already felt conspicuously out of place. The sweat on his brow appeared unnatural. There was protection under the shaggy camouflage, giving him a feeling of anonymous security.

"Keep your head up," Dave cautioned. "Look around and don't forget to check your six once in a while."

"My six?" Dominic asked.

"Six o'clock, behind you," Dave replied as he picked up the pace. Dominic hesitated, looking back into the emptiness. The satellite image had shown nothing where they planned to approach. Until they got within a quarter mile, they shouldn't encounter any human activity. They would approach just past a half mile and then set up. With Dave leading, the half-mile mark was approaching quickly. He stopped abruptly, signaling quiet and to suit back up. With purposeful steps they neared their objective, the welcomed shade of a large rock outcropping.

Dominic went to work as Dave surveilled the area. The roof of the hacienda was barely visible over low rising waves of barren desert. Dominic's program was sending them updates on the inhabitants. Inside was Sergio; ten others with cell phones patrolled within a few hundred yards of the property. A whir of motors caught Dave off guard as a drone suddenly appeared behind them carrying a box. The drone set the box next to Dominic and then moved back a few feet. Solar panels on the top split open for the drone to nestle itself inside protected from the harsh environment. Dominic reached into his pack for one of Mark's machined claymores, sliding it into a holder. "This one is done," he said as the hatch closed. "It should charge up pretty fast with this much sun. Let's go set the others and get out of here."

They repeated the steps, flying in the other five drones Ignacio had hidden along the road. The sun was an hour over the horizon as the last one nested for the night. Dave slid the last claymore into the box. The lid closed obediently as it sensed the explosive seat into its holder. He slowly stood up to stretch, reminded that not far away there were men with submachine guns. Tapping Dominic on the shoulder he gestured to his wrist. Dominic stepped behind a rock to check on Ignacio. His dot was still in town at the taqueria they had frequented the last few nights.

"How long do you think it will take to walk out?" he asked quietly.

"45 minutes to an hour," Dave replied.

Dominic sent a text with the pickup coordinates. "Ok, let's go," Dominic said impatiently. He was unaccustomed to such a chaotic and unplanned habitat. As much as he loved nature, he longed to see it from hiking trails and bike paths. Dave had been amused at how clumsy Dominic was in the wild. He was acutely aware of the steps he took and the noise they represented where Dominic plowed along unfazed. The human footstep was unmistakable in the woods of Colorado. The tourist hikers seemed to be able to kick rocks for miles, announcing their presence to every creature within earshot. That and their incessant need to talk. Hiking and hunting were nothing alike. There was nothing louder to a hunter than his own footsteps as he worked his way into an environment now mostly foreign to his species. The first morning of the season was a ritual re-schooling as the hunter stepped hundreds or maybe thousands of years back into his nature humbled by how far away he had wandered from it.

"You know," he half-spoke, half-whispered to Dominic, "with a .300 Win Mag and a decent hide, I could take out half of those guards at that ranch."

"I don't think that's necessary," Dominic replied.

"It would be tidier than splattering them with the claymores."

Dominic nodded nervously signaling for Dave to cut the

chatter and lead him out. Watching Dominic's general discomfort was worth bringing him along. Maybe the next time, with some experience, he would relax and not need as much coaxing. Maybe it was the thought of beer and tacos awaiting them in the truck for the drive back to the hangar that had him so restless.

With this part of the mission completed, they would make a quick stop in Cuernavaca to drop off Ignacio, a stop in California for Dominic, then a day in an empty house in Vero Beach before heading out to Eleuthera to meet up with Duncan and Derek. He was looking forward to a little quiet island time with two men he considered family. Derek would have stories of Colorado and working with Mark. There would be stories about whatever Paul had been up to. It was the only way he had to stay connected to his home. Hopefully, he could go back soon. At this point, he saw no reason not to other than staying with Duncan. Someone had to be around Duncan. If he was serious when he said he was planning to sell off the Vero property, then maybe he could return after that. Dave doubted he would. Kate was still a concern. Why didn't Duncan just tell her? Could she be made to realize that her boyfriend was a homicidal slave master?

"What is this?" Miguel asked as he dropped a photo on the coffee table in front of Kate.

She picked up the photo, trying to make sense of it. Miguel stood over her, waiting for her to come clean. He was already suspicious of her explanation before she had a chance to defend herself. She had to know her Uncle was fucking with him. She was hiding something from him. She was complicit in the loss of his men and probably the loss of Scott. At this moment, all he wanted was to reach down and pick her up by the throat. His eyes burned into her as she studied the photo in disbelief.

"I, I don't know," she stuttered. "Where did you get this?"

"Don't worry about where I fucking got that," Miguel shot back. "Why the fuck is that guy Dave at your Uncle's house? Are you fucking around on me?" he snarled. "You acted like you just met him at the bar. You know him. You knew him before, and you are bullshitting me!"

"I don't," she cried, "I only met him that day." She stood up, looking for comfort and trust but Miguel had none for her. Instead, he slammed his foot down on the top of the coffee table cracking it in half as Kate fell back into the couch trying to protect herself with any distance she could create between them.

"Your fucking Uncle had that guy follow me," Miguel screamed, kicking again at what was left of the table. "I knew I had seen him before." He spun around, denying her his eyes as Kate desperately tried to appease him.

"What are you saying? Do you think I would cheat on you? Why are you yelling at me? Cheating? Or being followed? I don't understand," Kate begged.

She needs this, Miguel thought. She needed to be afraid of him. To get her back in line and show loyalty. The three dead in the road and Scott made sense now. The old man was after him and Dave had helped. He knew about the farm. He knew that Scott was a cop. Somehow, he knew. This Dave guy must be following him all the time. When Marco pulled him over, that should have been enough to place him with Duncan. Why hadn't he thought this through? This guy and the other asshole at the bar had approached one of his crews as Brazilians looking for work. The fucking old man was trying to drive a wedge between him and Kate. That's what it was. The fucking old man was trying to take him down and destroy what he had built so he could keep Kate away from him.

Kate remained curled on the couch, fearful of another outburst. She searched her thoughts. Had she met this man before? Dave? She doubted herself and her memory. She wanted to tuck under a blanket and cry until Miguel calmed down. There had to be an explanation for everything, she trembled. She had seen Miguel angry, but never like this. She wanted to hold on to him and calm him. "I don't know," she continued to whimper repeatedly. Her face was buried in a pillow until the door slammed. He was gone.

"I want you guys to start working extra on everything we have around that house!" Miguel yelled into the phone as he tore down the road. "Keep your fucking eyes open and let me know when you see those two."

"Hey, boss," Pancho asked, "what about Kate? You think she will tell her Uncle?"

"I'll fucking kill her," Miguel replied coldly. "I need to make that clear with her. It's me or him now. You just keep that in mind. Those two assholes had something to do with the farm. Right now I don't care. Marco is at the house dealing with her." An angry quiet came over him, thinking about what to do next. "They probably killed Scott," he muttered.

"Nobody knows if he's dead," Pancho retorted.

"He's fucking dead," Miguel snarled.

"Hey girls, it's time to get ready for dinner," Derek called. His two mermaid-tailed daughters beached themselves giggling. He was happy. He felt like a father worthy of them again. As he ushered them into the house, he caught Gilberto by the shoulder. "How's our guest doing?"

"He is OK," Gilberto replied. "He has no idea where he is

or who I am. The cabin doesn't allow much sound out, so his yelling stays in. He yelled everyday for about a week when you brought him. Once in a while he cried, but now he just watches television."

"He can't get out?" Derek asked.

"No, if he does, Mister Duncan gave us permission to subdue him or eliminate him if we have to," Gilberto replied coldly.

Chapter 22

"Congratulations Dave, you are divorced," Paul's voice was loud enough for the room to hear. Dave stepped out into the courtyard, not as much for privacy but to alleviate his friends from the ills of his personal issues.

"That's it, huh," Dave replied. "Was it pretty easy?"

"She got the house as you wanted and half of everything else. A stellar deal for her," Paul said. "I am still playing dumb as to your whereabouts, so your half will be collected and managed by Mark and Sarah. The judge seemed to think that was OK. I am not sure it's legal, but that's divorce court. Who cares?"

"Yeah, I don't really care. It is odd. I thought I would, but I feel nothing," Dave replied.

"Then I will congratulate you again on your state of indifference. It is truly the opposite of love. Not hate. Pure indifference. It's a wonderful experience when you have to really put some thought into whether or not she actually existed in your life or she was just a bad Mexican food induced dream."

The phone went silent, Paul hesitating to go on. "And she's single."

"What? What happened to Stefan?" Dave asked.

"Not sure on that, but she has plans. She spent about fifteen minutes telling me how she is on a journey of self-discovery now that she is free and reborn," Paul laughed. "I am assuming it will involve India. She is from Boulder. Then, after she is railed by every anxious idiot with a good storyline she'll realize she is going to wait out death alone with the one person she thinks she knows the best, herself. Men are the problem, not her. God forbid she actually got to know herself. I don't believe her hubris would stand down against the reality of self-discovery. It is too strong in that one. She'll get a dog. That will help. She doesn't seem like she has enough self-esteem left for a cat. Wow sorry, maybe I can work on being more sympathetic. I am being overly harsh and cold."

"Man, that is harsh," Dave sighed. He knew it was true. Jessica was arrogant. He saw it now. She was the center of her universe, protected by an impenetrable force field of her self-perception. It was really a defense against deep-seated fear. But, he didn't care. He had realized in the last month that he didn't care if she was happy or miserable. It was surprising how content he had become. There was no hope or hate. There was only nothing. "Alright, well, thank you for that, I guess." Dave disconnected as he walked back into the living room, falling back into his chair. Duncan and Derek looked at him, expecting a story.

"You OK?" Derek asked.

"I am fine," Dave replied coldly. "What are we going to do about Scott?"

"I don't think we can reintroduce him back into society," Derek replied, wincing at the words coming from his mouth. To assume the responsibility of a criminal was the business of government. Although guilty of attempted murder, they lacked the will and the ability to hand him over to the law and due process. There would be no trial, no lawyers, no chance for him to thwart justice. He was unequivocally guilty. Execution was considered, but no one had the stomach for it. Derek's rear naked chokehold had brought Scott as near death as he would get for now. Beating him for information had left their knuckles and spirits bruised.

The final solution was to turn on the television and lock the door. He was a stubborn idiot who accepted no responsibility for himself, nor was he demonstrating any ambition towards improvement. When they had last interacted with him, he lectured from the position of his former privilege as a corrupt police officer and the power he assumed still came with it as if his plan was to rise back up, pin on a badge and exact vengeance upon them. It seemed to be his only ambition. However, isolation and satellite television now lulled him well enough.

"We got everything we needed to know," Dave reflected. "We beat the shit out of that guy and he was quick to give up. I was surprised how easy it was."

"Talking stopped the beating," Duncan replied, remembering the sounds of pain and crying. "His only real cause is self-preservation. I would guess all of Miguel's police henchmen are like that, focused on themselves and their personal ambition. Their power and a paycheck is something the state is irresponsible enough to give them."

"The world is average, Duncan," Derek interrupted. "An average world, run by average people to support an average system of maintaining nothing more than average. We live under a bell curve of average intellects, expecting them to be better than they are capable of. The problem is, it works. Why fix it? And these idiots will defend themselves to the death to stay average because they think anyone who doesn't think like them is an idiot. They have a whole support system to back up their ego-invested mundanity. They see what they want to see and what the news feeds them. It's as if there is no curiosity in them. No curiosity for truth. They put their hopes in politicians and a system proven over and over to be lying to them. They go into debt to display wealth they don't have. Wealth they did not create. They don't have love; they have relationships."

"What do you mean by that?" Dave asked.

"Relationships are transactions, Dave," Derek explained. "They have nothing to do with love. Relationships are what people have between them to get something from someone. And it works. Love is something you give without expectation of reward, without the requirement of reciprocity. That is why one of the highest forms of love is letting go. Or maybe being patient. Being kind to people at the moment you experience them in need without expecting anything in return is love. Telling someone the truth, knowing it will hurt, is love. It would be nice to have love and a relationship at the same time. I think it's pretty rare, though. For two people to both really love each other and be in a relationship? That would be like true friends who like to have sex with each other.

"I think I have something close to it with Alyssa now that we are near each other. However, there is still that shadow of transaction over us. We are becoming good at it. The give and take of it. But I don't know if she could really let me go if she had to. If she needs me too much, now that she has me. In reality, though, she doesn't know how much she has me. It is part of the game between men and women. The more a woman knows she has you, the less she thinks of you. It breeds contempt even in the most well-adjusted women. She may not leave you because of it, but she will grow too accustomed to you. She will lose her attraction for you.

"She cannot be the center of your world. She is like the moon, never the sun. The sun is a man's purpose. He orbits around that. This is truth a man can't relax on. It is exhausting playing this game but if you love her and want to be with her, it is a game you have to play. Men have to perform. The game is part of that performance. I used to joke that death was the only thing a man ever got to choose for himself."

"Suicide?" Dave interjected.

"Not necessarily suicide but the acceptance of his end. The comforting acceptance of no longer having to play the game. Finally, a chance to rest. He makes the choice long before when he seems to check out from the present. Then there are men who step away from it altogether and go into isolated hiding, but that is a game of avoidance. It's still a game. It takes a lot of effort to hide.

"We exist to recreate life and further the species. When our youthful viability to make children is gone, we continue to latch on to women and they latch on to us. For men, the idea of love is poetic. For women, I think it's a tangible need, an opportunity. Maybe a travel plan. They need to feel safe and secure and know where they are going. We don't. We, men, create our own safety and security. Women don't seem to be able to feel love without the things we create for them. We are useful until we are not. A woman can easily obtain another useful idiot. There are millions waiting in line to step into the role. She just needs to advertise an opening and maybe lower her standards.

"It's ironic that men, forever, have been inventing things to make women's lives better and easier. To make them less dependent upon us. Then, one of us invents hormonal birth control to hand over full control of reproduction. The unintended, ironic consequence of the pill was that it made a woman's body think it was pregnant, therefore influencing her to be attracted to less masculine men, men who were more willing to provide for her even though she wasn't pregnant. Her body said she was.

"Think of all the chump baby boomer assholes who were finally able to get laid because the women's hormones and attraction signals were chemically out of whack. And she didn't have to worry about getting knocked up by that chump. So it could just be good old, drunken fun. They then told their sons how to be sensitive because it worked for them. Some of this is my pure speculation. If this is actually true, it's both sad and hilarious. Making getting laid easier for weak men is like giving children keys to a theme park and telling them they own it."

"God that's cynical," Dave sighed. "It seems to be true. I think I have always known this. In the last few months, it has become apparent and I wish it weren't. When I took my marriage vows in front of the Priest, our families and God, I swore an oath. I was married to that oath and did my best to honor it. I think I was more married to the oath than to Jessica. She obviously was not. I eventually had the feeling that for richer or for poorer and for sickness and in health meant there had better not be any poorer or sicker, or else. If there was, she would find someone else. For me, it meant I would try, to the best of my ability, to improve the situation for the oath therefore for her. To tiptoe around whatever irritated her. Her affair made me feel really disposable."

"You were disposable, Dave," Derek agreed. "We all are. If you are not her best option, she will find it somewhere else. The problem with Jessica is that she and pretty much all women have as many dating options as they want. The more self-pride or hubris she maintains, the higher those options will have to perform for her. It's not good or bad. It's just truth. She can go the route of ditching men altogether, avoiding reality and retreating into herself. The system supports that with a general perception of safety.

"I fucking laugh every time a women tells me she doesn't need a man. She may not need one in her house, but she needs one in the middle of the night when her toilet is backed up, or her electricity is out, or she and her little dog hear scary things. Then she needs men. Lots of them. And she needs to pay them because she has retracted the currency she used to get these daily things from the one man she used to live with. Now, she needs money to support a tribe of men to fulfill her needs.

"Before, with one man who may have loved her, she needed only affection, loyalty, and enough sex to keep him attached. She gave that up for her independence from men. Ironically, she doesn't need a man; she needs hundreds of them to support her at the cost of her retirement account. Like it or hate it, but economics runs on sex. Men do everything for sex. They build themselves up, they build bridges, fight wars, invent dishwashers, till fields...

"When sex is on hold for the moment, all we want is loyalty, affection and peace in our homes. Our homes are our tribes we leave for our wives and children when we go out hunting. If we spend too much time in the tribe, we lose our value as a provider. Day-to-day, we spend way too much time with the women we love in modern society. It's unnatural. I learned this when I was working from home."

"Wow," Dave exclaimed, "I did the same thing. After Mark and I put a hold on the business, I had nothing to do. Mark and I spent most of our free time at the gun range, but I was home a lot more. That's when Jessica checked out. All I really wanted from her was some time to regroup. I felt like she gave me a week or two."

"Yeah, in general they have different timeframes and patience thresholds than we have," Derek responded. "Think about it, Dave. A woman is most sexually attractive when she is young, between 20 and 25, or maybe a little older. A man is useless at that age. He comes into his real value later. He has to learn patience. He is forced to. Finally in his mid-thirties, he is peaking while a woman the same age is in serious decline. I am talking about her ability to further the species, not anything else. She may have everything going for her, but at thirty-five, her eggs are giving up one by one. A man doesn't suffer this reality. He is as viable as he wants to be nearly his entire life. Look at Picasso. He was sixty-eight when his last child was born.

"When it comes down to it. Men don't need women for anything other than bearing their children and continuing a legacy. We don't need them for safety or support. I am using the word 'need' in the strictest sense. It's true that they complement our lives when we are with women who love us and respect us. They cannot love us without respecting us. They cannot be loyal to us without respecting us. But respect is something *we* have to earn constantly. It is our burden to earn and command respect. And I am repeating myself here, but it is fucking exhausting. Women will never understand how exhausting all this is for us."

"I don't think I want to have anything to do with them," Dave stated. "I'm done."

"I call bullshit," Derek laughed.

Duncan watched the exchange, amused and entertained. His age gave him the wisdom to know Derek was essentially correct. Although, he chose not to add to the conversation. It was a pointless topic for him at this time in his life. His concern for women was Kate and her wellbeing. She would never need a man. There was nothing her bank account couldn't take care of. Even her personal safety could be bought if necessary. Because of this, Duncan felt a sadness for her he could not describe. It was unnatural. The highs and lows of life's struggles made it worthwhile. She would continue through life insulated from the fullness of most of its challenges. It was true that she would never be hungry; she would never want or need for anything, but what would that accomplish in the end? It seemed like a hollow and pointless future to him. One that he had created.

A pensive silence fell over them as they reflected on the conversation. Derek thought of his fortunate discovery of Alyssa. She was a woman, but she seemed different. Was she a soulmate? As much as he wanted to, he didn't believe in soulmates. But there she was. It was easy with her. Chemistry was the only word that even came close to describing their connection. He loved her with all his soul. If the head malfunctioned and forgot her or the heart were to stop, he felt like his soul would continue.

As the moment passed and they returned to reality as it was, Dave was working up a plan. Something seemingly cruel and inspiring. A simple and brutish plan for Scott.

"I have it," he announced. "I have a plan for Scott... Hear me out. We give him some provisions for a few weeks and dump him on an island. There has to be one around here somewhere. We can find one off the beaten path where no boat will rescue him. At least not immediately. He will have to find a way to survive instead of being the parasite he has always been. Put up or shut time for Scott. What do you think?"

"That's something Paul would come up with," Derek laughed. "Fucking brilliant. How do we find an island?"

Duncan perked up, "Pete is flying out in the helicopter in a few days. Maybe we can ask the locals? Gilberto is becoming friendly with them."

"So that's it?" Dave asked. "You guys are good with that? I have another idea assuming we find an island, the right island. I'll go too."

Derek and Duncan looked at Dave in disbelief. "Why?" Derek asked.

"To watch him. I think it would be interesting to see how he does. If we have a big enough island, I can hide from him well enough. It doesn't have to be huge just have some difficult features to keep him from snooping around too much. I'll take the satellite phone and the right provisions so I don't have to make a fire, and I'll watch."

"We need to think about that," Duncan replied hesitantly, "What if he discovers you?"

"Glock," Dave stated coldly. "I will subdue him. I'll be fine."

Gilberto met Pete at the airport as the helicopter was being refueled from its long flight from Vero Beach.

"I'll show you the way to the house," Gilberto said as the fuel truck pulled away.

"Get in," Pete instructed. He helped Gilberto with his seatbelts before climbing into the pilot's seat. "Ok, I have one rule. Don't touch anything which includes with your feet and you will enjoy the ride."

"OK," Gilberto agreed cautiously. As the blades sped, the helicopter shook, yearning to separate itself from the tarmac. Pete put the machine into the air as Gilberto held on with a combination of fear and excitement. It felt like flying in a glass elevator, the ocean appearing below his feet as they broke free of the land. It would only take ten minutes to fly to the house. Enough time to decide how much he liked helicopter flight. They skirted the outer edge of North Eleuthera low enough to view reefs. Pete slowed the forward progress into a hover, tapping Gilberto on his leg and gesturing downwards towards a sizable Tiger Shark. It was menacing even from their height.

They flew on towards the house, landing on the remains of a tennis court. Pete reached over to put his hand on Gilberto's shoulder to keep him from exiting too early. "I'll let you know when we can get out." Gilberto sat patiently. As the rotors came to a stop and the engine slept, Pete unbuckled himself, gesturing for Gilberto to exit.

"Hello, Pete," Duncan said as he shook hands with the pilot. "We have an island in mind when you are ready to fly again. Good to have you here."

"Thank you, Duncan," Pete replied. "It's been a long day coming out here. Only one fuel stop besides this last one which I probably didn't need to make."

"Derek will show you to your room," Duncan announced. "We will have dinner around seven."

Inside the house, Dave was looking over the satellite images of the island they had chosen. According to the locals, the shore was approachable by nothing other than small boats, and although sustaining, no one lived on it. A rise of rock split the island in two. It would suit the experiment.

Pete stumbled into the kitchen at 6:45 waving off Derek's offer of Scotch. "No thank you, I assume we are flying tomorrow," he declined.

Derek poured himself a glass before showing Pete the way to the living room where Duncan and Dave were huddled over a map.

"You will have enough food and supplies for about four

weeks. We will put you here and Scott on this side, correct?" Duncan asked.

"Yes, that should be enough food. It looks like I can get up on this ledge to watch him," Dave replied. "The terrain is harsh in the middle of the island. If he is smart, he'll stay put on his side."

The plan was simple. Drop Dave off, fly back and get Scott. Whatever happened from then on, was up to fate. Dave was excited to be out of a house; back outside in the wild. It was the same anticipation he experienced before hunting camp with his father. Every autumn they chose a location and dealt with nature as it dealt with them. He had done it in groups, a few times alone. The time drag of being alone in the woods could be tortuous. The minutes ticked away at a maddeningly slow pace. Nature had a way of making every second count.

The next morning Dave, Gilberto and Pete took off early flying over the water towards a point on a map. Twenty minutes into the flight, a small green blemish in the water came into view. Pete flew around the northeast side of the island, looking for a suitable place to drop Dave. A small beach would suffice.

"You're going to have to jump out and wade," Pete said into the headset. Dave opened the rear door pushing his provisions out before dropping into the water. It was warm as he felt his head go under. The sand met his feet with a push, thrusting him back to the surface to waiting cases floating ahead towards the shore. He gripped the first one he could catch and began to kick. The island accepted him as he dragged the cases onto the beach.

Derek prodded a confused Scott with an aluminum baseball bat towards the helicopter as it landed on the tennis court. They had had a little scuffle over binding Scott's hands with rope and then again over a gag. The bat had become necessary for compliance.

"Get in if you want to make it out of today in one piece," Derek warned. Scott crawled into the helicopter, sitting in the seat Derek pointed out with the bat as Duncan strapped him in. In a moment, they were airborne. Scott watched out the window as the bandana wedged in his mouth soaked up saliva and sweat. Derek's conscience nagged at him. It was the solution they had agreed on. None of them had the stomach for executing Scott. It was impossible to release him. The Dave Solution, as they began to call it, was acceptable for the circumstance.

The island came into view as Pete descended towards the southern shore. Dave crawled to the top of the ridge to watch. As the door of the helicopter opened, Scott's feet appeared. He sat at the edge of the door, looking confused and broken.

Derek tapped the bat against the back of Scott's head to remind him where he stood. He loosened the rope binding Scott's hands enough for him to remove it. As the helicopter came within a few feet of the water, the spray of the blades flattening the small waves beneath, Derek leaned over and gave Scott some advice.

"You're going to want to think about water. Water to drink. You have enough for a while. There's already enough provisions stashed to give you a head start. Go find them. Good luck, fucker," he said as he planted his foot on Scott's back sending him face-first into the shallows. The helicopter immediately ascended and turned for home. Dave pressed the record on the camera; Scott flailed towards the beach dragging himself up out of the ocean.

It was at that moment Scott broke. He fell to the sand, blubbering. Dave felt a spectrum of pity and contempt as he watched. He had to look away; it felt wrong to him. His plan had seemed so fitting. How could he have sympathy for this man? Never in his life had he seen someone break like this. It was beyond the definition of despair. Dave thought, *he's going kill himself and I am going to have to watch it*. For Scott, his misery was the only thing his life had left to feel and endure.

Dominic checked the screen again for Kate's phone. It was dead. She had been at Miguel's. Now no signal. Miguel had come and gone. He had been out to the farm a few times. The only noticeable inconsistency was the amount of police presence at Miguel's home. Marco had been spending a curious amount of time there. New officers had taken up the chore of shadowing Miguel.

"Duncan, it's Dominic. You need to call me," he recorded on voicemail. Dominic texted Derek. There was silence in Eleuthera.

As the helicopter landed, Derek pulled out his phone, reattaching it to the WiFi, messages appeared. He jogged to the house as he read Dominic's message.

"Duncan!" he called as he entered the house. He found him asleep on a recliner. Shaking him awake, he held out his phone as it connected with Dominic.

"What are you doing?" Duncan asked, disoriented by sudden consciousness.

"Talk to Dominic," Derek instructed.

Dominic outlined his concerns while Duncan tried to think of rational reasons for Kate to be out of touch for almost a week. The inconsistency of it...

"And he is coming and going as usual?" Duncan asked.

"More or less, yes," Dominic affirmed.

"That is uncommon for her," Duncan agreed. "I am trying to rationalize this. Do we have cause for alarm? Have there been any ambulances? Just that Officer Marco? He's at Miguel's house?"

"Yeah, that's it," Dominic replied. "Maybe I am getting paranoid. Miguel has been quiet since the assault on you."

"He has," Duncan agreed. "Keep me posted. Let me know if her phone comes back on."

Duncan stood up to stretch out his nap. "How did it go with Scott?"

"Went fine. He is getting to know his new home," Derek grinned.

Chapter 23

Dave awoke as the sun glowed over the ridge between him and Scott. His head was still spinning from a long night of surveilling the scene of Scott's tirades. A full moon cast shadows of Scott standing then falling repeatedly to the sand flagellating himself against the earth. It appeared as though he were acting out a torturous penance against a demonic possession of his soul. A self-inflicted insanity teased and dangled suicide just out of his reach. He didn't deserve such an easy fate. What was left of any goodness in him was being taunted by his suffering. Dave grabbed for his camera and ran up the slope, apprehensive as to what the lens might capture.

Below lay Scott, lifeless. Gentle morning tidal waves clawed up the sand hoping to swallow him. As a wave teased his foot, it moved. Dave snapped a series of stills before grabbing the full scene. Video would quickly drain the rest of the battery but capturing the moment Scott gained consciousness would be worth watching later. As another wave slapped at him more assertively, the arms came to life pushing against the sand. He shot up, spinning himself around to face the ocean. The blue expanse between Scott and the rest of the world casually played with him as it splashed at his feet. Dave could feel the sorrow from his perch; Scott's head fell into his hands. It looked like an expression of bitter acceptance. It seemed too early for redemption. Dave's stomach tied up in knots. He had to look away.

Slipping back from the ridge, he left the camera and descended the path to make his first coffee and breakfast. He had enough fuel for a few weeks to cook freeze-dried and canned food. He forced himself to think about economizing on heat as much as possible; he ran a mental list of contingencies he might have to endure. Anything to concentrate on was better than thinking about Scott. The taste of the food didn't matter, only calories and preservation. He resolved to eat the canned food cold. The satellite phone blinked expectantly.

"Yeah," he said into it quieter than necessary.

"How'd it go? Is it alive?" Derek asked.

"He is alive," Dave responded. "It was a long night. I was convinced he was dead this morning, but I confirmed. He is still alive. He hasn't eaten anything yet. I don't think he has been off the beach or found the stash we dropped for him."

"He is going to get thirsty," Derek commented.

"That's for sure. That will kill him a lot faster than not eating," Dave replied. "I will guess he will be very happy to find the water jugs. If he plays it right, it should last two weeks. By then, maybe he will find a way to use what we gave him to capture water. We made it pretty easy on him with the sparker. He can make fire and use the cans to boil. I don't want to watch him shit himself to death from bad water. That would be sad to see."

"I will hold my opinion on that," Derek replied. "OK, if you need anything, let us know. It will take us a solid hour to warm up the helicopter and get out there. Are you sure he can't find you?"

"The ridge is brutal. It's better than I expected. If he has the energy to scale it, it's now. In a few weeks, he'll be too feeble and I haven't seen a good place to try. If I have to go down there, I have the rope and the ascender to get back up. Remember, I am from Colorado, not Florida," Dave laughed. "OK, I am hanging up so I can go see what he's up to."

Dave crept back to his viewing point with a fresh battery. Slipping into the shade of a bush, he scanned the beach. Scott was gone. *Maybe he found the stash*, he thought. Stepping carefully, he traversed the ridge until equal to the point where they had dropped supplies. Scott was there rummaging through the containers. He held up the sparker curiously. *Does he know what it is?* Dave wondered. Scott pulled the two halves apart and struck, as if to answer, shooting a flame into the sand.

He drank from the jug, water pouring out faster than he could take it in. Scott seemed to calculate his error. He searched around in the container finding a cup and carefully poured the rest of his ration. He seemed to be learning quickly or maybe had prior experience. He appeared to be someone who wanted to survive. His demeanor was a complete one-eighty shift from the night's tantrums. He was calm. Dave watched as Scott searched around for things to burn. Within twenty minutes, he had accumulated a huge pile of palm fronds and fall-down wood.

Dave slipped back to camp before the heat of the afternoon to bathe in the ocean. Refreshed, he hung his hammock slipping into a pendulum rhythm. His head was on Jessica wondering why her memory came to him now; the thoughts contaminated any rest he hoped to get. He had loved her. Nearly six years they had been married before she distanced.

He couldn't understand what he had done to drive her away. Was love and affection not enough? His stomach turned at the thought that he might repeat this over and over with women. Maybe Derek was right. Maybe women were just too exhausting to hang on to.

Even Derek kept playing as if he expected a favorable outcome in a game he said he couldn't win. Maybe Alyssa *was* different. Dave laughed to himself. He and every friend of his who had married said their girl was different. Until they weren't. Then to protect the investment they made, they all blamed themselves. They convinced themselves she was different, but they must have changed. Jessica was different until she wasn't. Something in him tried to feel bad for her thinking she probably blamed him for lost time. The ticking time bomb of female youth is precious. He still hadn't come to regret the time they were together. But it was lost. That time was gone. In retrospect, it could have been used differently. He still struggled to find regrets for getting married as if he were somehow a victim. But the experiences tallied had been more good than bad. Although, the bad had felt really bad and was too easy to remember.

A welcomed breeze picked up, gently oscillating him into a deeply needed sleep. Behind a door, there was a voice he recognized. It called him and distanced at the same time. He knew the voice and strained to visualize her face. His memory was faded as he strained to remember. His chest tightened in despair. *She is calling me*, he thought. *Who is she? I know her.* But she was getting further away from the door. Her voice was fading. He pulled and pulled at the door. "I can't open it," he yelled to her as he shook into consciousness.

A small bird he couldn't identify had perched on a branch near his foot. It fluttered away as he sat up sweating in the hammock, disoriented and thirsty. Reaching for a bottle, the warmth of the water did nothing to add satisfaction beyond its purpose. The sun was well past noon as Dave stumbled up the hillside along the markings of his newborn trail.

There he was. Scott sat straight-legged halfway into the gentle waves, staring out to sea. A fire roared behind him, too hot to create much smoke. He looked longingly to the east as if he had discovered the bitter realization that no boat could get near him. He had been released from the cabin only to be exiled behind a sunken wall of reef. Dave watched, trying in vain to divine Scott's thoughts. What had he done all that time in the cabin? The television had run day and night like a morphine drip reinforcing their collective opinion that Scott was a purposeless idiot. But at this moment, he seemed evolved. He appeared calm, thoughtful, almost divine, as if little birds would start landing on him chirping their affections into his ear. Dave laughed at the thought. Whatever was going through Scott's head, Dave thought, can only be navigated from my old beliefs like everyone else trying to guess the inner-thoughts, motivations and reactions of another. *Navigate from old beliefs.* He had heard that before.

Jessica had used it attempting to shame him once when her behavior had tempted him to call her out. He was old-fashioned, antiquated; therefore his defense, in a stunning triple flip of logical gymnastics, invalidated. She was an excellent shamer; he had become exceptional at concession. *What else would I navigate from*, he thought to himself. *Navigation requires a reference, a known point like the North Star.*

He pinched himself out of the logical rabbit hole dragging him under what she really meant. She wanted him to be more like everyone else. To be more uniform and predictable in his thoughts and more accommodating to her whims. She wanted her actions validated regardless of the incongruence with her words. She wanted him to feel like her, to stop defaulting so quickly to rationality. To listen to her as she lamented without solving the problems for her. Maybe that is what Stefan had done for her. He was a somewhat feminine guy dressed up like a man; he probably understood her better.

At this moment, Dave was doing everything Jessica had wanted. Just to listen and watch. To keep his judgment unexpressed and to himself. He couldn't guess what was going through Scott's head. The only thing he could discern from his vantage point was Scott's posture. Now it projected pain, regret and self-loathing.

Dave looked west. A little more than a finger between the sun and the horizon. He had more than enough time to get back to camp before sunset. He gathered up the camera and headed down the slope into the darkening shadows of jungle. He would eat and slip into the tent to read himself to sleep, leaving Scott to himself and a tarp. It didn't seem fair. Dave had to remind himself that, a few days earlier, they were considering whether or not to execute Scott. Would that have been better? Was offing him justified? Scott hadn't killed Duncan but he had intended to. Is it an eye for an eye when both eyes still see? Is vengeance only justified by outcome? What about intent? The satellite phone blinked when he arrived. *Coming out in the morning quietly. Look for me, Derek.*

Dave awoke the next morning anticipating his guest, worried that *quietly* wouldn't be quiet enough. Far to the north the helicopter hovered as a small speck hurried away towards him. An exceptionally quiet inflatable skimmed across the water bouncing gracefully over the waves. With skillful disregard for caution, Derek plowed headlong into the beach throwing Dave a line as he jumped out. The tiny craft was up the beach before they could break a sweat.

"Electric," Derek smiled. "Nice and quiet."

"Welcome to Scott's Island," Dave replied. "Hungry? I have some freeze-dried scrambled eggs."

"No, I am good, thanks. Coffee?" Derek asked.

"I have that," Dave grinned. He was happy to have a guest. While he poured a cup, Derek pulled a bag from the boat.

"More provisions," Derek announced as he fell into a chair. The scenery was different, but the feel of an early morning camp permeated him. Dave went about organizing for the day, packing away supplies and sweeping sand from the tent. Derek watched before commanding, "Show me the captive."

Dave led Derek to the edge of the ridge signaling for him to stay low and keep quiet. They settled in watching for Scott, who was nowhere in sight. The fire smoldered on the beach half-heartedly signaling distress. Out of the bush came Scott dragging a log. Dropping the end into the fire, he disappeared again. The log refused to ignite. In a few minutes, he returned stumbling with an armload of tinder. Kneeling before the smoldering embers, he fed them broken shards. He blew, then waved his hands, then blew again at a tuft of smoke until it relented into flame. He stood over it proudly satisfied. His next task took him to the water where he stood confidently with a spear made from a straightened stick. Dave and Derek watched as Scott cast the spear at whatever moved.

Derek gave Dave a surprised look. It had been a few days and their captive was already trying to hunt. He wanted to live, but for what? It was inspiring. And unsettling, the uncertainly of what they would ultimately decide to do with him.

"You think he'll make it?" Derek whispered.

"I don't know," Dave replied. "He's giving it a shot. The spear is new. He got a fire going pretty quickly, but we gave him the sparker. It's still a lack of water that will kill him. I haven't seen a fresh water source. If I were him, I would start using the tarp for collection. Once rain hits the ground it has to be boiled. I hope he knows that."

"You hope?" Derek asked.

"I don't want to think about what it would be like to die like that here alone. Your guts killing you from the inside as you essentially starve to death and dehydrate," Dave replied. "I am not so cruel to find joy in that."

Derek patted Dave on the back, gesturing for them to return to camp. "You sure you are OK out here?" Derek asked.

"I am fine," Dave replied. "It's easier than being alone in a hunting camp. I have a familiar creature to watch; someone from our species. It is sort of fascinating."

"That's true," Derek replied. "Ok, I gotta go. Send Duncan a text saying that I am heading out. Pete will pick me up," Derek instructed.

With a whisper, the electric motor powered Derek out beyond the reefs. The Atlantic was calm, giving him no fits. He had nearly disappeared from sight when the barely audible helicopter swooped down to hover. Dave returned to the ridge to watch Scott, who appeared to be engaged in some sort of meditation. He sat cross-legged, straight-backed at the waters edge. After about twenty minutes, he rose reaching his hands to the sky and elongating his spine before dropping to do pushups. Dave winced at the thought of extra effort. Living outside was taxing enough on your system. Scott returned to his fire as Dave left him. Returning to camp, he slid into the hammock to nap. *Was it Kate in my dream yesterday?* he wondered as his eyes gave in to the weight of his fatigue.

Chapter 24

I love you like salt.

"Dominic, what is this number?" Duncan asked. "The text came from it." The nervous energy in his voice barely had time to manifest.

"That's Marco," Dominic interrupted before Duncan could read off the final digits. "You got a text from him?"

"That's from Kate," Duncan replied hurriedly. "She needs me. *I love you like salt* means she needs me. It was a code we used when she was out at parties and couldn't drive or didn't feel safe."

"That's from Marco's phone. That's a fact. She must be still at Miguel's. Marco is at the house and has barely left the place since she went quiet," Dominic said.

"I knew I should have stayed in Vero," Duncan lamented.

Derek walked into the kitchen finding Duncan hunched over the counter staring down into his phone. Something was very wrong with him, his face ashen with regret and fear. He placed his hand on Duncan's shoulder, intending comfort. Duncan stiffened, startled by even the gentlest of gestures.

"I will call Pete and have him head out there now,"

Dominic's voice rose from the phone. "He is on stand-by and can be out there quickly. I will also call Dave on the satellite phone and let him know to be ready for a pick-up. Everything is going to be OK."

"What's going on?" Derek asked.

"There's a problem with Kate. She needs help," Dominic answered for Duncan. "The three of you need to go back to Vero Beach ASAP."

Derek spun on his heels, quickly returning to his room to prepare while Duncan ended the call. He was lost in worry and guilt for not warning Kate about Miguel's true nature. "How have things between them come to this?" he wondered aloud. "What is going on inside that house?"

The satellite phone blinked as Dave's coffee bubbled on the camp stove. Looking around cautiously out of habit, he answered.

"Yeah," he said into the phone.

"Hey, Dave, this is Dominic. Get ready to be extracted in a few hours. By the time Pete gets out there and fires up the helicopter we should be offshore about noon. He's already over water on the way in the Gulfstream. You are going back to Vero Beach with Duncan and Derek. It's about Kate."

"What about Kate?" Dave asked impatiently.

"She's been MIA for about a week. Duncan got a message from her this morning. She needs help. They'll fill in the details on the flight," Dominic instructed. "You might be gone from the island for a while."

"OK, I will be ready for the boat," Dave replied. His thumb pressed the End button as his head was already making a list of things he needed to pack away.

Tripping over tree roots he had gracefully been avoiding, his motor skills weren't catching up with his haste. He grabbed at his things before coming to the realization he had hours to wait. Settling down and getting control of himself, he took a breath. *I'll pack up most of the stuff then watch Scott*, he thought. *Then when I see the helicopter, I can head down to the beach. I can see far enough from up there.* It occurred to him that his thoughts seemed vocalized; that his speeches might be thoughts. There was no one to listen. He felt like he was losing it.

Scott was in the tidal pool with his spear, stalking corralled fish. The fire he built was so small it could only be for him. He was learning to conserve the energy nature provided him. Dave watched as Scott threw the spear, desperately missing and growing more impatient with each throw. The scene was further eroding his antipathy for Scott. The guy was trying to survive as best he could. Any energy he had left was no longer wasted on rancid tantrums. His efforts went towards water, food and what appeared to be meditation, maybe prayer. From Dave's vantage point, meditation and prayer looked the same. Maybe he was petitioning God for deliverance or seeking within himself answers to make sense of his captivity. He could be praying for an easy death. It was moving to watch as the picture of Scott ended his quiet devotions in a better, calmer mood than he began.

Dave quietly eased away from the edge to make the descent to the camp. He had come to realize that the freedom he had on his side wasn't unnoticed. Too much smashing about in the jungle would send up a storm of winged protestors. Small environmental changes observed repeatedly grew into theories. He hoped Scott wasn't becoming suspicious or at least curious about what existed past the wall of rock separating him from the North.

Finally, the distant sound of the helicopter shook Dave from a sleep he was trying to resist. Rubbing the fatigue from his eyes, he finished closing up the containers to wait for Derek. As the little boat neared, he felt his insides twist.

Derek didn't bother with a line. He gestured for Dave to jump as he navigated an artful turn in the shallow trough behind a breaking wave. Dave fell into the boat half-soaked as Derek throttled the motor, skipping over the waves out to the relative calm of deeper water.

"What's going on?" Dave asked.

"Kate is in trouble. Something happened with Miguel. She's been at his house all week. Then this morning, she sent Duncan a message from Marco's phone," Derek replied.

"Marco's phone? Why?" Dave asked.

"Her phone has been dead for about a week. Duncan has been getting more and more antsy about it every day. Then, the message. *I love you like salt.*

"I love you like salt? What does that mean?" Dave asked.

"It's a code she used to use when she was younger and needed him. You know, like when you're drunk at a party and need Dad or someone to pick you up," Derek replied. "Hopefully, Marco didn't notice."

As they approached the helicopter, Derek coached Dave through the process of climbing the rope ladder and securing the boat. It seemed easier than it became as the ladder swung in and out of reach until Dave was able to get a grasp. As he crawled into the cabin, the line tucked into his belt tugged him back towards the water. He anchored himself looking down at Derek, who made the pass from boat to ladder seem effortless. They both hauled hand-over-hand as the boat rose up and in.

Pete banked the helicopter towards Eleuthera, giving the throttle a full twist. Dave eased back to watch the waves speed by as his mind drifted to Kate. The abrupt change in lifestyle from hammock to leather seats alerted his senses to comforts he had missed. Derek was quietly pensive, unwilling to speculate on what they would find in Vero Beach. Fortunately the flight went by before they could fill the time with talk. As they came into land, the Jeep sat ready to move with Gilberto at the wheel. Duncan paced, his mind three hundred miles away.

Dave took Duncan's forearm in his hand looking the worried man in the eye, "It's going to be alright," he said calmly. "She is going to be OK." Duncan looked as if he was about to break, grabbing at Dave for balance and solace.

Landing in Vero Beach, Pete taxied directly to the hangar stopping short of the door. It was three o'clock. It had been decided they would wait for dark unless Dominic saw something from the data marking urgency. Miguel was at the farm. He had been leaving Marco overnight with Kate every day for a week. The history of movement showed Miguel had left his house soon after Kate's phone went dark. At first, it was nothing noteworthy, phones died but Kate had the means to replace hers. Then the text, leading to the assumption she was still there.

The three sat around the table at the beach house planning. Dave found a steel fence post pounder in the garage, filling the void with sand for added mass, he duct taped the open end. He presented it to Derek and Duncan as a battering ram capable of breaching Miguel's door. Derek heaved it up confidently.

"I'll smash the back door. You go in and get her. You are better with the gun than I am in case someone confronts us," Derek directed. "Dominic will let us know where Marco is, but you never know. I would just shoot anything that doesn't look like Kate."

"We are going to do this quick and efficiently," Dave

announced. "I will try to take out Marco if I have to, but a gunshot in that house is going to be heard even with the suppressor. Dominic, what's the cop situation around there this week?"

"Just Marco. There's a Sheriff's Deputy who lives a block over but he works at night. According to the log, he should be working today. That part of the island is the City of Vero. The county guys don't do regular patrols there," Dominic announced through the speaker.

"Anything else you can think of?" Derek asked.

"I was thinking if Duncan drops you off a few doors down and gives you time to get in the backyard, then he can pull up in front of the house. It wouldn't be a bad thing if that gets Marco's attention as you go in the back door. Did you guys get the home layout I sent?"

"We did," Dave replied. "We'll find her if she's in there." He stiffened realizing what he had said. "She's there," his eyes on Duncan as he corrected himself as confidently as he could.

As they approached, Duncan paused on the road. Derek and Dave slipped out and onto the sidewalk watching the SUV make the turn on the next block. The house was quiet. They slipped into the foliage between Miguel's house and the neighbor's. The light above the back door leading to the kitchen burned brightly. Dave and Derek melted into the shadows, waiting for Dominic to give the signal.

Marco should be inside. The first text signaled.

Duncan is rounding the corner. I'll tell you when to go.

Tension turned to mission focus. They were ready. "I smash, you go in gun up," Derek reminded Dave who stared steel-eyed at the back door.

Ok, go.

Derek hoisted up the makeshift battering ram, winding it up as he bore down on its target. The inertia of the mass crushed the door frame inward as Derek brought its wrath next to the doorknob. The door flew open as Derek stepped aside, giving way to Dave, gun drawn, looking for a target. The kitchen opened to the living room, where Marco was nowhere to be found. *The bathroom?* Dave reasoned. He glanced at an open door to the bathroom and saw nothing.

He moved cautiously through the house, pushing open doors and greeting the empty rooms with the muzzle of his gun. The handle of the master bedroom resisted. With a desperate kick the door flew open. There she was cowering in the corner, wide-eyed, holding a lamp like a club. "Kate, come with me," he said to her. She hesitated. "Come on, Duncan sent us. He is outside. You are safe." Her defeated appearance turned hopeful as she stood. Dave took her hand leading her out of the room towards the front door. He turned to Derek, who maintained watch at the back door.

A broad smile on Derek's face grew as he took a step towards Dave and Kate when a shot shattered the night. Derek's knees buckled under him, his body thrown limply against the floor. Dave ran to him as another shot came, burning across his shoulder. In the broken door, Marco stood considering how he would end both of them as Dave fell headlong into him. Marco's gun dropped to the ground as the neighborhood came to life. Dave struggled to pin down Marco throwing errant punches. He felt the battering ram against his leg as Marco was wriggling out from under him towards the fallen gun. As Marco scuttled across the patio, the battering ram rose above and hurled downward coming to a sudden stop as it crushed Marco's skull. Dave followed with another and another. His rage focused and automatic until he dropped the ram on Marco's lifeless back.

"No, no, no, Derek," he cried. Dave strained to lift his friend as he made a desperate run for the front door.

Kate stood holding open the rear door of the SUV, shocked by the brutality of her rescue as Dave fell in with Derek. "Go to the hospital!" he screamed at Duncan, who tore down the road.

"No," Derek whispered. "It's OK. It's OK. Take me home."

"No, you need a doctor now," Dave sobbed.

"It's OK, I am OK. I'm ready…"

"Your kids need you; what about Alyssa?"

"They'll be OK. They'll be OK," he repeated softly. "I know they'll be OK…"

Dave's head fell to Derek's motionless chest, listening desperately for life, "No, this can't happen," he whimpered.

Duncan punched in 1210 at the gate; the wheels turned solemnly up the cobbles.

Chapter 25

Baby, You have haunted my dreams since the first moment I saw you. We were torn apart by circumstance. Although, I left my heart in Colorado for you. I could never replace you as much as I halfheartedly tried. I thought it was the right thing to do. The normal thing. To accept the circumstances and go on. Try to forget you and give in. You know I am not much for giving in or giving up. I lived many years waiting to meet you, to have the chance to love you. I believe there will be a time when we reunite. I don't know when or how. What we had together was too real and beautiful to ignore and regret. I can't imagine not being with you at least one more time. I know it was difficult to say goodbye when I had to leave. I know your intentions were true to try to replace me. To fill the space I left you in. I hope you did. I hope you are happy. I hope you have found love again. I hope you were able to forget me and move on. I know you loved me as I love you. As you read this, fate has taken me somewhere. Something I can't explain compelled me to write this. Whatever happened, I don't know, but a piece of my soul is still alive and in love with you. Forever. If there is *a heaven, I'll be there waiting. Maybe that is where we were meant to be together all along. I love you, Derek*

Alyssa looked up at Paul through the tears. She felt numb. Derek's musky scent, still embedded in their sheets, tried to comfort her as she sobbed into her pillow when Paul called her. He had written the letter a year earlier, weeks after their separation. She had tried to replace him. She cursed him for leaving and moving to Florida, although she knew why he had to go. Nothing worked to erase him from her heart. When she had finally gotten to a point she could just go through the motions of life, there he was. He came back for her. What if she *had* moved on? He was standing there outside her work, fearless of having been replaced. That was Derek. He was irreplaceable. Distance meant nothing to him, stubbornly he carried the weight of it for the both of them. A weight too heavy for her, weakening her with ephemeral fits of desperation as she projected Derek into other men. She had everything she needed in life except for him. As much as she tried, she could never fully understand what love had meant to Derek. But he refused to give up on her. It was never in him to deny the undeniable in a superficial hope to feel at ease.

"We will put him where he can be close to you," Paul reassured her quietly.

"Thank you for being here; as you know, I am Chief Melissa Schmidt, Vero Beach Police Department. I will not be taking questions. As you know, we lost Officer Marco Sandoval while he was responding to a breaking and entering call last night. Officer Sandoval was a decorated professional dedicated to the City of Vero Beach. He will be missed. At this time, we ask that you keep his family in your prayers as we work through this case. If anyone saw anything, please call our 800 number. We have some strong leads we are working, and in due time, we believe we will bring this murderer to justice."

"Chief," a reporter spoke up, "what about Officer Scott Smith? Have you gotten anywhere with his disappearance?"

The Chief turned away from the reporters, ignoring their questions. The Public Information Officer stepped in to reiterate what the Chief had said to placate a persistent press.

Dave and Duncan pulled into the hangar ahead of Kate, Gilberto, and Ignacio. The makeshift bier bearing Derek's shrouded body pressed heavily into their shoulders as the men carried their friend to the plane. He would rest in Colorado on the last mountain his feet had stood. It was the practical thing to do. Practical and honorable for a friend who loved the outdoors. When his daughters were older, they would disclose the location where they could visit him, sit and talk. They would be met there by his friends. Friends they knew nothing about until they learned to ask. They would discover how people loved him as a friend and a comrade as strong as any familial essence of love.

Just as he had written to Alyssa, he had written to his daughters. The letters were in the nightstand next to his bed, left for someone to find. It was eerie to think Derek knew to prepare for the eventuality. He told them that he loved them. He spoke as if he was not gone but sidestepped into another realm, standing next to them as they continued on through their lives. He cried for their loss in the letter and asked them to be brave. To take care of their mother who he had loved. They were the gift of that love. He wished for them to know love for themselves; love for their own husbands and children. To recognize the blessings life would give them and to learn from its lessons. Most of all, he asked them to see life as it is with their own eyes and the conviction of their own thoughts and dreams.

They tried to talk during the flight to lighten the burden. How would Alyssa take to them or as they feared, turn against and blame them? They were fully embroiled in a clandestine war with casualties. They had become a gang embattled against another. Their enemy had the power of perceived legitimacy behind them. Their side had intelligence and vast sums of disposable cash. They had justice and the moral high ground, but they could never control the public narrative. The perception of legitimate power stood behind an impenetrable wall of distracting chaos and noise. Rogue justice would be seen as illegitimate no matter how righteous; the government held a monopoly on justice as much in the minds of its followers as its critics. Regardless of Miguel's culpability, he and his troops were sanctified in perceived legitimacy against the acts of vigilantes.

As the plane circled for the approach, the mountainside where he would be laid to rest came into view. Dave thought about Paul and Alyssa waiting up there for them. He was on the ground in Colorado, again. The place he loved and wished to return to was still finding ways to give him pain and would harbor that pain every time he returned. The plane taxied to the hangar where Dominic solemnly waited with two rented SUVs. Dave dreaded seeing Alyssa. His aching shoulder was nothing compared to how he envisioned their meeting. His chest tightened inch by inch as they neared the ranch. What could he say? He held his best friend, watching him die and could do nothing. Now, he was delivering what was left of him to the woman who loved him. He felt responsible.

The gate opened as they approached. A few more anxious minutes before they arrived in front of her. Alyssa came into view next to Paul as they cleared the small hill near the cabins. Dave couldn't speak. His eyes spoke for him as he stepped out and approached her. Trembling, he hesitated, expecting a barrage of anger. He was broken, his knees failing him. He dropped in front of her offering the back of his head for vengeance. Knelt there, he sobbed as she stood over him, her fingers digging into the back of his neck as she watched this man repent for a sin he hadn't committed.

"I am so sorry," he sobbed.

The rest couldn't bear to watch as Dave fell apart. They broke off into small groups to console each other. Mark, Duncan, Dominic and Paul carried Derek to the side of the grave as Kate knelt down next to Dave helping him stand.

His eyes met Alyssa's as she quietly reached to embrace him, holding his head against her shoulder. They wept together for her lost love. The man she had found was gone. All that remained of him were these people she didn't know.

Dave regained himself as best he could as they walked to the grave. He stepped down into the hole to comfort his friend for the last time, gently laying him into his final bed. Handful by handful, he slowly covered the body before his brother-in-law Mark reached down to pull him out. They each took turns placing shovel-fulls as the hole rose up to meet the forest floor.

Duncan cleared his throat to speak as Sarah knelt by the grave transplanting a kinnikinnick shrub she had found in the nearby woods. Dave knelt by his sister. She had always been his protector. He felt drawn to her maternal strength as he had when he was a child.

"We say goodbye to our friend. How do our crushed hearts make sense of this? There is sense to it if we look hard enough. Derek lived the ideal of an endless pursuit of truth. It was the truth that brought him back here to Alyssa. She was a truth his heart could not deny. When he asked to return to

Colorado, he shared a quote with me from the French moralist Francois de la Rochefoucauld, 'Absence diminishes little passions and increases great ones, as the wind extinguishes candles and fans flames'.

"Derek moved to Florida to be near his children. They needed him nearby. He stepped away from a business that had sustained him and his family for years. The truth of it was the business had changed and had become something he could no longer pursue.

"For a time, maybe too long, he felt lost and held on to a past representing all that had seemed right in his life. The truth of the past became something he could bear no longer. He opened his eyes and his heart to us and stood in the moment, the present. He embraced the inspiration of our nascent cause tightly. A few weeks ago he and I were talking late one night. He told me that if something were to happen to him along this path, we had to carry on because, as he said, 'the path is just; it is not mine to determine my fate. This moment and tomorrow belongs to the will of God. I can't spend tomorrow in regret; to regret the past is to suffer and remain in it'. He said, 'carry on Duncan'." Duncan stopped to gather himself. He looked around at the faces. They were quietly reflective through the gentle respite.

"He said, 'carry on Duncan. Carry on and help as many people as you can. If I am gone and can't see it, I will rest easy knowing you and Dave and the rest are there seeking the truth and helping people. Build on what we have started and follow the path of our just cause. The world can be as beautiful as it is horrible when the right people use their power for good. Sometimes, to see beauty, you just have to turn around and look for it another way. The right way. And learn to open your eyes every morning with a smile. Who is angry at a sunrise? Nobody I want to know.'"

Duncan breathed in deeply, looking out over the heads of his friends to the east where the sun would greet them in the morning. The birds chirped as a light breeze blew through the tops of the ponderosas. The world where they said goodbye to their friend was both simple and wild. Derek had been given back to it as someday they would be.

Scott coaxed a school of fish into the pool jumping in to scoop up as many as he could. His makeshift net flexed under four decent-sized mutton snappers. Dinner would be satisfying. The austerity of hunger he had forced on himself was finally becoming less reasonable as supplies dwindled at a slower pace thanks to fish and fruit. Still not a boat in sight. He hadn't heard the helicopter in more than a week. Really, he couldn't remember when he heard it last. What did it matter? He was surviving. Apart from the possibility of a land-swallowing storm, he was content to live as he was. If a hurricane came, he would fight it, leaving his fate to God. His guilt digested, he slept soundly now until the morning birds thought he had had enough. What he had been was dead. He was no longer Scott. He wasn't quite sure who he was but he was better.

He gutted his catch near the corral, offering their entrails back to the sea before sliding skewers through what remained. Awaken, tend to the fire, eat, boil found water, collect wood, fish, eat, and stay out of the mid-day sun. The simplicity of the system kept him alive; his head was occupied and innovating. In the evening, as the sun ducked below the ridge, he thought. As his eyes grew heavy, he prayed. He had never believed in an authoritative, conventionally religious god. He bent more toward the belief in something less explainable. Something existentially dwelling outside a material imagination; too far into the mystical for simplistic imaginations. His thoughts on the matter were new to him, conjured by his circumstance rather than a will to seek knowledge. He remembered what he was and where his ambitions had taken him. It was all bullshit. He had had no ambition. He had been holding out his hands, waiting for Miguel and anyone else to make something of him. He was one of the herd desperately trying to convince himself and others he was unique. He was like a limp puppet waiting to come to life seeking animation from its master. In that world he was nothing, a specter waiting for permission to be seen. It was obvious now. Miguel had looked straight through him. He was brought to life at Miguel's convenience. For too long, he had existed as such.

The island made him tangible. If it was making him more human, it was impossible to tell. His solitude forbade all it was to be human. He was nothing more than another of the island's animals surviving to survive. In that, he was unique from them. He took up space. They survived to replicate one nest of eggs at a time, one burrow of mice until the next. He was essentially extinct, consciously awaiting the finality. Even the hope of rescue had forgotten him. For the first few weeks, it taunted his sleep only to shake him awake to the repetition of survival. What could he go back to? How would he explain where he had been? Any lie he could fabricate would open up more questions until the truth was revealed. He had repented to God. Was repentance to people necessary? Could they only find satisfaction in punishing him?

Now, he was living *truth* and was productive. In the world from where he came every expenditure of effort, time and money he gave away meant he had less of those things. The island had harshly and unapologetically forced him to live within the confines of the present. He had nothing other than what was necessary for continued life. Every effort in thought and prayer gave him more. Was that what was so comforting about his circumstance? All the convenient lies he had told to himself were ridiculous jokes on the island. They were wastes of time and effort of thought better spent in the reality of his continued survival and spiritual evolvement. He felt like he was living in the precise moment hyper-aware of what was right in front of him. The future was an illusion. There was no Scott. Maybe there never had been.

"It's time to cut off the head," Dominic said bluntly as he took a sip of Scotch someone kept refilling for him. The bite of the drink tackled him when he was new to it; now, it slipped between his lips with ease.

Dave stared at the campfire, wondering if it would draw in county authorities. There had to be someone down the valley who could smell it. He couldn't remember a time in Boulder County where the smell of smoke relaxed anyone. Too many forest fires and burned dreams fueled a collective PTSD. The fire was small and well-contained. In an instant, they could bury it in water. "It is time to cut off the head," Dave echoed.

"Let's be done with this," Dominic continued. "We can track him wherever he goes. We know who follows him. I can deal with them. Unless Miguel or one of the deputies has been forthright with the County Sheriff or Police Chief on what has been going on, there may be one or two of them who knows who we are. Vengeance is right. It's ours to take."

"I agree," Dave spoke up. "It is time to blow this thing completely open. We have enough C-4 to make a statement. The feds would have to step in. The ATF would have to step in. Explosives get press and attention. They scare the shit out of people, especially the government. Except for when they are the ones dropping them on people. Who cares about the government? Let's make it clear they are useless and deal with this now. They can come around later and clean up."

"That's a terror attack," Paul spoke up. "If they trace it to you, you will be domestic terrorists and they will win the narrative game. They will chase you to the ends of the earth, isolate you and put you in legal limbo so long the world will forget you. There is no way around that. The government doesn't peel back the onion for truth. They parade it around then toss it in the garbage hoping it dries up and stops stinking in time for the next crisis."

"Then we won't get caught," Dominic smiled. "All of my new drones are fabricated using my electronics; they self-immolate if they have to. Who is going to piece together a bunch of burned parts readily available to everyone and every hobbyist? I can tell you, nobody. The only way they could pin anything on me, or us, is dumb luck or a preconceived agenda. I don't think we qualify for agendas."

"It's time to end this," Duncan agreed. "Regardless of the risk to ourselves, we will get that son of a bitch and let Derek rest."

Dominic opened his laptop, studying it briefly. "He is with that Courtney chick at her apartment. There is one cop parked out front and another within a few miles. The map history shows Miguel's cops have been trading off circling the area. That includes passing by your house, Duncan."

"What about the farm?" Dave asked. "We can't just off Miguel and leave those people out there."

Duncan thought for a moment. "We'll take Miguel first, then deal with the farm. How many are there?"

"When we were surveilling it, at least 50 to 60. Gilberto confirmed those numbers, although those barracks could house more," Dave replied.

"I have an old but still useful man camp out in one of our

fields in West Texas. It's not being used at the moment. We'll move them there."

"What's a man camp?" Dominic asked.

"It's barracks we set up for drilling," Duncan replied. "We can house them there until we figure out who they are and what to do with them. Paul, you send some of the foundation people we hired out there."

"No problem. I'll send out the bilingual caseworkers we have so far," Paul replied.

"Ok," Duncan said as he stood up, "We'll deal with the money problems with money. The rest with appropriate force."

Chapter 26

"Why didn't you just tell me?" Kate asked, her body aching with betrayal.

Duncan shifted in his chair before answering. The question was expected. He had watched Kate through the funeral and flight back to Vero Beach. She had been quietly pensive, taking in all that happened to her, patiently waiting to demand an explanation. The initial shock transformed into a bout of anger. As naturally graceful as she was, she could fight. Although there were no marks on her, Duncan knew Miguel had been forceful. Locking her in a room made sense if you were a strategist. He had to isolate her to mull over the next move and her fate. Maybe he had hoped she would come around and align herself with him or become useful for a future plan.

"Before you went missing, we had come to a conclusion that he wouldn't harm you," Duncan replied.

"You didn't think he would hurt me?" Kate exclaimed. "How could you think that if you knew what he was capable of?"

"A man capable of great evil is also capable of caring and

affection," Duncan replied. "I wasn't sure he knew it was us. I was wrong. But we *will* take care of him."

"Why don't you go to the police?" she pled. "Isn't there anyone you can go to?"

"We cannot. It's a fair question; we have been over that too many times," Duncan replied. "We have done some things that the authorities could spin on us. Since we feel confident we can handle this situation justly, we shall."

"Well, I want to be there," Kate demanded.

"You will play a role," Duncan acquiesced.

As the conversation took a relieving pause, Dominic and Dave entered the house through the kitchen door, dropping a large duffle bag as they fell into chairs.

"That was more stressful than Mexico for sure," Dominic exclaimed. "There are cameras everywhere. Can someone remind me later how much I hate those things? We were able to find a few more of those plate readers too. Those I really hate. They are being added to the system map for later."

"Did it go as planned?" Duncan asked. "Are they in place?"

"They are," Dave answered. "We have five drones in position."

"And they are armed?" Duncan asked.

"They are. And they learn. These have GPS on board but don't need it. GPS is sort of a backup to their thinking and remembering," Dominic grinned. "They also have a tiny radar distance sensor to keep them from crashing into things. And they can see in the dark like a cat. Better than a cat. They are like flying attack cats with super sensitive whiskers." The destruction the drones could create. Each one was a disaster waiting to happen for whoever they chose. Dominic looked at Duncan, the old man's calm nature under pressure was admirable. He led them without effort, without having to assert his authority. Duncan was open blue sky above the clouds, commanding the rainstorms below.

"Three are armed with claymores; the other two are made for distraction," Dominic continued. "They are all assigned with programmed contingency plans and can be changed if we need to. As long as they follow a simple plan, which is to blow up something or distract, they will function fine. One problem is getting them to ignore or choose to ignore certain data. I haven't figured out how to code that yet. Not sure if anyone else has either. That's why we keep their thinking simple; task oriented."

"What do you mean?" Dave asked.

"Human thinking has selective attention built in. It's probably evolutionary for survival. A thinking machine has a hard time ignoring inputs or at least choosing which ones to ignore. *Choosing to ignore* is not the right phrase for it. The machine seems to have to rationalize what to ignore where a human basically says 'screw it' and moves on hoping things will work out," Dominic answered. "Even if you make certain observations less important in the programming, the algorithm seems to spend a lot of time deciding where that data falls on the value scale. It's like asking someone who is irrationally ego-invested in some idea to just drop it. So I just give these little guys simple tasks; identify a target, move towards target ASAP and detonate or annoy. They're basically suicide bombers and they only hesitate on command from us. Otherwise, it's straight to hell."

"Theoretically," Dave responded. "We haven't used one yet."

"And gentlemen," Duncan stepped in, "we do not have collateral damage. I won't tolerate it. Our targets are known combatants only. We are not the US government. We are better than that and we have no willingly invested press to whitewash our reputations when we get sloppy. Therefore, we are not and will not be sloppy." He stood to stretch before retiring to his room for the night, the look in his eyes affirmed the seriousness of his rule.

Kate sat sideways across her chair, looking as though her world was ready to shut down for the night; her eyes heavy with thought and exhaustion. Dave stood to leave, a flash of impulse to carry her up to her room and lay her in her bed crossed his mind. He felt an innocence of caring for her he hadn't felt in a long time.

"Goodnight, Dave," Kate half whispered.

He and Dominic walked out the kitchen door towards the guesthouse into a gentle ocean breeze subduing what was left of the heat of the day. Added security Duncan contracted was in position for the night. Until recently, Duncan, with all of his wealth, wasn't well-guarded. He kept his life low profile and simple. His houses were the exception. The casual observer would regard them as palaces until they entered to experience their familial warmth. Even the Eleuthera house, with is exceptional price tag, was more about the land than the structures vying for attention.

The guest house was quiet and inviting. Derek's energy remained, possessing the air within. Dave was grateful for Dominic, finding him fascinating to listen to. An energy and passion for his work continuously poured from his small frame. Where Derek liked to discuss personal relationships and observations of human nature, Dominic talked about his relationship with the machines to which he gave life. He rambled on and on about the endless possibilities of machines to improve, becoming as human as we could make them finally surpassing us to become better than anything we could imagine.

Dave nodded goodnight to Dominic and headed straight

to his room. Calming his mind before bed had become his spiritual ritual each night. Asking *why* became a tiresome exercise. No one really knew why. 'I don't know' was the only honest answer he had. "I miss you brother," he whispered into the dark. "Thank you for being with me as long as you could. We will take your revenge."

"They are right next to each other in her apartment," Dominic said looking up at Kate as she sipped her coffee. Her eyes stared over the rim of her cup at the screen. Two dots on opposite sides of what she knew was Courtney's bed.

"I can't believe that bitch has been doing this behind my back the whole time," she snarled.

"He's been doing it too," Dominic added coldly.

Kate looked at Dominic with scornful indignation. Of course, she knew Miguel had been cheating on her. Not before she was given proof, but she had a feeling. But Courtney, she was a traitor who boiled thoughts of retribution in Kate she had only fantasized about. Until now, she had never gotten this close to a desire to hurt someone.

"Ok, call her," Dominic ordered.

Kate composed herself and dialed. The dot on one side of the bedroom moved quickly to the living room as she heard Courtney's hushed voice, "Hello?"

"Hey," Kate said happily, "how are you? Sorry I disappeared. My Uncle needed me to go to Colorado with him."

"Oh hey," Courtney replied, "How was that? I miss you."

"I know, me too. What are you doing later? Coffee?" Kate asked.

"Uhh, yeah, sure. At the usual?" Courtney asked.

"See you at 10:30?"

"Um, yeah, I'll see you then," Courtney replied. "Are you OK? I mean, you sound a little, I don't know…"

"No, I am fine; I will see you later," Kate replied impatiently. She was tensing up, anxious about how to act, ready to run from the conversation as fast as she could. The end of the call collapsed her onto a kitchen stool looking at Dominic for reassurance.

"That was good," he offered. "You are going to have a tough day. As we guessed, she didn't know you were being held at Miguel's. Well, let's hope she didn't for her sake."

"There's a lot of money in this town," Dominic commented as they watched Kate enter the cafe. They positioned themselves in the parking lot behind a row of shops and restaurants which could have been the back alley of anywhere. A half a block to the east, the ocean hid behind small dunes and opulent homes.

"None of it was made here," Dave scoffed. "What you see is the outcome of productive states being spent in Florida. Although, this town used to grow citrus before. It still does further west. Grapefruits."

"People still eat those?" Dominic asked.

"I guess," Dave replied as he kept his eye on the cafe door. "There she is." Courtney arrived, hesitating in the doorway to look right and left. She seemed to relax, then continued inside.

"I have her on the screen," Dominic said. "I don't see any of our cop friends following her around. But Miguel is headed towards the airport."

"Keep an eye on him," Dave cautioned.

"Hi," Kate greeted Courtney standing up from her table to hug her as amiably as she could. They each patted the other on the back limply displaying enough friendship for anyone who may be watching.

"How are you?" Courtney asked.

"I am fine. You know that Miguel and I are split for now, right?" Kate volunteered.

"I heard. I am so sorry," Courtney replied. "Are you OK?"

"I am, I guess," Kate sighed. "I thought he and I were inseparable. I think I was expecting more. Maybe I expected too much, but I just felt like we were made for each other. Have you ever felt like that? You never talk about guys, and you're so pretty. There has to be someone."

Courtney adjusted uncomfortably in her chair focusing on the menu as she worked up the words she thought would move the conversation. Kate kept eye contact on her like a predator assessing her prey.

"I go out. You know that, dating apps. I can always go out, but the guys in this town are either poor or rich, and the rich ones are so boring. They don't do anything," she lamented. "The ones I want everyone wants. Like, you have to fuck them immediately to get any attention or some other girl will. Even then, that's no guarantee. I hate the apps. I hate the bars. Seriously, do I have to start going to church? Is that where they are?"

"That doesn't work," Kate responded placing her hand on Courtney's. The waitress arrived to take their order giving them a welcomed pause. "I tried that," Kate resumed. "The guys were all nice. They did all the nice things, but something was missing. It didn't feel right. There was something that made me feel like it was all an act, sort of weird and creepy. Then I met Miguel. He seemed real. Like a guy who would protect me from anything, You know, a sweet guy most of the time who could be a badass when he needed to be. Maybe this break we're on will be good for us."

"I know what you mean," Courtney replied. She felt a tinge of guilt from her words, as if she might have outed herself. Did Kate know? Was she being played? Miguel had warned her that Kate could be ruthlessly two-faced. In the years they had been friends, she had never seen that side of her, but she trusted Miguel. He was secretly hers now. The secret was part of the excitement of winning him away. The months taken to go from a drunken hookup to what she had with him now was worth it. He was everything she wanted.

Kate asked, "Do you have someone in mind?"

"There's one guy," Courtney lied as their order arrived. "It doesn't matter. He doesn't know I exist and no matter what I do, there's always some girl with him."

"Seriously," Kate responded, "just talk to him. What's his name?"

"Brian, I think," Courtney replied. Her lie continued to build upon itself. "I don't know much about him. I just see him around and I like him." She felt like the hole she was digging was beginning to collapse in on her with every fabricated word. "It doesn't matter. What are you going to do with Miguel?" The act of diversion gave her hope.

"I feel like I should just wait," Kate replied. "He was a real asshole the last time we were together. There is something going on with him he won't tell me about. You know how I hate that." She stared directly over her coffee cup at the traitorous friend performing her best innocence. Kate felt pity for her. Courtney likely had no idea what Miguel was capable of. How could she? She hadn't. She had been wrapped up in the story of his life, interpreting it and admiring him like a work of art on a gallery wall. The artistry of his deception was breathtakingly real. A lie believed by the liar became impenetrable to anyone who accepted it. Belief in *something* was always more settling and comfortable than doubt.

Kate released her friend from talk of men and Miguel changing the subject to anything else. Courtney was a girl inhibited by her beauty and the average means of her upbringing. She hadn't grown up poor but had always been enslaved by want. There were always guys willing to provide her with perceptions of wealth. The habitual thirst of men expressed in material homage to her beauty.

Kate's anger with Courtney was evaporating. She and Miguel complimented each other. Courtney and Miguel was better than Kate and Miguel. She could live that without regret. Her only contrition was the idealized character she had created for him. It was a grand lie she desperately believed for too long.

"They've been in there a while," Dominic observed. "I wonder what they are talking about."

"Absolutely nothing," Dave responded dryly. "Not to sound sexist, but have you ever sat in on girl talk? They are the most intuitive creatures on Earth and, to a man, most of their conversations amount to nothing. But from that nothing, between the words, they understand things about each other and us men that we will never be able to explain. Try to step out of your male-centric rationalization and listen to them someday. It will blow your mind. And put you to sleep." Dominic rolled his eyes and laughed off Dave's comment.

Finally, Kate stepped through the door ahead of Courtney. They hugged each other warmly as they set off in separate directions. Dominic checked the screen for tails picking one up behind Courtney's car. Kate was free. Within minutes, she entered the gate of Duncan's house while Courtney headed towards the airport, one patrol car in tow.

Dave leaned over to watch. "Which cop is that?"

"Not sure, this is a new one," Dominic replied. They continued to watch from the parking lot as Courtney met Miguel. Their phones displayed the takeoff speed of the chartered jet to wherever they were going. From the car, they watched the plane pass overhead climbing up through the clouds, banking west.

"How was it?" Duncan asked. "Did you do what we discussed?"

"I did. I held it together. I wanted to strangle her and cry at the same time," Kate replied tearfully. "My friend is gone if she ever was my friend." Kate sat on the couch next to her uncle resting her head on his shoulder as the tears came. "That didn't accomplished anything," she sighed.

"I know," Duncan agreed. "You wanted to confront her. To see if she would come clean on what she has done to you. For her to volunteer her betrayal."

"How could she do that?" Kate cried. "The man I thought I loved made me a prisoner for almost a week and she had to know. She was my best friend. She was sleeping with him for months and you knew. And you didn't even tell me."

"We couldn't. There was no way to tell you without putting you in a worse position," Duncan apologized. "Sometimes it is better to hold information and let fate play out. You will find this as you get older. I don't mean to be patronizing, but we tend to be too impulsive and reactive when we are younger trying to force our will on an outcome. In this case, it was best to wait and see what happened. We had no idea he would lock you in his house. If it's any consolation, I doubt Courtney knew anything about it. I am sorry, kiddo. You didn't deserve this."

"It was awful. I felt so betrayed and alone. I couldn't reach you when I needed you. I was afraid he would come back to the house and really hurt me, but he just locked me up and discarded me," Kate sobbed now. Her wounded heart hurt. The feelings she bottled up for weeks exploded into tears on Duncan's shoulder. He hadn't seen her cry like this since she was a little girl tripping over things, skinning knees. He stroked her hair and let her cry. Time and new experiences would heal and comfort her.

"That one has a nicer ass," Sergio commented as Courtney stepped into the pool.

Miguel grunted his agreement. The heat at the ranch was brutal. Finally, the sun was working its way down promising a reprieve for the night.

"I don't know how you live here. I thought Florida was bad," Miguel commented.

"This is dry heat. It's different," Sergio replied. "This is why we need to keep our route. I don't want to lose any more to some coyote with a good idea. Fuck their good ideas. The route is the route. Your fucking Immigration forced us into it. Assholes. They think they're clever using dangerous terrain as a deterrent. Fucking assholes. You know how many we lost because of that? Before we found the route?"

"A lot, I know," Miguel replied.

"Even now when they have to carry a lot of water, they can't carry as much weed or fentanyl or whatever the fuck else is selling," Sergio answered. "It's a fucking problem."

"I don't really care what you do from this side of the border; just send me more. I need to rotate this group out. They are getting too familiar with the area and I don't trust them," Miguel warned.

Sergio went silent to think as his eyes followed Courtney's body through the pool. He took a long drink from his beer setting the bottle down hard. Miguel looked at him, expecting an outburst.

"I am thinking about drugs again on your side. Not just across the border," Sergio volunteered.

"You want to go back to that?" Miguel asked, dismayed at

what he was hearing. "Are you insane? These people we have are cash generators. Fuck the drugs. You want the Border Patrol and the fucking DEA after us? Plus the Mexican Federal Police? When one of ours gets caught, or ten or twenty, the fucking gringos quietly ship them back. Drugs they start investigating and eventually trace back to us. They are too fucking lazy to do that with humans even when they try to squeal on us. Putting photos in the press of a bunch of illegals makes them look stupid. It makes all that money and hype they put into border security a political joke. Pictures of drugs and cash make them look heroic. This administration wants drug busts to brag about at the border not in the suburbs. That's why you export only. You're good at it. Once drugs make it to the suburbs, they're a security failure. I don't have to remind you of my family history with drugs. Fuck drugs. Drugs kill gringos. Drugs don't mow lawns or clean up after people. What I still have to do with that shit already irritates the fuck out of me."

"They kill gringos but so what? The fucking gringos want drugs, drugs are simple and don't talk. They don't run away," Sergio lamented.

"This was your and Raphael's idea remember? May his soul rest in peace. Are you getting too old for this?" Miguel asked. "You two were the ones who originally said, 'fuck the drugs'. If you want to quit, then quit, but don't give me this drugs bullshit. Fuck the gringos and their stupid addictions. I am not going to be the one gardening for them and selling them coke or fentanyl or meth or whatever. And, I will add, that it's a whole other level of bullshit that I have to manage with the fucking cops. They are already costing us a shit ton of protection money north and south of the border. With a full-on drug business, these motherfuckers will be protecting us and stealing from us at the same time. Then they'll bust some of us once in a while to make themselves look good. It gives them way too much power."

"Keep it down," Sergio warned gesturing at Courtney.

"She knows the deal," Miguel replied. "She is not like that other one." He took a sip of his beer, watching Courtney float in the pool. Her body was enough to kill for. "This one has many faces," he continued. "She will be more useful than that spoiled, rich bitch. And fuck that Uncle. Hopefully he will go back under his rock where he belongs now that he got her back."

"What were you going to do with her?" Sergio asked.

"Honestly, I didn't know. I just locked her up. I was so pissed off I didn't know what to do. I couldn't kill her. Too high profile. I locked her up to figure out what to do. I still don't know how they found her. Lucky guess maybe? They would have had no idea there was anything bad going on between us. I don't get it. They have me bugged somehow. They might have you bugged."

"Don't be stupid," Sergio responded angrily. "What would they want with me? You know, I think that old man will fuck off now that things have calmed. He has lost a lot. He should just go back to his rich guy life and forget. Find a fucking hobby. That's what I would do. Didn't you say he still runs his oil business?"

"He does, mostly," Miguel replied.

"Then he has other things to do besides fuck with us," Sergio stated.

"Except for that Dave idiot," Miguel warned. "He is still around. One of my guys saw him a few days ago. What if we pop that guy?"

"Let it go," Sergio said. "Just let it go and let things calm down. If he's still a problem later, we'll deal with him. For now, get the old crew moved out and let's get new workers in.

Killing this Dave guy now will just be kicking the same hornet nest. There's been enough blood in that town in the last month. The Chief of Police doesn't need the pressure and we don't need any more pressure from her. Keep her fed and keep things quiet. This operation works in the quiet under a warm blanket of denial, ignorance and money. Remember that."

"So, no drugs then," Miguel circled back.

"If you calm things down, I will rethink it," Sergio replied.

"They are in Mexico at Sergio's," Dominic announced. "Miguel, Sergio, and Courtney are in the courtyard near the pool. My drones are itching to visit."

"Let the drones rest," Duncan responded. "There will be a time for them."

"What are you guys watching?" Kate asked, stepping up behind Dave; her hand lay upon his shoulder for balance sending shivers up his spine. He felt a tension well up he had missed. It was pleasantly distracting as he feigned focus.

"That is Miguel and Sergio," Dominic hesitated, "and Courtney." He winced, saying the name, but there she was on the screen, the third dot. There was no more holding back information from Kate. Duncan had given the order. She was to be in on everything. Trying to protect her feelings had caused everyone more harm than good. Kate was tougher than they thought, performing well when she had to. Now, she was part of them, fully invested.

"When that bitch comes back here, she is not going to enjoy our next meeting," Kate smirked as she turned to go to her room.

"What do you mean?" Dave asked.

"My Uncle spoke with Paul. He came up with a nice plan

to lure in Miguel." As she scaled the stairs, she held a flirtatious smile, her eyes locked on Dave's.

When she was gone, Dave looked at Dominic, wondering what the plan could be. Kate teasing them with Paul's plan revealed a new twist in the gang's dynamics.

Chapter 27

I *so grateful you are m friend*
I am on the way, Courtney replied.
Thank u, u r best, Kate texted back. *I m sooo drunk*

Kate glanced back at Paul with a devious curl to her smile. Dominic remained focused on the screen, waiting.

"She should be exiting any minute," Paul said quietly into his phone.

"Got it," Dave whispered. The insects were suspiciously absent from the foliage surrounding Courtney's apartment building. He had doused himself with repellant well enough to stay in the bush for hours. He felt like a jungle warfare experiment radiating a toxic forcefield as he leaned back against a tree. The pistol and suppressor jabbed into his side. Unholstering the gun, he laid it across his lap in a slow, methodical motion. By the time someone ran the security footage looking for clues, he would be gone or Dominic would have done his magic.

Dominic tapped Paul's shoulder pointing to the dot moving inside the apartment. One dot remained in the bedroom. Courtney's dot briefly hovered near the bed before making its way to the door. As she exited, Dave watched. She didn't seem hurried for someone called to rescue a drunk friend from lurking bar males and a potential drunk driving arrest. He would wait for the cue.

Kate stepped away from the bar to use the restroom as a pair of men sat down next to her. She left her phone upside down in her place, a signal she would be back. Giving them a flirtatious glance over her shoulder, she rounded the corner.

As Courtney turned onto the bridge leading to the island, Dominic changed screens on the laptop keying in a code that would unleash hell in Vero Beach. Five drones snapped to attention inside their hangars as the lids popped open. Three drones targeting police headquarters followed their preprogrammed flight plan landing on the roof of a mini storage nearby to await their next order while the other two hunted.

"Three are on point. The others are closing in on their targets," Dominic said to Paul as Kate sat back down in her chair. The two men looked at her as though their acknowledgment expected her to speak to them. She smiled politely, giving a sign to the bartender for the check.

"Can I buy you a drink?" the man closest to her asked.

"Sure," she replied. She redirected the bartender as the man engaged her in small-talk.

"What do we have for Miguel's security?" Paul asked Dominic, keeping his eyes on Kate.

"They are patrolling around the general area of the apartment. See?" Dominic answered, pointing to the red dots on the screen. "The drones for these two are sitting on the roof of this building nearby waiting. Send Kate the text. Courtney is getting close."

Paul picked up his phone; within seconds, Kate's phone vibrated. She stood up and walked out the front door, leaving her drink. Paul followed. As Kate sat down on a bench near the bar, Paul worked his way down the street, finding a location where he could loiter and observe. As Courtney's car turned down the street, Kate stood, stumbling towards it.

"I love you. You are the best," she stammered.

"Just get in," Courtney said through the window. "You're not going to puke, are you?"

"No, maybe, no," Kate mumbled. "Just take me home."

"That's done," Paul said as he sat down next to Dominic. The two men at the bar were beginning to realize that the drink and her tab was all that was left of Kate as she leaned her head against the passenger side window taking in the cool of the glass. Courtney pulled into Kate's condo complex, keying the gate code.

"Take me up then you go or stay or whatever," Kate drooled in a half-whisper.

Courtney said nothing. Visibly irritated, she thought of nothing but dropping Kate in bed and returning to Miguel. Kate fumbled with her keys adding to Courtney's impatience.

"How did you get so drunk?" Courtney asked accusingly.

The question went unanswered as she opened the door, dropping her purse and keys on the floor in the darkened apartment. Courtney followed Kate towards the bedroom, stopping in horror as she heard the door close behind her. She turned to see a Latin man holding a gun, making a shushing gesture. Her knees gave out from a kick from behind as a towel covered her mouth before she could scream. Death and rape flew through her mind as she stared down the dark end of the barrel. She was shoved to the floor by the attacker at her back who quickly gagged her methodically securing her hands with zip ties. Courtney kicked wildly, screaming through the gag and writhing about until her legs too were secured. The Latin man looked down at her with pity as he dragged her towards the couch, laying her down gently. Courtney convulsed in fear as he pulled a black hood over her head. She heard his pensive footsteps moving towards Kate's room.

"I don't like this," Gilberto whispered to Kate as he handed her Courtney's phone.

"Me either," Kate replied.

"Ok, Dave. Watch for Miguel coming out. It should be in a few minutes. If you have to take him there, do it. It's better that he gets in his car. Follow him from a safe distance. You know where he was going. We'll take care of the cops from here," Paul said quietly.

Dave said nothing as he ended the call. The bedroom light came on in Courtney's apartment. He watched as Miguel's silhouette paced back and forth in front of the window, gesturing wildly. The door to Courtney's apartment flew open as Miguel bound down the stairs towards his Land Rover. Dave remained in his hide as the SUV tore out of the parking lot.

"He's on the way," Dominic whispered to Paul. "Dave is a few minutes behind him."

"His cops?" Paul asked.

"They are both turning around and picking up speed towards the island. Time to unleash."

As two squad cars barreled through lights towards the bridge, drones assigned to them fell in pace behind. Three drones on the mini storage dove over the roof edge towards the police station, dropping down into the parking lot amongst a row of patrol cars. Dominic checked the map for any cell phones in the lot before sending the signal. The drones obediently set their payloads between the cars before running for the cover of their hangars. Dominic looked up at Paul grinning with the expectation of disaster.

"Kaboom," he smirked.

It was enough to shatter windows and blow out tires near the detonation. Two claymores upended the lot. As occupants of the station peaked out guns drawn, the third claymore detonated, sending them diving for cover. Dominic winced at the thought of hurting someone. He prayed the laptop screen told the truth.

The two patrol cars raced towards the island; their drones moved into position directly overhead, flying in formation only feet above. As they crested the arch of the bridge, the drones shifted forward in front of the windshields. The officers swerved to dodge as the drones followed their lead. The infuriating persistence of the drones kept them attached to the cars like gnats. As the cars cleared the bridge, they both accelerated in an attempt to shake them off. In response, each drone attacked with a burst of ten thousand lumen strobe lights into the eyes of the officers who swerved blindly. One patrol car caught the curb, sending it airborne into a row of trees. The other skidded sideways until the tires caught rolling violently over and over until coming to rest upside down on the road. Its engine struggled and coughed to turn over a few last rotations, finally giving up. Panicked bystanders scrambled around the cars making 911 calls to an already overwhelmed dispatcher. So far, the plan was working.

Miguel continued to call his backup as he closed in on Kate's apartment. Skidding to a stop in the parking lot next to Courtney's car, he looked again at the text.

I am crazy drunk and I'm going to kill this bitch. If you want her, come to my house and get her. BTW we are getting back together. XOXO, Kate.

Miguel drew his gun and raced quickly towards the stairs. He paused to text his security detail one last time, his foot ready on the first step.

"Ok, he is there," Paul yelled into the phone. "Bottom of the stairs. Dave should be there in one minute. He's headed up, he's headed up."

"Ok," Kate replied.

Paul looked uncharacteristically anxious. Dominic was in a haze, calmly packing up the laptop.

"No other cops on the way. They are busy. The city is under a terrorist attack. You should have seen the text I sent the Chief of Police. I wonder if she'll actually stop to think, 'Why would terrorists give a shit about Vero Beach?'," Dominic laughed.

"This is the point where I am getting a little nervous," Paul confided.

Dave parked along the street. He had shed his camouflage down to pants and a black tee shirt. His face still bore the smears of what was left of green and black paint. He quickly surveilled the area before stepping out with his gun tucked in his pants. There was no doubt there would be enough security camera evidence to identify and convict him of a federal firearms violation. In his left hand, he held an extendable baton.

"Open the fucking door, Kate," Miguel commanded.

NO! Kate replied stubbornly through a text message from Courtney's phone.

"I am going to kick this fucking door in!"

Miguel waited for a text. Kate was silent. He heard the door unlock. He hesitated waiting for the door to open; his phone received another text.

Come in

Miguel slowly pushed open the door. Following the shadow of his drawn pistol, he stepped over the threshold.

"Where the fuck are you?" he asked angrily into the blackened room. He flicked the light switch up and down. Frustrated, he inched forward aiming his gun deeper into the dark. Courtney's muffled screams for him through the gag drew his attention to continue forward.

Dave slipped in behind. Coming down on Miguel with all of his strength, he slammed the baton into side of his neck. The immediate shock to Miguel's nervous system involuntarily buckled his knees, collapsing him to the floor. Dave dove on top, pulling Miguel's arms back as he struggled to right himself. The force of Miguel's rage threw Dave off as he crawled desperately for his fallen gun. As he reached for the pistol, a foot slammed down on top of his hand, crushing it into the floor. He reflexively grabbed at his hand, looking up at Kate as Dave and Gilberto wrestled him back into submission. Miguel continued to fight with everything he had until Gilberto choked him to the edge of death. Kate pulled Dave outside by the hand closing the door behind her. She led him along the corridor, expecting to be confronted by curious neighbors. The complex was quiet.

She breathed heavily as the adrenaline eased. She looked up at Dave. Stepping into him, she grasped him by the waste to pull him close, her head rested gently against his shoulder. He could feel her tender lips searching his neck as he held her. He held her there against him as she trembled away the intensity of what they had done. Without thought, he reached to cradle her chin bringing her lips to his. He felt his heart race as she responded.

"He's in there," Dominic said as Paul drove into the

complex. Paul looked up as Dave followed Kate towards her condo.

"Looks clear," Paul said.

Miguel was hogtied and gagged on the floor at Courtney's feet as Dave and Kate entered.

"Tudo bem?" Dave asked.

"Everything is good," Gilberto replied in English. "Eles estão se comportando."

Kate looked inquisitively at Dave. "They are behaving," he translated. Her eyes remained on him as he stepped towards Miguel to remove the zip ties connecting his hands to his feet. Dave yanked him up into a sitting position as Paul stepped through the door followed by Dominic. Miguel stared angrily at Dave as if he were to be rescued soon. He would punish Dave himself.

Dominic sat down next to Miguel pointing to the laptop. "Your buddies are sort of splattered all over the road," Dominic laughed at Miguel. "You really need better cops to corrupt." Miguel glared coldly at Dominic, who reached over and patted him on the head. Courtney remained quiet, unmoving under her hood.

"What time is it?" Paul asked.

"It's 10:19," Dominic replied.

"Let's get these two to their next appointment," Paul commanded. "Got anything on the screen, Dominic?"

"Looks good, let's go," he replied.

The four men prodded Miguel and Courtney towards the Bronco parked on the street while Kate waited in a shadow of the parking garage for Paul and Dominic to drive her to her car. They would reunite at Duncan's house.

. . .

The Vero Beach waterfront was quiet as the Sikorsky S76 took off the next morning heading east out over the Atlantic. Pete flew low over the water before gaining a safer altitude to engage the autopilot. In about two hours, North Eleuthera passed underneath as they descended towards the island compound where Duncan waited. Pete reached over to awaken Gilberto, fast asleep in the copilot seat.

As the rotors came to a stop, Duncan opened the door, reaching up to give Kate a hand. Dave pushed Miguel towards the door. Paul and Dominic led Courtney out the other side whisking her away to the cabin formerly occupied by Scott. Miguel stood in front of Duncan, his eyes full of hate. He lurched towards Duncan with everything he had as Dave caught him by the zip ties binding his hands. After he had enough of Miguel's fruitless intimidations, Dave kicked the back of Miguel's knees buckling him to the ground. He defiantly tried to stand, only to be slammed back down at Duncan's feet. Dave yanked the gag off of Miguel's mouth.

"I am going to kill you old man," Miguel hissed.

Duncan stared down at Miguel. He was defeated in everything but his arrogance. Dave bumped the baton against the back of Miguel's head hard enough to remind him of his situation. Duncan slowly held up his hand to Dave.

"Miguel, you will be given a chance to work things out for yourself for as long as you can survive," Duncan said coldly.

"What the fuck is that supposed to mean?" Miguel asked.

"It means you will have only yourself and a partner for as long as you cooperate," Duncan explained. "Your little empire is going to have a staffing problem soon." Duncan looked at his watch. "Right now, your farm is being liberated, and your...employees? They are being loaded onto buses headed west. You should thank God that we didn't leave you to them."

"You can't do that! You are not the law!" Miguel screamed.

Duncan turned away to open a large wooden case. He withdrew an ornate curved-bladed sword pressing the tip against Miguel's throat. "I may not be the law you have come to know, but right now, I am the hand of justice," Miguel's eyes widened as Duncan moved the cold steel to the shoulder. Miguel's arrogance faded. Fear overtook him. Dave watched nervously, expecting a sudden burst of violence as Duncan slowly caressed the side of Miguel's neck with the steel. The blade moved up under Miguel's chin, lifting his contemptible face to meet Duncan. "I could care less if you took another breath," Duncan hissed. Miguel spit at Duncan defiantly. The sword came up above Duncan's head to strike; Dave recoiled. As the blade came down, it stopped inches from Miguel's head. In an instant, Miguel's head snapped back as Duncan's foot caught him in the chin, sending blood spurting from his mouth.

Dave and Dominic dragged Miguel to another cabin where they threw him to the concrete floor. Dave reached into his pocket; drawing out a pair of snub-nosed wire cutters, he dropped them next to Miguel's head.

"You can use these to free yourself. You will receive food through the hatch. Yelling is a waste of your time. We can't hear you, and we don't care," Dave instructed.

"Enjoy your stay," Dominic jeered.

Inside the other cabin, Courtney sobbed on the couch, still bound with zip ties. She looked up, hearing someone enter. "What are you going to do to me?" Courtney cried. Kate pinned Courtney to the floor, snipping the zip ties. The sound of the deadbolt locking was the only response she received as she pulled off her hood.

Chapter 28

Scott could barely hear the helicopter coming from the northeast side of the island. The ridge line masked the perception of its path. With shocking aggression, it careened over the trees, kicking up sand as it dropped low over the water one hundred yards offshore. The side door opened revealing a seated man wearing a black hood over his head. Scott winced at the memory of his first moments on the island.

"Ok, here we are," Dominic yelled over the engine. "I hope you can swim." As he cut the zip ties binding his hands, Dominic planted a firm kick between the shoulders, sending him face-first into the water. Scott watched as the man wrestled desperately with the hood as the helicopter moved towards the beach. A large case was pushed out. Then, as quickly as it arrived, the helicopter vanished. Scott sat back in the shade and watched. A passing thought settled within him; if the man drowned, he would have whatever was in the case to himself.

"I can't believe how much I hate you now," Kate yelled.

"Fuck you," Courtney spit. "You can't keep me here like this. This is illegal. It's kidnapping." A few desperate tears ran down Courtney's face as her eyes pierced Kate. "Why? Why are you so evil?"

"Me?" Kate replied. "You were sleeping with Miguel and acting like my friend. You were fucking a human trafficker and you knew it! And you think I'm evil?"

"You were fucking him too," Courtney countered. Kate turned away, stepping through the door as Courtney screamed for help to anyone who might hear. Kate turned for another look, slamming the door shut. Duncan was coming up the trail towards the cabin as she bolted the door.

"Any contrition?" he asked.

"None," Kate replied. "I still feel awful about this. I hate her but I feel bad for what we are doing to her."

"I am not sure we should have brought her here," Duncan sighed. "It was a lapse in judgment. Paul has a suggestion, but it's somewhat risky." Kate looked at Duncan contritely. "He thinks we should drop her off on an inhabited island. A place with residents who could help her. She will tell them her tale, and it will take some time for her to get back to the US. By then, things should calm down, and maybe she'll just decide to move on. He also suggests we give her a lot of cash and a kilo of cocaine. We will hide it in a suitcase we send with her."

"Where are we going to get a kilo of cocaine?" Kate asked.

"Paul has one. He brought it with him," Duncan answered. Kate stared at Duncan in disbelief. "I asked the obvious question. Paul said, 'you never know when you need a kilo of cocaine'. I was stunned. I had no idea he was like that."

"Like what?" Kate asked.

"Like a man who knows where to get cocaine," Duncan replied. "He told me he doesn't touch the stuff, but it is like money when money doesn't hold its value. 'More popular and better than gold,' he said."

Kate was silent, thinking about the people she was involved with. She had no idea her Uncle had such villainous friends; a conniving lawyer with drugs, a weird, skinny computer hacker who blew up things and Dave. What was Dave? She was drawn to him, but she couldn't explain why. He was at least ten years older than her. They hadn't spoken much or had much time together. She didn't know him at all, but she was drawn. There was something about him from the first moment she saw him at the Post Office. It was irrational, but she felt like he was a safe haven in the midst of the danger surrounding him. Kate looked up as Paul walked proudly up the path. She stepped back behind Duncan as he neared, impulsed to distance herself. In his hand, he carried a small travel suitcase.

"Here you go," Paul announced triumphantly. "The answer to the problem." He opened the case to reveal women's clothing. Pulling them to the side, he lifted a false interior panel with a taped-up package and five stacks of twenty-dollar bills hidden inside.

"Is that a kilo?" Kate asked.

"Quarter of a kilo," Paul smiled, "I am keeping the rest for emergencies. This will be enough to make our point. When the islanders find her, they'll take her to the authorities along with the suitcase. She can then explain how she has all this cash and cocaine while she's trying to explain a tall tale of abduction and torture by her best friend."

"We didn't torture her," Kate replied tersely.

"Not yet," Paul grinned. "It doesn't matter. If she felt tortured, she was tortured. Without this, they will believe whatever she says. This just adds to the mystery. And in my opinion, cops are lazy. I am guessing that goes for Bahamian cops too. They will take an easy, seemingly obvious bust over an investigation any day. It makes them look like heroes. Smart, efficient heroes. Besides, Courtney is a beautiful, young woman, it will give them an excuse to keep her around for lots of questioning."

Kate was uneasy. She felt her hatred thaw to sympathy for what Courtney was going to experience. She imagined her screaming to be believed as the Bahamian police ran her through the process of whatever it was they did to drug smugglers.

"I thought it out," Paul continued. "We'll use the boat and drop her off on at Sandy Point on Abaco. It's a haul, but the fast boat can get there and back. Dominic and Gilberto can take her."

Duncan nodded slowly in agreement as Kate stared at the cabin. She was reluctant to put Courtney through any more, but what was the alternative? Kate was involved in more than she expected. The initial rush of excitement had dulled giving her conscience space to take a small step forward. These men had been fighting a clandestine war around her, keeping it from her. She should be part of it but there was something about the situation hesitating her full commitment.

Dave watched Miguel flail around in the breaking waves. The case of provisions threatened to be dragged away as waves bounced against it. Getting his footing, Miguel stood in waste deep water staring out to sea in futile hope. Dave looked down the beach for Scott who was suspiciously absent. Before the helicopter arrived, Scott had been going about his daily chores. There was an ever-evolving confidence to his motions. Dave felt as though he was now just one of the other animals on Scott's island. He watched anxiously cheering for Scott to step out of the shadows and battle against the encroachment of his uninvited guest.

Miguel's soaked clothing hung off of him like a kid who was relegated to a wardrobe of oversized hand-me-downs. The weight of the water increased his shirt two sizes, his pants barely stayed up. For a man who was as attentive to his appearance and arrogant as Miguel, he was more than likely happy to believe he was alone. He trudged up dropping at the edge of the water. As he leaned against the case, waves slapped against it shooting spray into his face. He scowled then jumped up and brought a frustrated fist down on the case. His eyes turned upwards, scanning the ridge. Dave ducked, concealing himself behind a bush, as he had done many times with Scott. As he peered through the branches, he saw Miguel suddenly stiffen then take off running towards the tree line out of sight. The yelling was difficult for Dave to discern. Scott had revealed himself.

"You fucking asshole," Miguel screamed as he shoved Scott. "I thought you were dead." Scott was unprepared for an altercation. His body had shed unneeded mass in his effort to survive. As much as he tried, he did not have the strength to fight. Miguel was capable of inflicting more harm on him than ever. Scott fell to the sand and stayed there, his hand held up meekly between himself and Miguel's rage.

"Don't," was all he could say. He felt pathetic, ashamed of his frailty. The outside world had come to his door to chase him out of the daydream where he was King. A week before, he had killed a shark. Now he lay in the sand in fear of a man who had owned him; a man he could have physically crushed months before but feared nonetheless. "Don't," he repeated. The impulse to protect himself from harm with nothing more than a plea for pity made him feel nauseous. He turned away from Miguel, burying his head in his hands as Miguel kicked him in the ribs. Finally, after a flurry of punches, Miguel gave up as he spat on Scott's cowering back.

"You are useless," Miguel sneered, "always fucking useless." Miguel stomped off to retrieve the case before the ocean could claim it. Dave watched as he dragged it back towards Scott's encampment. He would have to move down the ridge to get a better vantage point although the late-day shadows were growing. It would be best to return to camp and pick up with Scott and Miguel in the morning. Whatever happened would be revealed after dawn.

Miguel pried open the case as Scott propped his aching body against a tree. He said nothing. He thought to himself how quickly he had fallen back into stepping quietly around Miguel's outbursts. How quickly he regressed into submission. Everything he had done on the island for himself seemed purposeless. He had survived, but for what?

Miguel rummaged through the case, pulling out food packets and a large tarp. There was nothing useful for building anything. No knives or a hatchet. He looked around Scott's camp, noting the fire pit. A small camp saw and hatchet leaned against a tree next to the striker. The fire smoldered when a light breeze moved the ash. Next to the fire was a large pile of wood and a jerry can. Miguel dug into the case pulling out a round plastic bag, 'solar still' printed on the outside. He threw it to Scott who said nothing as it bounced off him.

"What's in that?" Miguel asked, pointing to the can.

"Water," Scott muttered.

"Good, I'll need it for this food," Miguel replied as he tipped the can, splashing its contents into a plastic water bottle. Scott watched as the water he had worked for fell to the ground. The can had been full, but now there were two of them. The solar still was a welcome sight. The people who put him there must want him to die slower than he expected. Or perhaps killing him was the reason they sent Miguel.

Miguel mixed his food using a small aluminum spoon. He grimaced at the unsavory flavor of freeze-dried beef stew he had bigger hopes for. With an exasperated sigh, he dropped the stew in Scott's lap opting for trail mix. Scott hesitated to eat. *What will it do to my gut?,* he wondered. He had been on a diet of fish and fruit, but he was hungry. The discovery of his weakness was an unwelcome shock. Forced to compare himself to another, he realized how far he had fallen. With a little energy the stew gave him, he built a fire as the lengthening shadows crept over them.

Miguel seemed content next to the fire. He absorbed the heat happily as the perimeter outside the flames became unpredictably cold. The insects moved in immediately as he stepped away from the fire to relieve himself sending him dashing back to the relative safety of the smoke.

"How long have you been here?" he asked.

"I don't know," Scott replied. Miguel looked up impatiently. "I really don't know," Scott pardoned himself.

"They brought you here after the night you went to Duncan's," Miguel said.

"There was at least a week in a small cabin," Scott recalled.

"I was in there; I think they had Courtney in a different one," Miguel added. Scott remained quiet, wanting to avoid conversation of Courtney or anyone else associated with Miguel.

"How do we get off this fucking island?" Miguel asked. "It is an island, right?"

"I think so," Scott replied.

"You think so. Have you determined that?"

"I haven't gotten past this rock," Scott answered pointing up into the dark towards the wall and jungle that separated him from the north. "I think there's someone watching us."

"Who?" Miguel asked.

"I don't know. I just saw something move up there that didn't seem normal," Scott explained. "And the birds…"

Miguel thought a few moments before jumping to his feet. "We're going to make a fucking raft with these cases and the can there. A small one big enough to get around. We'll find out if someone is there. Maybe we can get off this thing." He jumped around like a hopeful child, imagining an impending battle.

The next morning, Miguel awoke wrapped in the tarp. He was stiff; the sun felt good on his skin, his muscles craved warmth. Scott was pulling fish from the ocean with ease as the fire roared. In a metal cup, Miguel heated water. Dropping a tea bag into it, he sat back to plan. All they needed was enough flotation for the two of them. Two empty cases on either end of a few logs and the jerry can in between should work. He would build it. Scott needed to save his strength so he would be useful in case of a fight. His food case had a few lengths of paracord. Scott had used his to build a sleeping structure off the ground. If there wasn't enough for the raft, he would pull the rest out of Scott's bed.

The day went by quickly as he worked. The raft came together with enough paracord to spare. A short length could make a formidable weapon in the right hands. Satisfied the raft would float, Miguel hid it in the trees in case Scott's suspicions were true. They would float it early in the morning towards the west where the cliffside ended in a plunge towards the water. He stirred water into some freeze-dried food, thinking he should share. He needed to put calories into Scott. Whatever it took to get some more energy into his accomplice. Scott's reluctance to eat foreign food gave way to a satiating swelling in his stomach as Miguel prodded him with calories.

"If there is someone there, we are taking all of his shit then we're getting off this rock," Miguel announced excitedly. "Why didn't you think of this? Didn't you want to leave?"

"I don't think I did," Scott reflected.

"You were always a little bit stupid. Stubborn and stupid," Miguel replied. "Thank God I got here. You would be sitting here staring at the ocean, eating fish like an idiot for the rest of your life or until a hurricane came along and erased this thing with you on it. Jesus, did you even think of that?"

Scott shrugged. He hadn't put any thought into it recently. He focused solely on the day-to-day survival of his body and his mind. Something Miguel hadn't had to consider yet. Everything was there for Miguel when he arrived; fire, water and a companion with experience. He had the luxury of looking for opportunity. Most of Scott's case of food was eaten while he learned to fish, build fires, collect fruit and survive the elements. In the remainder of his time, he thought through his life.

The struggle to live had weakened him for the world outside but for the island he was sufficient. He hadn't felt weak in strength nor in spirit. Not until Miguel arrived. Comparisons were disheartening when they dwelled within you out of context. Was that the thing he had been trying to discover there alone? It was brutally shoved in his face now. Once Miguel learned to survive, he wouldn't be needed. Would it come to blows? Would one have to perish for the other to live? Scott knew Miguel well enough to know that the only reason he was still alive was because he was needed.

Miguel poked at the fire with a long stick as they hid from

the midday sun. It seemed absurd to Scott to have a fire going, but Miguel insisted and he relented. Trying to look for the positive, Scott felt relieved that Miguel was occupied. It was another personal trait he had explored in his solitude, the compulsion to be positive. He realized his life had been one complacent shift from suffering to smiles over and over while trying to avoid the feelings of emotional pain. He had come to this thought the first day as he repeatedly threw himself at the sand. There was no positive. And there was no negative. There just was. There was no one to put up an act for. It was him, alone in the circumstance.

The tirade was just that, an act he had created for a perceived audience of people he thought should be watching and care. The thing he was used to. As he became at peace with himself, he accepted his setbacks and pain as valuable lessons. There was no one to perform for. He could only experience setbacks as they came; no longer able to reach out to others for a drug of accolades for enduring and overcoming them. All of that manufactured positivity had been shelved, replaced by reality. For every day he awoke alive, every fish he caught, every tree that gave him fruit he had nothing more to offer life than gratitude. He was conscious of all of it, like he was conscious of the stars at night reminding him of his miraculous, insignificant existence.

"We are getting out of here, and I am going to kill those bastards," Miguel spouted. "Maybe Sergio was right. Maybe drugs is the way to go now. Fuck those useless Mexicans."

"Aren't you Mexican?" Scott asked. "I thought most of your people were Hondurans."

"And Guatemalans," Miguel added. "I am Mexican in blood but not in mind. You wonder why these people come to America. What does it do for them? They have no fucking skills, so they come here to do shit work. They priced Americans, who would do the work, right out of the market."

"I thought Americans didn't want to do those things?" Scott replied. "Don't they come for opportunity? To make a living? What about escaping crime and poverty?"

"They don't come for opportunity. Maybe to escape crime. If that's it, they are fucking idiots. Opportunity is everywhere and criminals can be dealt with. There's opportunity in Mexico and Guatemala and everywhere else. They don't have the fucking balls or brains or power to seize it. They come here because they have been told about the advantages our middle class has. The ones who slave away their lives at a job. They equate that with being rich. They don't know that if you don't own your time, you don't own anything. These fucking aristocrats of suburban America get to feel superior when they see a bunch of immigrants mowing the lawns their soft, useless kids could mow. Really, all I am doing is selling them the arrogance and superiority complexes they need to maintain their ignorance."

"Ignorance?" Scott interrupted.

"The ignorant thinking that they are something more than their gardeners or maids," Miguel scoffed. "I will tell you how this started, and maybe you'll get it. When I was in college, I started a lawn care company. I hired some guys who I paid by the hour like everyone else does. Everything was legal, with a little fudging here and there on the taxes. After a while, I realized that most of my time was spent trying to keep my employees from stealing time from me. There was no end to how creative they were at fucking off. Because that's what most low-skilled workers are, fuck-offs. They have no ambition and all they do is work as little per hour for as many hours per day as they can get. Think about that statement for a minute.

"So I fucking had had it. I was bitching about it to Raphael, my roommate, Sergio's son, who said I should get some illegals. I told him I didn't want that. I didn't want the risk. He looks at me and says, you run more risk when they're free. I didn't understand what he was saying. Free from what? So he explains it to me. You have to own them. Control their movement, control their lives, control their exposure to the outside world while they're living in the middle of it. The fucking gringos don't know the difference between a legal wetback, an illegal wetback or a trafficked wetback. They only know if their fucking lawn is mowed. Then he put the numbers on paper and I woke up. That's not to say I liked it."

Scott watched Miguel become more and more animated as he recounted the past. His excitement took a pause and in a brief moment of consternation he seemed almost human.

"It was then that Raphael was hit. He was out riding his bike and some lady, illegal in the US for 20 fucking years, hit him and ran. No license, no insurance, fake plates. They caught the bitch and sent her ass back to Mexico where she promptly turned around and walked right back north. I saw her one day. You don't think that chick was going to live in Mexico, do you? She's been gone so long she doesn't know shit about that country." Miguel paused to take a drink of his tea. "I had met Sergio before. He somehow knew I had dealt some drugs in high school. After the funeral, he comes up to me saying Raphael had told him about our talk. I was saying how I didn't like that it was illegal. He says, 'Between what is legal and what is reality, there's a lot of profit; the work is going to get done by someone. You can make sure these people don't fuck up like that lady who killed my son. You can prevent these things.

"I started thinking more about it. Why do they want to come here? Opportunity? Maybe. That's sort of bullshit.

Maybe in a generation or two they can land some babies on this side who go to college. But the parents aren't bettering themselves and setting an example. They are slaving away at the shit jobs they are qualified for. Then they get to cheer for the first one in the family who goes to college and racks up a huge debt. Congratulations, your supposed opportunity is now your kid's debt slavery. I know this. That was me. I was that guy who was the first to go to college and leverage myself into the fucking dream.

"They don't come here for opportunity. That isn't the selling point. They come here for comfort. The envy of the illusion of comfortable America and its obsession with displayable luxury. Where everything, and I mean everything, has a talked-about, egotistical dollar amount attached to it. That is what America looks like to them. Then maybe, after a while, they discover that their suffering is America's comfort. Not theirs. They aren't any better off. The only thing that makes it remotely worthwhile is the ridiculous exchange rates their governments keep. It creates a constant influx of American dollars that the illegal labor is sending back to their families. That and the American infatuation with drugs.

"We are the biggest consumers of drugs in the world trafficking backwards billions to Mexico and the rest in cold, hard cash. They traffic drugs to us; we traffic dollars to them. You think the fucking Mexican Government wants to stop that? Dollars sent back to fucking Honduras are something like thirty percent of their gross national product. That's why Sergio is talking about drugs and he is up my ass every time something goes wrong. He is sick of dealing with products who run away, get injured and whatever else they can figure out in order to avoid work. I am guessing La Plaza needs a new Drug Lord and he thinks it's him."

Miguel jabbed the stick at the fire. "I don't care. He can

fuck around with drug plazas and Mexican corruption. I will just get new workers and ship my worn-out ones to Tennessee or the Northeast or wherever else non-linguals mow fucking grass. When I get a new batch, they all come with a debt price on their heads and motivation to pay it off as fast as possible. The more the idiot politicians fuck with the border, the better my business gets because you have to be an idiot to not realize that America was built on slaves and is still built and maintained by slaves. We're just more sophisticated about how we create and redefine slavery now. You get rid of the so-called illegal workers and construction collapses, fat kids have to mow lawns, restaurants shut down, meat packing plants go under, old roofs leak, and the list goes on, but the worst thing to happen to Americans is they lose the arrogant self-importance they rely on to feel like they aren't fucking slaves themselves.

"When it comes down to it, men do everything for sex and progeny. So you have to think their motivation is to come to this country to get what they need for sex back in Mexico or Guatemala. Forget getting any here. What chick wants to get with a ten dollar an hour lawn mower who can't speak the language? What kind of potential does that demonstrate? Even a crack whore has higher standards than that.

"So you gotta think he is planning to go back and get what he can in Mexico or Honduras, marry some village chick who doesn't know any better and sees him as her best option. That to me, is picking at the scraps, which is the same thing he does for these self-important gringos. What kind of fucking life is that? It's the life of a generally lazy fuck who is waiting for a handout or some miraculous golden scrap that lands at his feet. What you get in life is what you go after, plain and simple. Go after a pile of shit and you get shit.

"And fuck the gringos who put these idiots on some

heroic pedestal for the work they do, calling them hard workers. They work hard because they're scared. That doesn't sound fucking heroic to me. It just proves how clueless Americans are to what is right in front of them."

Miguel looked up from the fire at Scott, who had fallen asleep. He stood up against the heat of the flames to stretch out his legs. Incoming tidal waves curled against the beach, their frothy crests flickering against the moonrise. His speech had left him invigorated, ready for the coming day and revenge. He looked down at Scott still perplexed as to how and why he had not searched for a way to the other side if for nothing more than to look around. When they got off the island, Scott would be just another person who needed him and refused to acknowledge it.

Chapter 29

Gilberto gestured to slow the boat as the lights from the beach flickered across the waves. Dominic pulled the throttle back, watching the bow level off and begin to bob gently as they came to a drifting stop. Their trip had been planned to take a little over an hour, but the Atlantic refused to cooperate north of Eleuthera. Courtney had taken the brunt of the waves in her stomach so much so they had to take the blindfold off and and tie her below deck. With her gag removed, for the first time outside the cabin, she was allowed to breathe through her mouth. Screaming obscenities between her bouts of nausea, she had kept the men wide awake and entertained.

Gilberto slipped down to the cabin quietly behind where Courtney was tied to slip a gag over her mouth before covering her head with the black hood she was getting accustomed to. She writhed helplessly. Gilberto could only imagine what she had to be thinking. She had to have heard Miguel ruthlessly extracted from his cabin and dragged away to a waiting helicopter. What became of him, she would never know.

Freeing her from the seat, Gilberto helped her stand and find her balance as the boat pitched. The fight she still had in her was subdued by her unsure footing and the strong man guiding her without compassion. She kicked at the air as they lifted her into the cold of an inflatable raft. She could feel a hard object sitting between her legs, rocking back and forth with the waves. As the sound of a motor came to life, the man untied her hands giving her a hint of hope. She reached out for the sound, feeling the little raft recoil against her shifting balance. The dark swallowed the stern of the boat as she pulled the hood from her head. Alone, she cried as the waves pushed her towards a row of lights in the distance.

"Hey, wake up," Miguel prodded.

Scott rolled onto his back staring up at a starlit sky. Miguel, satisfied he had roused Scott well enough, began to stoke the fire.

"We gotta get going," Miguel insisted.

Scott stood looking into the dark towards the beach. The foreboding sound of pounding waves was more aggressive than it had been the night before. He knew Miguel's ambition and inexperience clouded his judgment. A do or die attitude could wait for calmer seas and an unsympathetic ocean would be better placated with patience than bravado. They had more time than Miguel could imagine.

"We need to wait," Scott warned. "Have you looked at the waves? If they are like this here, they will be worse near the rocks."

"Let's just fucking do it," Miguel insisted, overindulged with an ignorant sense of urgency and arrogance. His restless opportunism ground against Scott's reluctance. "I'll go by myself then," he threatened.

Scott said nothing. The habit of arguing with people like

Miguel had died in his solitude. Another blessing the island gave him. He didn't have to be right or explain himself to anyone. Fate would tend to that. The waves would vindicate and speak for him. "Go ahead," he muttered as he slipped back into his bed.

Miguel crashed through the remaining food case, tossing second and third choices to the sand as he looked for something to quickly satisfy his hunger. Scott watched, eyes half-closed. The burden of choice when it came to eating was a reality of a distant, complicated world. Miguel sat back against a tree with the bag of trail mix, unsatisfied. His eyes darted back and forth as he chewed, formulating a plan. He was too novice to be going mad already. Tossing the bag into the case, he took up his crudely constructed oar in a march towards the raft as the horizon began to glow. Scott, contented in the renewed silence he had taken for granted, slipped further into his bed hoping to avoid whatever came with the rising sun.

Dave awoke stretching his hand out into the dark to fumble with the stove. The click of the sparker followed by the rush of propane flame under the water pot felt like a good triumph for the morning. He drew his hand back into the tent to await the familiar sound of boiling. He wondered what was in store for Scott and Miguel today. Would they come to some level of cooperation? He couldn't imagine Scott's newfound competence for survival could bear much of Miguel's sense of superiority. Scott was the natural king of the island regardless of his unassertive nature. The way Scott accepted his captivity in the cabin led Dave to believe he would be dead in a week. His acting out the pathetic tantrums on the beach, then the desperate bouts of trial and error to catch fish. The first week, he seemed to be in a state of catatonia interrupted by short bouts of hysteria. Then, as his skills improved, Dave watched Scott begin to orate his adventure to himself. Every small win created constant chatter between himself, the birds and most fondly the marine life. He told the fish about everything, profusely apologizing to the ones he caught.

The waves pounded the beach relentlessly throughout the morning, apathetic to Miguel's impatience. It ate away at him. Things went his way. At least they had until Duncan and his goons decided Kate was too good for him. *Is that what it is?* he thought to himself. *Did the old man decide one day that I am not enough? Do a little prying and discover my operation then form some opinion about me? The oil business is high-level crooked and politically corrupt. Everyone knows that*, he thought. What made Duncan think he was so moral, so virtuous? It wasn't from running an oil company. They were the same, he and the old man. Duncan was numerically bigger, that was all. He was bigger and more people worshipped him, or feared him. More sycophants kissed his ass. The same sycophants who would never think to mow their own lawns or put their children through the social torment of being seen behind a mower. Comfort and luxury. That is what his poser clients worried about; maintaining an image of comfort and luxury and wealth by any means they could leverage. He felt the self-absorbed snobbery every time he spoke to them. His house was just as nice, his car paid for and still they looked down on him like he wasn't one of them. He wasn't good enough; just a better dressed wetback to them not a doctor or lawyer or some business dork with a title. He had a title, President; President of multiple small businesses. Still it wasn't enough. He had to buy his way into everything; into every level of social status. And he did, with their condescending money.

Scott stood up, stretching out his shoulders and back as he picked up a long stick he had hidden away from Miguel and the fire. "I am going to get some fish," he announced leaving Miguel in the shadows loosely demarcating the line between beach and jungle.

Miguel watched Scott slap at the water from the comfort of the shade. Already, the sun was intense regardless of the morning's cooling breeze. He studied the torn, almost stereotypical movie wardrobe shreds of clothing that clung to Scott's shrinking frame as the waves pushed him around. Shaking his head, Miguel sat back down by the fire. The sun seemed to rise slower here. It hung in the sky provoking him. He was sure that its plan was to torture him with boredom, dragging the reluctant days along behind as it beat down on him. The nights hurried by resetting the next day of life-crushing ennui. Over and over, it would be. "I will not be on this island very long," he vowed spitefully.

Scott threw down two gutted fish next to the fire. Miguel sneered at the sight, turning away as Scott skewered and placed them over the flames.

"You don't think I am going to eat that, do you?" Miguel scoffed.

"Suit yourself," Scott replied. "You can have some if you want. I can get more."

Miguel waved off the offer with an indignant flutter of his hand. He watched as Scott chewed the fish down to the bones. "Why aren't you asking or begging me for some of my food?" Miguel asked. "I would think you would want some of it."

"If I wanted it, I would just kill you and take it," Scott laughed looking up at Miguel for a reaction. During the night, he awoke from a dream where he had been king, sitting high upon a throne and looking down at his subjects far below. So far down, they couldn't reach up to kiss the ring he presented. They pled desperately for him to reach farther down so they could swear their loyalty. But to do so, he would have to climb off of the throne. It wasn't regal to do what his subjects wished, even if it was intended to glorify him. Nonetheless, he relented, one hand gripped on the throne, the other stretched towards his subjects as he slipped falling towards them and the rising floor. They parted as he neared; all he could see was marble tile rushing towards him. No one offered to stand between him and death. He jolted upwards in his bed just as he was about to impact at their feet.

"You should have killed the old man. You fucked that up and now we're here," Miguel retorted.

"It's my fault you are here?" Scott challenged. "You think you had something to do with it?" The triumph of the morning catch had emboldened something assertive in him. There was nothing worse Miguel could do to him but kill him. He had been choked unconscious. He survived. He had been beaten. He survived. He had been thrown out of a helicopter. He survived. Alone on the island, he had learned to survive on his wits and determination. It was his doing and his choices that made him survive the island. In his solitude, the fear of death had no power over him. Hunger pangs had held on to him tighter than death and he mastered them. Briefly he considered suicide but couldn't decide on a method. Without a sure and quick way to die, he hadn't been able to justify the risk of incapacitation followed by inevitable starvation and waning strength needed to finish the job. He shuttered at the thought of dying that way. That too was survival. He had successfully survived his own thoughts. A death coming from Miguel would be impulsive, quick. There was solace in that. It didn't matter. He was already dead to everyone he had ever loved.

"Your job was to protect the farm and me. I paid you and your boss well for that," Miguel spat.

"And the other cops, right? There are others besides Marco," Scott replied.

"There are," Miguel confessed.

"Why were they working for you? Same as me? Money? Something else?" Scott asked.

"Money. I paid them more than they were making in salary for doing nothing," Miguel answered. "All they had to do was drive around and watch my back. Once in a while, go deal with some shit at the farm. You know," he hesitated, "remove a problem."

"Kill someone," Scott inserted. "Kill one of your slaves. Last night you were talking about why they come to the States; comfort and luxury, right? To get their hands on what they think we have going for us? Isn't that just desperation? And maybe, at the worst, envy? Did you ever ask them what they go through in their own countries?"

"I know what they go through. Fuck you. I know," Miguel cursed. "They should clean their own house before they trash someone else's."

"OK, I think I know what you are saying," Scott replied. Hoping to de-escalate Miguel's anger, Scott stood up to retrieve water from the solar still. When he returned, Miguel was sitting by the fire, jabbing impatiently at a half-burned log. He handed him a water bottle. "You should drink as much as you can," he suggested. "Dehydration sneaks up on you."

Scott went about the day, relieved Miguel had postponed the raft idea as the waves persisted. The sky had become pleasantly overcast giving some relief to fish. He slapped at the water happily herding his flock into the corral where he could choose who to sacrifice. While Scott fished, Miguel sat looking at the raft then disappeared into the thin jungle below the cliff, unaware of being watched. Dave followed as far along the ridge as he could until his vantage point put him above but blind to his island inmate. He had grown accustomed to Scott going out of sight when he stepped into the jungle to retrieve wood and palm scraps. Miguel's disappearance sat heavily in his chest.

"Sergio is really leaning towards the dealing," Miguel grimaced at Scott as a fresh catch fell onto a palm frond near his feet.

"The drugs," Scott said

"Yeah, the drugs," Miguel replied impatiently, "of course."

"You will have to pay a lot more protection money for that," Scott warned.

"I know I will. I have already been paying for it. You just weren't cut in. And I only do the collecting and accounting not the selling of that shit. I don't want to get more involved. But if Sergio cuts off my flow of new labor, I might have to," Miguel complained.

"There is a ton of money in it," Scott replied. "People can't get enough. Just coke alone would make a killing."

"Like I said, I know," Miguel replied. "Maybe Sergio is right. But I hate drug dealers. They are some of the dumbest, laziest fucking retards out there. If it weren't for the money, they would all be doing low-life, useless jobs which is what they do now. They can thank corrupt cops like you and politicians for making their little businesses what they are on both sides of the border." Scott went distant, quiet.

With a jolt, Miguel stood up and dragged the raft close to him. He looked up towards the cliff for any sign of a watcher through the foliage before disassembling what he had built.

"What are you doing?" Scott asked.

"Fuck the raft," Miguel growled. "I found a spot we can

reach on the cliff. I am making a ladder. I can't believe you missed that. How long have you been here? What the fuck have you been doing?"

Scott looked away from Miguel towards the fish corral. The rock face up the ridge had never been a priority. Food, water, fire and thought had been enough. Now that there were two of them a new energy took over. Ambition. Miguel had brought ambition to the island that Scott alone couldn't afford, and it wasn't sitting well. He remembered the last time he felt like he was feeling now. The day he decided to break up with his girlfriend. She had been full of ambitions for him. She wasn't responsible for his job with Miguel but she benefitted. His need for her approval and affection drove his need for Miguel.

When he decided to end it, Scott was surprised to be overcome with a feeling of relief even though he was about to hurt her. Thinking about it was better than doing it. After he let her go and escaped the crying, the yelling then the shaming, he knew he had done the right thing. He was surprised how little guilt he felt. There was contentment in solitude without her, without the drive to please her. He had felt the same before Miguel arrived. Now the entrapment of the island felt like a complaint bomb set to go off at random times. It wasn't like that when he was alone. It was the same feeling he had with her.

"Fucking answer me," Miguel yelled.

"What?" Scott responded sheepishly.

"What the fuck have you been doing?" Miguel stared at him with piercing hate. Scott had nothing to explain or defend against something that had never motivated him. Climbing the cliff was never a thought.

"It wasn't something I cared about, I guess," Scott

muttered in his defense. "You are being pretty harsh on me for nothing."

"For nothing? It's obviously not nothing. You had all that time and no fucking motivation," Miguel snarled. "It was like when you fucked up the job. There were times I thought you had it, but then you would fuck something up and I had to pay for it. You are the reason I am here. It's fucking you!" Miguel glared unblinkingly for so long Scott was afraid to cut their eye contact, but that was what Miguel wanted, submission. Scott's eyes moved to the fire hoping the flames would take sympathy on him. At that moment, he began to regret his unexplored suicidal plans. What he had become on the island was falling apart. A deep, internal shame gripped him as it had when he was merely an instrument of Miguel's ambition. The torrent of anger he deserved to unleash upon Miguel sat idly dammed up behind his shame. He felt useless. He felt the irony of his thought about the girlfriend. If she could see him now, she would be so relieved and vindicated. Laughter burst out thinking of it.

"What are you laughing at?" Miguel asked impatiently.

Scott walked away towards the water to bathe himself in the waves, hoping they would carry him out to sea. He felt powerless; it indescribably hurt. Once again, he was along on someone else's ride. It was the role he knew and kept getting called for.

"It's beautiful," Dave said quietly into the satellite phone.

"Here too," Kate replied. "You are sure you are OK out there alone?"

"I am fine," Dave reassured her. "I have the two guys to entertain me. And there is plenty to do around the camp."

"There is no way I could do that," Kate replied.

Dave paused to reply. The course of the conversation was seemingly too familiar and comfortable for as little time he and Kate had spent together. There was an aura of care coming from her he hadn't experienced from a woman in many years. It felt good, but he remained suspicious. He liked her, but what if they were not compatible? He thought she liked him well enough. She was a few weeks off a relationship. A good time to play around for most women. It could be the end of him and Duncan. It was bad enough there seemed to be something growing between him and Kate. If he took the steps forward, he would have to commit to it. He did not know the snowball effect a relationship with Kate would have but intuitively knew she would determine it; she and the social situation he was in. Something new inside of him cautioned against this. He had been carried around by the wind enough in his life. It was time to determine his own direction.

"Tell Duncan all is well. I gotta get back to what I was doing," Dave said abruptly before disconnecting. He immediately regretted his impetuousness, second guessing it as the timid act of a timid man. *I should call her back*, he thought, trapped in the residual flow of his former self. He threw the satellite phone into the case and walked to the beach to watch the sunset. It seemed an impossible task to become indifferent to her. "I have to be careful," he muttered.

"Come on. Let's go," Miguel commanded.

Scott stood to follow. He had resolved to stay on the island, as ridiculous as it seemed. If there was a way off, he had no interest in it. This was his island. His energy maintained it. The best he hoped for in crossing over the cliff was to claim the other side. He fantasized about Miguel being swallowed up by the sea or falling to his death freeing him again for solitude. Reluctantly, he followed into the shadows cast by jungle and rock.

The ladder shot up into a dark crevice above. With each moment, the setting sun obscured their ascent as Miguel led them to a small resting point where the ladder ended and a notch in the rock began. The sky glowed above, calling them upwards. Miguel crested the cliff; he waited.

"That was easy," he taunted Scott. There was no need to elaborate. The message was clear enough. As Scott sat down next to Miguel, he felt an assertive backhanded strike against his shoulder. His eyes followed the hand to where it pointed, a small glow in the jungle.

"You were right," Miguel whispered, "there is someone." He motioned for Scott to follow as they crept opposite the light. "We'll go along the beach."

Twilight cast the last rays on the day as Miguel and Scott moved cautiously down the slope of the ridge. The jungle eased its grip on their progress as they neared the beach. Settling behind a large rock between themselves and where they had seen the glow, they waited. After he regained calm over his nervous energy, Miguel signaled for Scott to follow as he hugged the edge of the beach and jungle. They moved in unison with the ever-growing darkness until the light abruptly stopped Miguel causing Scott to bump into him. Miguel pushed Scott back away deeper into the shadows as he crouched down to watch.

There, they saw him moving around in the light of a small lantern. As they crept forward, details of the camp became apparent. There was a small tent. A hammock swung between two palms. Cases of what had to be more food were stacked nearby. The man turned to reveal a profile as Scott grabbed at Miguel's arm.

"It's that Dave guy," Scott whispered. Scott could sense

Miguel go rigid, staring at Dave. He waved Scott on to follow as he moved from a slow stalk to a full run. He burst out of the shadows in ambush. As Dave reached for a boiling pot, an impact of surprise and crushing momentum upended him. His face was driven into the ground; he fought against the earth for air as blows came unrelentingly from above. Each punch driving his face deeper into the compacting sand until it was done.

"There's a lot of activity near Sergio's," Dominic announced as he walked into a darkened living room where Duncan and Kate sat in the glow of a single lamp.

"What kind?" Duncan asked as he motioned for Dominic to sit.

"It's government mostly; Mexican Army. They haven't been around there until recently," Dominic replied. "Sergio has been the only trafficker in that area since I have been watching."

"Curious," Duncan said as he tapped his fingers together. "Keep watching and see if you can figure out where these phones have been before. Do you have historical data on them?"

"I don't, but we can get it, "Dominic replied. "It will cost us."

Duncan nodded the go-ahead for Dominic to spend the money. He had the authority to spend what he needed but felt more at ease when Duncan signed off. He quickly compiled an email to his source while Duncan fiddled with a ring he always wore on his index finger. A cheap stainless steel ring bearing markings Dominic couldn't discern and Duncan never spoke of.

"That's that," Dominic said looking up from the laptop.

"I'll have the data probably by the morning. I am going to bed."

"Good night," Duncan said as he reached for a glass next to him. Kate was slipping in and out of consciousness. She had faded off as Dominic had begun to speak. With a sudden shudder she awoke as if the world had ended and she missed it. Gathering her composure, she stood to kiss Duncan on the cheek.

"Good night, dear," he said, looking up at her.

"Don't stay up too late," Kate cautioned. She stepped through the doorway of her room ill-at-ease over something illusory and distant. She had begun to dream on her chair, half-conscious and aware of Dominic while on the edge of another world. The dream, unmaterialized, lingered on the edge of her consciousness as she prepared for bed. As she slipped between the taut sheets, she hoped sleep would be gracious enough to reveal the secret. As tired as she was, her thoughts fantasized about Dave. There was something she couldn't describe about him. The pull she felt towards him at the Post Office, then the bar. And again, as he broke through the bedroom door, commanding her to run out to Duncan as gunfire exploded through Miguel's house. She had seen him in more emotional pain than she had seen any man as he held his best friend through to the last breath. The memory of that night…

Dave slowly regained consciousness. Becoming aware of his incapacitation, he tried to right himself. He struggled with his bound arms and legs to turn towards the stars, his right eye hopelessly swollen shut. Sand caked against the side of his head conglomerated with hours-old blood. He managed to turn himself around to face the tent where he could hear someone tossing to adjust in his sleeping bag. The hammock swayed under the weight of another against the moonlit waves. He hurt so much it took him moments to realize who they were. Scott and Miguel, who else could they be? They had found a way to his side. He quietly tried to wriggle out of the cord binding him with no luck, only adding to his pain. A wave of suffering came over him. He prayed for relief that came from unconsciousness. Quieting his mind took all of his will. In the end, the pain and exhaustion blessed him with sleep.

"Good morning," the voice from the satellite phone taunted.

"Who is this?" Duncan asked as he sat down.

"You know who this is. Figure it out, old man," Miguel replied. Duncan stared at the coffee cup in front of him, hoping he was hallucinating. "Hey! Old man! Wake the fuck up!" Miguel yelled into the phone as he kicked Dave in the ribs to wake him.

"What do you want?" Duncan asked anxiously.

"I want the fuck off this island! What do you think I want?" A gunshot rang out. Duncan's heart stopped as he feared what Miguel had done. "You get me off this island, or I put the next round through Dave's ugly fucking head!" The phone connection cut as Duncan frantically tried to reconnect.

The phone rang. "I will call you; don't call me," Miguel sputtered before disconnecting again.

"Dominic! Dominic!" Duncan yelled into the quiet of the house.

Miguel dragged Dave by his arms to a tree, propping his weakened frame against it. He bent down face-to-face before striking Dave with an open hand. "Wake up!" he commanded.

Scott was going through the food cases as Dave slowly came to. His burned hand seared with pain behind his back as chunks of dried blood and sand fell from his face. He stared spitefully as Miguel poured himself some coffee.

"We are going to give the old man some time to worry. Maybe he'll have a heart attack. Then who will save you?" Miguel taunted. "Not that other asshole, right? From the bar?"

Miguel stood up to open a package of cookies. He held one in front of Dave just out of reach. Satisfied, Miguel sat back down to stare at his captive. "You really fucked things up for me, Dave. I really want to kill you, but you are my leverage. Duncan will come for you. He will submit like a bitch to me and Scott, and we will leave this little prison of yours."

"I am not going back," Scott spoke up.

"Are you fucking stupid? Of course, you are," Miguel yelled.

"I am not. What difference does it make if I go?" Scott yelled.

Miguel paused, facing the water. Turning, he said, "You are right. You are a liability to me." He quickly pulled the gun up and pulled the trigger. The round struck Scott's shoulder, flinging him to the ground.

"Stop!" Dave yelled as Scott rolled in the sand, desperately trying to get away from Miguel. The gun came up again. Dave forced himself to his feet throwing his shoulder into Miguel's back.

"Why do you care?" Miguel yelled as he righted himself. He stood pushing Dave's face against the sand with his foot as he fired taunting shots at the sand near Scott. Another round grazed Scott's leg. "There. Now you can stay here all alone and die in pain."

Scott gave up. He lay face down in the sand, his breathing

heavy. Dave fell quiet; he shuddered at what he was witnessing.

Miguel picked up the satellite phone, "Old man, get that helicopter here now."

"It will take at least an hour before we can take off then at least another hour before we arrive," Duncan responded.

"There is no 'we'. The helicopter and the pilot only. You will pick me and what's left of Dave up. I will finish him off if you pull any shit," Miguel warned.

"Understood," Duncan replied reticently.

Miguel sat in a camp chair gloating at Dave. He was beaten but would live long enough to be useful.

"There are clotting bandages in that," Dave said motioning as best as he could towards the case nearest Miguel. "At least put some on him." Miguel sighed reluctantly retrieving the dressings along with a medical bag. He dropped them in the sand next to Scott before returning to his chair. Miguel tapped the pistol on the chair arm impatiently as Scott struggled to dress his own wounds.

The satellite phone rang. Miguel stared at it before answering, "You don't fucking listen old man. I call you."

"The helicopter will leave in thirty minutes. I want to know that Dave is alive," Duncan ordered.

"He's alive," Miguel replied. "Your pilot will see him with me on the beach, as I said." Miguel abruptly disconnected before throwing the satellite phone at the tent.

He stood up to get some food out of a case when he suddenly stopped and retrieved the phone. "Duncan," he said calmly, "Along with the pilot, I want cash. Ten thousand."

Duncan hesitated, "OK," he conceded quietly.

"Does this thing go faster?" Dominic yelled over the engine.

"It is all the way," Gilberto yelled. "We can get there. Pete will wait. It's not that far, anyway. They just think it's far."

The boat sped towards the south side of the island, bouncing in the chop. As they neared, Gilberto slowed to help Dominic into the electric inflatable. "Good luck. I will stay around this side with the phone."

"OK!" Dominic yelled back as he motored towards the beach, slowing to pick his way through reefs rising up to capture him. His heart pounded with every wave trough turning the sea black and jagged. Inside the barrier reefs, he sped around the coral heads to the eastern edge of the beach, diving out onto the sand as a wave toppled him. He ran desperately back into the water to retrieve his rifle bag from under the overturned boat.

"He is on the island," Gilberto said into the phone.

Dominic ran along the edge of the jungle, remembering Dave's account of how Scott lived. The cliff jutted out over an area of trees Dave had described as Scott's camp. Dominic fell into the trees at the base of the cliff searching for any signs of how Miguel and Scott were able to get to the other side. He broke through the underbrush until there it was, a crude ladder. Dominic stared upward his heart pounding; he slung the rifle on his back and began to climb. The rungs twisted under his impatience threatening to send him to the jungle floor. His hand reached up finding a good hold as one turned under his feet. "Slower," he coached himself. "It's OK. You gotta calm down." He moved methodically through the rocks at the ladder's end, topping the cliff. "Breathe, breathe," he chanted in a whisper. There were signs of a path Miguel and Scott had taken to descend. Recalling Dave's description, he slipped across the ridge line to the west. As he settled above where the camp should be, he called Pete. "I am here," he whispered.

The din of the helicopter broke the morning calm as it flew low over the camp before turning towards the ocean to hover off-shore.

"Old man," Miguel said into the phone. "Do you have my money?"

"There's ten thousand in a bag inside. Give the pilot your instructions once you are onboard," Duncan replied.

Dominic slipped through the jungle, desperately trying to calm his nerves. He was foreign to guns. Duncan had assured him that the scope was sighted and warned him to pull the trigger as calmly as he could. "Aim for the center of mass," Duncan had instructed, pointing to his heart.

"Center of mass," Dominic repeated to himself. "I can do this." As he crept through the underbrush, he couldn't see Dave or Miguel anywhere. He nervously turned in a circle, hoping they weren't behind him as the helicopter hovered between breaking waves and the beach sending spray and sand into the air. There they were. Dave's arms were bound, his legs loosely hobbled causing him to fight the sand with every step. Miguel prodded him along with quick jabs of the pistol, keeping Dave between himself and the helicopter.

Dominic steadied the rifle on a tree limb as he found the center of Miguel's back in the scope he squeezed. The trigger froze. There was nothing. *It doesn't fucking work!*, he panicked. "Breathe," he said to himself as he searched frantically for a solution. "The safety!" he said aloud as his thumb found the lever. Miguel pushed at Dave, coaxing him the last steps to the helicopter as the bullet pierced his shoulder blade. Dave felt the muzzle of the pistol press against his back, Miguel's weight pushing him against the lower frame of the open door. Dave leaned his body into the helicopter as a hand closed on the back of his neck, pulling him to the water. Miguel's bleeding chest heaved as he held Dave's face under.

Dave writhed to surface; to take a breath. His strength faltered with every inhalation of sea water he desperately tried to expel as Miguel pushed him under by the throat. A grey cloud closed in on him as he faded.

"It's OK; you are alive," Dave thought he heard as his good eye fluttered open. Dominic bent over him. "Scott, Scott got to you before I could."

"What?" Dave asked.

"He saved you. He smashed Miguel's head in with a rock. I have never seen anything so gruesome," Dominic shuddered. Dave looked towards the water where Miguel's lifeless body floated face down in a pool of blood.

"Where is he?" Dave asked.

"He's in the hammock over there," Dominic pointed. "Pete had to pull away. Gilberto is coming around with the boat." Dominic looked over Dave trying to dab away the blood that remained over his swollen eye. "Scott wants to stay here."

"What? Help me up," Dave said.

Dave stumbled to the hammock. Holding on to the straps for support, he looked down at Scott. "You are coming with us," he insisted. Scott looked up from his pensive gloom to Dave's eager and battered face.

"Nobody wants me there," he replied. "They all probably think I am dead. I may as well stay here and let myself die the way I want."

"You have too much in you to spend it here alone," Dave smiled. "Come with us; it will be worth your time. You can start a new life as a Brazilian."

"What? Why Brazilian?" Scott asked.

"Why not?"

Chapter 30

"Ignacio, are you ready?" Dave asked.

"Ready."

"OK. When you hear it, start coming towards the house. Hopefully we will be there at the gate," Dave instructed. "You sure this is when they were planning it, Dominic?"

"They are heading out right now," Dominic replied. "There are five vehicles, at least fifteen men from what I can tell from the phones."

The Mexican Humvees sped along a dark, rutted road towards Sergio's ranch, bouncing in and out of shallow arroyos. Dave looked over at Scott giving him the thumbs up as they inched their way towards the house.

"Birds are in the air," Dominic announced.

"We gotta get behind something," Dave warned. Scott pointed towards a small gully to their right. As he and Dave settled in, the drones took position behind them four hundred yards from the ranch. They could see the headlights of the Mexican military crashing through the desert. The ranch house was quiet. Sergio had sent the few men he had into town for supplies. It was a perfect time for the military to move in.

The gate crashed open as the first armored vehicle entered the grounds. Lights came on; dogs barked into the night as the column drove in a whirlwind of dust around the house coming to a cloudy halt. A loudspeaker yelled for Sergio to come out as warning shots peppered the side of the house.

"Stay down!" Dominic's voiced blasted through their earpieces.

The drones came in the same as the column of Humvees, circling then hovering in place. Their payloads were pointed and ready. As stunned faces turned towards the noise of the drones, they swooped in detonating C-4 behind a wall of buckshot. The devastation was immediate and thorough. Stray shards of metal peppered the area around Dave and Scott as an ominous cloud of dust and smoke built around the house.

"Let's go," Dave commanded. Brandishing his pistol as Scott took up his AR-15, they ran towards the remains of the scene. A burning truck overwhelmed their night vision goggles; they both tore them off their heads. Scott reached the ranch gate first clearing the area before moving forward behind a surviving tree. He caught sight of one of the military attackers moving towards the main door. Rifle raised, he dropped the man on the threshold as Dave ran ahead towards a door leading to the courtyard. The military squad had been utterly annihilated, but Sergio was still expected to put up a fight. As Dave and Scott entered the courtyard, they could see the shadow of someone moving through the kitchen. Dave slipped down through the hallway through the east wing past closed bedroom doors.

Scott pounded on the door, "Open up, asshole!" Bullets flew through the wood as Scott jumped behind the protection of a planted palm. As the door swung slowly open ahead of another hail of bullets, Scott responded with a double-tap of rounds.

The house went quiet for a moment. Then another burst of gunfire through a window over Scott's head, glass shards bounced past him towards the pool. Dave crouched low behind the kitchen counter waiting for Sergio to return. He listened to the stomping of cowboy boots coming down the hall from the west wing, eager to end the assault. From his hide he could see Sergio turn to fire randomly through a second window. An empty magazine dropped to the floor as the mechanical sound of another clicked into place. Then, another burst. In the confused noise of gunfire, Dave slipped in behind Sergio his pistol ready for anything. Sergio focused on the attack coming from outside as Dave struck the back of his head knocking him face first to the floor. Kicking at Sergio's rifle, he sent it skidding across the tiles then drove the muzzle of his pistol menacingly into Sergio's temple as he bore down on him with all his weight.

"Get up," Dave commanded. "If you try anything stupid, I have orders to eliminate you." Sergio hesitated. "I know you speak English. Get your ass up," Dave repeated.

Scott came running in, forcing Sergio up onto his knees; he frisked him and bound his hands. Sergio spat at Dave as Scott wrestled him to his feet and pulled a gag tightly into his mouth.

"That's not necessary," Dave scolded. "You should behave yourself. It's your lucky day, Sergio."

"Ignacio, we are ready," Scott said into the radio.

The van skidded to a stop outside the gate as Dave and Scott threw in their captive. Sergio glared at Dave as his head bounced in unison with the van along the back roads to a secluded airstrip.

"You know we just saved your ass, pendejo," Dave said, reaching over to release the gag.

"I can handle myself. I don't need your fucking help," Sergio protested arrogantly.

"We have been trying to contact you, but you keep ignoring us," Dave replied. "So we came to get you. Apparently, the Mexican Military wanted to come along. Are you not paying your protection? Does someone not like you trying to take over La Plaza?"

"Where are we going?" Sergio asked. "You better not be taking me to the US."

"You'll find out," Dave replied. "And we aren't that stupid."

The van came to an abrupt halt. As the doors opened, the shrill whine of jet engines pierced the night. Scott led Sergio to the plane pushing him up the steps as they followed him in. With Sergio ratchet strapped to his seat, Dave and Scott fell asleep while the plane made its way south. As the sunrise peeked over the central Mexican mountains, the landing gear locked startling Dave awake. He looked over at Sergio, who looked like he had been dragged behind a horse. The trafficker's attitude was as malignant as ever.

"Welcome to Cuernavaca," Dave said. "Ever been here? It's really nice."

"I have a fucking house here, idiot," Sergio sputtered. "Why am I here?"

"Duncan wants to have a talk," Dave replied.

About the Author

Richard Light is the author of psychological and vigilante fiction that examines the tension between justice, morality, and human endurance. With a focus on character-driven storytelling and moral complexity, his work challenges readers to confront the gray areas of right and wrong. When he's not writing, he studies human behavior and the forces that drive people to seek their own form of justice.

richardlightbooks.com

- instagram.com/rlight7777777
- amazon.com/author/richardlight7777777
- tiktok.com/@richard.light26

Also by Richard Light

The King's Game

Killer Interviewing

www.ingramcontent.com/pod-product-compliance
Lightning Source LLC
LaVergne TN
LVHW041744060526
838201LV00046B/910